Crime Files Series

General Editor: **Clive Bloom**

Since its invention in the nineteenth century, detective fiction has never been more popular. In novels, short stories, films, radio, television and now in computer games, private detectives and psychopaths, prim poisoners and overworked cops, tommy gun gangsters and cocaine criminals are the very stuff of modern imagination, and their creators one mainstay of popular consciousness. Crime Files is a ground-breaking series offering scholars, students and discerning readers a comprehensive set of guides to the world of crime and detective fiction. Every aspect of crime writing, detective fiction, gangster movie, true-crime exposé, police procedural and post-colonial investigation is explored through clear and informative texts offering comprehensive coverage and theoretical sophistication.

Published titles include:

Maurizio Ascari
A COUNTER-HISTORY OF CRIME FICTION
Supernatural, Gothic, Sensational

Pamela Bedore
DIME NOVELS AND THE ROOTS OF AMERICAN DETECTIVE FICTION

Hans Bertens and Theo D'haen
CONTEMPORARY AMERICAN CRIME FICTION

Anita Biressi
CRIME, FEAR AND THE LAW IN TRUE CRIME STORIES

Clare Clarke
LATE VICTORIAN CRIME FICTION IN THE SHADOWS OF SHERLOCK

Paul Cobley
THE AMERICAN THRILLER
Generic Innovation and Social Change in the 1970s

Michael Cook
NARRATIVES OF ENCLOSURE IN DETECTIVE FICTION
The Locked Room Mystery

Michael Cook
DETECTIVE FICTION AND THE GHOST STORY
The Haunted Text

Barry Forshaw
DEATH IN A COLD CLIMATE
A Guide to Scandinavian Crime Fiction

Barry Forshaw
BRITISH CRIME FILM
Subverting the Social Order

Emelyne Godfrey
MASCULINITY, CRIME AND SELF-DEFENCE IN VICTORIAN LITERATURE
Duelling with Danger

Emelyne Godfrey
FEMININITY, CRIME AND SELF-DEFENCE IN VICTORIAN LITERATURE AND SOCIETY
From Dagger-Fans to Suffragettes

Lee Horsley
THE NOIR THRILLER

Merja Makinen
AGATHA CHRISTIE
Investigating Femininity

Fran Mason
AMERICAN GANGSTER CINEMA
From *Little Caesar* to *Pulp Fiction*

Fran Mason
HOLLYWOOD'S DETECTIVES
Crime Series in the 1930s and 1940s from the Whodunnit to Hard-boiled Noir

Linden Peach
MASQUERADE, CRIME AND FICTION
Criminal Deceptions

Steven Powell (*editor*)
100 AMERICAN CRIME WRITERS

Alistair Rolls and Deborah Walker
FRENCH AND AMERICAN NOIR
Dark Crossings

Susan Rowland
FROM AGATHA CHRISTIE TO RUTH RENDELL
British Women Writers in Detective and Crime Fiction

Melissa Schaub
MIDDLEBROW FEMINISM IN CLASSIC BRITISH DETECTIVE FICTION
The Female Gentleman

Adrian Schober
POSSESSED CHILD NARRATIVES IN LITERATURE AND FILM
Contrary States

Lucy Sussex
WOMEN WRITERS AND DETECTIVES IN NINETEENTH-CENTURY CRIME FICTION
The Mothers of the Mystery Genre

Heather Worthington
THE RISE OF THE DETECTIVE IN EARLY NINETEENTH-CENTURY POPULAR FICTION

R.A. York
AGATHA CHRISTIE
Power and Illusion

Crime Files Series Standing Order
ISBN 978–0–333–71471–3 (hardback)
ISBN 978–0–333–93064–9 (paperback)
(*outside North America only*)

You can receive future titles in this series as they are published by placing a standing order. Please contact your bookseller or, in case of difficulty, write to us at the address below with your name and address, the title of the series and one of the ISBNs quoted above.

Customer Services Department, Macmillan Distribution Ltd, Houndmills, Basingstoke, Hampshire RG21 6XS, England, UK.

James Ellroy
Demon Dog of Crime Fiction

Steven Powell

palgrave
macmillan

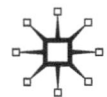

© Steven Powell 2016

All rights reserved. No reproduction, copy or transmission of this publication may be made without written permission.

No portion of this publication may be reproduced, copied or transmitted save with written permission or in accordance with the provisions of the Copyright, Designs and Patents Act 1988, or under the terms of any licence permitting limited copying issued by the Copyright Licensing Agency, Saffron House, 6–10 Kirby Street, London EC1N 8TS.

Any person who does any unauthorized act in relation to this publication may be liable to criminal prosecution and civil claims for damages.

The author has asserted his right to be identified as the author of this work in accordance with the Copyright, Designs and Patents Act 1988.

First published 2016 by
PALGRAVE MACMILLAN

Palgrave Macmillan in the UK is an imprint of Macmillan Publishers Limited, registered in England, company number 785998, of Houndmills, Basingstoke, Hampshire RG21 6XS.

Palgrave Macmillan in the US is a division of St Martin's Press LLC, 175 Fifth Avenue, New York, NY 10010.

Palgrave Macmillan is the global academic imprint of the above companies and has companies and representatives throughout the world.

Palgrave® and Macmillan® are registered trademarks in the United States, the United Kingdom, Europe and other countries.

ISBN 978–1–137–49082–7

This book is printed on paper suitable for recycling and made from fully managed and sustained forest sources. Logging, pulping and manufacturing processes are expected to conform to the environmental regulations of the country of origin.

A catalogue record for this book is available from the British Library.

A catalog record for this book is available from the Library of Congress.

Typeset by MPS Limited, Chennai, India.

UNIVERSITY OF SUNDERLAND LIBRARY ML	
11112857549	
Askews & Holts	
813.54 P59	
	ND15001938

*For Diana,
who started the journey*

Contents

Acknowledgements	ix
Introduction	1
1 Lee Earle Ellroy and the Avon Novels	8
The last days of Lee Earle Ellroy	9
Brown's Requiem: death and rebirth	11
Clandestine: the anti-private detective phase	23
Stray dogs: 'The Confessions of Bugsy Siegel' and *Killer on the Road*	33
The Avon characters and new writing styles	46
2 The Lloyd Hopkins Novels: Ellroy's Displaced Romantic	49
'L.A. Death Trip': the genesis of Lloyd Hopkins	49
Blood on the Moon	54
Because the Night	69
Suicide Hill	78
The Lloyd Hopkins novels: the incomplete series	88
3 James Ellroy, Jean Ellroy and Elizabeth Short: The Demon Dog and Transmogrification in *The Black Dahlia*	91
'You are free to speculate': Ellroy and the Black Dahlia	93
The Black Dahlia	100
'I wrote the last page and wept': Ellroy's Continuing Black Dahlia Narratives	111
'Now we know who killed her, and why': Ellroy and the Black Dahlia true-crime sub-genre	114
Perfidia: Ellroy's Black Dahlia legacy	122
4 Developing Noir: The Los Angeles Quartet	129
After *The Black Dahlia*: the evolution of Ellroy's writing process	134
The Big Nowhere and 'Man Camera'	139
L.A. Confidential and Ellrovian prose	147
White Jazz: apocalypse noir	157
The legacy and return of the LA Quartet	164

5 **The Narrative of Secret Histories in the Underworld USA Trilogy** 169
  American Tabloid 171
  The Cold Six Thousand 190
  Blood's a Rover 201
  Conclusion: 'I have paid a dear and savage price to live history' 212

Bibliography 216

Index 223

Acknowledgements

This book began as a thesis, and I am deeply grateful to Professor David Seed at the University of Liverpool who was a generous and inspiring PhD supervisor. Also at Liverpool, Dr Chris Routledge has always been a good friend and a source of sound advice. I am deeply indebted to my family for their support, especially to my wife Diana, without whom this book would not have been possible. I should also mention a fine group of people whom I regard as my second family – my colleagues at the Sydney Jones Library. I would like to extend my thanks to my friends Daniel Slattery and David Harrison who have endured my Ellroy obsession with good humour. At Palgrave I would like to thank Clive Bloom, Paula Kennedy, Keith Povey and Peter Cary; they have all been extremely helpful. In a scholarly study of this kind, the critic must keep some objective distance from his subject, but I would be remiss if I did not mention the kindness and generosity of James Ellroy in consenting to be interviewed by me and allowing me access to his papers at the Thomas Cooper library, University of South Carolina.

STEVEN POWELL

Introduction

James Ellroy was born in Los Angeles in 1948. He grew up in the epicentre of American noir at the height of the classic film noir period: 'I remember feeling that things were going on outside the frame of what I was seeing. The language I got partly from my father, who swore a lot. It was an older L.A., a man's L.A., where everybody smoked cigarettes and ate steak and went to fights' (Kihn 1992: 32). This experiential, inchoate knowledge of Los Angeles was to prove Ellroy's most valuable education. He absorbed what he saw at home and on the streets, and culturally he gravitated towards this world more than any other: 'My passion for movies does not extend beyond their depiction of crime. My filmic pantheon rarely goes past 1959 and the end of the film noir age' (Ellroy 1997a: xvii).

The city and the era had an enormous influence on his formative years and on his identity as a crime writer. One of Ellroy's main aims as a crime novelist has been to revisit and reimagine this noir era in the LA Quartet series. Noir presents a world where politics is a byword for corruption, individuals are morally compromised, and protagonists are resigned to their fate knowing there will be no happy endings. It is noir's darkness which makes it so attractive, and Ellroy's historical fiction has captured the essence of this noir paradox. Yet even though his writing style is nostalgically drawn to film noir and detective fiction in the era of the 1940s and 1950s, Ellroy's noir vision deconstructs both the perceived glamour and social conservatism of the era: his LA is a city riven with organized crime and LAPD corruption.

The history of Los Angeles and its cinematic identity was just one inspiration for Ellroy. He would also draw on biographical elements of his own life in his fiction, including, most notably, the unsolved murder of his mother Geneva Hilliker Ellroy in 1958. Ellroy would entwine LA narratives with that of his mother's death to deepen, contextualize, spiritualize and fictionalize his mother's influence on his life. Ellroy's childhood discovery of the Black Dahlia case, the most famous unsolved murder in LA history, while reading Jack Webb's *The Badge* (1958), was also significant. Before he reached adolescence, Ellroy had discovered the two main obsessions of his literary career: his mother's murder and the Black Dahlia herself – Elizabeth Short.

Ellroy's path to becoming a writer, however, was to be an unconventional one. With his father's death in 1965, Ellroy lost all restraining influences. The next few years of his life were characterized by drug and alcohol abuse, homelessness, petty crime and several stints in the LA County Jail. It was a brush with death that finally persuaded Ellroy to reform and start writing. In 1975, Ellroy suffered a mental and physical breakdown, which he has described as 'post-alcoholic brain syndrome', but he did not stop substance abusing until he nearly died of pneumonia and a lung abscess (Kihn 1992: 25). In 1977, he joined Alcoholics Anonymous which became a turning point: employment followed sobriety. His first novel, *Brown's Requiem*, was published in 1981. Ellroy slowly and steadily built his reputation as a crime writer. His breakthrough came with his seventh novel, *The Black Dahlia* (1987), in which he created a fictional solution to the murder of Elizabeth Short and allusively explored his obsession with his mother's murder. Since then, Ellroy has become one of the most prominent of contemporary crime writers through the publication of a series of novels merging noir with historical revisionism in the LA Quartet and Underworld USA trilogy.

In parallel to his work as a novelist, Ellroy has developed a public persona as the self-styled Demon Dog of American Crime Fiction. Through interviews, Ellroy found an outlet for his literary persona, elevating standard publicity opportunities into a form of creative performance, building and deconstructing narratives which in turn play with the semi-biographical as well as the purely fictional narratives of the novels: 'As critical acclaim and response has built up, every interview I give is a chance to puncture the myth I've created about my work and refine it' (Hogan 1995: 60). The documentaries *James Ellroy: American Dog* (2006) and *Feast of Death* (2001) feature scenes with Ellroy at his favourite LA restaurant, the Pacific Dining Car, holding court with his contacts in the LAPD alongside fellow writers such as Bruce Wagner and Larry Harnisch and show-business friends Dana Delany and Nick Nolte, discussing unsolved cases and LA history. Few crime writers could match Ellroy in terms of clout and his ability to generate publicity, but by his own admission much of what he says should be taken with a degree of scepticism. Ellroy is an author at ease with his own sense of celebrity, but, in one of the many contradictory sides of his character, he relishes his self-crafted image as an outsider – too edgy, unpredictable and maverick to ever truly belong to the Hollywood or publishing establishment. He can be an intimidating figure to some journalists, as Iain Johnston wrote during one interview: 'The myopic stare of James Ellroy, too, reveals much about his character – his suppressed anxiety, resolute obsession, locked down concentration, fierce determination and wild, black humour, are all detectable there' (Johnston 2014). In his public appearances, Ellroy cuts a striking figure, often dressed in garish Hawaiian shirts, spouting outrageous right-wing views and barking like a dog. This manic behaviour might seem to contradict his reputation as an acclaimed historical novelist, but in part Ellroy maintains his creativity and uniqueness by eschewing respectability.

At times, critics have found it difficult to distinguish James Ellroy the man from his Demon Dog persona. However, such a neat dividing line overlooks the subversive quality of his character: Hans Berten and Theo D'haen have commented, 'Ellroy aims to be serious all the way. There is nothing funny or laid-back about his characters, most of whom show the same kind of assertiveness and tenseness Ellroy himself projects in his public appearances and in the photographs that his publicity agents distribute' (Berten and D'haen 2001: 96). The Demon Dog persona preceded Ellroy's literary celebrity rather than coming later as an adjunct to it, and as such, it is integral to an understanding of Ellroy as a writer. There may not have been one distinct moment when Ellroy invented the persona, but there are two events examined in this book which are evidence of its genesis: a meeting with editor Otto Penzler early in Ellroy's writing career when the author declared himself the 'Demon Dog of American Crime Fiction' and Ellroy's invention of 'Dog' humour with his friend Randy Rice.

Ellroy's work has been examined in studies of crime fiction such as Lee Horsley's *Twentieth Century Crime Fiction* (2005) and Andrew Pepper's *The Contemporary American Crime Novel: Race, Ethnicity, Gender, Class* (2000). In *The Street Was Mine: White Masculinity in Hardboiled Fiction and Film Noir* (2002), Megan Abbott refers to 'a project that has, in a large part, been taken up by James Ellroy's novels', which she describes as 'A pointed demythologization ... made by targeting the misogyny, or racism or homophobia at the heart of the tough guy figure' (Abbott 2002: 194). But this demythologization works two ways;

by reinventing the tough guy figure of the noir period and moving his less attractive features to the fore, Ellroy's portrayal becomes more nostalgic: 'he [the white tough guy] solidifies his status as a beloved nostalgia icon, a figure from an antiquated dream, a recurring white fantasy that persists still' (Abbott 2002: 189). No matter how antiquated it might seem, and despite his protestations to the contrary, Ellroy has never been able to turn his back on noir. As his reputation as a literary figure has improved, Ellroy has not rejected noir but placed the genre in a cycle of reinvention which has solidified the status of characters such as Dudley Smith and Pete Bondurant as 'beloved nostalgia icon(s)'. His LA, as Abbott states, is 'deglamourized', but on a different level it is romanticized. Ellroy says of his protagonists, 'they either are somewhat redeemed by love, or fully redeemed by love, or die looking for love. And that's why I love 'em' (Powell 2008b: 171). Equally, his Underworld novels are a celebration of America as much as an indictment: 'the bad things [about America] are tremendously exhilarating to me. It annoys me when people say that my books are depressing because they're not. I think they're exhilarating. I think they're easily the most passionate crime books ever written and I'm a relentlessly positive, hopeful, optimistic, almost utopian person' (Duncan 1996: 84). Ellroy's warped utopia, however, placed conspiracy at the heart of an outwardly democratic political process through his portrayal of American history from the 1940s to the 1970s.

Although there are still relatively few full-length studies of Ellroy's work, his contribution to the genre is frequently referenced in critical overviews of American crime fiction, which suggests he has been successful in establishing himself as a character within the history of the genre. Significantly, most of the scholarship on Ellroy focuses on his literary career from *The Black Dahlia* onwards: the LA Quartet and the Underworld USA trilogy have dominated critical discussions of Ellroy's body of work. Ellroy's first six novels have generated considerably less interest. Much has been written about how the details of his extraordinary life have influenced his fiction. In his study of Ellroy, *Like Hot Knives to the Brain: James Ellroy's Search for Himself* (2005), Peter Wolfe attempts to tie Ellroy's fiction to specific moments in his life, as though the novels are a form of memoir. Anna Flügge's full-length study, *James Ellroy and the Novel of Obsession* (2010), frames Ellroy's work in a genre or sub-genre of obsession narratives.

This study, the latest volume in the Crime Files series, however, is an examination of the diverse narrative styles Ellroy has embraced and experimented with over a significant period of his career. *James Ellroy:*

Demon Dog of Crime Fiction is divided into five chapters which examine different stages of Ellroy's career and trace the evolution of his prose style, novel structure and literary influences. Each stage of Ellroy's career has been fairly distinct. This is partially a consequence of Ellroy writing novels which are part of an ongoing series, but it can also be attributed to the author's penchant for being dismissive of his past work at the beginning of each new project. However, Ellroy has created complex and extensive links from novel to novel in his fictional worlds, and I explore both the stylistic and structural connections between the LA Quartet, the Underworld USA trilogy and the Second LA Quartet. In this study I have tried to redress the balance of critical work on Ellroy by devoting the first two chapters to the six novels which preceded *The Black Dahlia*. The anthology *James Ellroy: A Companion to the Mystery Fiction* by Jim Mancall (2014) is an invaluable guide in this regard, providing insight into early characters such as Fritz Brown and Lloyd Hopkins.

Another issue in critical discussion of Ellroy's work is how to disentangle Ellroy's labyrinthine plotting. In his review of *The Black Dahlia*, Peter Messent wrote, 'If my analysis focuses so much on the complexities of the plot, this is because it is plot that drives this novel, and it is through plot and what it reveals (not through character and authorial point of view) that the text's social critique becomes most apparent' (Messent 2013: 192). Although I agree with Messent that plot drives Ellroy's novels, I have tried as much as possible to avoid discussion of plotting so complex it could warrant multiple volumes in itself. Instead, I focus on the evolution of Ellroy's prose style from novel to novel.

Chapter 1 examines three novels Ellroy wrote early in his career. *Brown's Requiem*, *Clandestine* and *Killer on the Road* were not breakthrough works for Ellroy, and his professional relationship with Avon was not entirely to his liking, but his burning ambition is apparent in his exploration and reinvention of the Raymond Chandler-inspired private detective model in *Brown's Requiem*. The Chandler influence was quickly discarded in *Clandestine* as Ellroy adapted the unsolved murder of his mother into the narrative and capitalized on other themes close to his personal life, such as protagonist Freddy Underhill's longing for transcendent 'wonder'. *Killer on the Road* is more radical still: written from the perspective of a serial killer, it acts as the culmination of Ellroy's work for Avon. In the three Avon novels, Ellroy mixes high and low culture, from references to classical music to comic-book characters. Such a strange and potent mix indicates his desire to carve out a reputation as a literary, as well as genre author.

In Chapter 2, I examine the three novels of the Lloyd Hopkins series. Ellroy wrote the Hopkins novels under editorial pressure to write a popular, lucrative series character, but he struggled to adapt his writing style to the genre conventions that he had, after *Brown's Requiem*, determined to avoid. Lloyd Hopkins is Ellroy's displaced Romantic, a man out of place in a 1980s crime novel, who finds the consumerism of his era deadening. Yet Ellroy contrasts Hopkins' rejection of contemporary culture with criminals who, having abandoned contemporary society's morality and culture, are portrayed as Hopkins' mirror image. The Lloyd Hopkins novels reveal a division between Ellroy and his colleagues regarding the direction of his writing career. This conflict, neatly paralleled in the themes of the novel, existed between Ellroy the self-styled Romantic and Ellroy the commercially viable genre author.

The third chapter focuses exclusively on Ellroy's Black Dahlia narrative. Its scope, however, is not limited to the fictional union between Ellroy, his mother and Elizabeth Short that the author creates through the novel *The Black Dahlia*. Rather, I argue that Ellroy has been developing the Dahlia case into narrative since he first learned of it at the age of eleven. A larger, uncontainable narrative external to the novel emerges when Ellroy's engagement with the Dahlia mythology is seen in its full context.

In Chapter 4, the last three novels of the LA Quartet are discussed by examining the writing style Ellroy adapted during the gruelling revisions forced upon him in the editorial process. For *L.A. Confidential*, Ellroy cut hundreds of pages of text, excising words sentence by sentence, but ultimately retained every scene he had envisaged in the original outline. This proved a turning point in his style as a writer and the style of the genre itself. Although steeped in noir, the Quartet novels are works of experimentation, culminating in *White Jazz*, the novel Ellroy conceived as a symbolic end to noir itself.

The fifth and final chapter is an examination of the Underworld USA series. Ellroy moved beyond noir boundaries and its classic 1950s LA setting in *American Tabloid*, a book in which the State, through the bureaucratic rivalries of competing departments, is shown to be every bit as corrupt as the criminals profiting from the system. In *American Tabloid* and its two sequels, Ellroy portrayed fifteen years of American history through a crime fiction narrative that covered the major events of the late 1950s to the early 1970s through the prism of Ellroy's noir style. By the end of his most ambitious writing project to date, Ellroy had, through fiction, developed noir as a form of historical revisionism.

Having just embarked upon the project of writing a Second Los Angeles Quartet, Ellroy seems determined to prove that his best work lies ahead of him. This study demonstrates how critical opinion is divided between reviewers who still marvel at Ellroy's experimentation and narrative risk taking, and those who feel the Demon Dog persona has become an encumbrance on Ellroy's writing. As an author who thrives on controversy and publicity, Ellroy, I believe, would appreciate the critical schism.

1
Lee Earle Ellroy and the Avon Novels

'James Ellroy' came into being with the publication of his first novel *Brown's Requiem* in 1981. Before that, Ellroy was known by his name at birth, Lee Earle Ellroy. The name change marked a significant moment in his long transition from alcohol- and drug-addicted vagrant to author. Yet despite this remarkable metamorphosis, and Ellroy's strong and powerful writing in his early novels, much of his early literary career was plagued by missed opportunities and messy compromises. Ellroy was able to find a publisher for his first novel remarkably quickly, bypassing the often long struggle aspiring writers face getting their work published. Yet he was unsatisfied in his ambitions: he had hoped he would achieve a new crime-fiction style with his early work.

Part of Ellroy's frustration lay in his sometimes difficult relationship with his first publisher, Avon. Against his better judgement, Ellroy was pushed into several editorial decisions, mostly concerning how the novels should comply with the conventions of the crime fiction genre. Avon published Ellroy's first two novels, *Brown's Requiem* and *Clandestine* (1982), before rejecting his third novel. After a short crisis in his career when he was unable to find a publisher, Ellroy began his professional relationship with the Mysterious Press, who published the Lloyd Hopkins novels. Ellroy returned to Avon to write his sixth novel *Killer on the Road* (1986). One of his most bizarre works, it would also be the last novel Ellroy would write for the publisher.

The lack of recognition Ellroy received as a newly published author drove him to constantly reinvent and refine his writing style during this period. The three Avon novels have been critically overlooked despite the fact that as Ellroy's only stand-alone, non-series novels, there is a greater capacity for stylistic experimentation between each novel than in his later work. Ellroy would draw on his past, often harrowing, experiences as Lee Earle Ellroy for material in the Avon novels. The narratives are suffused with elements of his personal history. However, it would be a mistake to think of the Avon novels as merely a form of fictional autobiography. They also reflect how Ellroy, even during periods of homelessness and recidivism, had developed a sophisticated understanding of the complex history of the genre, and here lies the genesis of his Demon Dog persona. The other side to Lee Earle Ellroy, less apparent than the drug addict, alcoholic, voyeur-burglar and periodically homeless criminal (but in a curious sense dependent on it) was the aspiring author: 'I spent much more time reading than I ever did stealing or peeping. They never mention that. It's a lot sexier to write about my mother, her death, my wild youth, and my jail time than it is to say that Ellroy holed up in a library with a bottle of wine and read books' (Rich 2008: 181).

The last days of Lee Earle Ellroy

Although they were never close, the death of Ellroy's father, Armand Lee Ellroy, in 1965 precipitated Ellroy's decline into addiction, homelessness and crime which lasted until the mid-1970s. Years later, when his literary reputation was rising, the manic, aggressive performances Ellroy would give in interviews and book readings were drawn from the knowledge that his unusual early life could be adapted to suit his identity as a crime writer, an identity that would eventually make him a key figure in the history of the genre.

Before the age of seventeen, Ellroy had endured the trauma of his mother's unsolved murder, was expelled from the predominately Jewish Fairfax High School for fighting and truancy, volunteered for the US Army and then faked a nervous breakdown in order to secure a quick discharge, and had even briefly been a member of the American Nazi Party. Ellroy became an alcohol and substance abuser, drinking gin, Romilar CF cough syrup and using amphetamines and Benzedrix inhalers. In his interviews and memoirs, Ellroy candidly describes his attempt to recast himself as an eccentric LA character, sleeping rough in parks and (by his own account) carrying around a bust of Beethoven for company. This striking juxtaposition revels in both low life and high culture, which Ellroy would attempt to merge throughout his career. By the late 1960s, Ellroy's criminality was fuelled by his sexual voyeurism. He would break into the houses of wealthy families who lived in Hancock Park, taking food and drink from their kitchens, rifling through drawers and sniffing women's panties, 'circumspectly, very, very cautiously, [and with] great concern to cover my tracks' (Powell 2009: 196). Even in breaking the law, Ellroy finds room to deviate from and thus rewrite the criminal type, and his moderate 'circumspect' approach to criminality seems out of keeping with the fervour he invested in almost every other pursuit. Yet the voyeurism that he developed in these early years would be a continual motif in his works.

As he was learning about crime by indulging in it, Ellroy was also nurturing another obsession which would come to define him in later years, an obsession that had the potential to help him give up his criminality and imbue it with a sense of narrative meaning:

> I was always thinking about how I would become a great novelist. I just didn't think that I would write *crime* novels. I thought that I would be a literary writer, whose creative duty is to describe the world as it is. The problem is that I never enjoyed books like that. I only enjoyed crime stories. So more than anything, this fascination with writing was an issue of identity. (Rich 2008: 181)

Ellroy offers an image of himself as a wild man and then undermines it. By distancing himself from his earlier disclosures, the more extreme aspects of his life that he capitalized on to promote his novels are debunked in his desire to be viewed predominantly as an aspiring author rather than a criminal. The two identities would merge in the gradual formulation of his literary persona. Ellroy has crafted an image of his younger self as ambiguous and undefinable, neither fully a criminal nor an author. From its inception, the Demon Dog persona was always subversive, and not subservient, to Ellroy's 'creative duty' to realism. Against the odds, crime fiction would be Ellroy's conduit into becoming a 'literary writer', but his ultimate ambition was to both embrace and transcend the crime fiction genre.

None of Ellroy's difficulties, even his criminal record and jail time, deterred him in his ambition to become a writer. Quite the contrary: 'Booze and drugs ... are powerful inducers of fantasy' (Meeks 1990: 21). Yet although these fantasies and obsessions drove him, he always maintained an objective distance as an observer and outsider. Speaking about his time in jail, Ellroy explained, 'I always had some germ of circumspection that said, "White boy, don't open your mouth." I think I should've been in grad school somewhere' (Kihn 1992: 30). Ellroy's humour is rooted in his self-embodiment of high and low culture: he mimics the language of the streets, which is demeaning to him, 'white boy', and pairs it with a reference to 'grad school' that makes him sound snobbish. The internal dialogue implies the author sees his past self as a character, and all characters, even real-life ones, are there, in Ellroy's words, 'to be manipulated', an important point when approaching Ellroy's countless autobiographical admissions (Duncan 1996: 81). Ellroy's ambition was to tease out the circumspection which was blocking his complete assumption of a criminal life, and yet still apply some of his criminal experiences to narrative. In 1977, Ellroy started attending Alcoholics Anonymous, and the following year he began making notes for a novel that had been 'churning in his subconscious for years' (Kihn 1992: 31). He had been aware, even during his darkest periods, that his experiences contained the potential for narrative.

Ellroy found his first regular job caddying, although it did not begin smoothly as he was fired from the Hillcrest Country Club for fighting with another caddy. He then began to work for the Bel-Air Country Club where the clientele included several Hollywood celebrities (Milward 1997). It was at this time that he began outlining his first novel, but panic quickly set in: 'I stopped because I was afraid I might write the book and not sell it; I was afraid that I might fail in general' (Kihn 1992: 31). It was an act of faith that persuaded Ellroy to start writing: 'on January 26, 1979, he went out onto the green, stared up at the sky, and prayed: "Please, God, let me start this book tonight"' (Kihn 1992: 31). In other sources, Ellroy has given this anecdote a hint of irreverence: 'I was on the golf course. And I actually sent up a prayer to my seldom sought, blandly Protestant God. "God," I said, "would you please let me start this fucking book tonight?"' (Meeks 1990: 22). Ellroy's profane supplication to a 'Protestant God' makes his faith, such as it is, a subversive and creative act. Ellroy is both iconoclastic and traditional, and his approach to writing has been to bring the two into direct conflict.

Brown's Requiem: death and rebirth

Caddying combined some of the desperation of Ellroy's earlier life with a new insight into how the underbelly of society services the elite: '95 percent of most country club caddies ... are alcoholics, drug addicts, and compulsive gamblers' (Swaim 1987: 16). His experiences as a caddy were to be an integral part of *Brown's Requiem*, but a brief unsuccessful interim in detective work was also an influence: 'I had quit caddying for a spell, to work for an attorney service. Basically I was a processor server, but I couldn't make any money at it, because it was contingency work, and I wasn't very good at finding people' (Silet 1995: 42). Ellroy's emotional investment in failed men would help form the characters of would-be private detective Fritz Brown and his deranged client Freddy 'Fat Dog' Baker.

Fritz Brown is an ex-policeman turned repossession agent, 'Repoman', who has officially registered as a private investigator merely as a tax front. 'Fat Dog' Baker, a corpulent golf caddy, hires Brown to investigate the middle-aged Jewish businessman Sol Kupferman. Kupferman is paying for the music lessons of Baker's sister Jane, a cellist, and the anti-Semitic Fat Dog fears he may have designs on her. Brown finds himself attracted to Jane, and they become lovers, but disturbed by what Jane tells him of her brother, Brown begins to investigate Fat Dog. Brown learns that Fat Dog was implicated in a nightclub firebombing case which killed six people but was shielded from prosecution by corrupt LAPD Lieutenant Haywood Cathcart, who has been using Fat Dog as an enforcer. Events appear to be heading towards a showdown between Brown and Fat Dog, but Ellroy unexpectedly closes down this storyline halfway through the novel with the sudden death of Fat Dog, and gradually pivots events so that the climax is a deadly confrontation between Brown and Cathcart.

Ellroy has repeatedly stressed the autobiographical side to the narrative: 'Here's a guy [Brown] who looks exactly like me, has a German-American background, likes classical music, came from my old neighborhood, gets involved with a bunch of caddies. All that's me' (Duncan 1996: 64). But what Ellroy has not explicitly stated is that both the protagonist and the antagonist were based on aspects of his own personality. Fat Dog is a caddy who sleeps rough on golf courses. Ellroy was caddying at the time of writing the novel and, years earlier, spent time sleeping in LA parks. The criminal, shambolic and anti-social Fat Dog might seem like the more natural parallel with Lee Earle Ellroy than Brown who, despite the occasional moral lapse, is a former policeman turned moderately successful businessman. Ellroy, however, has insisted on distancing himself from Fat Dog: 'I invented a nice Arsonist … I knew a caddy who was called Fat Dog who slept on golf courses' (Rich 2008: 182). Fat Dog's nickname foreshadows Ellroy's Demon Dog persona; however, Fat Dog's name is rather ironic as although he dreams of owning racing dogs, he enjoys torturing animals. Ellroy, however, is a dog lover. Indeed, Fat Dog is Ellroy's nemesis as much as he is Ellroy's former self, as his anti-Semitism and voyeurism connect directly with Ellroy's own containable, but nonetheless questionable, obsessions. Fat Dog's anti-Semitism extends towards an adulation of Nazism, but Ellroy was never a Nazi ideologue, using it instead as a prod 'to infuriate and sicken his peers and teachers' (Rowston 2012). However, his brief association with the party was a source of guilt. He began a relationship 'five months into my first book' with a woman named Penny in June 1979: 'She was Jewish. That appealed to me. It would force me to atone for prior anti-Semitism' (Ellroy 2010: 57). Redemption and rebirth are major themes of the novel as Ellroy was compelled to make Jane Baker and Fat Dog partly Jewish, and it is later revealed they are the illegitimate children of Kupferman. That Fat Dog's father was Jewish and his adoptive parents were Russian Jews who anglicized their name is Ellroy's way of mocking the dead man, rendering his racism ludicrous, and by extension, further atoning for his own past bigotry.

Despite his dislike of Fat Dog, Brown sympathizes with him and recognizes how their different upbringing pushed Fat Dog to his fate: '[I] was tempered with some love and gentleness. ... All he knew was anger, hatred, and meanness. ... He deserved better' (Ellroy 1981: 121–2). Brown's ambivalent relationship with Fat Dog mirrors Ellroy's identification with him. Peter Wolfe argues Ellroy has an 'urge to be fair ... he will safeguard the integrity of his books against *his* evil side. One familiar countercheck is his tactic of identifying with scurvy characters' (Wolfe 2005: 15–6). Brown's sympathy, which places him in Fat Dog's shoes, is extended through their names: Brown and Fat Dog share the same initials, FB.

Ellroy's personal experiences also inform the romantic sub-plot of the novel. Brown and Jane's relationship reflected Ellroy's sexual frustration following his recovery from drug addiction: 'I wanted sex. I wanted all that stuff and I wasn't getting any, and that's what really informs that book [*Brown's Requiem*]' (Duncan 1996: 64). As with his voyeuristically motivated housebreaking, Ellroy's obsession with what he could not have spurred him to follow female musicians around LA:

> Symphony concerts ended around 10 p.m. Women with violins and cellos scooted out rear exits. I was a tongue-tied stage-door Johnny. Most of the women met their husbands and boyfriends. They wore tight black orchestra gowns with cinched waists and plunging necklines. They looked anxious to shuck their work duds, belt a few and talk music. Single women walked out, lugging heavy instruments. I offered to help several of them. They all said no. (Ellroy 2010: 49)

Ellroy has never been afraid to cast himself in a bad light, yet his dubious behaviour around female musicians and involuntary abstinence is not transplanted onto Brown, whose sexual relationship with Jane begins fairly soon after their first meeting, making him more of a fantasy version of Ellroy than a direct portrayal. This is apparent in Brown's somewhat laughable boasting. After inviting Jane back to his apartment on the pretext of listening to chamber music, he reports 'in the end we didn't listen to chamber music, we made our own' (Ellroy 1981: 90). By contrast, Fat Dog, unkempt and ugly, 'looked like a refugee from the Lincoln Heights drunk tank', and appears at first to be sexless (Ellroy 1981: 12). However, his sexual tastes are animalistic, as Brown discovers Fat Dog owns a collection of extreme pornography. Fat Dog is unable to separate sex from perversion, anger from sadism.

Ellroy's voyeuristic obsession with classical musicians is suggestive of his striving for critical superiority. The novel's original title, 'Concerto for Orchestra', eventually became the title of the fifth and final section of the novel (Ellroy 1980). The title was changed to *Brown's Requiem*, which suggests both music and death, at Avon's insistence. The publisher wanted a novel grounded in the genre, whereas Ellroy desired to rise above crime fiction: 'At the time I was reading some recent crime fiction and rereading some of my old favorites, and I had this sneaking suspicion that I could do better' (Silet 1995: 42). Ellroy was fiercely ambitious and fantasized about surpassing established authors in the genre. Yet because Ellroy did not have full creative control of *Brown's Requiem*, he felt thwarted in his creative ambitions. Unable to discard the private eye model, he attempted to visually distance his work from it by suggesting the front cover depict a woman holding a cello: he was again overruled (Ellroy 2010: 49).

Despite his desire to escape the confines of crime fiction through classical music, *Brown's Requiem* also pays homage to Raymond Chandler, and it reflects the style and conventions that Chandler had developed and Ellroy had learned to imitate through his wide reading of the genre. When Brown walks into the Westwood hotel, his first-person narration directly references Chandler:

> Walking into the hotel was like walking into another era. The flat finished white stucco walls, ratty Persian carpets in the hallway and mahogany doors almost had me convinced it was 1938 and that my fictional predecessor Philip Marlowe was about to confront me with a wisecrack. (Ellroy 1981: 193)

Despite Ellroy's meta-fictional reference to Chandler's influence, with Brown describing Philip Marlowe as his fictional predecessor, Ellroy's Brown is an errant offspring of Marlowe. Ellroy liberally imitates, hyperbolizes, and somewhat mocks Chandler's style in his use of colourful first-person prose and unusual similes: 'I was never a child. I came out of my mother's womb full-grown, clutching a biography of Beethoven and an empty glass. My first words were "Where's the booze?"' (Ellroy 1981: 129). The first section of the novel is titled 'I, Private Eye', which acts as a form of introduction to Brown's first-person prose. The title is a doubling of Brown, separate from his parallels with Fat Dog, which refers to the distinction between the image and reality of the character as a private detective. Dennis Porter has identified the characteristics of Marlowe's witticisms: 'The quintessence of Chandler's style is what came to be known as a "Chandlerism". That is, in the finality of his one- or two-liners that elevates the wise-crack of an American, urban folk tradition to the level of a hardboiled conceit.' (Porter 2003: 105) Rather than 'elevate the wise-crack', Brown's one-liners veer towards parody in their homage to Marlowe. Ellroy's overt Chandler references imbue Brown with what Porter dubs a 'finality' as a character, as though he cannot break free from the pastiche. The references are an oppositional movement to the classical music theme which seeks to raise the narrative out of the genre. The location also blurs the lines between author and fiction, as the Westwood hotel, which reminds Brown of Chandler in its furnishings, was the location where Ellroy was living in LA, in a $25-a-week room, when he outlined and drafted the novel (Meeks 1990: 21).

The death of Fat Dog half way through the novel throws Brown and the narrative into a flux, and Ellroy breaks from the Chandler model here at least in terms of plotting. Instead of a violent showdown with Fat Dog, Brown is forced to confront Haywood Cathcart, the crime boss who ordered Fat Dog's murder. Brown finds the slain Fat Dog in Mexico, and against his better judgement, feels compelled to bury his mutilated corpse:

> I was somewhat inured to violent death and stiffs, but Fat Dog's was too much: the stench crept through the wadded-up Kleenex and my eyes stung from the acidity of rotting flesh. I grabbed the corpse by both wrists and pulled. The left arm came loose at its socket, flying up in the air, spraying decomposing matter. I lost my balance and almost fell, letting out a strangled cry when a viscous glob of rented flesh flew up and hit me in the cheek. (Ellroy 1981: 123)

Brown decides to bury Fat Dog out of a quixotic sense of honour. From his professional viewpoint, there is nothing to be gained from burying the man he would himself have killed in different circumstances. Indeed, he initially leaves the scene of the crime only to return to show the body to a relative of one of Fat Dog's victims, Omar Gonzalez, who was also planning to kill Fat Dog. Whenever he is close to Fat Dog, Brown is in danger, and this applies even after Fat Dog's death. While he is moving the body, the two hit-men who murdered Fat Dog return and kill Gonzalez, and a shoot-out ensues in which Brown manages to kill the two men but is left deeply shaken. Through the characters of Brown and Fat Dog, Ellroy is metaphorically using one part of his personality to bury the other part. This inner struggle is embodied in the corpse of Fat Dog which still seems to be fighting with Brown and even in death manages a comically disgusting insult: 'a viscous glob of rented flesh flew up and hit me in the cheek.' Ironically, Brown does not bury Fat Dog as he had planned. Accepting that Gonzalez was by far the better man, he moves his corpse into the hastily dug grave and burns Fat Dog's body alongside those of the two hit-men. The chaos of the circumstances leads Brown to continually reassess his course of action, and by extension, both his and Fat Dog's moral identity.

Brown's feelings towards Fat Dog are ambiguous, but Fat Dog's death sends the character into an uncharacteristic, depressive state of inaction. One factor that motivates Brown into renewing his investigation is a bizarre encounter with some hippies on a beach who cook and eat a dead dog:

> 'I toast all of you,' I said. 'Truly you are the survivors of both capitalism and the rapacious, fanatic counter-culture it spawned. When I said earlier that I envied you your freedom, I was bullshitting. I thought you were just another cadre of dumb hippies. But I was wrong to condescend. I apologize. In a small way, you have life by the ass and I salute you.' They didn't quite know how to react. The joint was passed to me and I inhaled deeply. I was expecting more applause and laughter. Instead, through the blazing fire I got warm smiles and puzzled looks. (Ellroy 1981: 136)

The encounter with the hippies acts as a metaphoric exorcism of his depression after the death of Fat Dog. Specifically, the eating of the dog meat is symbolic of the regeneration of the private investigator in Brown, as he will further investigate Fat Dog's crimes and also avenge his murder in the final confrontation with Cathcart. The dog meal suggests how society has exploited the underclass that Fat Dog belonged to, a literal rendering of 'dog eat dog'. Fat Dog's life of crime can therefore be construed as his revenge on the social system. The hippies, who are by no means violent like Fat Dog but who are similar to him in their earthiness, are oblivious to the hypocrisy that Brown sees, especially as it is they who instigate the eating of the dog. Brown has always been dismissive of, even hostile to, left-wing culture. Although Brown and Fat Dog are both right wing, Fat Dog took this to extremes whereas Brown is a moderate conservative, even a 'bleeding heart' compared to some of his former LAPD colleagues (Ellroy 1981: 122). Brown is defensive of being perceived as soft though, and states categorically, 'I'm no liberal' (Ellroy 1981: 121). Brown's conservatism is rooted in a distinct hatred for large swathes of contemporary culture as a prior visit to Berkeley 'gave me the creeps: the people passing by looked aesthetic and angry, driven inward by forces they couldn't comprehend and rendered sickly by their refusal to eat meat' (Ellroy 1981: 7). Brown equates aestheticism with a puritanical anger; the hippies, by contrast, lead a hedonistic, counter-cultural lifestyle. They are more 'rapacious' and 'fanatic' than the capitalism they object to, insofar as they have coherent views, for Brown recognizes the need to protest is instinctually easier than the murky compromises he makes in his job. Brown's identity is the antithesis of hippy belief. He is proud to be an ex-cop and businessman: in their eyes, the embodiment of capitalist authoritarianism. Yet, the hippies are welcoming and friendly to Brown, and it is he who is morally shocked at their form of consumption.

If Fritz Brown and Fat Dog were both drawn from facets of Ellroy's own character, there is one character in *Brown's Requiem*, Walter, who was based on an important friend to Ellroy. The novel is dedicated to Randy Rice, the inspiration for the Walter character. Rice had shared several of Ellroy's addictions before helping him overcome them. Ellroy and Rice also had the same obsessions: 'We used to spend HOURS hashing over the Black Dahlia case and talking about crime fiction' (Swaim 1987: 15). Ellroy suffered a bout of what he himself dubbed 'post-alcoholic brain syndrome' at Rice's apartment (Kihn 1992: 21). Rice called an ambulance, an act which probably saved Ellroy's life: 'Randy Rice told him later that he twitched and writhed for twelve hours straight' (Kihn 1992: 25).

Walter is Fritz Brown's closest friend. He is an unemployed alcoholic who lives with his mother, but he is the embodiment of Brown's conscience in the novel, even though his character has no direct bearing on the mystery narrative. Despite his shortcomings, Walter's intense, forceful personality holds great sway with Brown:

> Walter has taken fantasy into the dimension of genius. His is pure verbal fantasy: Walter has never written, filmed, or composed anything. Nonetheless, in his perpetual T-Bird haze he can transform his wino fantasies into insights and parables that touch at the quick

of life. On his good days, that is. On his bad ones he can sound like a high school kid wired up on bad speed. I hoped he was on today, for I was exhilarated myself, and felt the need of his stimulus: the power of a Walter epigram can clarify the most puzzling day. (Ellroy 1981: 20)

The ability to stretch and expand a genre was what fascinated Ellroy about his friend. Ellroy credits Rice with co-creating a vital component of his Demon Dog persona: 'Dog' humour, which Ellroy described as 'the crassest, vilest, most offensive [humour]' (Jayanti 2001). The seeds of Dog humour are present in *Brown's Requiem:* Brown's Chandlerisms and wisecracks are contrasted with Fat Dog's unrelenting bigotry. Walter possesses what Ellroy and Rice clung to during their addictions, as it distinguished them, in their own view, from other addicts: an inner talent which could create 'insights and parables that touch at the quick of life'. Brown and Walter grew up in the same neighbourhood in LA, but Brown moved on and assumed several identities – policeman, private detective and businessman – whereas Walter stayed in the neighbourhood, permanently unemployed and seemingly frozen in time. Walter's decline could have been Brown's or even Ellroy's: he is a victim of life whose abilities were greater than his achievements. Walter dies prematurely of cirrhosis of the liver leaving Brown devastated. Ellroy has spoken little of what became of Randy Rice, but in the documentary *Feast of Death* Ellroy comments, 'Sometimes I miss him', which suggests he may have met the same fate as Walter (Jayanti 2001).

Although his presence appears incidental, Walter's emotional hold over Brown affects Brown's approach to the investigation. When Brown begins tracing the background of the two hit-men he killed in Tijuana, seemingly by chance he spots a young Mexican woman he recognizes as a performer in the pornographic material that had belonged to Fat Dog. Brown ponders this coincidence: 'Walter used to tell me that *everything* in life was connected. I didn't believe him. Now I did. It was eerie, almost like proof of the existence of God' (Ellroy 1981: 145). Brown, through Walter's creative inspiration, ponders the role of a supernatural agent, clarifying and connecting but also giving meaning and reason to seemingly unrelated events. Significantly, Brown does not put all the pieces of the mystery together solely by intellect: some events of the novel appear to occur by chance or, Brown implies, by divine intervention.

Ellroy uses Brown to test the limits of crime fiction. Indeed, Brown's musings on God read like an authorial comment on the crime-fiction genre. The novel was published fifteen years after Tzvetan Todorov's influential essay 'The Typology of Detective Fiction', in which he argued that a detective novel essentially tells two stories: the story of the crime and the story of the investigation. Everything that is related to the reader should connect as part of a larger whole, 'the structure of the whole', as though all the action and dialogue are pieces of a puzzle which when arranged correctly and coherently serve to solve the mystery (Todorov 1966: 52). Ellroy's intentions were more expansive than Todorov's definition as none of the 'types' of detective fiction Todorov identifies – 'whodunit', 'thriller', 'adventure story' – quite fit Ellroy's methods of storytelling in *Brown's Requiem*.

However, Todorov's explanation of the connectivity of the two stories, crime and investigation, in the 'whodunit' style bears some similarity to Ellroy's debut novel: 'This first story, that of the crime, ends before the second begins. But what happens in the second? Not much. The characters of this second story, the story of the investigation, do not act, they learn' (Todorov 1966: 52). Todorov allows the first half of the story for action, the second for thought. Brown is trapped in a state of inaction for a period after Fat Dog's death, but the investigation eventually changes course and begins again. Brown is not the intellectual equal of the detectives Todorov uses as examples, Hercule Poirot and Philo Vance. Therefore, as a form of narrative connectivity, chance plays a larger role in his investigation out of necessity. The link between the two halves of the novel is complex because Brown is never fully certain of what he is investigating or what he hopes to achieve. The farce surrounding the burial of Fat Dog and Gonzalez develops Brown as a man who can be both brave and honourable but still confused and indecisive. Ellroy has a 'romantic fascination with the intangible', and the subtly revealing parallels between Brown and his two nemeses, Fat Dog and Cathcart, tears down Todorov's neat dividing lines between crime and investigation (Powell 2012b: 161).

Ellroy's early plotting style, which allows Brown's investigation to take a sudden emotional detour, led to criticism from some quarters. Paul Duncan said of Ellroy's debut, '*Brown's Requiem* contains the embryo of the later Ellroy: the fallen cop anti-hero who's an orphan, the *noir* heroine, the machinery of corruption. But its prose outshines its plot' (Duncan 1996: 31). Brown is in awe of events bigger than himself. This is, in itself, a plot device as the reference to 'God' suggests both an omniscient narrator and a mystery storyline in which everything connects. Brown, however, is an inadequate detective. He cannot unravel mysteries intellectually and fulfil this convention of the genre. Brown's shortcomings as a detective are ironic considering he is a cultural snob.

His passion for classical music is equalled only by his passionate hatred of rock music, and by the coda this leads to his biggest humiliation as a character.

Brown's Requiem does not fall comfortably into either Todorov's codifying of the detective novel or the Chandler model of private detective to which Ellroy admitted to being 'heavily indebted' (Hogan 1995: 58). As an echo of this debt, the ending of the novel explores the implications of following great men. Ellroy may imitate Chandler's cynical style, and Brown shares Marlowe's limited capacity for action against larger forces at work, yet Ellroy never set out to replicate Chandler's manifesto for how the hardboiled detective should act in 'The Simple Art of Murder':

> Down these mean streets a man must go who is not himself mean, who is neither tarnished nor afraid. The detective must be a complete man and a common man and yet an unusual man. He must be, to use a rather weathered phrase, a man of honor. He talks as the man of his age talks, that is, with rude wit, a lively sense of the grotesque, a disgust for sham, and a contempt for pettiness. (Chandler 1950: 44)

At the beginning of the novel, Brown displays very few of these admirable qualities. Brown, like Marlowe, is weathered and possesses a ready wit, but he is often passive to the extent where he is afraid. Ellroy would later admit that the Chandler influence was 'one that I've had an apostasy regarding' (Hogan 1995: 58). For a first-time writer, Chandler's style, Ellroy commented, 'is easy to adapt to the personal prejudices of the individual' (Hogan 1995: 57). Ellroy limited the overt Chandler influence to this single novel. He would come to regard Chandler negatively, perhaps even bitterly, as a limiting influence on crime fiction that was too easily imitated.

> Down these mean streets the single man who can make a difference must go. There is an institutionalized rebelliousness to it that comes out of a cheap liberalism that I despise. It's always the rebel. It's always the private eye standing up to the system. That doesn't interest me. What interest me are the toadies of the system. (Duncan 1996: 85)

In echoing Chandler's prose in his attack, Ellroy exposes the contradictions of the Chandler model. By the 1980s, a single man standing up to the system was such a cliché that Ellroy dubs it 'institutionalized rebelliousness'. By moving away from this model, Ellroy would nurture his own radicalism, ironically, by portraying the profitable submissiveness of the 'toadies of the system'.

Despite Brown's acknowledgement that he is a pawn in the system, his Romantic beliefs make him less cynical than Philip Marlowe. Brown follows nihilism with spontaneous creativity. After a paid sexual encounter with a prostitute bores him, Brown suffers from nightmares. He awakens suddenly after a poem comes to him in an instant:

> There's an electric calm at the
> Heart of the storm,
> Transcendentally alive and safe and warm.
> So get out now
> And search the muse,
> The blight is real,
> You have to choose,
> The choice is yours,
> Your mind demurs,
> It's yours, it's his, it's ours, it's hers.
> Moral stands will save us yet,
> The alternative is certain death. (Ellroy 1981: 230)

Brown creates this poem from thin air rather than labouring over its construction, which is entirely in keeping with his character as a detective who relies on epiphanies. To 'search the muse' is a method of investigation as well as a creative act. He thinks of the poem again on the eve of his confrontation with Cathcart. He is fully aware that his life is in danger on this course of action but the 'moral stand' is a form of salvation as the alternative is a 'certain death' even worse than what Cathcart can inflict on him. In the dream that precedes the poem, Brown sees himself and Fat Dog in a reversal of roles: 'Fat Dog, wearing a blue uniform and a gun stopping jaywalkers on Hollywood Boulevard, and me carrying golf bags' (Ellroy 1981: 230). The role reversal symbolizes Brown's assumption of both roles, and by extension, Ellroy's affinity with the two characters. Brown will never be as morally repugnant as Fat Dog, but by killing Cathcart he is avenging his former nemesis and standing by his ideal that even Fat Dog deserves justice, albeit extra-judicial, along with Cathcart's other countless and nameless victims. Justifying his vigilantism, Brown once again invokes God when his planning of Cathcart's assassination goes smoothly and efficiently:

'It was so perfect that I almost collapsed in gratitude. Maybe there was a God' (Ellroy 1981: 233).

Poetry is not the only art form that takes on greater importance as Brown prepares himself for his defining moment with Cathcart. Brown's usual passion for music had been soured after Fat Dog's death. When the case comes to an apparent dead end, his love of music evaporates as it no longer makes sense to him. When Brown finally confronts Cathcart, he is shocked to discover they share an admiration for the work of Anton Bruckner, further signalling his disillusionment with the form. Cathcart admonishes Brown about the meaning of Bruckner's music:

> Good. You love Bruckner. But you don't understand him. What his music meant. It's about containment. Refined emotions. Sacrifice. Purity. Control. Duty. The muted melancholy throughout his symphonies! A call to arms. A policeman who loves Bruckner and you can't feel his essence. He never wed, Brown. He never fucked women. He wouldn't expend one ounce of his creative energy on anything but his vision. *I have been Anton Bruckner,* Brown. You can be, too. You come from good stock, you're a big strong man. You can be of service, it's just a question of reeducation. I'll tell you what I'll do. I'll... (Ellroy 1981: 240)

Brown shoots Cathcart dead before he can finish his speech, repulsed that the music he had loved has been used to justify a lifetime of crimes. Cathcart's malevolence could just as easily have been formed in Brown, and his embodiment, in its extreme interpretation of the composer's work and values, '*I have been Anton Bruckner*', creates a pattern for replication: 'You can be, too'. Brown fears such a single-minded and controlling interpretation. His love for classical music is more natural, and he prefers to experience it through his feelings, as with his romance with the cellist Jane. Cathcart, however, views it academically. Bruckner's music is a type of disciplining method. It advances his criminal career by allowing him to shed sentimentality and replace it with 'Refined emotions. Sacrifice. Purity. Control. Duty'. Brown has an openly emotional attitude toward music; he can remember the day, 2 September 1967, when he first listened to Beethoven's Third Symphony, and his reaction was to immediately give up on his dreams of being an academic and pursue a career in the LAPD. Music 'went through me like a transfusion of hope and fortitude. ... I had found truth, or so I thought, and a strange metamorphosis took place' (Ellroy 1981: 67). However, after killing Cathcart, the metamorphosis is reversed, and Brown's love of music contributes to his decline. He loses a fortune after an ill-advised investment in a restaurant selling 'jumbo sandwiches named after composers' and his visit to the Bayreuth music festival ends disastrously when he gets into a fight with two 'British yobs' (Ellroy 1981: 246). Music has come to symbolize his degeneration into both violence and consumerism.

By the coda, Brown concedes that rather than being in control of the narrative or the Requiem of the title: 'I was part of the insane, tragic music of so many people's lives. That summer was my concerto for orchestra – each instrument in the orchestra having a voice equal, yet distinct from all the others' (Ellroy 1981: 248). These closing words shed light on Ellroy's intention with the novel's original title 'Concerto for Orchestra'. *Brown's Requiem* is an intriguing play on words as it suggests Brown's death, although, as it is possessive, the title also implies Brown's authorship of the Requiem. However, Brown concedes that the circumstances, 'the music', drive the story. Music is also a comment on the novel itself: the characters perform in a specific way for the pieces of the mystery to fall into place, just as every instrument in an orchestra is reliant on the others. In the final line of the novel, Brown retreats to the simplicity which is the genesis of his obsessions: 'I listen to a lot of music' (Ellroy 1981: 248). Music no longer reflects the complexity of events that Brown was embroiled in as he is now living comfortably off an investment in a liquor store, which, as Jim Mancall points out, is rather ironic: 'selling a commodity that killed Walter and against which Brown has struggled all his life' (Mancall 2014: 59). But then just as he ate dog meat shortly after Fat Dog's death and visited Bayreuth after killing the Bruckner devotee Cathcart, Brown finds redemption in what is destructive to him. His requiem is both literal and metaphoric, covering the death of his former self and the actual death of Fat Dog. In both these characters, James Ellroy the crime writer was born.

Clandestine: the anti-private detective phase

Ellroy began writing what became his second novel, *Clandestine*, one month after completing the manuscript for *Brown's Requiem*, and he was well into the drafting stages when his debut work was being edited. According to Ellroy, 'I wrote *Brown's Requiem*, and I had a tremendous revelation when I finished it. I realized that all modern private-eye novels are bullshit, and that I would never write another one' (Silet 1995: 44). However, with this statement Ellroy appears to put the drafting of his novels in an overly neat chronological order. Ellroy was juggling the two projects at the same time, and there would inevitably be some thematic and stylistic overlap, such as the use of first-person narration and the sudden, unexpected plot detour halfway through the novel. *Brown's Requiem* had not achieved much critical impact, or for that matter brought him fame: 'It sold scant copies. ... The cover sucked Airedale dicks. Fuck – a man with a gun and a golf course' (Ellroy 2010: 66). Avon's cover choice put Ellroy more comfortably in the genre which he was trying to transcend. Judging from his initial elated response at the publication of his first novel, Ellroy had been expecting a degree of celebrity: 'With his first check as an author, Ellroy got a hooker, paid his back rent, bought a cashmere sweater and a $500 1964 Chevrolet Nova, and took his girlfriend away for the weekend. By Monday, he was broke' (Kihn 1992: 31). His initial excitement would turn to disappointment. Only a few years into sobriety he was still nurturing a wild-man persona, but as yet, he had not found a way to make it financially lucrative.

In *Clandestine*, Ellroy attempted to build a bigger profile for himself as an author in a genre that he was already beginning to view with disdain. Paul Cobley accurately identified Ellroy's emerging attitude towards the private-detective novel in the crime genre: 'For Ellroy and others, the private eye genre is – by comparison with preferred narratives about the police – a complete confection and thoroughgoing conceit' (Cobley 2000: 100).

Ellroy's problem with the generic Chandler-inspired private eye he had used in *Brown's Requiem* was its lack of authenticity:

> The reader out to sate his dark curiosity and inform himself on the violence that surrounds him will want a hero, or antihero, who meets the requirements of a realistic vision. In one of the 87th Precinct books, McBain's hero Steve Carella ruminates that the last time he ran across a private eye investigating a murder was never. (Tucker 1984: 9)

In *Clandestine*, Freddy Upton Underhill is Ellroy's attempt to meet 'the requirements of a realistic vision' in a 1950s LA setting. Underhill is neither a hero nor anti-hero but a man operating in a world of unclear moral guidelines. A draft dodger during the war, he has hidden his past to build a promising career in the LAPD: at the age of 27 he becomes the youngest officer to join the Detective Bureau. Underhill's charm and apparent decency mask some uglier habits. He is a serial womanizer, and at least one casual sexual encounter comes back to haunt him. Ellroy's new vision stipulated Underhill would not be a private detective, but through the course of the novel he becomes one of sorts. Four years after he is forced out of the LAPD, he conducts a private investigation, albeit with no client to represent. He is motivated purely by his conscience.

Underhill's name symbolizes some of the changes his character experiences over the course of the novel. His name is also suggestive of his underhandedness: Underhill is clandestine, both in his sexual life and as an investigator. Peter Wolfe argues the name echoes Underhill's rise and fall as a character, as he is at first (Up)ton and latterly (Under)hill (Wolfe 2005: 65). The symbolism of the title *Clandestine* is meta-fictionally revealed at key moments in the text. One character uses the word 'clandestine' to describe his role in Intelligence operations during the war, a couple in a forbidden affair 'love clandestinely', and there is even a religious cult 'The Order of the Clandestine Heart' (Ellroy 1982: 265). The constant reappearance of the word and the different connotations of each usage allude to the many different forms of illegitimate identity which are unmasked in the narrative.

One major theme is the continual shifting and reordering of family units. Underhill, an orphan, finds himself an interloper in several unusual families. Underhill's main love interest is the Jewish attorney Lorna Weinberg, whom he meets in the dining room of a golf club (another carry-over setting from the previous novel). Their attraction is sparked by their opposite personalities. Underhill is young and fit; Lorna is older and has a deformed leg after her pelvis was crushed in a car crash at the age of thirteen. Underhill has typically authoritarian views for a policeman, whereas Lorna is a liberal who naturally distrusts the police. Another attraction between them is their shared suffering. Underhill never knew his parents, and Lorna had a difficult relationship with her mother. Underhill and Lorna cannot start a family together as Lorna is barren. When both their careers fall apart, and they are at their lowest ebb, they decide to marry. The marriage soon runs into difficulties and they separate. Underhill only manages to reunite with Lorna when he gains a proxy son and finally starts the family he never had.

In *Brown's Requiem*, Ellroy had drawn on disparate elements of his own life for material. The mystery narrative of *Clandestine* was based on a single event in his life, the murder of his mother Geneva Hilliker Ellroy. It is not a straight retelling, however. Ellroy splits this single murder into two separate murders in the narrative, set in two distinct time periods of the novel, 1951 and 1955. In the first two-thirds of the novel, the action takes place in the 1951 setting, and then it shifts to the 1955 setting after Underhill's murder investigation collapses and he is forced out of the LAPD. It is a narrative break as radical and sudden as the death of Fat Dog in *Brown's Requiem*. In the prologue, Underhill introduces himself to the reader at some indeterminate point many years after the main events of the narrative. From his opening words it is clear that Underhill is a man who has grown hardened and cynical through the events he is about to describe:

> Nostalgia victimizes the unknowing by instilling in them a desire for simplicity and innocence they can never achieve. The fifties weren't a more innocent time. The dark salients that govern life today were there then, only they were harder to find. (Ellroy 1982: 1)

This is the beginning of Ellroy's first attempt to revise the classic noir period in his fiction. Underhill is talking about the 1950s as an era, but through him Ellroy is commenting on the noir genre as an author writing in the 1980s. Ellroy knows that noir is subliminal, the 'dark salients' are more hidden than in his previous, contemporarily set novel. As a narrator looking back on events, and presumably having witnessed the rapid liberalization of American society from the 1960s onwards, Underhill recognizes the apparent conservatism of the era, but adds the caveat, 'The fifties weren't a more innocent time'. This is an important precursor to Ellroy's later novels of the LA Quartet in which the fictional unveiling of history is deliberately at odds with the conventional perception of an era. Underhill's narration reveals him to be an embittered man who never realized his grand ambitions. Indeed, his career in the LAPD looks so promising at first that his love of life is encapsulated in a concept which seems to be the antithesis of noir: he calls it 'the Wonder'. Underhill is not entirely sure what the wonder is, but he loosely describes it to Lorna as 'the wonderful elliptical, mysterious stuff that we're never going to know completely' (Ellroy 1982: 135). However, like the repeated use of the word 'clandestine', every time 'the wonder' appears in the text it takes on a new meaning. In the prologue, Underhill states that he realized the wonder is a metaphor for every person's narrative, essentially the music the characters are moving to, 'my willingness to move with and be part of a score of hellishly driven lives in clandestine transit was the wonder – as well as my ultimate redemption' (Ellroy 1982: 3).

Underhill's closest friend in the LAPD, Herbert 'Wacky' Walker tells him the wonder is rooted in death, or more specifically as Wacky is a war hero, the experience of taking life. Underhill refuses to believe him. Even after Wacky is killed in a shoot-out and Underhill avenges him by shooting dead his two killers, Underhill is still unwilling to give up on the idealism of the wonder. As the narrative progresses, however, and Underhill's optimism falls away, the wonder becomes a darker concept: 'Wacky was right. The key to the wonder is in death. I had killed, twice, and it had changed me. But the key wasn't in the killing, it was in the discovery of whatever led to it' (Ellroy 1982: 80). In the novel it is not just the 'dark salients' of noir that are subliminal in the period, but the wonder itself is hidden in the murder mysteries that obsess Underhill. As the setting is immersed in a sense of innocence and nostalgia that is a façade, Underhill must ironically find the wonder beneath the idealized surface of 1950s American society.

For Ellroy, the wonder is a deeply autobiographical concept. He discovered the feeling living with his father after his mother's death:

> The upstairs left back apartment. 4980 Beverley Boulevard, LA, California. That's the place where I discovered the wonder. That's the place I came to live with my father after my mother's murder. That's where I read sixteen trillion crime books between the years of 1958 and 1963. I watched crime movies there. I stared out the window onto Beverley Boulevard and wondered what it all meant. (Jud 1998)

The wonder is a childlike emotion devised by the young Ellroy, which was ironically driven by his growing adult-like obsession with the darkness of the 'crime books' and 'crime movies' he immersed himself in after the unsolved murder of his mother. Although the wonder is an allusive, autobiographical reference to his youth, Ellroy more directly based several characters on members of his family. In an interview with Laura Miller, Ellroy described *Clandestine* as a 'chronologically altered, greatly fictionalized account' of his mother's murder (Miller 1996). It is not only the chronology but also the roles that are altered. Through writing the novel, Ellroy becomes the detective: 'I solved the case in that book', rather than the helpless child unable to avenge his mother. Ellroy's father was the inspiration for the killer 'Doc' Harris, which seems a rather unusual decision considering the father–son relationship was never overly antagonistic. Ellroy has claimed he simply 'doesn't know' why he cast his father as the killer in *Clandestine*, although he is clearly inviting Freudian speculation, as he has been candid in interviews regarding his taboo feelings for his mother shortly before she died: 'At the time of her death I was heading toward puberty and was sexually obsessed with her' (Duncan 1996: 66; Silet 1995: 46). At this early stage in his career, Ellroy was not famous enough for many readers to grasp the autobiographical connections, and this was exactly his intention: 'I wanted to get rid of the story. I wanted to prove myself impervious to my mother's presence and to get on with it' (Miller 1996). Ellroy was afraid of being typecast as the crime writer whose mother was murdered, and *Clandestine* was designed to be his last word on the matter, although it was a decision he would later reverse: 'I didn't know at that time that you can't run from such an overweening presence' (Miller 1996).

Early in the novel, Underhill has a one-night stand with a woman ten years his senior named Maggie Cadwallader, the first of the two murder victims who together form a fictional composite of Ellroy's mother. He constructs a false identity to make the sexual encounter as casual as possible, describing himself as an insurance salesman named Bill Thornhill. Maggie is later found murdered and Underhill's sense of guilt and his subsequent investigation into her death are the focus of the first 200 pages of the novel. The pseudonym Thornhill is convenient as it closely resembles his own name, but more symbolically, Maggie becomes a metaphoric crown of thorns to Underhill. The pleasure of sleeping with her is soon dissipated as he is overcome with guilt, which remains until he solves the case four years later, thereby gaining his redemption. However, the murder that is more precisely based on the murder of Geneva Hilliker Ellroy does not occur until more than halfway through the novel, by which time Underhill has been forced out of the LAPD and has given up hope of finding Maggie's killer. Marcella Harris, the second victim, is murdered in a way that precisely replicates the murder of Ellroy's mother. Marcella is strangled to death. Her corpse is discovered in 'a line of scrub' outside Arroyo High School in El Monte, all of which is identical to Ellroy's mother's murder (Ellroy 1982: 209). One notable difference is the date: Marcella is murdered in 1955 whereas Ellroy's mother was murdered in 1958. The latter half of the novel is set in 1955 and Marcella's murder marks the return of Underhill as an investigator, albeit now in an unofficial role.

A twenty-page section titled 'Time, Out of Time' transitions the novel between the 1951 and 1955 settings and is essentially an exposition of the aftermath of Underhill's expulsion from the LAPD and his rash marriage to Lorna and its breakdown. There are no significant details in this section which tie into the mystery storyline, and Underhill drifts through it in a purgatorial haze, rather like Fritz Brown between the death of Fat Dog and the eating of the dog meat. Underhill goes into a funk after leaving the LAPD, which he describes as 'years of regret and introspection; years of hitting hundreds and thousands of golf balls'

(Ellroy 1982: 199). However, the influence of golf appears to be more positive here than in *Brown's Requiem*, as though Ellroy is looking back on his former identity with more affection. Caddying is portrayed as a sleazy, desperate profession in Ellroy's first novel. But for the golfer, Underhill, it is a means of escape from the drudgery and squalor of police work: 'Golf was breathtaking cleanliness and simplicity' (Ellroy 1982: 1). He meets Lorna at a golf club and his friendship with Wacky begins when they bump into each other while both carrying golf bags. The simplicity Underhill finds in golf is replicated in his post-detective identity. Underhill gets a job as a bricklayer at one point and tells Lorna '"Our brains are a curse, Lor. I want to use my muscles and not my brain."' (Ellroy 1982: 203) However, Marcella's death serves as a rebirth of Underhill. He cannot simply repress his intellectual side. When he meets a boy who closely resembles a younger version of himself, it rekindles his desire for answers.

Underhill poses as an insurance investigator to investigate Marcella's death. He meets her ex-husband William 'Doc' Harris and a ten-year-old boy, Michael, who is supposedly Marcella's son from her marriage to Doc. From his first meeting with Michael, Underhill knows there is something special and unusual about the child:

> Michael Harris got to his feet, unsmiling, brushing the grass from his blue jeans. When he stretched to his full height I was astounded – he was almost as tall as I. The boy looked nervously at his father, then at me. Time froze for a brief instant as I recalled another brown-haired, fiercely bright boy of nine playing in the desolate back lot of an orphanage. It was over twenty years ago, but I had to will myself to return to the present. (Ellroy 1982: 234)

Ellroy based Michael on himself as a boy, thus by extension, Underhill is imbued with facets of Ellroy's own character, as he can recognize his younger self in the boy. When Michael looks nervously between Doc and Underhill while 'Time froze for a brief instant', it is as though he is questioning his own parentage, and rightly so as it transpires. The connection between Maggie and Marcella involves a complex and illegitimate interweaving of the two family lines. The similarity of their forenames is striking, and the dubious maternal role Underhill sees in the older Maggie during their night of passion foreshadows Michael's illegitimate parentage. Underhill insists on watching Maggie put her diaphragm in, noting, in a childlike fascination with her body, that he has never seen a woman do this before, echoing Ellroy's sexual fascination with his mother. Then in their foreplay, or more accurately in this case petting, Underhill pretends to be a dog around Maggie, barking to gain her attention and affectionately licking her face. Underhill eventually discovers that Maggie is the biological mother of Michael and that Doc Harris forced Maggie into handing over Michael to him after Marcella had a miscarriage and the doctors declared her unable to have children. Doc later murders both Maggie and Marcella. Therefore, in the deliberate blurring of the family roles, the matriarch Geneva Hilliker Ellroy is a presence in Ellroy's composition of both female victims.

Basing the character Doc on his father might suggest feelings of enmity on Ellroy's part, but the influence of Armand Ellroy on his life was much more ambiguous. Ellroy claims to have resented his father for giving him the first name Lee, which, combined with Ellroy, sounded like Leroy, a name he detested for its lower-class associations. Ellroy's name change, however, cannot be wholly seen as a repudiation of his father's will, as Ellroy still referenced him in his new identity: 'James' was taken from one of his father's pseudonyms, 'James Brady', and he retained Ellroy as his surname. Ellroy's father conceded before he died that he had given his son a bad 'nigger-pimp name' (Ellroy 1996: 107). Ellroy embraced a fictional version of his father in his name, although Ellroy has maintained his choice was 'just a simple name that goes well with "Ellroy"' (McDonald 2001: 123). Doc shares many of the attributes of Armand Ellroy: he is physically imposing, handsome and a skilled liar who easily manipulates people. Yet Doc's intellect (he attended medical school but dropped out when he discovered crime to be more profitable) is in stark contrast to Ellroy's father who was chronically lazy and broke. Ellroy's portrayal of himself in Michael also focuses on intellect. Michael is abnormally tall with a sharp intelligence to match any adult. Through Doc, Marcella and Michael, Ellroy constructs a fictional representation of his family life in the 1950s. However, this illegitimate family does not hold, and the composition is reordered at the denouement when Underhill kills Doc and unofficially adopts Michael, becoming reconciled with Lorna in the process.

Although families can be reconstituted, other potential families never come into existence. Lorna and Marcella are both barren. Underhill discovers that Doc was formerly an abortionist, often killing the pregnant woman as well as terminating the foetus. The car crash that broke Lorna's pelvis also led to the death of her pregnant mother. Badly injured in the crash, Lorna's mother was informed that her baby had died in the womb, but she refused to believe it or take medical advice to have the baby removed, and she died shortly afterwards with the dead baby inside her. Families also hide perversion and criminality. Eddie Engels, Underhill's original prime suspect in Maggie's murder, admits to his homosexuality under police interrogation and claims that he was brought out of the closet when his lesbian sister forced him to have sex with her.

Although the composition of families is a major theme of the novel, the role of individual friendships is less important than in the previous novel. Ellroy's friend Randy Rice was an influence on *Brown's Requiem* through the character of Walter. In *Clandestine*, there is a minor character named Randy Rice whom Underhill informally interviews after Marcella's murder, but here he is a boorish, pathetic alcoholic devoid of any of Walter's talent. The early chapters of *Clandestine* represent a form of buddy–buddy narrative following Underhill and 'Wacky' Walker, another possible Ellroy–Rice incarnation. Underhill is working incognito when he meets Rice and introduces himself as 'Herb Walker'. Underhill uses a variety of aliases but this is the only incident where he uses Wacky's real name, and it is significant as when he does so, he is introducing himself to the character Randy Rice (Ellroy 1982: 220). In one scene, Wacky declares a stray dog a genius after it dances to a saxophone tune, and Underhill adopts the canine naming it 'Night Train' in honour of its dancing skills. Underhill and Wacky's shared love of Night Train may allude to Ellroy and Rice's friendship and how they saw in each other the potential for genius, expressed most forcefully in Ellroy's Demon Dog persona. Their shared outsider status was central to the relationship of Brown and Walter in *Brown's Requiem*.

Wacky's death occurs early in the novel and Underhill never finds an equivalent close friendship outside the constant reordering of families forced on him through events. By comparison, Brown's friendship with Walter lasts longer in narrative terms in *Brown's Requiem*, as Walter only dies at the end of the novel. Even Brown and Fat Dog shared a friendship of sorts as their rivalry was tempered by a form of empathy. Despite the removal of any close friendship in the narrative, Wacky's memory is still an influence on Underhill. As he becomes more jaded by events, Underhill's view of the wonder moves closer to Wacky's view that it is reserved for those who have killed. The wonder increasingly comes to represent the opposite of Underhill's original idealism and awe of life.

Ellroy has said of his characters that 'men and women involved in these webs of intrigue will continue to pay the moral and psychological cost of having engaged the horror' (Powell 2008a: 168). Underhill kills to avenge Wacky and finally kills Doc to avenge Maggie, Marcella and his countless other victims. Through killing he finally understands the wonder, but at a terrible emotional price. Whereas the wonder is initially tied to imagination, raising the individual out of their circumstances, 'the horror' carries a significant burden. It is a forbidden engagement with evil in the world, but Underhill has to endure it as the only way to achieve justice after he leaves the LAPD, and as a way to atone for manipulating Maggie for sex prior to her murder. Underhill acknowledges the emotional limits of his lifelong atheism: the wonder cannot combat the horror. The unknown and the possible, however, do exist for him as a beacon of hope as the concept of family is restored by the coda in new forms.

In their final confrontation, Underhill outwits Doc Harris and enacts a poetic justice. Doc has made a fortune from drug dealing, and Underhill forces him to consume morphine. Harris is not afraid of death, choosing unemotionally to kill himself with a knife before the morphine causes his heart to explode. As he is dying, he justifies his life through his dark philosophy: 'I've been to mountaintops that you and the rest of the world don't know exist. There's a certain solace in that' (Ellroy 1982: 322). Harris believes in the wonder, although he does not use that particular word. Like Underhill and Wacky, he believes the wonder relates to death. But whereas Wacky and Underhill kill in the line of duty, Doc murdered to be above conventional morality. This redefinition of the wonder allows him to justify murder through intellectual superiority, but by extension, Underhill regards Doc as so evil he must become a vigilante and murder him. Underhill will never hold Doc's Nietzschean views, but by killing for justice he transgresses his old view of the wonder and moves closer to Doc's vision.

After Doc Harris' death, a family is formed from the surviving characters. Underhill has killed an illegitimate paternal figure to become one himself, and his adoption of Michael gives Lorna the child she could never have. It is an unconventional family by 1950s standards; a previously estranged couple raising a child who is not their own. The mother is disabled, the son is physically and socially awkward and Underhill himself is an ex-cop vigilante fraught with emotional problems. Nevertheless, the concept of family has been reinvented and survived, imperfect but intact. Underhill knows that his marriage can work again as he and Lorna love each other more because they can recognize the flaws and limitations of their own characters. This is in contrast to Doc whose entire life has been devoted to achieving the perfection 'you and the rest of the world don't know exist'. Doc's dying words echo Cathcart's death scene in *Brown's Requiem* in which he declares '*I have been Anton Bruckner*' (Ellroy 1981: 240). Both novels end with the revelation that protagonist and antagonist share the same passions, Bruckner in *Brown's Requiem* and the wonder in *Clandestine*, yet they hold radically different views of the concept, with Cathcart and Doc Harris using it to justify their criminal lives.

Ellroy's experimentation with villains such as Cathcart and Doc Harris who regard themselves as a Nietzschean *Übermensch* reached its peak in his third and final novel for Avon, *Killer on the Road*, in which serial killer Martin Plunkett is the main focus. In contrast to *Brown's Requiem* and *Clandestine*, there is no heroic protagonist in *Killer on the Road* to share a more palatable view of Plunkett's philosophy.

Stray dogs: 'The Confessions of Bugsy Siegel' and *Killer on the Road*

Avon rejected the manuscript for Ellroy's third novel and dropped him as a client. His agent dropped him shortly thereafter. He then began the manuscript of a historical novel, 'The Confessions of Bugsy Siegel', which he would never finish. The novel aimed to cover the life and death of the Jewish gangster Benjamin 'Bugsy' Siegel. Ellroy completed 398 pages of the novel, which consisted of Book I and II, titled 'Benny and Meyer [Lansky]' and 'Dreams and Experience' respectively. He planned to write the concluding Books III and IV, which were to be titled 'City of Gold, City of Dreadful Night' and 'Torch Song', but dropped the project. Ellroy has been dismissive of the unfinished book in interviews: 'I was just a kid running amok. Thirty-four years old, which is not a kid, but I mean I was running amok in New York City, and I was just holed up one winter and wrote half of this thing.' (Powell 2008b: 174) A more ambitious project than *Clandestine*, 'The Confessions of Bugsy Siegel' was Ellroy's first attempt at historical crime fiction on an epic scale, and it featured many historical figures as characters.

Even in this failed manuscript, there are the seeds of Ellroy's grand literary ambitions which would be realized in later years. 'The Confessions of Bugsy Siegel' begins with an epigraph from Saul Bellow's *The Adventures of Augie March* (1953). The novel haunted Ellroy; in an interview he stated it inspired the theme of *The Cold Six Thousand*: 'As Saul Bellow wrote in *The Adventures of Augie March*, "Everybody knows there is no fineness or accuracy in suppression. If you hold down one thing you hold down the adjoining." That's what these guys ultimately learn in *The Cold Six Thousand*' (Simon 2001). The content of 'Bugsy Siegel' would stay with Ellroy: the unfinished novel features a quote from the A.E. Houseman poem 'To an Athlete Dying Young', and the final novel of the Underworld USA trilogy, *Blood's a Rover*, takes its title and epigraph from Houseman's poem 'Reveille'. As with his later works, Ellroy transposes some of his sexual obsessions and experiences into the first-person narrative: 'My most urgent curiosity would take me into bedrooms, where I felt the storing of haphazard tides of passion and great sadness and disillusionment' (Ellroy 1983a: 3–6). By creating a high-ranking mobster who is also a voyeur, Siegel had the potential to be one of Ellroy's most fascinating characters; an outsider who is also a major figure in the criminal underworld. Siegel would have been Ellroy's first main protagonist who is a career criminal. Brown's and Underhill's minor crimes appear incidental to their character until they finally kill to achieve justice.

Once he abandoned 'The Confessions of Bugsy Siegel', Ellroy began to rebuild his career writing the Lloyd Hopkins novels for the Mysterious Press. His return to Avon with *Killer on the Road* is an oddity in his career on a par with 'Bugsy Siegel'. A stand-alone novel published between the more ambitious Hopkins trilogy and the LA Quartet, Ellroy regarded *Killer on the Road* as 'the only book I ever wrote for the money, because I needed some dough' (Rich 2009). Considering he has been paid for every book he has written, Ellroy's dismissal of *Killer on the Road* is not quite as critical as it might seem, but whereas the author regards his other works as commercial and artistic ventures, *Killer on the Road* holds no such place in his estimation. However, the novel should not be critically dismissed because Ellroy has come close to disowning it. By experimenting with a variety of narrative techniques, Ellroy used the novel to once again probe genre boundaries. The title *Killer on the Road* most likely refers to the rock song 'Riders of the Storm' by The Doors. The line reads 'There's a killer on the road. His brain is squirmin' like a toad' (Mulholland 2005). The song was inspired by the crimes of the American hitchhiker and murderer William 'Billy' Edward. The title on Ellroy's 24-page outline for the novel and the title during the drafting stage was 'What the Thunder Said: Journal of a Serial Killer' (Ellroy 1984c: 4). Ellroy transitioned from referencing poetry – 'What the Thunder Said' is taken from T.S. Eliot's *The Waste Land* – to a rock song, yet neither of these titles was chosen for the first edition. Ellroy reluctantly accepted *Silent Terror* at Avon's request. Not for the first time, Ellroy had found himself at odds with Avon, but he got his way eventually as the 1990 republication and all subsequent US reprints of the novel have been titled *Killer on the Road*. This change was a condition Ellroy insisted on for the republication: 'They foisted it upon me [*Silent Terror*]. When they reprinted the book—rejacketed the book—they wanted to be nice to me, so they called it *Killer on the Road*, which is *my* title' (McDonald 2001: 123). This admission undermines his claim that he wrote the novel solely for the money. Both of Ellroy's preferred titles explore the high and low culture divide. The novel is littered with many varied and disparate cultural and media references. It switches between rock songs, comic-book characters, and in one of the strangest scenes, environmental documentaries to reflect serial killer Martin Plunkett's journey across the US. The narrative voices include two character viewpoints, a memoir, diary entries and newspaper articles.

In cult circles, *Killer on the Road* has given Ellroy the rather unlikely status of a serial-killer expert. Serial killers are an important feature of Ellroy's early work, although none is explored in as much detail as Plunkett, who is the first-person narrator and the lead character of *Killer on the Road*. However, Ellroy later professed himself to be bored with the concept: 'serial killer novels are just as dead as private eye novels', and justified *Killer on the Road* by arguing, 'at least it's strictly from the serial killer's viewpoint and not a *roman policier* on any level' (Silet 1995: 44). But even this qualification is not strictly accurate given the late introduction in the novel of Thomas Dusenberry, an FBI agent who reveals through his journal how he came to capture Plunkett.

Ellroy's work as a serial-killer 'expert' has been peripheral to his main literary output and includes two of his most obscure pieces. There is his role as narrator and executive producer of the gruesome documentary *Bazaar Bizarre* (2004) about the Kansas-based serial killer Bob Berdella which featured re-enactments of Berdella's crimes. Ellroy would later disown the film: 'a horrible movie and a horrible performance on my part. ... It's a bad, vile movie' (Powell 2013). The film features several forgettable songs by the short-lived 'The Demon Dogs Band'. Prior to this, Ellroy wrote the introduction to the equally obscure anthology *Murder and Mayhem: an A to Z of the World's Most Notorious Serial Killers* (1992). Ellroy is the only credited author of the book, and is even credited as editor of *Murder and Mayhem* in the comprehensive bibliographies which preface his later novels such as *American Tabloid*, but it is unlikely that he wrote or edited anything beyond the introduction of this curious work. His author's biography for the book closes with the line: 'Mr Ellroy's knowledge of serial killers is held in high regard' (Anon 1992: i). However, this paratextual detail appears to contradict the actual content the author supplied for the book, as Ellroy was not aiming for respectability in his introduction:

> Woooooo, daddy-o! Feel the thrust of your curiosity edging you forward, wishing this introduction concluded so that you can get to the stories inside? Do you know what it is that you ultimately wish to

know? Do you feel some queasy undertow reaching for you – slithering around your soul, making your blood pump spasmodically and send tingles out your extremities? Are you experiencing a certain ambivalence: The desire to snout in the gutter of twisted psychopathology while remaining morally superior to the fiends you are about to meet on paper?

You are experiencing these things? Good. (Ellroy 1992b: 9–10)

Ellroy taps into the public's combined fascination with and repulsion from serial killers while also noting their status as a commodity in a consumerist, tabloid-obsessed society. Ellroy paints himself as a form of circus ringmaster to a public that hungrily devours information about serial killers. He directly addresses his readers as voyeurs, wanting to indulge some dark fantasy but with the 'morally superior' reassurance that they are not participating.

In *Killer on the Road*, Ellroy tries to break down any sense of moral reassurance through the manipulative narrative voice of Martin Plunkett. The plot is deceptively simple: it is styled as a confessional narrative by Plunkett of his psychopathic crimes, or achievements as he would put it, as his narcissism is deeply ingrained in the text. He commits his killing spree on a road trip across the US, taking advantage of jurisdictional rivalry and the lack of communication between police departments to avoid capture. Parallels can be drawn between Ellroy's life and the fictional serial killer. Plunkett's modest upbringing in LA, caught between a deluded, alcoholic mother and lazy, uncaring father is reminiscent of Lee Earle Ellroy's early life. Orphaned after his mother's suicide, Plunkett tentatively begins a criminal career breaking into expensive homes in LA, looking for sexual gratification by spying on other people's sex lives. A one-year stint in the Los Angeles County Jail brings Plunkett into contact with the criminal class, whom he holds in contempt. A jailhouse meeting with Charles Manson arouses his curiosity, but ultimately Plunkett considers himself far superior to every criminal he encounters, until late in the narrative when he starts a brief and disastrous love affair with a fellow serial killer. Ellroy's arrest sheet records fourteen arrests between 1968 and 1973 for offences such as burglary, petty theft and driving under the influence, leading to his own spell at the LA County Jail which informed the writing of these scenes (Tucker 1984: 10). There are several other parallels between Ellroy and Plunkett. Plunkett is left parentless with the death of his mother in 1965, the same year Ellroy's father died. If a special insight into the mind of serial killers was falsely accredited to Ellroy, his lifting of biographical details from his own life to create Plunkett was a significant factor in gaining him that reputation.

As events unfold in the novel, it becomes clear that Plunkett is just as devious as he is psychopathic, and cannot be fully trusted as a narrator. However, Plunkett wants the reader to believe the work is a personal, secret history as he is divulging information that he has withheld from the police. Plunkett is writing from his prison cell, 'I have everything I need …: world-class typewriter, blank paper, police documents procured by my agent', and it is clear there is a mystique regarding his case. The authorities are still unsure as to how many murders he has committed. Plunkett boasts their 'estimated body count was low' (Ellroy 1986a: 7). Just as Plunkett is devious in how he tells his story, Ellroy was slippery, planting both direct and allusive links in the novel to his own life. When Plunkett finally confronts a memory from his childhood which he has been repressing for most of his life, it reads as the justification for his actions. As will be discussed later, the incident Plunkett has been repressing ties directly to something that happened to Ellroy himself, which he only revealed 24 years after the publication of *Killer on the Road* in his memoir *The Hilliker Curse*.

From his early teens, Plunkett develops the habit of creating internal 'brain movies' featuring his favourite comic-book characters. This behaviour severely damages his ability to distinguish fantasy from reality, as one of the most dominant characters becomes his partner in crime:

> His name was the 'Shroud Shifter,' and he was a recurring bad guy in 'Cougarman Comix.' He was a supercriminal, a jewel-thief hit man who drove a souped-up amphibious car and snarled a retarded version of Nietzsche in oversize speech balloons. Cougarman, a moralistic wimp who drove a '59 Cadillac called the 'Catmobile,' always managed to throw Shroud Shifter in jail, but he always escaped a couple of issues later. (Ellroy 1986a: 18)

Plunkett's affinity with the Shroud Shifter stems from the character's villainous nature, whereas the hero, Cougarman, was 'a moralistic wimp'. But the Shroud Shifter transcends the role of a mere childhood literary hero: he interacts with Plunkett in his brain movies, controlling an increasing number of his actions and inciting him to kill. When Plunkett spies on couples having sex, he imagines their limbs rearranged in his brain movies, tying his thirst for blood with the desire to integrate himself into other people's sexual relationships. Plunkett admits that Shroud Shifter was 'ridiculous trash' (Ellroy 1986a: 19). However, like many adults looking back on the pop-music or comic-book culture that captivated them in their youth, Plunkett is fond of Shroud Shifter precisely because it is hokum. Its failings in narrative mirror his socially awkward identity and sexual inadequacy, hence his reason for invoking Shroud Shifter in his sex murders. He notices in the Shroud Shifter's car 'a gleaming angularity – all brushed steel, all mean business'. Even as an adolescent, he is able to merge culture and consumerism into potential weapons with bladed edges that could strike out unexpectedly. Elements of Nietzschean philosophy, at least a 'retarded version' of it, is a common thread in the villains Ellroy created for the Avon novels, manifesting in music, the wonder and finally a comic-book character. In an interview I conducted with Ellroy, he specifically denied the link: 'I don't associate classical music with odious philosophy ... I wasn't trying for that at all' (Powell 2008b: 169). However, the methods by which Cathcart, Doc Harris and Plunkett dismiss traditional morality and commit crimes in a strictly functional manner suggest Ellroy was adapting the *Übermensch* concept into narrative. Nietzsche is directly referenced by Plunkett. Ellroy's own experiences taught him that the *Übermensch* as 'supercriminal' was an absurd idea, but whereas his previous villains are all eventually outwitted by the protagonist, *Killer on the Road* is almost entirely from Plunkett's viewpoint, and even after his capture, Plunkett maintains the totality and fanaticism of his Nietzschean views.

Plunkett's childhood is lonely and insecure, further emphasizing how his obsessions began through emotional insecurity rather than intellectual superiority. When his father deserts the family, his mother's obsessive nature ends in tragedy when she commits suicide:

> My mother was lying dead in her bathtub. Her gashed arms were flopped over the sides, and the tub was full to the top with water and blood. A half-dozen empty Phenobarbital bottles were strewn across the floor, floating in inch-deep red water.
> I skipped down the hall and called Emergency, telling them in an appropriately choked-up voice my address and that I had a suicide to report. While I waited for the ambulance, I gulped down big handfuls of my mother's blood. (Ellroy 1986a: 23)

The death of his mother is a transitional moment for Plunkett. Her erratic behaviour is made worse when he quietly replaces her medication with Benzedrine. By his teens, Plunkett has already become an expert manipulator, and his mother is his first victim. He has taken her life without needing to resort to the hyper-violence of his later murders. His child-like behaviour around the corpse suggests excitement at his new-found power: 'I skipped down the hall'. His acting, however, shows a mature understanding of the difference between what is socially expected and how he feels: he has to affect 'an appropriately choked-up voice'. This is, again, similar to Lee Earle Ellroy: on the day his mother died 'I felt relieved. I remember forcing myself to cry crocodile tears on the bus going back to L.A.' (Kihn 1992: 29). What distinguishes Plunkett from being just an unusually cold-hearted son is his act of vampirism, a kind of participation in the death which alludes to the genesis of his later obsession with trophies and branding of his murder victims with the initials SS, for Shroud Shifter. Plunkett continues his vampirism when he murders a stray dog and licks its blood off his hands. For Plunkett, watching violence is an enlightening precursor to the act. He wanders into a cinema in San Francisco showing a documentary film on seal clubbing, and while the young audience looks on in horror, Plunkett himself sheds tears of joy. His fellow audience members console him, unaware of his true feelings. The film is directed to make the audience feel sad, sympathetic and morally outraged, but through his brain movies Plunkett can manipulate the violent images to give him the opposite emotional response.

After the death of his mother, Plunkett lives with his Uncle Walt, but the restraints on his behaviour are effectively removed. He breaks into houses and begins an acquaintance with two hippies, Flower and Season. He has an abortive sexual encounter with Season and becomes intrigued by both women's devotion to their leader, 'Charlie'. Plunkett finally meets the enigmatic 'Charlie' in the LA County Jail. Season and Flower are members of the Manson Family, and Plunkett is initially impressed by Manson's ability to gain followers through his apocalyptic ideas, but upon seeing how pathetic and obnoxious Manson is in person, Plunkett decides he has to verbally destroy Manson to assert his own superiority:

> Shroud Shifter interrupted the music by superimposing CASTRATE HIM across Charlie's forehead. I reached for a deep draft of cool and said: 'I fucked Flower and Season at your place by the Strip. They were lousy fucks and even worse recruiters, and they used to laugh about your little one-inch dick.'
> Manson hurled himself at the bars and started screaming; I picked up my broom and began sweeping my way down the catwalk. Hearing clapping on the tier above me, I looked up. A group of deputies were applauding my performance. (Ellroy 1986a: 81–2)

Plunkett's alter ego, Shroud Shifter, prompts him to humiliate Manson, helping to negate the shame he feels at formerly admiring him. His order, 'CASTRATE HIM', reveals the essence of Plunkett's anger at the world and his victims, feelings of hatred stemming from sexual inadequacy, which he, in turn, projects on Manson. Plunkett's verbal abuse is nonetheless a 'performance' – he is aware of his audience – and he wins momentary respect from legitimate authority figures in the prison. Ellroy and Manson were both inmates at the LA County Jail, but they never met. Manson's indirect impact on Ellroy's criminal life – Ellroy decided to end his spate of burglaries as a consequence of widespread paranoia in LA following the Manson Family murders – feeds into Plunkett's desire to humiliate Manson in *Killer on the Road*. Plunkett is just as dangerously deluded as the cult leader: the schizophrenia that encourages his obedience to the Shroud Shifter makes it easier for Plunkett to justify his murderous rage.

Released from jail, Plunkett moves to San Francisco where he ingratiates himself with a young couple, Steve and Jill. His killing spree begins when Jill walks out of the bathroom, towel wrapped around her head, excited to reveal her newly dyed blond hair:

> I unclipped my self-sharpening, Teflon-coated, brushed steel ax and swung it at her neck. Her head was sheared cleanly off; blood burst from the cavity; her arms and legs twitched spastically; then her whole body crumpled to the floor. The force of my swing spun me around, and for one second my vision eclipsed the entire scene – blood-spattered walls; the body shooting an arterial geyser out of the neck, the heart still pumping in reflex; Steve frozen on his feet, turning a catatonic blue. (Ellroy 1986a: 100–1)

Plunkett describes himself almost as a superhero armed with a 'self-sharpening, Teflon-coated, brushed steel ax', who displays remarkable physical strength: 'Her head was sheared cleanly off'. Reliving the scene also gives it a cinematic quality, with events going into slow motion so as to experience every detail. This leaves the reader with questions over Plunkett's reliability as a narrator. He may see himself as a superhero, and his victim's partner as awed, but his obsession with detail is somewhat banal. This is in stark contrast to Manson who justifies his actions through a mish-mash of pop culture and mysticism. Manson is unique and stands out, whereas Plunkett is ordinary and overlooked, a characteristic which helps him to avoid detection for longer. Manson is apprehended partly as a consequence of the media storm he has created. Plunkett's description of the murder is more focused on the features of the weapon than on the murder. His obsession with hardware appliances persists throughout the novel and has its genesis in his admiration for Shroud Shifter's car. The tone is reminiscent of a narrator of television commercials rather than a memoirist promising revelations, and Plunkett comes across as a salesman who sounds authoritative but always leaves the impression he cannot be trusted. Indeed, Jill quotes the cruelly ironic dialogue of an 'old Clairol ad' only seconds before she is murdered: 'If I've got only one life, let me live it as a blonde' (Ellroy 1986a: 100). Therefore, the violence is merely a continuation of the sales talk. For Plunkett, it is the completion of the transaction. He does not, however, specify to the reader why the potential sight of blond hair is the catalyst for the violence. This revelation comes later.

Plunkett's schizophrenic reliance on the Shroud Shifter begins to fade when he develops a physical relationship with another man. After Plunkett commits a murder in Wisconsin, he is befriended and protected by a fellow serial killer, Police Sergeant Ross Anderson. Anderson is falsely credited with solving a murder case in a newspaper article titled, '"WISCONSIN WHIPSAW" INVESTIGATION ON THE BACK BURNER; DEAD MAN KILLER?' (Ellroy 1986a: 157). The upper-case lettering of the headline foreshadows Ellroy's now well-established method of embedding different types of media formats into the text as narrative devices. Articles are taken from the *Milwaukee Tribune*, the *Kentucky Herald* and the *Illinois Eagle*, three different papers from three states, to reflect the breadth of Plunkett's road journey and killing spree but also the lack of communication between police departments. The newspapers perpetuate misinformation, inadvertently allowing Plunkett and Anderson to kill unhindered. Anderson is given a false moral platform through the media, who perceive him as a hero detective: '"The Whipsaw case took a lot out of me. It's going to be nice to get a change of scenery, to ply my trade in new places"' (Ellroy 1986a: 159). The rather hackneyed clichés 'change of scenery' and 'ply my trade' seem perfectly innocent in the context of the article, but to the reader of the novel, who is aware that Anderson is the real Whipsaw and has framed one of Plunkett's victims for the crime, they carry a different message: a form of murderous *double entendre*. Anderson enjoys this double-speak. Indeed, his teasing of the authorities is the trademark of the serial killer attempting to gain recognition for his crimes.

Ultimately, it is mutual attraction as much as their murderous rage that draw Anderson and Plunkett together. Anderson sees in Plunkett what Plunkett himself cannot see: 'Ross leaned forward and kissed me on the lips. I leaned into it and tasted wax on his moustache and bitter coffee on his tongue, and when he broke contact and about-faced through the door, I was flushed and hungry for more' (Ellroy 1986a: 154). Anderson has deduced Plunkett's homosexuality and their shared urge to murder. Anderson prefers to kill brunettes whereas Plunkett's obsession is with blondes: 'Apples and oranges', as he puts it, but their sexual appetite is for each other (Ellroy 1986a: 153). Anderson is manipulative; his weapon is his charm, breaking off the physical contact at a moment he knows will leave the socially awkward Plunkett tantalized. Ever since his meeting with Charles Manson, Plunkett has considered himself superior to every other criminal. By giving into Anderson's seduction, however, he exposes himself to betrayal. Plunkett, blinded by love, is unable to foresee it. Anderson is not an exact double to Plunkett, as when he is caught by police, rather than protect him, he helps the authorities capture Plunkett in a plea to avoid the death penalty. Plunkett is beyond reason and is more fanatical in his murderous obsessions than Anderson. Plunkett's self-styled integrity is very important to him: in fact, it is the only moral compass he has. He refuses to cooperate upon his capture and consoles, or deludes himself into thinking that he was only caught due to Anderson's cowardice and not because he was outwitted by a superior intellect in Agent Dusenberry. Through his delusion, he unwittingly reveals the same arrogance and hypocrisy of Manson that he once claimed to detest. Plunkett had said to Manson regarding capture, 'don't rationalize their failure through mystical jive talk', and of murder, 'it's so good that you never have to tell anyone about it' (Ellroy 1986a: 81). Both are values he ultimately abandons with no degree of shame.

Plunkett's meeting with Anderson and the self-realization of his homosexuality is not the most revelatory detail with regard to Plunkett's pathology, although it seems to be the scene which has left the biggest impression on critics. Paul Duncan notes, 'it [*Killer on the Road*] doesn't deserve to be ignored, which is what some critics seem to have done' (Duncan 1996: 67). Duncan, one of the few critics who have discussed the work, regards *Killer on the Road* as 'one of the best serial killer books you're likely to come across', and refers to the meeting with Anderson, 'About halfway through Martin (Plunkett) is caught—then Dog delivers a twist which had me gasping' (Duncan 1996: 67). A late scene where Plunkett reveals he was the victim of sexual abuse as a child was designed by Ellroy to be the shocking revelation which much of the narrative is working towards, but it does not have the same dramatic effect as Plunkett's meeting with Anderson. It was not until the release of Ellroy's second memoir that the autobiographical aspect of the scene became apparent.

Ellroy had expended so much of his literary celebrity on revealing his life story that it seemed unlikely there would still be previously undisclosed revelations as late as 2010. However, Ellroy revealed in *The Hilliker Curse* how he was once the victim of sexual abuse. Ellroy claims it happened on New Year's Eve 1957, while on a visit to his mother's family in Wisconsin. They left him with a German babysitter who 'emitted Hitler-Jugend vibes' (Ellroy 2010: 10):

> She tucked me in last. The bedroom door was shut. Her fluttery presence felt un-kosher. She sat on the edge of the bed and patted me. The vibe devolved. She pulled down the covers and sucked my dick.
>
> I dug it and recoiled from it in equal measure. I withstood thirty seconds and pushed her off. She talked a Kraut blue streak and bolted the room. I killed the lights and brooded out the bad juju.
>
> I felt sideswiped, more than assaulted. I recalled the magic-spell book. I figured I could brew a blank-memory elixir. I could create X-ray eye powder at the same time. I got bilked on those glasses. My secret eyeball blend would set that straight. (Ellroy 2010: 10)

Ellroy was still too young to fully comprehend what had happened, and he takes solace in a pair of children's X-ray eye glasses which were a present from his father on his ninth birthday. The glasses help him draw a 'blank-memory elixir', but the incident would not be completely forgotten as it recurs in narrative form years later in *Killer on the Road*. It is important not to overstate Ellroy's repression of the memory as his style does not suggest he is writing a 'misery memoir' and inviting sympathy. He admits to a mixed physical reaction to the fellatio when it occurred, and the language suggests an aggressively irreverent attitude, noting the woman talked a 'Kraut blue streak', preferring to trivialize events rather than grasp at profundity. The repression is deliberate as Ellroy's description of the Wisconsin trip in his earlier memoir *My Dark Places* passes by without incident, and he dates his first sexual experience later, claiming it was an act of mutual masturbation with another boy. An act he described as 'shameful, exciting, loathsome and motherfucking scary' (Ellroy 1996: 113). Thus, the X-ray glasses simultaneously stimulate his imagination and help him repress the incident. It was a method he would repeat in narrative through Plunkett's habits of creating brain movies and his development of the alter ego Shroud Shifter whose extrasensory perceptions are not unlike those Ellroy fantasized about as the abused child with X-ray glasses.

The back cover of the 1990 reprint of *Killer on the Road* prepares the reader to think that Plunkett's pathology hinges on a single event from his childhood: 'Beneath his calm veneer, his mind is filled with raging voices that spring from the one defining moment in his life, a moment so shocking he has buried it for thirty years.' The incident in *Killer on the Road*, which Ellroy based on his own experience of abuse, occurs as a direct result of Plunkett's adulterous father. One evening Plunkett's father brings home one of his lovers after a fancy-dress party. The woman takes an interest in Plunkett who, as his memory slowly awakens to the incident, reveals he was only four or five years old:

> Tick tick tick tick tick as she moves on the bed, straining with her lips around me; tick tick tick tick I shut my eyes; tick tick tick tick she's biting me and I open my eyes, and my mother is there swinging a brushed-steel spatula and frying pan, and I pull away, and the woman is bleeding at the lips. She pushes my mother and runs, losing her wig; my father snores and my mother holds the wig over my face, and I fall asleep pushed into suffocating liquor breath that goes tick tick tick tick. (Ellroy 1986a: 243)

The woman is wearing a garish white wig. She had insisted to Plunkett's father that they keep their wigs on during sex for a thrill. The young Plunkett spies on them and is aroused, but, being pre-pubescent, is unable to ejaculate. Plunkett's discovery of sex is through voyeurism, as he spies on the adultery. However, sexual deviancy follows, as afterwards the woman quietly performs fellatio on him while his father sleeps. The woman is in the middle of the sex act when she is beaten away by Plunkett's mother, evoking images of castration as she pulls back from Plunkett 'bleeding at the lips'. Plunkett's attention to the weapon, 'a brushed-steel spatula and frying pan', echoes his later fixation on turning household implements into murder weapons. The recurring motif of the clock, 'Tick tick tick tick tick', explains the build-up to this revelatory detail about Plunkett's childhood, and suggests the incident had such a profound effect that a murderous rage grew inside him waiting to explode like an alarm clock. 'Tick tick tick' also alludes to the squeaking of the bedsprings as couples have sex. This rhythm synchs with Plunkett's murderous rage in later life so that sex and violence appear in tandem in his mind. The memory only comes back to him after his relationship with Anderson is fully consummated. Like his father's lover, he insists on keeping the light on during sex, as though to be a voyeur as much as a participant in the coupling. Ellroy's repression, from the public at least, of his first sexual encounter suggests that as an author and public figure there was only so much he could clearly reveal, preferring instead to fictionalize the event in *Killer on the Road* through Plunkett, a narrator as manipulative as he is psychotic.

Plunkett ends his narration and the manuscript in his prison cell with a final vow to choose death over incarceration:

> So you look for cause and effect; you partake of my brilliant memory and absolute candor and conclude what you will. Build mountains out of ellipses and bastions of logic from interpretations of the truth I have given you. And if I have gained your credibility by portraying myself honestly frailties and all, then believe me when I tell you this: I have been to points of power and lucidity that cannot be measured by anything logical or mystical or human. Such was the sanctity of my madness.
>
> It's over now. I will not submit to the duration of my sentence. With this valediction in blood completed, my transit in human form has peaked, and to subsist past it is unacceptable. Scientists say that all matter disperses into unrecognisable but pervasive energy. I intend to find out, by turning myself inward and shutting down my senses until I implode into a space beyond all laws, all roadways, all speed limits. In some dark form, I will continue. (Ellroy 1986a: 280)

Even in his capture, Plunkett does not admit defeat, preferring to think of his mental superiority and ability to control the situation: 'I will not submit to the duration of my sentence', and 'in some dark form I will continue'. He will follow in the footsteps of his radically religious mother and commit suicide, which he sees as a victory; the excessive use of personal pronouns reveals his narcissism. He had murdered his victims in their prime, to assume their strength and to stop the decline that comes with advancing years. At the age of 37 he will end his life but as a way of limiting people's knowledge of him. By shutting down his body he is committing an act of repression, but whereas his sexual repression once drove him to murder his last act is to commit suicide. Anderson, who once understood Plunkett, has through cowardice shown himself to be no longer worthy of being his equal. Instead, Plunkett associates himself with a higher, unstoppable power of science. This 'unrecognisable but pervasive energy' is what ultimately destroys Plunkett's nemesis, Thomas Dusenberry. Dusenberry commits suicide once he has brought Plunkett to justice, unable to cope with unlimited evil and his wife's adultery. Dusenberry has the prospect of rapid promotion, but Plunkett mentally tortures him, refusing to show any remorse or give any explanation for his murder spree. Dusenberry had evaded his own emotional problems for years by dedicating himself to the capture of serial killers, but the arrest of Plunkett triggers his emotional collapse, allowing the serial killer to destroy one more victim from behind bars, and triggering a parallel between the two men as they both commit suicide. As the novel ends with Plunkett switching himself off as author by taking his own life, it leads to another question regarding the authorship of the text. Ellroy's method of interspersing newspaper articles and journal entries into Plunkett's supposed memoir may suggest there are passages that are not entirely under Plunkett's control. However, the newspaper articles may be seen as Plunkett's editorial decision, and he does make reference to an agent assisting him. He may have collected them on his journey as souvenirs of his work and then arranged them in his manuscript to highlight his triumphs. Plunkett also states that his manuscript is 400 pages long, but the novel is just under 300 pages. The novel also features journal entries of Dusenberry, which Plunkett would not have access to, disclaiming Plunkett's complete authorship, and undermining his self-proclaimed intellectual powers. *Killer on the Road* begins as the first-person narration of a serial killer. By the end, it reads as a fragmentary manuscript possibly belonging to a broader, and just as incomplete, archive. Ellroy employs archives as a narrative device to a much greater extent in the LA Quartet and Underworld USA trilogy, but its genesis lay here, in the almost forgotten serial-killer novel he wrote 'because I needed some dough' (Rich 2009).

The Avon characters and new writing styles

There is an intellectual arrogance to the characters Ellroy wrote for Avon which is not present in his other novels. Plunkett claims, 'I have been to points of power and lucidity that cannot be measured by anything logical or mystical or human.' This echoes Haywood Cathcart's dying boast in *Brown's Requiem* 'I have been Anton Bruckner' and Doc Harris' last words in *Clandestine* 'I've been to mountaintops that you and the rest of the world don't know exist' (Ellroy 1981: 240; Ellroy 1982: 322). These characters are connected in thought and deed as they derive power from the complete ownership of other people through violence and murder. In the LA Quartet and Underworld USA novels, characters are motivated by the pursuit of wealth and political power. In this world, every character is more noticeably part of the established order and limited by its constraints. Ellroy's Avon characters are outsiders who do not possess any real influence in society: Cathcart, it may be argued, is an exception as he is an LAPD lieutenant, but his links to Fat Dog push him to the fringes of society as Fat Dog is the ultimate outsider.

The Avon characters are driven to extreme violence as a way of taking revenge on a society which has never accepted them. For this reason, the early Avon characters, whether they be the protagonists or villains of the piece, were drawn more from modulations of Ellroy's own character, members of his family, and friends such as Randy Rice. The Avon characters reflected the status in society of Lee Earle Ellroy, the drunk, drug-addicted vagrant who displayed flashes of creative brilliance. Even Fritz Brown and Freddy Underhill are only relatively accepted by society and live, to a certain degree, as outsiders. Both are forced out of the LAPD in disgrace and wrestle with a number of emotional problems.

In his introduction to *Murder and Mayhem*, Ellroy suggests, 'Think of the line between us and them [serial killers] as fragile and in need of jealously guarding' (Ellroy 1992b: 10). Reading *Killer on the Road*, it appears Ellroy has ignored his own advice for the sake of artistic experimentation and deliberately blurred the line between his role as author and Plunkett's as murderer. Ellroy draws attention to the fascination society has with serial killers. However, he views public interest as disproportionate to the actual impact of serial killers on crime statistics: 'They represent a miniscule percentage of this country's overall homicide rate and capture a maximum amount of national attention. You're much more likely to run into a crazed crack addict devoid of interesting psychology' (Ellroy 1992b: 7). When fascination veers towards the adulation that Plunkett craves the moral divisions fall apart and serial killers are elevated above their victims, a status the outsiders of the Avon novels aspire to. Plunkett has the entire manuscript as a forum to justify his actions, and Ellroy uses it as a hook to indict the readership which is drawn to the novel through a fascination with serial killers.

This chapter has identified some of the key stages in the evolution of Ellroy's style: in *Brown's Requiem* the autobiographical influence is apparent in the dichotomy between Fritz Brown and Freddy 'Fat Dog' Baker as both protagonist and antagonist are imbued with opposing facets of Ellroy's personality. The constantly shifting boundaries of the family unit in *Clandestine* symbolize the complexity of Ellroy's own family history and apportion guilt for his mother's death based on an individual's role in the family. In *Killer on the Road*, the parallels between Plunkett and Ellroy, serial killer and author, are present but naturally limited, and yet Ellroy only revealed the most important similarity years after the novel was published. As the three novels Ellroy wrote for Avon were stand-alone works, and as he was not yet in the public eye, his Demon Dog persona was less evident during this stage of his career as there was less need for it. However, it is still notable as a feature internal to the narratives. Ellroy did not simply arrive as a major figure in the crime-writing genre with the Quartet in the late 1980s: there was a gradual formulation of his persona as a distinct identity in the Avon novels, often as the residue of Lee Earle Ellroy, that had evolved to a fully thought-out and exploitable profile by the time his work was becoming internationally successful. Laura Miller described Ellroy as 'a publicist's dream. He's got a dynamite story, loves doing press and has no discernible sense of shame' (Miller 1996). In the early novels, Ellroy began his writing style by adapting his life story into the novels and developed it until it became a more complex form through which he would forge a new style in the genre.

2
The Lloyd Hopkins Novels: Ellroy's Displaced Romantic

James Ellroy had planned to introduce and kill off the maverick police detective Lloyd Hopkins in a single stand-alone novel titled 'L.A. Death Trip'. But 'L.A. Death Trip' never saw publication in the form Ellroy had originally conceived. A series of events forced Ellroy to radically revise his literary plans, and Lloyd Hopkins eventually became the lead character in three novels: *Blood on the Moon* (1984), *Because the Night* (1984) and *Suicide Hill* (1986). Ellroy was already a published novelist when he began writing the Lloyd Hopkins novels, yet he has described the period as a time when he was still 'learning how to write' (Jud 1998). Ellroy's task of finding a publisher for the first Hopkins novel, and the complex process of converting the nihilistic and apocalyptic 'L.A. Death Trip' into the more conventional and publishable novel *Blood on the Moon*, was a difficult stage in his writing career. He was to engage in more complex stylistic experiments and build a bigger profile than in his novels for Avon. Ellroy's departure from Avon and his subsequent renaissance as a crime writer for the Mysterious Press, guided by Otto Penzler and Nat Sobel, is the focus of this chapter. As with the Avon novels, Ellroy's Lloyd Hopkins novels have been critically overlooked in comparison to his later work. However, despite their flaws, the Lloyd Hopkins novels feature constant narrative experimentation and, in this regard, Ellroy's later work is indebted to them.

'L.A. Death Trip': the genesis of Lloyd Hopkins

Ellroy moved from LA to New York in 1981. In his memoir, *The Hilliker Curse*, Ellroy describes this period of his life and the difficulty he faced in finding a publisher for the 'L.A. Death Trip' manuscript:

> My publisher rejected my third novel. They found the sex-fiend cop and his feminist-poet girlfriend hard to believe. They were right. I wrote the book in a let's-ditch-L.A.-and-find-*HER*-in New York fugue state. My quasi-girlfriend agent sent the book to 17 other publishers. They all said nyet. My quasi-girlfriend dropped me as a client and pink-slipped me as a quasi-boyfriend. (Ellroy 2010: 67)

Ellroy's humour masks his professional failure. He mimics the tone of a comedian, reducing his new pariah state to a punch line. His first two novels had moved from manuscript to publication with relative ease. He had never experienced the rejection many authors come to regard as a rite of passage. Now, having already rebuilt his life and started a new career, he found himself back at the beginning. It is both Ellroy the author and Ellroy the man that receive the double insult, as the Romantic idea, the 'fugue' outpouring, is rejected and romantic love demystified – turned into a business transaction – through his girlfriend's 'pink slip'.

'L.A. Death Trip' was rejected by Avon and turned down by seventeen publishers. To put it diplomatically, the fact that his agent was his lover at the time suggests Ellroy was not receiving objective advice. He had ignored the advice of two male agents who had urged him to do extensive rewrites. Ellroy's luck eventually changed after a meeting with renowned crime fiction editor Otto Penzler. In a 1990 interview with Fleming Meeks, the meeting is described in a manner which underplays the sense of crisis which preceded it:

> In 1981, Ellroy moved across country to a basement apartment in Eastchester, N.Y., close by the Wykagyl Country Club, where he soon resumed work as a caddy. On his first trip into Manhattan, for lunch in midtown with editor Nellie Sabin, who bought his second book, *Clandestine* (1982) for Avon, he happened onto the Mysterious Bookshop on West 56th St. Overhearing a conversation in the store about its owner, mysterymeister Otto Penzler, Ellroy marched upstairs to Penzler's office and introduced himself, 'I'm James Ellroy,' he announced, 'the next King of American crime fiction.' Penzler, he recalls, replied coolly, 'Mr. Ellroy, would you excuse me if I reserve judgment on that?' (Meeks 1990: 22)

This appears to be a sanitized account of the meeting, casting Ellroy in a more powerful position than he was in at the time. Ellroy's literary career was in danger of ending before it had really begun. It also seems odd that Ellroy would be lunching with Nellie Sabin when his professional relationship with Avon appeared to be over. Meeks adds a casual tone to Ellroy's sales pitch: he merely 'happened onto' the bookshop and '[overheard]' a conversation about Penzler.

Nat Sobel, Ellroy's agent, whom he met shortly after the first meeting with Penzler, has claimed the visit to the Mysterious Bookshop must have been planned in advance by Ellroy:

> Otto had this wonderful bookshop where crime writers came in all the time, and he would send writers to me who asked how to get an agent. So we started the Mysterious Literary Agency. We did a whole thing where our letterhead had no address and no phone number. If you wanted to find us, you had to solve the mystery. *New York Magazine* did a little thing about the Mysterious Literary Agency. James saw that. James had had two paperback originals published and his agent had given up on him. (Ferrari-Adler 2008)

Note that in this account Sobel clearly states that Ellroy had been dropped by his agent before the fateful meeting with Penzler. Sobel also differs from Meeks' account in the phrasing of Ellroy's introduction to Penzler: '"I am the demon dog of American crime fiction." Otto said, "I've never heard of you"' (Ferrari-Adler 2008). Whether Ellroy called himself the 'next King' or the 'Demon Dog of American crime fiction' is disputed, but what is significant is that both Sobel and Penzler, who eventually published *Blood on the Moon*, were taken aback by Ellroy's abrasive working style and did not at first understand the persona that Ellroy was then nurturing. When Penzler recalled the meeting he admitted, 'I never thought for a moment he wasn't going to be a monster' (Kihn 1992: 32). And Sobel said of him:

> I wrote Ellroy a rather lengthy editorial report about that first novel I represented. I got back what looked like a very lengthy kidnap letter. It was written in red pencil on yellow legal paper, and some of the words on it were like an inch high: I AM NOT GOING TO DO THIS. I thought, 'Oh, I've got a loony here. Somebody who calls himself the demon dog? Maybe he is a demon.' (Ferrari-Adler 2008)

Ellroy's defensiveness about *Blood on the Moon* is remarkable considering the difficulty he had in selling the manuscript. However, he had not told Sobel or Penzler that his literary career had stalled: 'Of course neither Otto nor I knew that James' previous agent had had seventeen rejections on this novel. But we had done a lot of work on the book' (Ferrari-Adler 2008). The novel was extensively redrafted despite Ellroy's objections. The Demon Dog persona had been crucial to getting Penzler and Sobel's attention but also to defending his point of view as an artist when they disagreed with him. Ellroy was not conciliatory. Disagreements about the novel were a trigger for abrasive behaviour. A series of rejections had forced Ellroy to formalize a literary persona which would become a lucrative publicity device.

The publication of *Blood on the Moon* led to one of Ellroy's first interviews, titled simply 'An Interview with James Ellroy', which appeared in *Armchair Detective* in 1984. However, during a routine copyright request, I corresponded with the credited interviewer, Duane Tucker, who claimed he had never conducted the interview. Tucker further suggested that Ellroy may have used his name for it to be published (Powell 2012a: x). Circumstantially, the evidence suggests that this is plausible: Tucker and Ellroy were close friends, and the original 'L.A. Death Trip' manuscript is dedicated to him (Ellroy 1983b). Ellroy later dedicated *Killer on the Road* to Tucker, and the name Duane Tucker even appears in *Blood on the Moon*: in a police report Hopkins reads, Tucker is listed as a witness who was interviewed about a suspicious suicide (Ellroy 1984b: 165). Ellroy, who would develop into an energetic and shrewd publicist of his own work, would not at this early stage of his career have had many publicity opportunities. However, Penzler was also the editor of *Armchair Detective* at the time and has strongly denied the interview was fabricated. Ellroy has neither confirmed nor denied whether he wrote the interview, stating that he has 'no recollection' of it (Powell 2012a: x).

Examining the interview in light of these revelations, there are a few indicators which suggest Ellroy may have been its sole author, possibly deceiving Penzler in the process. First, the introduction to the interview features the term 'contrapunctually' (Powell 2012a: x). Ellroy coined the term to describe the parallel narrative of cop/killer in *Blood on the Moon*, which would be more commonly described as contrapuntal. Ellroy reused 'contrapunctually' in the prologue to *LA Noir*. Given that Ellroy originated this word, it is unusual for it to appear in the section of the interview which was supposedly written by Tucker. Secondly, there is the repeated use of the term 'ikon', with the distinct 'k' spelling – 'My instincts, however, tell me that the cop will replace the private eye as the hardboiled ikon' (Tucker 1984: 8). As Ellroy's prose style has evolved, he has occasionally employed heavy use of alliteration, including replacing a 'c' with a 'k' to create a sharp-sounding alliterative effect.

Although it is a fairly common feature in American English, there are early signs of Ellroy's fondness for using the letter 'k' in alliteration in *Blood on the Moon*, with the terms Kathy's Kourt and Kathy's Klown. It is possible that 'ikon' and 'contrapunctual' were both planted in the introduction of the interview by Ellroy and not Tucker. Again, the word 'ikon' appears in the novel, suggesting its reappearance in the interview is not coincidental. When Hopkins is examining the books Kathleen McCarthy keeps in her apartment, he notices 'volumes by Lessing, Plath, Millett and other feminist ikons' (Ellroy 1984b: 156).

The technique of an author interviewing himself is not without precedent. Prominent literary figures such as Norman Mailer authored interviews with themselves, and other authors have reviewed their own works under pseudonyms. Mailer wrote an interview of himself for *New York Magazine* only a few years prior to the Tucker interview, and it may have influenced Ellroy. The interview is titled 'Before the Literary Bar', and is structured as a conversation between Mailer and a courtroom prosecutor. Mailer is defending his book on Marilyn Monroe, *Of Women and their Elegance*, from the charge of historical inaccuracy. The subhead to the interview reads 'In which the author puts his new Marilyn Monroe book on trial – before the critics do' (Mailer 1980). Mailer was known for his combative interview style, but here he is using the platform to pre-empt attacks on his work, by employing the argument that historical accuracy is not relevant to the novel. Ellroy would develop a similar argument in defence of his later work, but he was also looking for critical attention of any sort. The style he was developing in the Lloyd Hopkins novels was worthless without a strong readership, and he viewed the Demon Dog persona as its guarantor.

The interview could be read as a manifesto of Ellroy's ambitions as a novelist. He mentions several novels he planned to write, only one of which came to fruition – *The Black Dahlia*. The most revelatory moment comes when he divulges his view of Romanticism and how it is communicated through his characters:

> I'm interested in people who tread outside the bounds of conventional morality: displaced romantics ill at ease in the 1980s; people who have rejected a goodly amount of life's amenities in order to dance to the music in their own heads. The price of that music is very, very high, and no one has ever gotten away without paying. Both cops and killers fall into that category, to varying degrees, walking the sharpest edges between their own music and the conventional music that surrounds them. (Tucker 1984: 5)

There is a degree of autobiography in this statement. Ellroy had lived and almost died by an unconventional morality which included drug abuse and crime. During the late 1960s and early 1970s he was 'walking the sharpest edges' between a criminal life and his dreams of becoming a writer. Even after sobriety and his first publications he was still a 'displaced romantic' living modestly on his caddying salary while pursuing his writing career. When these ideas are transplanted to the text of *Blood on the Moon*, elements of Ellroy's own character can be seen in both Hopkins and his nemesis Verplanck. Romanticism feeds an obsession which can be either righteous or psychopathic in the characters' determination to 'dance to the music in their own heads'.

Although Ellroy's interview with Tucker displayed the Demon Dog's authoritative, persuasive and self-preserving qualities, it is important to note that Sobel and Penzler overruled Ellroy on key editorial decisions during this rebirth of his writing career. Martin Kihn suggests Ellroy may have been willing to sacrifice 'L.A. Death Trip' and the Lloyd Hopkins character in favour of his first serious attempt at historical fiction, 'The Confessions of Bugsy Siegel'. His new agent and editor however felt otherwise: 'During a meeting at Penzler's store, Sobel and Penzler told Ellroy that Siegel was out to lunch but Death Trip could be reworked' (Kihn 1992: 32). Penzler in particular felt that 'L.A. Death Trip' would need to be improved, if only to rein in the prose style and rework the plotting: 'I thought, "This is an extraordinary original talent who doesn't really know how to write a book." A very powerful stylist, but they weren't particularly well constructed plots' (Kihn 1992: 31). Penzler's description of Ellroy's writing style matches the personality of the author at the time, brimming with talent and energy but lacking in discipline. In the long term, it would be through personality or the veneer of an unhinged persona where Ellroy would find his literary identity. But had it not been for the exhaustive redrafting and editing stages of the novel, overseen by Sobel and Penzler, *Blood on the Moon* would have remained unpublishable.

Blood on the Moon

Blood on the Moon is a fairly generic detective novel in its premise. Lloyd Hopkins is an LAPD Detective Sergeant who begins to see a connection between twenty unsolved, apparently random, murders of women going back several years. His private investigation brings him closer, chapter by chapter, to the deranged psychopath Theodore Verplanck who believes he is murdering women to preserve their chastity. The closer Hopkins gets to Verplanck the more parallels emerge between the two men. Despite its clichés, Ellroy envisaged the novel as being strikingly different from his first two novels which were 'a private eye story and a period cop story' (Ellroy 1997b: i). Moving away from well-known genre tropes, *Blood on the Moon* was conceived as being more ambitious, 'a contemporarily set, contrapunctually-structured novel about a sex obsessed cop tracking down a sexually-motivated killer'(Ellroy 1997b: i). The Hopkins novels do not read particularly as a trilogy of novels, as Ellroy admits, 'I hadn't planned a trilogy at first. I did not possess the long-range planning skills I possess today' (Ellroy 1997b: i). At various times throughout the drafting of the three Hopkins novels, Ellroy planned to write a quartet or quintet of novels with the series title 'Hopkins in Jeopardy'. As late as 1995, Ellroy was still referring to the novels as the 'Hopkins in Jeopardy' series, and when asked how many books he had planned to write in the series, Ellroy answered, 'Three, four, or five' (Silet 1995: 45). Ellroy did write an outline for a fourth Hopkins novel, titled 'The Cold Six Thousand', which he would later use as the title for the second novel of the Underworld USA trilogy. With the Hopkins series, Ellroy never committed himself unduly to planning or structure between novels, rather the character allowed his writing style to be in a state of constant experimentation.

As Ellroy has come to view the Hopkins novels as his apprenticeship, it is not surprising that he is 'a bit embarrassed by' the main protagonist (Jud 1998). Part of this critical reaction stems from *Blood on the Moon* unwittingly finding its home within an emerging genre: 'I didn't know that the mano-a-mano duels of cops and serial killers would soon become a big fat fucking cliché' (Ellroy 1997b: i). For Ellroy, in his desire for originality, it was not only the 'cliché' that frustrated him, but also the fact that the novel found its way into a sub-genre mastered by another author. Thomas Harris' novel *Red Dragon* (1981) was to leave such a strong impression on Ellroy that he decided to write a whole series of Hopkins novels: 'I finished *Blood on the Moon*, read *Red Dragon* and wanted another shot at making Sergeant Lloyd Hopkins as great a character as Thomas Harris' Will Graham' (Ellroy 1997b: i).

An influence on *Blood on the Moon* and the Hopkins series is alluded to in the dedication: 'In Memory of Kenneth Millar 1915–1983' (Ellroy 1984b: 11). Kenneth Millar, who wrote under the pseudonym Ross Macdonald, was the author of the Lew Archer novels. Although Ellroy had disowned the influence of Chandler after the publication of *Brown's Requiem*, and Hopkins was created as reaction against this model, 'my antidote to the sensitive candy-assed philosophizing private eye',

Macdonald's Archer was heavily indebted to Chandler's Philip Marlowe (Ellroy 1997b: i). Ellroy has acknowledged the influence of the Archer novels on his early work: 'there's some elements of his [Macdonald's] lost child motif, and the webs of violence going back generations, in my earlier books' (Hogan 1995: 58). Ellroy even took the aborted series title of the Hopkins novels from a Lew Archer anthology of novels, *Archer in Jeopardy*, which was published in 1979, two years before Ellroy published his first novel.

Hopkins differs from both the Chandler and Archer model of lead character as he is a maverick detective at odds with many fellow police officers in his department and not a lone private investigator. But although private detectives and maverick police detectives are common in genre fiction, Ellroy distinguishes his creation from these recognizable forms through the narrative structure. Hopkins' moral ambiguity is rooted in the striking parallels between his life and the killer he is chasing, Theodore Verplanck. Characterization is developed through what at first glance is Hopkins' mirror image.

The novel alternates between the subjective third-person viewpoints of Hopkins and Verplanck. Ellroy's stylistic experimentation is contained within this framework. Hopkins and Verplanck attended the same high school and share romantic feelings for the same woman, and both men were subjected to a sexual assault in their youth. Ellroy invests both characters with a Romantic vision which, to varying degrees, reflects his own Demon Dog persona. Here Ellroy is repeating a technique he explored in *Brown's Requiem*, whereby protagonist and antagonist, Fritz Brown and Freddy 'Fat Dog' Baker were both heavily invested with facets of his own character. Thus, their rivalry is driven more by the characteristics they share than what separates them, although in their roles, as detective and serial killer, Hopkins and Verplanck could not be more different. This theme of similarity made more complex by assumed difference is reflected in the structure of the novel, with each chapter alternating between the two characters' viewpoints 'killer–cop, killer–cop, and so on' until they meet in the finale (Tucker 1984: 5).

Part one of *Blood on the Moon*, 'First Tastes of Blood', opens on Friday, 10 June 1964, 'the start of KRLA golden oldie weekend' (Ellroy 1984b: 17). Ellroy evokes nostalgia only for it to be followed by horrific violence. This day will be the catalyst for Theodore Verplanck's murderous existence. Verplanck is not named in the scene and is referred to simply as 'the poet'. Verplanck is continually referred to by this rather vague, non-threatening title until Hopkins discovers his identity in the latter half of the novel, as if through Hopkins, Verplanck is defined. The name 'the poet' is never capitalized, which emphasizes Verplanck's anonymity and how inconsequential he is to wider society. A student at Marshall High School in LA, Verplanck provokes two of his violent fellow students, Larry 'Birdman' Craigie and Delbert 'Whitey' Haines, by writing poems mocking their masculinity in the Marshall High Poetry Review.

Birdman and Whitey ambush and physically assault Verplanck. The situation becomes more violent when Whitey unexpectedly finds he is sexually aroused. Ironically, their adrenaline-fuelled hatred for the poet's effeminacy has led them to a shared homosexual experience:

> When the poet's face and bare arms were covered with blood, Whitey stepped back to savor his revenge. He pulled down his fly to deliver a warm liquid coup de grace, and discovered he was hard. Larry noticed this, and looked to his leader for some clue to what was supposed to happen. Suddenly Whitey was terrified. He looked down at the poet, who moaned 'scum,' and spat out a stream of blood onto the steel-toed paratrooper boots. Now Whitey knew what his hardness meant, and he knelt beside the poet and pulled off his Levi cords and boxer shorts and spread his legs and blunderingly plunged himself into him. The poet screamed once he entered; then his breathing settled into something strangely like ironic laughter. Whitey finished, withdrew and looked to his shock-stilled underling for support. To make it easy for him, he turned up the volume on the radio until Elvis Presley wailed into a garbled screech; then he watched as Larry delivered his ultimate acquiescence. (Ellroy 1984b: 21–2)

What should be the end of a violent, but ordinary, high school beating becomes a life-defining moment for the three characters. Whitey experiences a revelation and leads his underling into the homosexual world with him. The course of the attackers' lives is changed by this violent confrontation, with both becoming homosexuals. Likewise, the victim begins his transition from sensitive, socially awkward teenager to sadist and murderer. He screams in agony during the rape, but before it is over he seems to accept or even enjoy the assault as he releases 'ironic laughter'. The laughter reverberates throughout the text as one ill-timed erection produces an onslaught of violence over a generation. Moments before the rape, Whitey and Birdman are terrified as they mistakenly believe they have killed Verplanck. They are overcome with laughter and relief when they realize Verplanck is still breathing, but Whitey's unexpected arousal will lead them to a far more damning fate than if they had killed Verplanck through the beating. Whitey first appears as the more sensible of the two, taking a strong dislike to Birdman's vulgar attitude towards women. He hated to hear 'nice girls blasphemed' (Ellroy 1984b: 18). Whitey's shift from straight to gay in the opening chapter sets the stage for a novel in which the parallels between characters ebb and flow with the circular nature of their fates. One of the poems Verplanck wrote mocking Whitey had been styled as a requiem, and ultimately both men drag each other to their doom.

Ellroy describes *Blood on the Moon* as his attempt to find 'the strongest possible voice' (Tucker 1984: 5). The strongest voice for Ellroy is never singular as the viewpoint alternates between Hopkins and Verplanck. The central narrative of the novel is structured around the relationship of these two characters who will only ever meet once. Although Verplanck is not referred to by name as the victim in the rape scene, it is difficult to assume the narration is entirely the third-person viewpoint of Whitey and Birdman. The prose seems too sophisticated to be accurately conveying the thoughts of the two thugs, with phrases such as 'coup de grace' suggesting the scene is partially the subjective third-person viewpoint of the more eloquent 'poet'.

As the assault is winding down a new song, slower in pace, is playing on the radio. 'Cathy's Clown' by the Everly Brothers is symbolic of the poet's anonymous love for Kathleen McCarthy, and of the many songs referenced in the novel it is the only one which is a specific clue to the mystery narrative: 'I die each time / I hear this sound: / "Here he co-o-o-o-omes. That's Cathy's clown"' (Everly 1960). The clown of the song is being rejected and humiliated in love just as the poet has been emotionally and physically humiliated through being brutalized. But the poet is also literally 'Kathy's Klown'. He is in love with McCarthy, a fellow student at Marshall High who runs a poetry reading group known as 'Kathy's Kourt', which consists of sexually abstinent female students. Several members of the group have 'Klowns': male admirers whom they deliberately reject out of feminist superiority; thus, in a less brutal way, the Kourt adds to the poet's emasculation, using physical and emotional rejection more effectively than Whitey and Birdman's assault, just as the poet had used his mastery of the written word against the two thugs. The word 'co-o-o-omes', when applied to Verplanck, is also sexual innuendo, alluding to ejaculation. As a comment on Verplanck's humiliation the song combines his rape and involuntary celibacy – to give him a violent yet 'poetic' purpose: the women Verplanck murders are sacrificed in honour of the 'pure' Kathleen McCarthy, who stayed true to her ideals while the rest of the Kourt drifted away.

Yet Verplanck also drifts away from his original ideals, rejecting the intellectualism of poetry for the brutality of his fantasies. In the original manuscript of 'L.A. Death Trip', Verplanck is raped by five attackers: Whitey, Birdman, Tim Hunchley, Ely Garcia and Joe Garcia (Ellroy 1983b). But Ellroy's decision to reduce it to two in *Blood on the Moon* focuses the narrative, as Verplanck balances his voyeurism between stalking and murdering women and keeping tabs on Whitey and Birdman. He derives power over women through the murders, but his power over his brutal rapists is ironically more passive. Although he eventually kills Birdman, symbolically shooting him in the groin and anus, he gains his revenge from a distance, voyeuristically following how dysfunctional his attackers have become in adult life.

Ellroy follows Verplanck's rape by immediately moving to one of the defining moments in Hopkins' life: 23 August 1965, the day the Watts riots break out in LA. Ironically, with every parallel that exists between the two characters comes a form of divergence. Hopkins is able to enact vigilante justice almost immediately after the horrors he witnesses, and, therefore, he is not as traumatized as Verplanck. The scene is set about fourteen months after the assault on Verplanck. Hopkins is a Private First Class (PFC) in the National Guard, and he hopes his experiences in the riots will be his 'Baptism by fire' (Ellroy 1984b: 26). The shocking violence Hopkins encounters in the riot will alter his character and set him on a path that parallels Verplanck's life.

Ellroy described Verplanck and Hopkins as 'displaced romantics' (Tucker 1984: 5). For Verplanck, this is delusion. He believes that by murdering women he is preserving them in honourable chastity. Hopkins has no illusions of people's innocence, be it chaste or childlike. Hopkins takes, rather, the opposite view, that children should be denied innocence for their own preservation. When he first hears of the riots, he is building sand castles for a group of children on a Malibu beach. In a reference to his Irish Presbyterian heritage, Hopkins describes himself to the children as a brave Loyalist who must rescue the damsel in distress from the evil clutches of his Nationalist brother Tom, who is also at the beach. Although the idyllic qualities of this beach scene and fairy tale might suggest Hopkins entertains Romantic notions of life, Ellroy shatters this illusion by Hopkins' highly inappropriate choice of subject: Irish sectarianism. Hopkins believes that by deliberately exposing the vulnerable to the ugly truth of life, he is destroying the innocence he sees as weakness. Much to his wife's displeasure, his bedtime stories to his daughters consist of uncensored accounts of his police cases. Hopkins' Romanticism stems from his loss of innocence early in life, freeing him to embark on a full engagement with the world in the role of detective/protector. Yet his version of protection is distinct from Verplanck's murderous preservation.

Hopkins' whimsical take on sectarianism is contrasted with the stark reality of the racial dividing lines in the boundaries between the wealthy, predominately Caucasian area of Malibu, and the economically depressed African American district of Watts. Hopkins' nemesis in the riots, however, is not one of the black rioters, but a white man and fellow National Guardsman, Sergeant Richard Beller. Hopkins agrees to go on a scout patrol with Beller ahead of the main unit, armed with some of Beller's illegal weapons. But Hopkins soon finds himself caught in a visceral nightmare: when Beller brutally kills several black people in a church, Hopkins traps the racist murderer through his bigotry. Hopkins switches on a radio and by playing 'rhythmic soul music' fools Beller into thinking there are more blacks in the vicinity:

> Beller burst out the door of the outhouse seconds later, screaming, 'Nigger! Nigger! Nigger!' Blindly, he fired off a series of shots. The light from his muzzle bursts illuminated him perfectly. Lloyd raised his .45 and aimed slowly, pointing at Beller's feet to allow for recoil. He squeezed the trigger, the gun kicked and the elephant clip emptied. Beller screamed. Lloyd dug into the dirt, stifling his own screams. The radio blasted rhythm and blues, and Lloyd ran toward the sound, the butt end of his .45 extended. He stumbled in the darkness, then got down on his hands and knees and bludgeoned the music to death. (Ellroy 1984b: 43)

Beller is an overt racist who detests Hopkins because of his comparatively liberal views, although Ellroy described Hopkins as a 'fascist fuckhead' (Ellroy 1997b: i). It is this contrast between Beller's unmitigated hate and Hopkins' struggle to control his darker instincts from which the novel draws its moral compass. Beller dislikes Hopkins' intellectualism as Hopkins (who is nicknamed 'the Brain') is a graduate of Stanford University. Beller states, 'Brains are overrated. Guts are what counts', failing to realize that Hopkins' intelligence bolsters his personal courage (Ellroy 1984b: 30). In character, Beller and Hopkins are anatomically contrasted as 'Guts' and 'Brains', just as Verplanck and Hopkins are intellectually contrasted as 'The poet' and 'The Brain'; by this comparison, however, Hopkins seems closer to Verplanck the serial killer than Beller the racist killer. Hopkins' racism is tenuous and owes more to the rhythm of his manic character; before the riots, he affects a 'Negro's shuffle' and 'broad dialect', then lambasts his fellow Guardsmen as 'nigger scared' when they refuse to laugh at his antics (Ellroy 1984b: 25–6). Thus, Hopkins' murder of Beller is rooted in his conviction that the victims of murder, whatever their race, must be avenged.

After killing Beller, Hopkins 'bludgeoned the music to death'. In the opening chapter, music is playing on the radio throughout the brutalization of Verplanck to cover up the crime. In the second chapter, Hopkins uses music as a device to lure and kill his enemy, and by extension, to graduate to manhood. Throughout the narrative, Hopkins expresses unease whenever he hears any music being played. Ellroy teases the reader with this recurring detail until it is finally revealed that Hopkins was also subjected to rape and torture when he was only eight years old, and his hatred of music stems from his attacker playing radios at full volume to drown out Hopkins' screams of pain. Thus, music is a revelatory device in the narrative and Hopkins' use of it to trap Beller seems particularly brave given the awful memories it evokes. For both Hopkins and Verplanck music returns them to the exact moment which forged their pathology. By killing Beller, Hopkins is also killing a part of himself, that which is deferential to the law and would have attempted to arrest Beller, and this is when the music stops. Hopkins interprets the law as a merely arbitrary rule, tangential but not essential to his moral actions. The carnage of the Watts riots is reminiscent of a war zone, and in an area where law has broken down, Hopkins can issue his own form of justice. His duel with Verplanck is different as in the 1980s setting the law is firmly in place, but the institutions have failed the victims: Hopkins is the only LAPD detective that sees the connection in a series of murders and has to exceed his remit to ensure justice is done.

Hopkins' sense of vigilante justice is shaped by his Romanticism. Ellroy has been careful never to precisely state what he means by the term Romantic, but his view of the crime genre gives an insight into his own Romanticism: 'I think crime fiction at its best is touching the fire and getting your hand burned' (Silet 1995: 45). By leaving the term vague and undefined, it gives him the opportunity to explore characters like Hopkins and Verplanck whose obsessions will push them right to the boundaries of society. In her study of Ellroy, Anna Flügge identified some of the conventions of Romanticism which come the closest to a definition which would be applicable to Ellroy's work:

> In Romanticism, the protagonists are often artists or scientists who put their profession above everything else. Their desire to transgress

human and ethical limitations makes them great in the eyes of some, but also vicious since they risk utter destruction for their personal quests. They accept that they are alone on their quest, taking others only if they can use them. (Flügge 2010: 31)

Verplanck and Hopkins are 'ill at ease in the 1980s', but their ambitious individualism might read more as a product of the 1980s rather than a rebellion against it (Tucker 1984: 5). Flügge comments that the protagonists put their 'profession above everything else'. Yet Hopkins and Verplanck put their obsessions above everything else, which pushes them to levels of intellectual brilliance but also to an emotional unpredictability that is distinctly unprofessional. Neither man is interested in money; in this sense, their individualism is unusual in the decade of Reaganomics, as it is based on ideals rather than on wealth. Both men seem to be anachronistic and contradictory figures, capable of both piercing intelligence and cold-blooded murder, yet always at the mercy of the obsessions that drive them, so much so that 'they risk utter destruction for their personal quests'.

There are moments in the novel when Hopkins allows his emotions to cloud what should be the objective reasoning of a detective, such as when he discovers the female corpse of one of Verplanck's victims, which has been tied up at the ankles and hanged upside down:

'You'd better leave her like that for the Coroner, Sergeant.'
Lloyd said, 'Shut the fuck up,' and cut through the nylon cord that bound Julia Lynn Niemeyer at the ankles. He gathered her dangling limbs and violated torso into his arms and stepped off the bed, cradling her head into his shoulder. Tears filled his eyes. 'Sleep, darling,' he said. 'Know that I'll find your killer.' Lloyd lowered her to the floor and covered her with the robe. The three cops stared at him in disbelief. (Ellroy 1984b: 116)

The other cops are more conventional, using black humour as a coping skill to offset their emotional reaction. Hopkins has to be unconventional in his behaviour to be true to his Romantic beliefs. His vow to the victim is quite specific: 'I'll find your killer.' He promises neither justice nor vigilantism; the latter would be unwise as there are other policemen in the room, but his words imply a personal unorthodox investigation which will largely disregard procedure. The tender regard he shows towards the corpse, physically and verbally, is contrasted with the obscenities he aims at his colleagues. He does not want her to hear their crude jokes, but he is happy to use foul language at them. The corpse is the most important person to him in the room; he talks to her, shields her from colourful language and tries to physically comfort her. The social conventions he ignores for the living do apply to the dead. At the crime scene, Hopkins discovers lonely hearts adverts which are so desperate and lewd it makes him despair of the entire human race. He knows that many people are dead in their soul; therefore, he treats the dead as living. By cutting the body down and cradling the victim in his arms as if he were her father, he is composing the corpse on his own terms, banishing the ghoulish image of Verplanck's work.

Hopkins' refusal to follow crime scene protocol is an indication of what is both original and absurd about the Hopkins novels. They are ostensibly police procedural novels about a policeman who seldom follows procedure. According to Eddy Von Mueller's writing on the subgenre, this would exclude the Hopkins novels from being classified as police procedurals:

> We also should also set aside the majority of 'rogue cop' tales, so dramatically epitomized by Clint Eastwood in Don Siegel's 1971 *Dirty Harry*. The rogue cop is, by definition, an outsider, and difficult to contain within the regulations and routines that delineate the procedural. Many a procedural ensemble, however, includes an unruly cop, or even a rogue, in the same way as a protagonal collective might have a quirky genius numbered with its company. But ultimately, the rogue, like the token great detective, becomes a disruptive force that most often has to be tamed or driven out in order for the integrity of the police unit as a whole to be maintained. (Von Mueller 2010: 99)

As the narrative of the series progresses, it becomes apparent that Hopkins is capable of cooperating with fellow policemen in the LAPD when he needs to. His closest professional relationship is with Dutch Peltz, who helps to mitigate Hopkins' unconventional behaviour. In *Suicide Hill*, Hopkins' 'rogue cop' status even helps to stabilize the LAPD, which has become unduly influenced by the presence of devout evangelicals in senior positions. As Lee Spinks argues in his essay 'Except for Law', 'Ellroy's fiction consists in its transition from a classical to a modern structure of exception in which exception has now become the normative logic of juridical and political processes' (Spinks 2008: 126). For Hopkins, Romanticism is rooted in his intense individualism as a Romantic detective, so he would never envisage or desire his methods to be the 'normative logic' of police procedure. Hopkins is a radical outsider, within a predominantly conformist police department. Only in his LA Quartet novels would Ellroy portray criminality as a fairly widespread LAPD phenomenon, and here it is related more to corruption in the form of institutionalized racism and detectives taking payoffs from organized-crime figures. Hopkins sees his law-breaking as a form of higher good.

Ellroy breaks the established structure of the narrative and character arcs in the final part of the novel titled 'Moon Descending'. The previous section of the novel, 'Convergence', carries a double meaning in that the parallels between the two characters deepen as Hopkins' investigation brings him literally closer to Verplanck. But in the following section, a moral divergence is established even as the two characters' experiential similarities are increased when Hopkins reveals to Kathleen McCarthy that he was raped as a child. Hopkins describes how at the age of eight he was beaten up by his older brother Tom and tied to a chair in their father's workshop. When Tom tells their parents Hopkins has run away, they leave the house in search of him. Trapped in the workshop all alone, Hopkins is visited by a supposedly harmless, shellshocked old man named Dave, who lives in a tent at the nearby Silverlake Power Plant:

> I was scared at first, but then the door opened, and it was Dave. But he didn't rescue me. He turned on every TV set and radio in the shack and put a knife to my throat and made me touch him and eat him. He burned me with tube testers and hooked up live wires and stuck them up my ass. Then he raped me and hit me and burned me again and again, with the TVs and radios going full blast the whole time. After two days of hurting me, he left. He never turned off the noise. It grew and grew and grew. ... Finally my family came home. Mother came running into the shack. She took the tape off my mouth and untied me and held me and asked me what happened. But I couldn't talk. I had screamed silently for so long that my vocal chords had shredded. (Ellroy 1984b: 228)

This revelation is the payoff to several carefully placed clues earlier in the narrative that Hopkins has been subjected to a traumatic childhood experience. Hopkins' story of how he was raped by a local man contextualizes his inflexible hatred of music, and music, the trigger for his psychological and physical trauma, is always present during the most dramatic moments in the novel. The 'music' played during the rape, a clash of loud TV and radio which is devoid of both meaning and structure, alludes to the moral horror of the novel. It is only loud noise. At one point the mental torture blasting out of the electrical appliances becomes physical torture as Hopkins describes how Dave 'hooked up live wires and stuck them up my ass'. Technology is attacking Hopkins in an extension of the inhuman act. The functionality of the machines mirrors how, as a rape victim, Hopkins must disassociate himself from the act to go on living, but emotional disassociation is anathema to the Romantic Hopkins. The danger is not only of sensory overload but also of not feeling anything at all. Dave is mentally disturbed: he is the natural body that commits action without feeling or sympathy. Hopkins has tried to shield himself from the memory, but he slowly reveals himself to Kathleen until she fully extracts the memory from him. During their lovemaking, Hopkins thinks he ejaculates blood, but it is actually Kathleen's menstruation. She decides, 'if I am going to be his music', then she must make him reveal his childhood trauma (Ellroy 1984b: 224). Kathleen is the conduit through which the reader sees the parallels of Hopkins and Verplanck. Both men take solace in her after their rape, but ultimately she is unable to change the music they are dancing to. Kathleen naively begs Hopkins not to kill Verplanck, whom she remembers as a 'very kind boy', completely oblivious to the fact that he has murdered over twenty women in her name (Ellroy 1984b: 229).

Hopkins' rape feels like a complete betrayal as his absent family's electrical appliances cover up the crime, implicating technology and culture in the act. This partly explains Hopkins' complete disinterest in contemporary culture. His sense of isolation from the music and culture of the 1980s setting adds to his Romanticism. After enduring an extreme noise during the rape, Hopkins is reduced to physically imposed silence. It would become a moral silence for most of the novel, with Hopkins acting out his role as the 'fascist fuckhead' and the parallels between him and Verplanck ever deepening (Ellroy 1997b: i). However, the revelation of Hopkins' rape deepens the physical parallels between the two men while forcing a moral and emotional divergence. Hopkins bears the same scars as Verplanck, but he has emerged comparatively righteous and heroic in his worldview.

For much of the novel, Ellroy leads the reader to believe that Hopkins' 'baptism by fire' at Watts was his defining moment. Hopkins' revelation to McCarthy, however, revises the two leading characters' similarities. Hopkins came to view vigilantism as a legitimate form of dispensing justice before his experience at Watts. Hopkins' mother discovers him in the shack after the rape. He writes down what happened to him, becoming literally the 'author' of his own narrative, as the damage to his vocal chords has left him mute. She swears him to secrecy about the rape and walks down to the power plant where she calmly murders Dave, shooting him six times with a pistol. Hopkins witnesses the revenge attack as he has secretly followed her: 'She took me to bed with her that night and gave me her breasts' (Ellroy 1984b: 229). Hopkins' brutal rape is followed by acts of maternal nurture which are, by any measure, taboo. His mother expresses her love for her eight-year-old son through murder and then breastfeeding, both acts probably contributing to Hopkins' insatiable womanizing. His mother murders the author of the homosexual act to give new birth to the heterosexual Hopkins. Verplanck is offered no such opportunity, and his sexuality and psychopathic behaviour are forged entirely by one event, his rape. Another divergence between the two leading characters is that the nature of Hopkins' job, homicide investigation, acts as an aphrodisiac to him whereas Verplanck kills to repress his sexual feelings. Fifteen years after his rape, Hopkins activates this dormant vigilantism by killing Sergeant Beller at Watts and finally the narrative comes full circle with an extra-judicial showdown between Hopkins and Verplanck at the Silverlake Power Plant.

Peter Wolfe argues that the similarities between Hopkins and Verplanck create a constantly shifting moral ambiguity in the narrative which only begins to clarify itself towards the denouement of the novel.

> With so little to choose between Verplanck and Lloyd, one worries if Ellroy miscued by letting Lloyd survive at his mirror-image's expense. One needn't worry for long. The answer is no, as is seen in Verplanck's killing of one Joanie Pratt the same night Lloyd has sex with her. The adultery the big police sergeant committed by bedding Joanie, though wrong, is less sinful than murder. (Wolfe 2005: 98)

When he considers Hopkins' relative moral stature, Wolfe does not take into account that in the original draft of 'L.A. Death Trip', Hopkins is killed by his 'mirror-image' who also dies. The moral differences between the two versions have been clouded by Ellroy himself, who has made misleading statements regarding the ending of 'L.A. Death Trip'. Martin Kihn's profile of Ellroy states that 'L.A. Death Trip' ends when 'L.A. burns to the ground' (Kihn 1992: 31). Ellroy has been open about his original intention to kill off Hopkins and Verplanck, but he exaggerates what happens directly afterwards, speaking figuratively about LA burning as though he is killing the genre by destroying its most iconic location. In his interview with Silet, Ellroy repeats his terse summation of the bizarre ending to 'L.A. Death Trip': 'In the first draft the cop, Hopkins, and the killer, Teddy Verplanck, kill each other and L.A. burns to the ground' (Silet 1995: 44).

The ending was not as apocalyptic as Ellroy has publicly stated. A limited explosion is caused by Hopkins committing suicide with a grenade launcher at the Silverlake Power Plant:

> Lloyd smiled. He felt the love he was receiving and felt even more the love he was about to give. He aimed at Dutch's voice and pulled the trigger, and in the last split second of his life saw the world consumed by flames. (Ellroy 1983b: 418)

Ellroy's description of the ending corresponds to the very last thing the dying Hopkins sees, but it does not accurately explain the narrative as clarified in the epilogue to the manuscript. In both 'L.A. Death Trip' and *Blood on the Moon*, Hopkins is initially losing his duel with Verplanck, but in 'L.A. Death Trip' he is even more grievously injured, losing several fingers when Verplanck attacks him with an axe. Hopkins' life is saved when Verplanck is shot dead by a marksman from a police helicopter. But in one stroke, Hopkins commits suicide and, in another parallel to Verplanck, becomes a mass murderer as he fires a grenade launcher into the power plant. In doing so, he kills his best friend, Detective 'Dutch' Peltz, the crews of five police helicopters and numerous National Guardsmen. The motivation for Ellroy's original bloodbath of an ending can be traced to his admission in his memoirs that he wrote 'L.A. Death Trip' in an anti-LA and anti-genre frame of mind. He was also interested in making a name for himself through shock value: 'I wanted to write the ugliest and most explicit cop/psycho-killer book of all time' (Silet 1995: 44). In 'L.A. Death Trip' Ellroy appears to have grown contemptuous of the characters and narrative by the end of the novel, and felt obligated to kill the entire cast, as though he was killing the genre itself: 'I look back now and think, "Holy shit, is this moribund"' (Silet 1995: 44). To end the novel with a mass murder instigated by the detective is radical, and it is as ugly and explicit as Ellroy intended. However, it is also implausible, and it vindicates Sobel and Penzler's determination to shift the plotting more firmly back to the conventions of the genre. One of the legacies of 'L.A. Death Trip' is that Ellroy has repeatedly claimed that the ending was more hyperbolically violent than it was, distancing himself from the text on the one hand while simultaneously buttressing his credentials as an experimental stylist.

In the novel's extensive redrafting, Ellroy would assume some of the more practical aspects of the genre (such as the Detective's final triumph over the serial killer), and as a consequence, write a much improved story. The original manuscript expresses a more unbridled and confused intensity: Hopkins' suicide near the location where he was once raped could be interpreted as a redemptive, cleansing act, but taking his life in a manner which kills dozens of innocent people is incompatible with his role as a detective. However, this violent response closely parallels Verplanck and the consequences of his rape. In this final perversion of emotion and reason, violence is more than just a vigilante means to an end, it is an expression of love, with Hopkins regarding firing the grenade launcher as 'the love he was about to give'. When Hopkins' mother murders Dave it is a justifiable act of love that starts her son's journey toward vigilante cop. The ending to 'LA Death Trip' cannot be justified as vigilantism. By deliberately triggering the explosion, Hopkins becomes an indiscriminate murderer, and destroys any semblance of morality that remained.

It is fitting that the last thing Hopkins sees before his death is 'the world consumed by flames', which alludes to the original epigraph taken from the T.S. Eliot poem 'Little Gidding', the last poem of the *Four Quartets*: 'We only live, only suspire / Consumed by either fire or fire' (Eliot 1942: 42). Death here is also the essence of life. And Verplanck and Hopkins conform to different Romantic passions – fire – but with the same result – fire. Hopkins' fiery and murderous suicide symbolically wipes out every trace of his authoritarian identity: Dutch, the LAPD and National Guard.

In the final confrontation of the novel, the parallels between detective and killer continue even in death. Dutch saves Hopkins' life by arriving at the power plant just in time and killing Verplanck. In a highly symbolic act, the wounded Hopkins is then given an immediate blood transfusion from Verplanck's corpse: in death the killer becomes life-saver. The parallels continue as both Hopkins and Verplanck are ultimately denied the love of Kathleen McCarthy, who leaves LA to escape the violence caused by the two men both of whom, in their different ways, loved her.

Ellroy's decision in *Blood on the Moon* to leave Hopkins alive, though physically and psychologically exhausted, showed his new willingness to embrace the structures of crime fiction and turn his back on the anti-genre mood of 'L.A. Death Trip'. This was an uncharacteristically conventional decision by Ellroy, but his new professional relationship with the Mysterious Press had rescued his career and steered him away from sudden, radical shocks in his writing. Ellroy's stylistic evolution, both on the page and as the Demon Dog, would continue within the framework of the detective genre in the short term, with two more Lloyd Hopkins novels.

Because the Night

The second Lloyd Hopkins novel, *Because the Night*, was published the same year as *Blood on the Moon*, 1984. The rapid production turnaround of *Because the Night*, which clearly did not go through as many drafts as *Blood on the Moon*, indicated Ellroy's increasing confidence and impatience as a writer. The plotting is more ambitious but less focused than in *Blood on the Moon*. Hopkins' investigation veers between a triple homicide at a liquor store and the disappearance of an LAPD detective. Both crimes point to psychiatrist Dr John Havilland, who is capable of manipulating people to commit murder on his orders. As with the previous novel in the series, Havilland is partly motivated by a traumatic childhood experience, and like *Blood on the Moon*, he also nurtures a chaste love with Hopkins' romantic interest. Linda Wilhite is one of Havilland's patients. Hopkins starts a relationship with her partly as a means of gaining information on Havilland: Ellroy again uses a woman to deepen the connections between protagonist and antagonist.

Another similarity with *Blood on the Moon* is the alternating subjective third-person viewpoint between Hopkins and his chief suspect. However, Ellroy has abandoned his method of linking the pathology of both leading characters to a single defining event. Back-story is a factor in the plotting and character motivation, but the interaction and rivalry between Hopkins and Havilland unfolds in a less rigid structure. Unlike Verplanck, Havilland is less adept at committing physical violence himself, which is partly a reflection of his higher, and more visible, status in society. Ellroy claims he wrote the novel after reading Thomas Harris' *Red Dragon,* and there is a strong parallel between the two novels as Havilland is a murderous psychiatrist not entirely dissimilar from Harris' most famous creation, Dr Hannibal Lecter.

Aside from the psychiatrist-turned-killer, the symbolism of colour is one theme which loosely links the two novels. The title *Red Dragon* is taken from *The Great Red Dragon* paintings by William Blake: the serial killer Francis Dolarhyde is obsessed with the paintings and tries to develop the same colossal strength as the dragon. In *Because the Night*, colour represents a variety of emotions, including psychological triggers to violence. This is established right from the very first scene when an unnamed criminal commits a liquor store robbery which quickly escalates into a triple homicide:

> A scream was building in his throat when he saw the beige curtain that separated the store from the living quarters behind it. When a gust of wind ruffled the curtain he did scream – watching as the cotton folds assumed the shape of bars and hangman's nooses.
> Now he knew.
> He jerked the girl and the old man to their feet and shoved them to the curtain. When they were trembling in front of it, he dragged the counterman over and stationed him beside them. Muttering, 'Green door, green door,' he paced out five yards, wheeled and squeezed off three perfect head shots. The horrible beige curtain exploded into crimson. (Ellroy 1984a: 284)

The neutral, everyday colour of beige is ironically the catalyst for the gunman, later revealed to be Thomas Goff, who first sees the universal colour for go, 'green', before committing the murders. It is revealed that beige is a trigger for Goff early in the narrative. During a stint in Attica state prison, Goff's cellmate committed suicide by hanging himself with a beige trash bag. Goff was trapped in the cell for hours. A light was flickering outside the cell intermittently illuminating the corpse, and creating a form of cinematic horror show. Now, the mere sight of beige induces both horrific memories and the compulsion for violent acts in Goff. The splattering of blood on the curtain turns the repressive beige into a liberated crimson. The sentence seems to suggest that the curtain entirely changes colour in one moment from beige to crimson. As the action is contained with a single sentence, it reads as a single action instead of three separate gunshots and deaths, creating a kind of linguistic barrier to the true nature of Goff's actions. Rather than describing bullets tearing holes into bodies and the random spraying of blood, the subjective third-person narrative encapsulates the horror into a rather unintimidating fact: the curtain changing colour. The singularity of the action compresses the timeframe of the already fast moving scene and makes it more cinematic, as though the concluding sentence is a camera cutting away from the murders to the curtain, which itself is evocative of cinema, as it suggests if the curtain was drawn back an onscreen image would be in view. In this case, it is a distinctly violent image. Goff has been programmed by Havilland to commit the robbery and murder, but the limitations of the 'man as machine' model are laid bare almost immediately as he is surprised to find two people hiding behind the store refrigerator: 'nothing he had been taught had prepared him for three' (Ellroy 1984a: 284). Ultimately, even when Goff does not have Havilland's direct instruction or influence, he is still under the sway of the psychiatrist and commits even worse acts of violence.

Green is an important colour in the therapy techniques employed by Havilland, as he encourages his patients to go 'beyond the beyond' or 'beyond the green door', meaning that they should push themselves to the limits of their physical and psychological capabilities. The phrase is also reference to the 1957 song 'Green Door' by Jim Lowe:

> They had an old piano and they played it hot behind the green door! Don't know what they're doin', but they laugh a lot behind the green door! (Lowe 1960)

The lyrics allude to the smoking of marijuana as green is the colour of a marijuana plant and in American slang 'green' refers to someone who is inexperienced. Ellroy references the song to explore the nature of voyeurism. In the song 'Green Door', voyeuristic pleasure is always secondary, as the singer never discovers what exactly is going on behind the green door. There is forbidden pleasure on both sides of the green door, as the singer's imagination gives him transference, being both tantalized and tormented by the activities from which he has been excluded. Ellroy would reference Lowe's song again in *The Cold Six Thousand*: in the novel, a motel room with a green door contains camera equipment which is covertly recording trysts in the adjoining room. Walls and doors act as metaphors in Havilland's teaching as the simple act of walking through a door 'the dividing line between his old life of fear and his new life of power' becomes a symbol of transformation and conversion from past failures to Nietzschean strength (Ellroy 1984a: 283).

Lowe's 'Green Door' is not the only music reference in *Because the Night*. The title of the novel is taken from the 1978 song of the same name written by Patti Smith and Bruce Springsteen for the Patti Smith Group. The title is used by both Hopkins and Havilland in subjective third-person accounts of their back-story, which serves as the intellectual justification for their actions. It also acts as Ellroy's payoff to the reader for using such a strange title. Ellroy builds a form of artificial mystery around the title which is resolved mid-way through the novel when the back-story of the two leads is revealed. Unlike Hopkins' literal similarities to Verplanck, the rogue detective has more intellectual parallels with Havilland, and both men, in their different ways, share a philosophy that they are above conventional morality and have a deeper understanding of the world. But in *Because the Night*, the Romanticism has become bitter and cynical, with Hopkins and Havilland so disconnected from other people that they have become misanthropic.

Havilland's misanthropy began after an intensive study of the work of Alfred Kinsey:

> The most profound truth lay in the labyrinths that coiled behind a green door in the interviewee's mind the very second that Alfred Kinsey said, "Tell me about your fantasies"; and, two, that with the proper information and the correct stimuli he could get carefully chosen people to break through those doors and act out their fantasies, past moral strictures and the boundaries of conscience, taking him past his already absolute knowledge of mankind's unutterable stupidity into a new night realm that he as yet was incapable of imagining. Because the night was there to be plundered; and only someone above its laws could exact its bounty and survive. (Ellroy 1984a: 325)

Havilland's psychology is a form of academic voyeurism, his observations being a codified self-indulgence. The patient's so-called 'break-through' is the exposure of their secrets and passions rather than a self-revelation, and Havilland takes advantage of his position as an absorber of their weaknesses. Rather than allowing the patient a cathartic confession leading to identification and self-empowerment, Havilland's patients are moved further toward enslavement as Havilland exploits his new knowledge and position of power to manipulate them into committing crimes. The philosophical justification of these acts is expressed in an unusual reversal of basic sentence structure: 'Because the night was there to be plundered.' The conjunctive adverb 'Because', comes at the beginning of the sentence, but it is not preceded by the cause which should reveal Havilland's justification. By reordering the sentence structure, Ellroy presents a moral code which has been turned upside down. Acts are measured not by whether they fall within the law, but by the individual brilliance with which they are applied because 'only someone above its laws could exact its bounty and survive'. Havilland notices early in his career that he can shed people of their fantasies and turn them into 'loving, boring, happy human being(s)', but with Goff and others, he develops the opposite effect by forcing his patients to reject conventional morality and, as a consequence, develop criminal fantasies. For all his brilliance, Havilland is blind to the one thing that will destroy him. Havilland regards himself as above his patients, neither stripped bare of fantasy nor beholden to it: 'He could look out and see all; no one could look in and see him' (Ellroy 1984a: 324). Hopkins understands Havilland because, despite their moral differences, he is his intellectual equal.

In contrast to Havilland's parasitic and manipulative voyeurism, Hopkins' moral code is to fight for Romantic dreams and noble causes. The only relevant back-story provided for Hopkins in *Because the Night* describes his upbringing in Silverlake. Because of its close proximity to an animal shelter, Silverlake is nicknamed 'Dogtown'. Dogs frequently manage to escape from the shelter through a wire fence, only to be killed by the drunken joy-riders who frequent the area. As a fourteen-year-old (six years after his rape), Hopkins stays up all night listening to howling dogs. Hopkins is deeply affected by the sound of dogs dying when they are hit by cars and also by the smell of their corpses the next morning. Hopkins knows he cannot spend his nights agonizing over how many dogs are suffering so close to him. He sets up camp in a sleeping bag on 'Dead Dog Curve'. As a 'peewee member of the Dogtown Flats gang', he engages in fights with bikers twice his size and age who play 'chicken' on the roads endangering the dogs (Ellroy 1984a: 436). These acts of foolhardy courage earn Hopkins the nickname 'Dogman', 'Saviour' and 'Conquistador', the first title not unlike that of his creator, The Demon Dog of American Crime Fiction.

Hopkins shows more courage and determination than seems humanly possible for a young teenager:

> Lack of sleep drew Lloyd gaunt that fall of fifty-six, and he knew that he had to act to reclaim the wonder he had always felt after dark. Because the night was there to provide comfort and the nourishing of brave dreams, and only someone willing to fight for its sanctity deserved to claim it as his citadel. (Ellroy 1984a: 436)

One of the songs referenced in *Blood on the Moon*, 'Cathy's Clown', specifically links Verplanck to Kathy's Kourt and the motivation behind his entire killing spree. In *Because the Night,* a song links Hopkins and Havilland unwittingly in their thoughts. The awkward construction, 'Because the Night', is employed by both men when they are ruminating on their own nature. The Springsteen/Smith song is not specifically named in the text nor is it a component piece of a mystery puzzle. The foundation of Hopkins' Romanticism is rooted in his teenage love of dogs and his need to protect them. Hopkins' affinity with dogs only emphasizes his difficulty at communicating with people. As a child Hopkins felt 'the wonder ... after dark', and he longs to return to this place where he can turn inward, away from other people he sees as threatening and cruel. His philosophy, however, pushes him into constant engagement with the world, denying him rest. As with his rape in *Blood on the Moon*, the back-story here establishes Hopkins' bravery as both a death and rebirth. Whereas Havilland indulges in the pain of others, Hopkins' punishing ordeal has made him look gaunt and deathly. But through his sleepless nights fighting on the streets, he has found his philosophy and purpose. Hopkins is driven not for reasons of sexual fantasy and death like Havilland, but to protect life: his version of 'Because the Night', to 'provide comfort', is in complete contrast to Havilland's narcissism.

With the success of the LA Quartet and Underworld USA novels, Ellroy's Demon Dog persona became associated with his manic, publicity-hungry performances in interviews and at book readings. But in the early novels, Ellroy's fondness for dog motifs was a sly narrative reference to his literary persona. The symbolic importance of canines to the back-story is striking in *Because the Night* and its follow-up *Suicide Hill*. It is significant that Hopkins' nickname, Dogman, and his gang's name 'Dogtown Flats', echoes Freddy 'Fat Dog' Baker in *Brown's Requiem* and that the young Hopkins' enemies also take pleasure in killing dogs. Ellroy's technique of referencing his persona in his novels is split between protagonist and antagonist, the heroic and malevolent.

Whereas Hopkins' Dogman identity is connected to Ellroy's Demon Dog persona, Havilland most likely takes his nickname, 'The Night Tripper', from the American musician Malcolm Rebennack Jr. Rebennack has composed and performed in many musical genres, and from 1968 to 1971 he performed under the stage name 'Dr John the Night Tripper'. During this period, he specialized in New Orleans rhythm and blues merged with psychedelic rock. Rebennack is not specifically referenced in the novel, only the stage name he used for a relatively short period of his career. Havilland picked up the name in college from 'a Creole who shrieked odes to dope and sex' (Ellroy 1984a: 326). A short online biography of Rebennack references the link with Ellroy's novel (Anon 2011). Given the psychedelic music Rebennack experimented with under the stage name, Ellroy may have considered it apt to evoke his name to describe a villainous character that specializes in psychological manipulation and seems to use and discard creative references with the same ruthlessness he applies to people. Havilland wants more than to just 'dance to the music' in his own head. He tricks others into dancing to his tune as well, and to go 'tripping' with him, as he has a college sideline in 'manufacturing LSD and liquid methamphetamine' so that users become mentally dependent on him (Tucker 1984: 5; Ellroy 1984a: 326). Like Haywood Cathcart in *Brown's Requiem* and Doc Harris in *Clandestine*, Havilland uses Nietzschean philosophy to justify his crimes, feeling 'tremors of love' when Goff quotes the German philosopher (Ellroy 1984a: 330).

Havilland is only referred to as the 'Night Tripper' at specific moments in the novel to describe his euphoric state after recovering from the shock of extreme violence. The early crimes in the novel are committed at night and go relatively smoothly. The violent acts in the latter half of the novel happen in the daylight and spin out of control. One of the few violent acts Havilland commits personally occurs as day turns to night. When corrupt LAPD Lieutenant Christie attempts to dominate Havilland, Havilland cannot control his response. Christie's mistake is to liken their relationship to that of father and son. For Havilland, who is obsessed with being a stronger man than his father, the reference is a psychological trigger to murder:

> Havilland reached for his waistband and pulled the gun free, then closed his eyes and aimed at where he thought Christie's face should be. He pulled the trigger twice, screaming along with the explosions, then opened his eyes and saw that Christie's face was not a face, but a charred blood basin oozing brain and skull fragments. He fired four more times, eyes open and not screaming, ripping Christie's badge from his belt just as the last shot sheared off his head and sent him pitching over the railing to the rocks thirty feet below. Drenched in blood and inundated with horror and memory, the Night Tripper ran. (Ellroy 1984a: 454)

Christie's uncouth and tactile behaviour physically dominates the awkward Havilland. Christie has no respect for psychiatrists, claiming to have fooled several in the LAPD during his evaluations. To Christie, Havilland is just a quack who never got past his college addiction to a psychedelic nickname and bite-sized Nietzschean philosophy. The realization that he has to beat Christie on physical terms and the father reference escalate the situation to violence, which quickly becomes surreal from Havilland's viewpoint. Havilland has his eyes closed, willing night time and thus a disguise. He has previously relied on his followers to commit violence on his behalf: they have been his disguise. Therefore, the spontaneous murder of Christie is an unveiling of sorts. Even though Havilland still tries to mask this through closing his eyes and screaming so as to deny the sensory confirmation of the murder, its image and noise. When he eventually opens his eyes, what Havilland sees is not real but fantasy, as it is unlikely that Christie's corpse would still be standing after the first two shots or that the next four shots would cleanly decapitate the body: 'the last shot sheared off his head'. Part of the pleasure of Havilland's repression is the final fulfilment of the action, and he adds to his satisfaction by taking a souvenir in the form of Christie's badge, so as to ruminate on the memory. The scene ends by confirming his indulgence, 'drenched' and 'inundated' indicating the completeness of his gratification in the moment, but also the continuity of the violence through 'memory'.

Ellroy uses the medium of film to as a metaphor for voyeurism. Havilland manipulates a prostitute, Sherry Shroeder, into appearing in a pornographic film which, unbeknownst to her, will end with her being murdered by one of his patients, Richard Oldfield. Havilland then tricks his patient, Linda, for whom both he and Hopkins have romantic feelings, into watching the film, telling her it is part of her therapy:

> The screen went blank, then filled up with a long shot of the blond woman, now dressed in her nurse's uniform, leaning against the bedroom wall. Suddenly a man, also clothed, threw himself on top of her. The screen again went blank, then segued into an extreme close-up of a transparent plastic pillow. The muzzle of a gun was pressed to the pillow. A finger pulled the trigger and the screen was awash with red. The camera caught a close-up of a man's face. When Linda saw the face she screamed 'Hopkins!' and fumbled in her purse for the gun. Her finger was inside the trigger guard when the lights went on and the man from the movie jumped out of the closet and smothered her with his body. (Ellroy 1984a: 522)

Havilland employs memory to heighten the events: as the film recreates Linda's mother's murder, Linda experiences a 'replay' of her worst memory in a form which has hitherto been urban legend, a pornographic 'snuff' film. Havilland can relive events from his past with precise visual accuracy through a technique he calls the 'time machine'. He recalls as a child seeing his father tie a pregnant woman to a large roulette table and perform a bloody abortion/murder. The scene is so horrific that the young Havilland is unsure as to whether it really happened until he finds confirmation after his father's death that he murdered at least eighteen women this way. He has a 'Cinemascope and Technicolor replay of the Caesarean birth' but the boundary between fantasy and reality has been blurred by his recollection of the event as film (Ellroy 1984a: 517). It is this blurring which he recreates for Linda. Linda views the movie with the director, Havilland, standing over her, and the 'actor', Oldfield, waiting to attack her. Film and reality intermingle as the set piece layers the levels of experience. When the pornographic film cuts to a close-up of Oldfield, it is as though he is in the same room as Linda and will walk off the screen and attack her. Linda shouts Hopkins' name upon seeing Oldfield onscreen but her motive is open-ended. On one level she is shouting for Hopkins' help, but she also regards him as a threat. Before the film starts, Linda tells Havilland she has fantasies about being 'menaced by the same type of man I used to have the hots for' (Ellroy 1984a: 521). The fantasy ends with her shooting her attractive assailant. Oldfield's face is revealed on film after he has shot Sherry and, as if on cue, he appears in the room once Linda says Hopkins' name. However, instead of coming out of the screen, he 'jumped out of the closet', which is equally symbolic of the sexual inadequacy driving the violence.

Moments of violence in *Because the Night* are always accompanied by an all-consuming image which blots out the preceding image. The beige curtain is turned completely red by blood in the liquor store holdup, and the bulky frame of Oldfield smothers first Sherry then Linda. This jumping between images, often with stark colour contrasts, as opposed to blurring, is similar to cutting from scene to scene as in a film, whereby the camera cuts from one image to another. In the subjective third-person narrative, Linda views her own assault cinematically. To restrain Linda, a man of Oldfield's strength would need only to grab her by the arm or head, but Oldfield is obsessed with sexual domination, which is motivated by his impotence. Oldfield affects the role of masculinity to shield the failure of his manhood.

The climactic scene of the novel is set in Havilland's Malibu beach house. The tranquillity of the coastline is in contrast to the shocking violence that unfolds. It was on a Malibu beach where twenty years previously Hopkins was called out to the Watts riot. Despite a violent climax, the story appears, quite deliberately, to be incomplete. Oldfield escapes and Havilland is left incapacitated after a vicious beating by Hopkins – the brilliant psychiatrist is deprived of the use of his mind, a cruelly poetic justice for the man who once laughed at 'mankind's unutterable stupidity' (Ellroy 1984a: 325). Hopkins later discovers that after being attacked by Oldfield, Linda managed to persuade him that he was being manipulated by Havilland and that they should escape from both him and the police. Therefore, by Linda's account, Hopkins has unnecessarily entered the beach house to attack Havilland. Linda has achieved more than Hopkins through her non-violent methods. She has also made a mockery of Havilland, achieving more control over Oldfield through persuasion when Havilland thought he had Oldfield under complete psychological control. Linda further degrades Hopkins' estimation of himself as a policeman by saying that his assault on Havilland made him more brutal than Oldfield. Linda's opinion of Hopkins and Oldfield is a role reversal of policeman and criminal, which begins with her ambiguous calling of Hopkins name during the snuff film. Her protection of Oldfield is almost maternal, which is ironic considering killing Sherry was a deliberate re-enactment of her mother's murder. The novel ends with Hopkins vowing to Linda that he will find Oldfield and arrest him for the murder of Sherry Shroeder. The outcome of this pledge forms the prologue of *Suicide Hill*.

By the end of *Because the Night*, Ellroy had established a more complex form of paralleling between protagonist and antagonist which he had previously developed in *Blood in the Moon*, and before that in *Brown's Requiem*. The film within a novel is the climax of a series of cinematic techniques in Ellroy's writing. Ellroy was becoming a cinematic novelist. The visual images of *Because the Night* act as a precursor to the LA Quartet's film noir setting and milieu.

Suicide Hill

A number of titles were considered for the third Hopkins novel, all of which seemed more suggestive of the hardboiled genre than the titles of the previous two novels. Ellroy considered returning to the 'L.A. Death Trip' title he had discarded when writing the first Hopkins novel. 'For the L.A. Dead' was also briefly considered before Ellroy decided on *Suicide Hill* (Ellroy 1983b). All of these titles allude to some form of death, be it collective, individual (suicide) or even psychedelically induced. Ellroy's early establishment of the theme of death in *Suicide Hill* serves as a form of requiem for Lloyd Hopkins, or more precisely the Lloyd Hopkins novels.

Suicide Hill is a long cement embankment in inner-city LA used by the local gangs as a motorcycle gauntlet. The area has spawned many urban legends. A local criminal, Joe Garcia (originally the name of one of the five rapists in 'L.A. Death Trip'), takes inspiration from one of the Suicide Hill myths and is trying to write a song about the area set to the tune of Fats Domino's 'Blueberry Hill'. Garcia's attempts to rewrite the lyrics of the song mirror how the characters try to manipulate the reality of relationships and events to suit their own self-deceiving beliefs. Garcia believes a story that a Second World War veteran by the name of Fritz 'Suicide' Hill lived in a tent at the embankment and started an LA chapter of the Hell's Angels. According to the legend, Hill was a heroic motorcycle highwayman who finally developed terminal cancer after years of exposure to chemical fumes. Rather than succumb to the disease, Hill chose to commit suicide through a daredevil motorcycle stunt. Garcia has been unable to complete the tribute song, only managing to produce a few lines. Garcia's unfinished song is unintentionally symbolic of his shambolic existence. Characters in the novel are self-destructive and make bad decisions out of misplaced love and loyalty. There is a lack of completion: songs go unwritten, dreams unfulfilled, yet people believe in false, absurd urban legends. This trait is not limited to Garcia and his criminal accomplices; Hopkins is also at the nadir of his career and suffering from depression.

Suicide Hill is the only novel of the series which begins with Hopkins as the immediate focus, albeit he is not the main actor but the subject of the prologue, which is written in the form of a psychiatric evaluation of Hopkins commissioned by the LAPD. This method of beginning the narrative with an official document works on two levels: it foregrounds some of the pathological issues facing Hopkins as a theme of the novel, and it questions the more conventional structure of the previous Hopkins novels. Hopkins is less important to the narrative of this novel than any other of the series as Ellroy had finally decentralized events from being caused by or directly affecting him. It was a further reaction against the Chandler model he had imitated in his first novel and foreshadowed the complex series structures of the Quartet and Underworld novels. Hopkins also faces his most sympathetic criminal adversary in car thief and bank robber Duane Rice, a chronically unlucky but likable recidivist who, unlike the psychopaths Verplanck and Havilland, is morally worthy of the extra focus which Ellroy gives him. One of the first things the reader discovers about Rice is that during a prison sentence he gained 'Class A' status allowing him to work as a firefighter. Ellroy details Rice's courage from the beginning of the novel so as to heighten the tragedy of what he could have achieved if he had not turned to crime.

The prologue recaps some of the events of *Because the Night* and brings greater resolution to the narrative. Hopkins traced Oldfield to New Orleans. At Oldfield's arraignment, an emotionally fragile Hopkins is forced to admit he broke numerous police regulations in the investigation. *Suicide Hill* is the most convincing novel in the Hopkins series, as it is clear Hopkins' career in the LAPD will soon be over. Hopkins may even face prison, as Internal Affairs are investigating his role in the Watts riots twenty years prior to the setting of the novel, and they are on the brink of gathering enough evidence to charge Hopkins with the murder of Richard Beller. As the plot lines are returning to the event which first introduced Hopkins in *Blood on the Moon*, it suggests that the Hopkins narrative is reaching its natural conclusion: the downfall of the maverick, racist cop.

In the novel, Hopkins' views on race are less problematic than the increasingly fractious influence of religion within the LAPD. There is tension between Hopkins, who is notionally Presbyterian, and Internal Affairs Division Chief Dean Gaffaney, who was raised Catholic but has converted to Evangelical Christianity. The nominal faith either man has in the religion of their upbringing does not stop them from using sectarianism as one more reason to hate each other. Through this sub-plot, Ellroy keeps Hopkins occupied and largely detached from Duane Rice, and subsequently distant from the most dramatic events of the narrative.

Duane Rice holds an unconditional love for his girlfriend Vandy, although it is obvious to everyone but himself that the feelings are not reciprocated. Rice is provoked into extreme acts of violence whenever anyone slurs her name and the plotting loosely revolves around the increasingly violent and anarchic events which ensue when Rice uses his criminal connections to try and build a career for Vandy in the music industry. The first and second chapter introduce several criminals into the narrative, but Hopkins does not appear in person until the third chapter. Unlike the previous Hopkins novels, *Suicide Hill* follows the viewpoint of several characters: Duane Rice, the Garcia brothers and finally Hopkins. Hopkins has only one confrontation with Rice, an inconclusive shoot-out with no dialogue. Ellroy is less interested in 'cop/killer' parallels in a 'contrapunctually' structured narrative, and more concerned with portraying multi-character perspectives loosely tied to a series of events. Thus, the narrative does not contain a long-running duel between Hopkins and Rice as there was in the previous novels between Hopkins and Verplanck, and Hopkins and Havilland, respectively.

Rice first appears in the novel awaiting release from the LA County Jail. Despite all his apparent flaws, and lack of intellect in comparison to Verplanck and Havilland, Rice still considers himself to be street smart enough to 'outthink, outgame and outmaneuver any cop, judge or P.O.', and he hides this natural intelligence behind a veneer of toughness, affecting a walk in prison 'that allowed him to keep his dignity *and* look like he fit in' (Ellroy 1986b: 573–5). He is moved to a cell which contains an unnamed biker type who immediately tries to provoke him. However, Rice was taught martial arts by a Japanese correctional officer who warned him about 'never initiating an attack' (Ellroy 1986b: 576). Rice shows restraint by at first ignoring the insults, but when the biker accuses his girlfriend of promiscuity it provokes an extreme reaction:

> Rice saw everything go red. He forgot his teacher's warnings about never initiating an attack and he forgot the ritual shouts as he swung up and out with his right leg and felt the biker's jaw crack under his foot. Blood sprayed the air as the big man crashed into the bars; shouts rose from the adjoining tanks. Rice kicked again as the biker hit the floor; through his red curtain he heard a rib cage snap. The shouts grew louder as the electric door slammed open. Rice swivelled to see a half dozen billy clubs arcing toward him. Brief thoughts of Vandy kept him from attacking. Then everything went dark red and black. (Ellroy 1986b: 576)

As in *Blood on the Moon* and *Because the Night*, colour is symbolic of danger and violence. Upon hearing the biker slur Vandy's reputation, Rice 'saw everything go red'. Colour is reflective of Rice's psychological reaction to the speed of events, not the trigger to violence which it had been for Goff in *Because the Night*. Red is not mentioned as the colour of the blood which is spraying the air, but Rice can hear things through a 'red curtain', red being evocative of his immense anger, and the curtain is a block between self-discipline and unthinking physical brutality. When Rice is knocked unconscious by the prison guards everything turns 'dark red and black'. Ellroy's confident use of a range of colours in this scene and throughout the series is another reference to the history of film noir. In his study of the genre *Somewhere in the Night* (1997), Nicholas Christopher examines the transition from black-and-white to colour filming that helps to distinguish the classification of film noir and neo-noir:

> This reliance on orange, apparent in colour film noirs through the 1950s and 1960s and in the neo-noirs right up to the present day, functions in place of the chiaroscuro of the black-and-white films. Orange provides the sort of deep-contrast, low-key photographic effects previously achieved with black-and-white contrasts. (Christopher 2006: 100)

Christopher identifies orange as the colour closest in symbolic value to the black-and-white imagery of the classic noir period. Ellroy, however, uses a multi-coloured approach to display a wide range of emotions. Each character resembles a gaudy eighties image of a classic noir motif. Vandy is the lounge singer *femme fatale* who lacks the style and seductiveness to make her immorality alluring. Duane is the doomed protagonist without the self-awareness which makes the performances of Fred MacMurray in *Double Indemnity* (1944) and Robert Mitchum in *Out of the Past* (1947) so appealing. Ellroy intentionally devalues noir through his hideous portrayal of the entertainment industry in a commercially obsessed 1980s society.

The influence Vandy has on Rice's physical and psychological behaviour is not entirely negative, as the thought of her stops Rice from fighting back at prison guards which could delay his release. Rice's relationship with Vandy is a classic noir paradox. On one level she is his redemption from a life of crime, the only woman he has loved and is willing to risk everything for. However, Rice is pushed into increasingly audacious and insanely violent crimes in order to win her love. Vandy does not have the beauty or cunning to drive a man to self-destruction; she uses her promiscuity as a way of scoring cocaine, not of controlling men. Yet despite this, Rice destroys himself by refusing to stop loving her. Through Vandy, Ellroy reimagines the *femme fatale*, moving the seductive and destructive power away from the woman to the feelings of love which consume Rice through self-delusion.

Rice is adept at merging his criminal enterprises with acts of personal revenge. Rice, Joe and Bobby Garcia rob a bank where Rice knows that his former prison guard Gordon Meyers has taken a job in security. Meyers slept with Vandy within earshot of Rice's cell:

Rice saw the whole bank shake in front of his eyes. His voice sounded like it wasn't his, and the people cowering at their desks looked like scary red animals. He turned around so he wouldn't see them, and saw Sharkshit Bobby talking trash to a young woman teller. He was wondering whether to stop it when Gordon Meyers walked out of a door next to a vault.

And he knew.

Rice raised his .45; Meyers saw him and turned to run. Rice squeezed off three shots. The back of Meyers' white shirt exploded into crimson just as he felt the three silencer kicks. The dinged-out ding jailer crashed into an American flag on a pole and fell with it to the floor. The bank became one gigantic blast of noise, and through all of it, Rice heard a woman's voice; 'Scum! Scum! Scum!' (Ellroy 1986b: 719)

Rice becomes strangely detached whenever he is on the verge of committing acts of extreme violence: 'His voice sounded like it wasn't his.' His conscious thoughts become erratic and jumpy – he sees the people in the bank as 'scary red animals' despite the fact that they are visibly scared of him. Red symbolizes the onset of violence which terrorizes Rice, even when he instigates it. Unlike Havilland's psychological approach to colour, Rice tries to repress the colours, rather than push through the 'green door', as he knows he cannot control the chaos that will ensue. He begins to lose his cool when Bobby makes some sexually crass comments to a terrified woman. Sexual humiliation reminds him of his own betrayal by Vandy. Rice is about to commit an act of kindness by stopping Bobby from intimidating the woman when another memory of Vandy shifts him back to violence. Seeing the object of his revenge, Meyers, gives both victim and murderer a sudden shared clarity: '*And he knew.*' The three italicized words appear in a single line which comes between two five-line paragraphs. All of the action is happening within a timeframe of seconds. But the narrative slows the action down to explore the thoughts motivating the scene. Rice sees Meyers and *knows*; Meyers sees Rice and *knows*. Ellroy uses a similar technique in the opening murder scene of *Because the Night*, when Goff decides to kill the three people in the liquor store; 'Now he knew' appears in a single line in the middle of two larger paragraphs (Ellroy 1984a: 284). Rice's knowledge differs from Goff's in that Goff is manipulated by Havilland, but Rice is willingly self-deceived. Rice kills Meyers because he thinks Meyers violated Vandy's honour. But Vandy willingly had sex with Meyers in exchange for cocaine. Goff has a form of epiphany when he realizes the liquor store robbery must become a multiple murder, as does Whitey in *Blood on the Moon* when his unexpected erection leads him to rape Verplanck. Rice's murder of Meyers, however, is motivated by denial and not enlightenment. The violent impulses which he cannot control at the thought of Vandy cuckolding him share some similarities with Verplanck in *Blood on the Moon*, who also resorts to violence after a sexual humiliation. But Verplanck is a psychopath on a murderous quest, whereas Rice by contrast is a luckless criminal who has the potential for redemption.

Meyers' corpse falls into an American flag which crashes to the floor. The flag is a recurring symbol throughout the novel of the institutions and nature of American society. Meyers is a 'dinged-out ding jailer' and corrupt security guard. The 'ding' cells Meyers supervised in prison were considered the worst of the worst. Meyers is 'dinged-out', repulsive in appearance, and has managed to commit acts of brutality in the name of the law which equal, or even exceed, Rice's violent acts as a criminal. Meyers' death, wrapped in a blood-soaked flag, reads as a caustic comment on his opportunistic authoritarianism.

The symbolism of the American flag is also seen on the lapel pin of Dean Gaffaney. Gaffaney has been mentoring several fellow evangelicals in the LAPD, and he has plans for evangelicals to hold all of the LAPD's senior positions. Gaffaney's religiosity in *Suicide Hill* stands in contrast to his views in *Blood on the Moon*, where he appears as a minor character and specifically states his faith does not influence his decisions as a policeman (Ellroy 1984b: 144). Gaffaney's officers all wear a lapel pin which features a crucifix set against the backdrop of the American flag. In this instance, the flag is a symbol of the pervasive influence of a religious group based within a state institution. The evangelicals are ruthlessly ambitious, but they are at least idealistic, as they want the LAPD to be changed in accordance with their beliefs, as opposed to Gordon Meyers, who has no apparent beliefs and only wants to exploit the system for his own ends.

The violence of the bank robbery initiates a whole sequence of increasingly violent events as more characters become embroiled in the hunt to find Rice. Rice makes his escape from the bank robbery and murders two police officers who arrive at the scene. One of the policemen happens to be the son of Dean Gaffaney, and Rice is now marked for death by Gaffaney's allies in the LAPD. After the murder of Meyers, Rice kills again out of his delusional love for Vandy. Rice believes that Bobby Garcia attempted to seduce Vandy. In reality, Bobby's brother Joe has started a relationship with Vandy, and the couple are planning to leave LA with the help of Hopkins, who believes Joe is capable of reform.

Rice finds Bobby trying to atone for a lifetime of violence by stuffing stolen money into a charity box in a Catholic church:

> The poor box was on the side wall near the rear pews, ironclad, but too small to hold sixteen K in penance bucks. Bobby started shoving cash in the slot anyway, big fistfuls of c-notes and twenties. Bills slipped out of his hands as he worked, and he was wondering whether to leave the whole bag by the altar when he heard strained breathing behind him. Looking over his shoulder, he saw Duane Rice standing just outside the door. His high school yearbook prophecy crossed his mind: 'Most likely not to survive,' and suddenly Duane-o looked more like a priest than the puto with the alligator fag shirt.

> Bobby dropped the bag and fell to his knees; Rice screwed the silencer onto his .45 and walked over. He picked up the bag and placed the gun to the Sharkman's temple; Bobby knew that defiant was the way to go splitsville. He got in a righteous giggle and 'Duhn-duhn-duhn-duhn' before Rice blew his brains out. (Ellroy 1986b: 782)

Bobby, a compulsively violent and sexually deviant criminal, is as genuinely sincere in his Catholicism as Gaffaney is in his Evangelicalism. *Suicide Hill* is Ellroy's only novel in which religion is a direct subject. The novel appears at first to have a strongly anti-religious undertone to the narrative. Of the genuinely religious characters, one is a psychotic and the other is an ambitious, ruthless policeman. Bobby and Joe use religion as a scam, impersonating priests to solicit donations from elderly Catholics. Yet, *Suicide Hill* is a novel about redemption. All of the characters are searching for redemption in different ways: Rice through love, Hopkins by protecting innocence and Bobby through his final confession before Rice kills him. Bobby even sees his impending murder as a better atonement than the absolution just granted him in confession: 'Duane-o looked more like a priest than the puto with the alligator fag shirt.' In this world, religion has become as commercialized as everything else and Bobby laments the fashionable but disrespectful dress sense of the last priest he will ever see in his life. The possible homosexuality of the priest unnerves Bobby, as he wants to confess to sexually touching Joe when they were both very young. He regards this as the worst of all his crimes as, regardless of the effect it had on Joe, he wallows in self-disgust at his own potential homosexuality. Bobby settles for Rice as his redeemer, rather than physically resist his own murder. He does give a 'righteous giggle', taunting Rice, but he is also grateful that he is going to die. This moment is the fulfilment of the lamentable destiny given to him in his high school yearbook: 'Most likely not to survive.' This flippancy becomes profound when Bobby accepts his fate. Bobby does not consider his redemption to be totally contrary to his criminal side. The last thing Bobby does is to hum the 'Shark' theme from the movie *Jaws*, as a nod to his 'Sharkman' street name. Redemption and defiance are the contrary but interwoven emotions of Bobby in his last few seconds alive.

Rice's death comes when he is accosted by Gaffaney's police officers and taken to Suicide Hill:

> A fuzz type in a cheapo suit in front of him, blotting out his view of the terrain. The grip on his arms tightened. Rice saw a weird lapel pin on the fuzz type's jacket and a .357 Python in his right hand, and he

knew he was going to die. He tried to think up a suitable wisecrack, but 'She was a stone heartbreaker' came out instead. And I loved her was about to come out, but three slugs from the magnum hit him first. (Ellroy 1986b: 819–20)

Rice begins the scene dreaming he is once again joyriding in stolen cars. When he wakes, he realizes that he is at Suicide Hill, where he once performed daredevil motorcycle stunts. Yet this time there is no thrilling sensation of cheating death. One of the last things Rice sees before he dies is 'a weird lapel pin' on Gaffaney's jacket – a clue more for the reader than for Rice, who is unaware his executioner is an Internal Affairs Captain and the father of the man Rice murdered in the bank heist. The crucifix/flag design of Gaffaney's evangelical group oddly connects with Rice's highly symbolic physical position at the moment of his death: Rice is being held upright by both arms as though tied to his own cross. Rice has been taking ecstasy to keep him awake while he is on the run, but it gives him hallucinations culminating in the heavy religious symbolism surrounding his death. Suicide Hill is a place of urban legend, where one mythical suicide supposedly took place, and the area has become a form of urban LA holy ground. It is Rice, rather than the Evangelical Christian, who is portrayed as Christ-like, a telling subversion that shows how far Gaffaney's group have corrupted the LAPD.

When Rice knows he is about to die, his instinctual response is one of defiance like Bobby: 'He tried to think up a suitable wisecrack, but "She was a stone heartbreaker" came out instead.' Rice's last words are a lyric he wrote to describe his love for Vandy, but his almost involuntary utterance of them in this moment is a revelation that his love was in vain. Vandy's contempt for Rice, her 'stone loser', becomes clear to him moments before his death. Yet his inability to complete the song is his final humiliation. Ultimately, if his love for Vandy was redemptive, in that a criminal would act from unselfish motives, it was also never fully realized, as with his unfinished song, which is echoed by Joe Garcia's unfinished tribute to Suicide Hill.

A now depressed Gaffaney hopes to provoke Hopkins into murdering him. While waiting for Hopkins, Gaffaney ruminates on his conversion to Evangelical Christianity. As a uniformed policeman, Gaffaney encountered a German-American homeless alcoholic who preached to the bikers at Suicide Hill. The evangelist handed out tracts which featured a cross set against a background of the American flag. Gaffaney considered the man a lunatic at first, and when the man claimed that his life was being threatened by a biker gang known as the Demon Dogs, Gaffaney ignored his request for protection. When the evangelist is later found dead – decapitated and then hung, drawn and quartered by four bikers at Suicide Hill – Gaffaney is plunged into a guilt-ridden despair which leads to his conversion. The lunatic tramp was right, and the idealistic young policeman was wrong and negligent. The backstory of Gaffaney, which is only revealed towards the very end of the novel, destroys the myths which have been created out of Suicide Hill. Gaffaney does not reveal the name of the evangelist, but he is almost certainly Fritz 'Suicide' Hill, the same man Joe Garcia is trying to write a song about. Thus, Hill did not commit suicide: he was murdered, and the bikers who supposedly committed stunts of spectacular bravery are in fact the gangsters who tortured a man to death. Years later, Gaffaney, the Christian policeman, shoots dead the murderer of his son at the same myth-laden location. Ellroy creates a world in which morality seems to be constantly and almost pointlessly going around in circles, rather like the bikers driving round and round Suicide Hill.

When Hopkins finds Gaffaney in a suicidal state, he is dismissive of his old rival at first, advising Gaffaney to kill himself as he refuses to murder him. In the last few lines of the novel, his tone changes to conciliatory and he comforts the grieving parent:

> Lloyd said no and walked down the hall to the bathroom. He was clenching the edge of the tub, staring at the cross and flag logo, when he heard the shot. His hands jerked up, ripping out jagged chunks of porcelain, and then there was a second shot, and another and still another. He ran back to the study and found Gaffaney on his knees, holding the gun and an armful of framed photographs to his chest. He was muttering, 'I've got nothing. I've got nothing.'
>
> Lloyd helped him to his feet. The mementos he was grasping made the embrace cumbersome, but he was able to get his arms around the sobbing man anyway. The simple act felt like mercy for all their lost ones, all their stone heartbreakers. (Ellroy 1986b: 848)

Without the cross and logo, the symbols that kept them apart, Gaffaney and Hopkins share a common humanity and a common grief: 'their lost ones'. Even the distinction of names slip away as the two characters move physically and emotionally closer to each other. The wording here is significant, 'their stone heartbreakers', as Gaffaney was puzzled by Rice's last words and had asked Hopkins if he knew what Rice meant. Hopkins did not know, and yet, both men adopt the term in a conscious association with the murdered man. Hopkins and Gaffaney, like Rice, have sealed their fate through years of self-destructive behaviour, which is itself a form of emotional suicide. By the end of the novel, Gaffaney has contributed to the further mythmaking of Suicide Hill, as Rice's murder is reported as a suicide. Gaffaney escapes punishment for Rice's murder, but his career with the LAPD is over and the guilt of murdering Rice rather than trying to forgive him weighs heavily with his Christian beliefs.

Ironically, *Suicide Hill* does not feature an actual suicide, and yet the original ending to 'L.A. Death Trip' featured Hopkins' suicide which was also a mass murder. The deaths of two characters are reported as suicides, but both were actually murdered, and Gaffaney unsuccessfully attempts to commit suicide. The first supposed 'suicide' in the timeline of the narrative is that of Fritz Hill. Lies and misconceptions have been built around the murdered man's name, and yet he serves as the moral compass of the novel once the truth of his death is revealed. Hill is also strongly associated, more than any other character in the novel, with the author's persona through his German-American heritage and his murder at the hand of the Demon Dogs. The Fritz Hill legend connects to a recurring theme of the Hopkins novels: how institutions, individuals and beliefs continue to function despite their flaws. The LAPD is corrupt, the religionists push the institution further into crime (rather than their anticipated role of cleaning it up), love is given but never returned, and yet the final image of Hopkins comforting Gaffaney is an ambiguous but moving coda.

The Lloyd Hopkins novels: the incomplete series

After the publication of *Suicide Hill*, Ellroy was advised by Otto Penzler and Nat Sobel to continue the series to a fourth and fifth novel (Duncan 1996: 71). Ellroy completed an outline for volume IV of the Hopkins in Jeopardy Quintet before he abandoned the series. The fourth novel was to be titled 'The Cold Six Thousand', a title Ellroy was to return to many years later for the second novel of the Underworld USA trilogy (Ellroy 1984d). In the 84-page outline, Hopkins is investigating a series of murders of high-class hookers. Lynn Dietrich is a hooker working for New Age Enterprises, the legitimate front for a prostitution ring. Her dream in life is to save six thousand dollars and then emigrate to the town of Xuatapul, Mexico, where this exact sum can buy a year of luxury living. Whenever she is close to reaching the required amount, she wastes too much of her savings, thus she is periodically sabotaging her own ambitions. In *The Cold Six Thousand*, the meaning of the title stems from a similarly allusive sub-plot in which Wayne Tedrow is paid six thousand dollars to kill a black pimp named Wendell Durfee. Tedrow allows Durfee to escape only for Durfee to rape and kill Tedrow's wife. Overcome with grief, Tedrow plunges himself into several criminal conspiracies while occasionally searching for Durfee. Near the end of the novel, he finally finds and kills the pimp and fulfils the contract. In both the unfinished Hopkins novel and the second novel of the Underworld USA trilogy, the six thousand dollars alludes to recurring themes of the Hopkins series, namely self-destruction and incompleteness.

The outline to 'The Cold Six Thousand' concludes with Hopkins hiring an arsonist to burn down New Age Enterprises headquarters, but unbeknownst to Hopkins, both Lynn and the man who has been murdering the prostitutes, Chaz Minear, are in the building when it is set on fire. Both escape, but with serious burns. Lynn later kills Minear in self-defence. In the course of the story, Hopkins' younger partner on the case, Bob Disbrow, falls for Lynn, and Hopkins gives the couple the six thousand dollars to move to Xuatupul, a sum Hopkins obtains by extorting money from corrupt police captain John McManus, who has himself been accepting money from organized-crime sources to fund his congressional election campaign. McManus, however, has information on Hopkins' involvement in the New Age Enterprises fire, which allows him to exact a measure of revenge on Hopkins, demoting him to a uniformed position.

By reading *Suicide Hill* next to 'The Cold Six Thousand' it is possible to see parallels between the unpublished work and the completed novels. Hopkins repeats his kindness to Joe Garcia and Vandy by helping Lynn and Disbrow start a new life outside of LA. Likewise the stalemate between McManus and Hopkins reads much like his relationship with Gaffaney. 'The Cold Six Thousand' also features plot ideas that Ellroy would continue to develop in his later novels. Lynn Dietrich, the hooker who dreams to escape into a new existence, is not unlike Lynn Bracken in *L.A. Confidential*.

Ellroy said of Hopkins, 'I wanted to do a limited series with him, chart his psychology over a set period of time, and then abandon him on some sort of ambiguous note' (Silet 1995: 45). Ellroy slowly withdraws from Hopkins in *Suicide Hill* as the maverick cop is no longer the leading character. By the end of the novel, Hopkins is moved even further from the action: he is a has-been, a ghost of his former self. With a fourth and possible fifth novel, Ellroy would have further explored Hopkins' marginalization until the series was no longer about him.

By purposefully leaving the Hopkins novels with many narrative issues unresolved, Ellroy allows for the option of a sequel, and it also suggests that he regarded the Hopkins series as largely unplanned, experimental narratives which would be abandoned abruptly. It is ironic then that the Hopkins series is relatively conventional when compared to the later LA Quartet and Underworld USA series. Each Hopkins novel is a direct sequel to its predecessor, whereas Ellroy's later novels, which were more rigorously outlined, displayed a looser, more fluid connectivity within a series.

Over the course of the three Lloyd Hopkins novels, Ellroy experimented with a number of narrative styles. The 'contrapunctual' style of *Blood on the Moon* involved switching between the perspective of detective and serial killer and slowly drawing out the parallels of the two men, particularly with regard to back-story. *Because the Night* suffers in comparison to *Red Dragon*, but the multiple references to music and colour are a testament to how Ellroy was developing his own identity as a stylist. In *Suicide Hill*, Ellroy marginalized Hopkins as a character and took a sharp thematic departure, and its most direct link to the previous novels lay in its subtle references to Ellroy's literary persona. The legacy of the Lloyd Hopkins novels for Ellroy's more successful work has been largely ignored by critics and underplayed by Ellroy himself. Ellroy's plans for a fourth Hopkins novel contained themes and plot ideas that would later appear in *L.A. Confidential* and *The Cold Six Thousand*. His intention for LA to 'burn to the ground' in 'L.A. Death Trip' was later realized, in more symbolic terms, in *White Jazz*, which, as we shall see in Chapter 4, was the genre-ending novel he had been trying for when he first created Lloyd Hopkins. The most immediate legacy, however, was in his first novel published after he abandoned Hopkins, *The Black Dahlia*. Just as Hopkins was marginalized as the series wore on, Elizabeth Short is never a living character in Ellroy's novel on the Dahlia case, yet her influence on the author's life and the lives of the characters was huge. In *Suicide Hill*, Lloyd Hopkins is at the periphery of events but still essential to the narrative, and Ellroy takes this idea even further with Elizabeth Short acting as the ghost and moral compass of *The Black Dahlia*.

3
James Ellroy, Jean Ellroy and Elizabeth Short: The Demon Dog and Transmogrification in *The Black Dahlia*

On 15 January 1947, the tortured and dismembered corpse of Elizabeth Short was discovered at an abandoned lot at Thirty-Ninth and Norton, Los Angeles. The unsolved murder of Miss Short, dubbed the 'Black Dahlia murder' by the LA press, would become the most enduring and fascinating mystery in LA history. One year after the Black Dahlia murder, on 4 March 1948, James (Lee Earle) Ellroy was born to Geneva (Jean) Hilliker Ellroy and Armand Ellroy. More than any other public figure, James Ellroy has explored, created and refined the myths around the Black Dahlia murder through various mediums, including interviews, documentaries, memoirs, true-crime books, short stories and most significantly his novel, *The Black Dahlia* (1987). Ellroy grew up with an experiential knowledge of LA as a noir city, where Elizabeth Short spent her last years, and it would be through noir that Ellroy formed his Dahlia narrative. The closeness between the dates of the Black Dahlia murder and the birth of Ellroy is coincidental but significant as, over time, circumstances would create ties between the murder-myth and the myth-shaper, leading to what Ellroy termed the 'transmogrification' of Elizabeth Short and Jean Ellroy.

On 22 June 1958, the body of Jean Ellroy was discovered on an ivy strip just outside Arroyo High School, El Monte, 22 miles from LA. She had been strangled with one of her own stockings. Like the Black Dahlia murder, the case would go unsolved, and as with the Dahlia, Ellroy would re-imagine and reformulate the murder into narratives throughout his literary career. Ellroy discovered the Dahlia case less than a year after his mother's death, and the similarities between the two cases sparked his fascination with the Dahlia, which in turn led him to emotionally reassess his relationship with his mother in narrative form.

There are two terms which recur in this chapter regarding Ellroy's approach and communication of his Dahlia obsession through narrative: 'meta-narrative' and 'transmogrification'. Meta-narrative refers to how Ellroy constructed his novel *The Black Dahlia* from the original Dahlia case, building not just on the facts but also on the already abundant myth and speculation surrounding the murder of Elizabeth Short. Ironically, Ellroy's fictional account of the Dahlia has influenced the work of several true-crime authors, which has to a certain extent, created a form of meta-narrative to the novel. Ellroy has crafted the Dahlia narrative as a *grand* narrative, encompassing not just the events of his own life, but also the defining moments in the history of LA and noir. Ellroy's extraneous work on the Dahlia case, his publicity tours, his involvement with true-crime authors and the presence of subtle Dahlia narratives in his other works culminated in the recent publication of *Perfidia*, the prequel to the first LA Quartet which features several characters from *The Black Dahlia*, including Elizabeth Short. Since the publication of *The Black Dahlia*, Ellroy has continued the Dahlia narratives in spinoffs and minor pieces, introductions to separate texts or even the frequent retelling of the Jean Ellroy–Betty Short connection in hundreds of interviews. These continuation Dahlia pieces comprise Ellroy's ongoing meta-narrative: a complex narrative about the Dahlia narrative.

Ellroy has used the term 'transmogrification' repeatedly in relation to his mother's murder and the Dahlia case. In Ellroy's work transmogrification refers specifically to the ever-changing identity of individuals within a three-way relationship, tied together by circumstances or emotions, a noir unholy trinity. Ellroy's transmogrification began with his discovery of the Black Dahlia case a year after his mother's murder, which led him to not only mentally associate the two women who had never actually met, but also to include himself in the union. The idea of the trinity continues within *The Black Dahlia*, through the shifting trios of characters contained within it, such as Madeline Sprague, Bucky Bleichert and Kay Lake, but also through those external to the text: Ellroy joins his mother, Short and himself, only to reshuffle the narrative when a cinematic version of his novel was released. Ellroy introduced the director of *The Black Dahlia* adaptation Brian De Palma to his own quasi-spiritual relationship with Betty Short: 'I followed her lead. Brian De Palma brilliantly followed mine. My novel. His film. My world as his visual record' (Ellroy 2006a: 367). Yet like all of Ellroy's trinities, these bonds can be slackened and remerged with new unions or in reinterpreted forms.

The first section of this chapter will focus on how Ellroy sustained his Dahlia obsession throughout his young adulthood, beginning with his childhood discovery of and subsequent fascination with the Black Dahlia case, which evolved into early fantasies and nightmares about the murder that would constitute Ellroy's initial attempts at adapting the case into an internal, psychological work of fiction. In his early novels, Ellroy made tentative Dahlia references and included one distinct Dahlia sub-plot as a way of building his confidence before writing his definitive novel on the case. The second section moves to an analysis of the novel *The Black Dahlia* and examines how Ellroy wove the themes of sexual obsession and the unresolved personal trauma of his mother's murder into the narrative. I will then detail some of Ellroy's first attempts at Dahlia narratives following the publication of *The Black Dahlia*, including his friendship with the actress Dana Delany and how this inspired the novellas published in *Destination Morgue!* The final section is drawn from material published in an article by this author, '"Betty Short and I Go Back": James Ellroy and the Meta-narrative of the Black Dahlia Case' in *Cross-Cultural Connections in Crime Fictions*, and expands upon it to include new research. Ellroy's attempts to control the Dahlia narrative by tying the story inextricably to his own experiences and his Demon Dog of American Crime Fiction persona began to fall apart when he became involved with two historical researchers on the Dahlia case, Larry Harnisch and Steve Hodel. The fifth section concludes the chapter by looking at how Ellroy's *The Black Dahlia* and the Dahlia meta-narrative have influenced his body of work, and how, with *Perfidia*, and the forthcoming novels of the Second LA Quartet, he has embarked on a major expansion and revision of the Dahlia story after it seemed, for a time, that he was ready to close the subject for good.

'You are free to speculate': Ellroy and the Black Dahlia

Ellroy was only ten years old at the time of his mother's death, and when he first learned of the Black Dahlia case shortly thereafter, he immediately recognized the literal and emotional parallels with his mother's murder:

> My father bought me Jack Webb's book *The Badge* for my eleventh birthday. It contained a piece on the Black Dahlia murder. Jean Hilliker and Betty Short – one in transmogrification. (Ellroy 2006a: 363)

The Badge included a twelve-page synopsis of the Black Dahlia case written, unusually for the stern and straight-faced Jack Webb, in a somewhat irreverent tone mocking the frustration and inability of the chief detective Finis Brown to solve the case. Webb summarizes the case on the blackly comic final line, which in its cynical invitation seems to have stimulated Ellroy's imagination: 'you are free to speculate. But do him a favour – don't press your deductions on Finis Brown' (Webb 1958: 35). For Ellroy, the discovery of the Dahlia case in *The Badge* gave him free rein to speculate and fantasize. Yet his exploration of fantasy, history and memory resulted in the blending of fact and fiction and the blurring of relational and historical lines in his desire to create a narrative for both women. Ironically, Ellroy's consuming obsession with the Black Dahlia case was in stark contrast to what had been initially an emotionally detached response to his mother's murder. It was only through examining Elizabeth Short as a complete stranger that he in turn appreciated Jean Ellroy as his mother. It is this secondary, surrogate understanding of his mother that allowed Ellroy to develop a mixture of sympathy and sexual feelings towards her.

Cultural references to the Dahlia case, such as Webb's *The Badge*, would become very important to Ellroy as he sought to draw from, and ultimately surpass, them with his own Dahlia narrative. From the very beginning, the Black Dahlia was more than a murder case to Ellroy; it was an amalgam of crime and fiction. Even the 'Black Dahlia' sobriquet may have been a reference to the noir genre, a genre which would ironically later contain works on the Dahlia. *Los Angeles Times* columnist Jack Smith has been credited with originating the term 'Black Dahlia' on account of Elizabeth Short's black hair and habit of wearing dark clothes (Hodel 2004: 381). However, it is possible that the name was also a reference to the film noir *The Blue Dahlia* (1944), which is mentioned in Ellroy's novel, although there is little to connect the film with the murder other than the similarity in names: the Blue Dahlia of the film is a nightclub rather than a murdered heroine (Ellroy 1987: 105). *The Blue Dahlia*, like *The Badge*, has sustained its historical importance not by artistic merit but due to the web of connections to the Dahlia case, and by extension, its connection to Ellroy.

There is another Dahlia reference which pre-dates *The Badge* and is influential for Ellroy as it stems from a deeply personal, family source. Ellroy claimed in a Zocalo Public Square lecture in 2007 that the Black Dahlia murder was an event his parents 'thought', 'ruminated' and 'cognified' on when he was a child 'in ways I will never be able to fully discern' (Ellroy 2007). This contradicts his more widely quoted story that he first discovered the Dahlia case in *The Badge* which he read after his mother's death. It is possible that *The Badge* sparked in him some memory of his mother discussing the case, or, it was simply a more convenient narrative revision to have Jean Ellroy reference the Dahlia murder personally, unaware that it foreshadows her own demise and forging another connection between the two women. Although 27 years would elapse between his mother's murder and the publication of *The Black Dahlia*, the young Ellroy instantly forged an emotional connection between the two unsolved murders and was already beginning to form narratives, however crude, out of the Dahlia murder from the moment he read of the case in *The Badge*:

> My Dahlia obsession was explicitly pornographic. My imagination supplied the details that Jack Webb omitted. The murder was an epigram on transient lives and impacted sex as death. The unsolved status was a wall I tried to break down with a child's curiosity.
> I applied my mind to the task. My explication efforts were entirely unconscious. I simply told myself mental stories.
> That storytelling worked counterproductively. My daytime tales of death by saw and scalpel gave me terrible nightmares. They were devoid of narrative lines – all I saw was Betty being cut, slashed, probed and dissected. (Ellroy 1996: 103)

Ellroy's description of the murder as an 'epigram' alludes to these fantasies as beginnings to a broader, more ambitious narrative. As a child he would create scenarios in which he would rescue Elizabeth Short or catch her killer. But these small narratives and fantasies also formed a part of Ellroy's emerging sexuality; aside from imagining himself in a heroic role as Miss Short's lover or rescuer he also developed an 'explicitly pornographic' mental picture of the murder. For as much as he wanted to be the saviour of Elizabeth Short he was also morbidly fascinated with her murder and corpse. Jack Webb's open-ended synopsis was unsatisfying; without resolution there is only the repetition of the facts. Ellroy's nightmares were one form of continuation, but his darker tales of sex and violence, 'I simply told myself mental stories', suggested a need for answers, and as a young storyteller, fictional ones would suffice.

Ellroy's mental stories would become increasingly psychedelic and surreal as he became a serious abuser of alcohol and drugs. This apparent contradiction of narrative building amidst an emotional disintegration would prove influential to Ellroy in his creation of Dahlia narratives. In the novel *The Black Dahlia*, Bucky Bleichert's investigation into the murder is paralleled by a traumatic self-exploration. Bleichert begins his narration by saying of Elizabeth Short, 'I reconstructed her as a sad little girl and a whore, at best a could-have-been – a tag that might equally apply to me' (Ellroy 1987: 3). This echoes Ellroy's description of his early fantasies working 'counterproductively', as fantasy could not resolve the emotional issues at stake. For Bleichert and Ellroy, Elizabeth Short is the starting point of the emotional journey. Bleichert has a relatively stable, middle-class career, something Elizabeth Short never achieved. However Bleichert knows that much of what he has achieved is built on fraud, such as informing on Japanese-Americans during the war in a deal to keep his father, a Nazi sympathizer, out of trouble, and he sees in the victim someone who has paid the most horrific price for other people's sins. The transmogrification occurs in the parallels between Bleichert and Ellroy, and Elizabeth Short and Jean Ellroy. Both women are murdered, and to a degree Bleichert and Ellroy feel responsible. Bleichert knows he has the same flaws as Short but whereas she is 'a sad little girl and a whore', his social advantages and gender protect him. After his mother's death, Ellroy indulged in many of her vices, including alcohol, only with even less restraint. Knowing that his gender, luck and changing social attitudes allowed him to live more freely than his mother, Ellroy sought to redeem and reclaim Jean Ellroy through the Black Dahlia, thus the factual and fictional, Ellroy and Bleichert, converge.

Ellroy had given some thought to making the Black Dahlia murder case the central plot of his first novel, but the critical and commercial success of John Gregory Dunne's *True Confessions* deterred him from attempting such an ambitious task at the beginning of his literary career:

> In 1977, just as I was getting sober and was about to change my life, I read John Gregory Dunne's wonderful, if fanciful novel, *True Confessions* ... I thought the success of Dunne's novel precluded anyone else ever writing about the Black Dahlia. I didn't realize at the time that, *au contraire*, if you have a big, hit book like that, it spawns a great many imitators. And so I wrote my first six books, learned how to write in the process. (Silet 1995: 47)

The influence Dunne's novel had on Ellroy should not be underestimated: the upshot of the delay in writing his 'Dahlia novel' was that it became more natural for Ellroy to view the Dahlia murder as a lifelong narrative, present, to varying degrees, in many of his other works.

From his very first novel, *Brown's Requiem*, the Black Dahlia case is referenced. The title character Fritz Brown discusses the Dahlia murder with his alcoholic best friend Walter. Walter asks Brown, 'Who do you really think killed the Black Dahlia?', knowing that the question is unanswerable (Ellroy 1981: 21). In Ellroy's second novel, *Clandestine*, the Black Dahlia murder investigation forms a significant part of the back-story. In a scene which later reappears in *The Black Dahlia* in a revised form, LAPD Lieutenant Dudley Smith brags to lead character Freddy Underhill about his rather unusual role in the Dahlia case. Smith describes how he acquired 'a fine-looking young female stiff' from the morgue, stripped the body naked and dyed the hair black so that it resembled Elizabeth Short, and then rounded up a group of violent lunatics who were notionally suspects and allowed them to mutilate the body in an attempt to make the Dahlia killer inadvertently reveal himself (Ellroy 1987: 125). The bizarre theatrical setup suggests Smith is motivated by more than just his role as an investigator: 'I was looking for a reaction so vile, so unspeakable that I would *know* that this was the scum that killed Beth Short' (Ellroy 1982: 125). Smith is unwittingly revealing his own violent fantasies. His reaction is more vile and unspeakable than the lunatics who are unable to carry out his demands. It is not just the murder he is trying to recreate, but Elizabeth Short herself by proxy through his acquisition and studied composition of the corpse. This is a recurring theme of Ellroy's Dahlia narratives. Characters and the author himself try to integrate Short into their fantasies through re-enactment or replication with other women. For both Ellroy and Smith the 'other woman' is also dead. Smith is an outwardly corrupt character on many levels, but the murder of Elizabeth Short has driven him to display a veneer of justice, albeit only through a self-righteous attitude to extremely violent and sexual acts, which he experiences vicariously through the acts of others: 'I went home and prayed to God and to Jesus and to the Blessed Virgin to let me have the strength to do it again and again, if I had to, in the name of justice and the church' (Ellroy 1982: 125).

Smith's Black Dahlia anecdote in the novel amounts to merely three pages of text, but it signified Ellroy embracing greater complexity in his Dahlia narratives, and he would return to the theme of a proxy Dahlia cadaver in the novel and to the need of men who are haunted by Elizabeth Short to actualize their obsession onto other bodies. The

Dahlia back-story in *Clandestine* is secondary to the main murder investigation, which was based on his mother's murder, and is another early example of how Ellroy regarded the two cases as inextricably connected in narrative terms.

Prior to writing *The Black Dahlia*, Ellroy would attempt one more minor Dahlia narrative which warrants discussion here. In the contemporarily-set *Blood on the Moon*, Detective Lloyd Hopkins is investigating the murder of a woman and believes the killer's profile bears similarities to the Black Dahlia killer, although he can only speculate as to who the Dahlia killer was:

> Lloyd felt his thesis take on the form of what he called the 'Black Dahlia Syndrome,' a reference to the famous unsolved 1947 mutilation murder. He was certain that a middle-aged man who had never killed before, a man with a low sex drive who had somehow come in contact with Julia Niemeyer, whose persona somehow triggered his long dormant psychoses, and eventually led him to plan her murder carefully. He knew also that the man was physically strong and capable of manoeuvring on a broad-based societal level: a solid citizen type who could score heroin. (Ellroy 1984b: 107)

Hopkins' thinking goes further than an immediate desire to solve the murder he is investigating: he creates a 'thesis', giving academic weight to his conjectures and establishing a prototype and a profile for other murders that follow. But if Ellroy toyed with the idea of developing Hopkins' rather prescriptive 'Black Dahlia Syndrome' into *The Black Dahlia*, he would later jettison these plans. In *The Black Dahlia*, Elizabeth Short is murdered by a man and a woman. The former is deformed and the latter is an alcoholic, so even though one of them is respectably middle class they are no longer able to move 'on a broad-based societal level'. The murderers are also former lovers, which contradicts the 'low sex drive' supposition. However, some of Hopkins' theory does seem to transition to *The Black Dahlia*, suggesting Ellroy retained elements of the psychological profile, as Elizabeth Short's personality does trigger the killer's 'long dormant psychoses'.

After nurturing an obsession to write a novel on the Dahlia case for years, Ellroy began a period of intensive research on the case on 5 May 1984 at the Stephen A. Schwartzman Building, New York Public Library. He must have appeared a somewhat eccentric figure to the library staff, carrying, as he did, $300 in quarters in three triple reinforced pillowcases and ordering through inter-library loans microfilm copies of the original Los Angeles newspaper coverage of the case in 1947 (Powell 2012b: 164). Ellroy would personally conduct more research for this novel than any other novel in his career. For later novels, Ellroy hired researchers. The formal research for *The Black Dahlia*, and the outlining, drafting and re-drafting of the novel, lasted approximately three years. His aim was to recreate a fictional but historically accurate portrayal of Los Angeles in the late 1940s, revealing how the police investigation unfolded and merging this with his fictional characters. This historically detailed recreation was partially rooted in his need to create a strikingly different narrative from Dunne's *True Confessions*. Dunne had not followed the facts of the original investigation for his novel. He used the Dahlia murder to explore the themes of his own Irish-American identity, transposing the Irish culture and demography of 1940s Boston onto an LA setting. Dunne even renamed the victim Lois Fazenda, dubbing her 'the Virgin Tramp'. Ellroy purposefully did not include any prominent Irish-American characters to avoid any direct comparisons with Dunne's book. Instead, the lead character of *The Black Dahlia*, Bucky Bleichert, and several supporting characters are German-American, in a reference to Ellroy's own ethnic heritage. Ellroy claimed *True Confessions* 'wasn't a direct stylistic influence', and this is true in so far as Ellroy went to great lengths to make his Dahlia narrative significantly different from Dunne's novel (Powell 2008a: 163). Dunne's main protagonist Tom Spellacy is a natural cynic, whereas Bucky Bleichert is always emotionally involved with his work. The case unravels less dramatically in *True Confessions*, and the violence, when it comes, is blackly comic. Ironically one of the key influences *True Confessions* had on Ellroy was a reductive one, first stalling his writing and then forcing him to leave out the fictional Irish-American Lieutenant Dudley Smith in an effort to avoid any hint of similarity with Dunne's work. Despite his absence in *The Black Dahlia*, Smith would become one of the most prominent characters of the LA Quartet and re-emerge in another Dahlia narrative, *Perfidia*, over twenty years after the publication of Ellroy's 'Dahlia novel'.

However, despite Ellroy's conscious efforts to distinguish his novel from Dunne's, in the dedication to *True Confessions*, it is possible to see a theme which Ellroy would adapt as his own:

For   DOROTHY BURNS DUNNE
                 JOAN DIDION
                 QUINTANA ROO DUNNE
Generations.   (Dunne 1977: i)

Dunne pays tribute to the three generations of women in his life: mother, wife and daughter. Ellroy's dedication, '*Mother: Twenty-nine Years Later, This Valediction in Blood*', also references generations in that Ellroy's dedication links Jean Ellroy and Elizabeth Short through the author's desire to find resolutions for their unsolved murders (Ellroy 1987: i). The transmogrification which had come to Ellroy following his mother's death and stayed with him from childhood onwards involves a woman killed in the 1940s, a woman killed in the 1950s and the writer avenging them 30 years later. Although Jean Ellroy is not specifically referenced in the main text, the character of Elizabeth Short is a metaphorical stand-in for his mother's unsolved slaying, as Ellroy noted 'I wanted to honor Elizabeth Short as the transmogrification of Jean Hilliker Ellroy' (Rich 2008: 185). Thus, Ellroy's *Generations* are rooted not in a direct family line, but in a complex union wherein James Ellroy, Jean Ellroy and Elizabeth Short are one.

The Black Dahlia

Bucky Bleichert is the first-person narrator of *The Black Dahlia*, and the story is told simply as his recollections. There are shades of metafiction in the novel: allusions to the text being a manuscript written by Bleichert as his secret memoir of the Dahlia case: 'since I owe her a great deal and am the only one who does know the entire story, I have undertaken the writing of this memoir' (Ellroy 1987: 3). However, the ending, which will be discussed later, appears to undermine the notion of the novel as Bleichert's autobiography. Bleichert begins his reminiscences with his time at LAPD Central Division during the war. It is here that he meets police officer and fellow boxer Lee Blanchard. They are wary of each other at first as they have opposite reputations. Blanchard is a celebrated heavyweight boxer whereas Bleichert is distrusted because of his German-American heritage. However, they forge a close friendship during the Zoot Suit riots of 1943, and after the war, Bleichert and Blanchard agree to fight each other in a politically motivated boxing match. During the build-up to the fight, Bleichert meets Blanchard's lover, Kay Lake. The three become very close, although Bleichert's loyalty is tested when he finds himself strongly attracted to Kay.

When the narrative moves to the investigation of Elizabeth Short's murder, Bleichert and Blanchard are working on a separate case they believe may be connected. Blanchard's relationship with Kay begins to fall apart, as he becomes paranoid and obsessed with the Black Dahlia case as it reminds him of his sister's murder when he was a child, and he eventually disappears. Bleichert marries Kay but they separate after he develops his own all-consuming Dahlia obsession at a time when interest and resources devoted to the case are beginning to wind down. Bleichert's obsession with the Dahlia case is only heightened by his passion for Madeleine Sprague who bears a stunning physical resemblance to Elizabeth Short. When Madeleine introduces him to the eccentric Sprague family, Bleichert finds himself close to solving the Dahlia murder. The novel ends with Bleichert planning to reunite with Kay and start a family, but even after this conclusion Ellroy was planning for his personal Dahlia narrative to continue in other forms.

The valediction of Ellroy's dedication to the novel, although it precedes the events of the main narrative, is neither a beginning nor an end to the transmogrification. Ellroy is locked with his mother, and by extension Short, in an ongoing narrative: 'My mother and I are a continuum and we will continue' (Sublett 1997: 98). In a similar way, Ellroy created relational trinities throughout the narrative. Ellroy's trinities, however, are not harmonious: each carries a disturbing emotional, psychological or physical scar, which passes from one character to the next. They are a source of attraction and also repulsion.

Bleichert, Blanchard and Kay Lake form the first trinity of the novel. The first six chapters show their friendship at its height, with Kay acting as the lover/friend/mother figure to her two boys. Cracks in the trinity begin to appear after a police shooting in which Bleichert and Blanchard kill four men. They return to Blanchard's home before he abruptly departs leaving Bleichert alone with Kay:

> Kay was standing nude under the shower. Her expression stayed fixed in no expression at all, even when our eyes met. I took in her body, from freckled breasts with dark nipples to wide hips and flat stomach, then she pirouetted for me. I saw old knife scars crisscrossing her backside from thighs to spine, choked back tremors and walked away wishing she hadn't showed me on the day I killed two men. (Ellroy 1987: 71)

Kay's direct sexuality is exuded through her nude posing. Her fixed expression admits a sense of being watched, which is heightened by her performance: her ballet-like pirouette. Kay's revealing of her scars provokes an ambiguous sexual response in Bucky as he 'choked back tremors' possibly through anger at what she has been through but also in guilt, as the scars could become emotionally deeper if he betrayed Blanchard. His lustful admission, 'I took in her whole body', is abruptly altered by her movement 'then': Bleichert's reaction to violence is not that of a professional detective. It is emotional and personal, and at the mercy of Kay who has lured him to the bathroom in a classic seduction technique, as she runs a bath leaving Bucky 'feeling the steam, knowing it was all for me' (Ellroy 1987: 71). In this moment, preceded by violence and arrested by violence, the trinity begins to reformulate. Yet Bleichert's association of Kay's scars with the murdered men shows death is not an aphrodisiac for him, despite the obsession he later develops with the desecration of Elizabeth Short's body. The scars are also a portentous omen of the imminent discovery of Elizabeth Short's corpse as the man who slashed his mark onto Kay's flesh, her former pimp Bobby DeWitt, has the same initials (BD) as the Black Dahlia.

Blanchard's attraction to Kay stems from his guilt over the disappearance of his younger sister Laurie at the age of nine. Blanchard always thought she would have been a high achiever had she lived – 'Prom Queen, straight A's, her own family' – but time makes him numb to the pain of losing her, and he starts imagining her as a 'floozy' (Ellroy 1987: 51). Blanchard suffers from a false duality which is suggestive of Ellroy's emotional relationship with his mother and Elizabeth Short. Blanchard regards women as either whores or angels, and despite Kay's former profession, their celibate relationship transitions her in his mind to the latter. Blanchard's mental association of Kay with Laurie makes his relationship with Kay, if consummated, incestuous. Blanchard is motivated by guilt, and he distorts his relationship with Kay because of the other woman in their union, his sister.

Strong relationships exist between opposites: Blanchard and Bleichert's respective pugilist nicknames are Mr Fire and Mr Ice, but their wildly different personalities lead them to be good friends and professional partners. In sexual terms, ice implies frigidity, but Bleichert becomes increasingly sexually active in comparison to the chaste Blanchard. There are several other factors in which the polarizing opposites in the two men's characters bring them emotionally closer. Carole Allamand has noted that Bleichert and Blanchard are derived from German and French words for whiten, and Ellroy's choice of the names implies an innocence the two policeman clearly do not possess but aspire to through authoritarianism and chastity (Allamand 2006: 358). Kay's surname 'Lake' is a straight reference to water, alluding to the purifying effect the weary cops hope she will give them through love. This is in direct contrast to Elizabeth Short, the 'Black' Dahlia. Yet the characters operate in worlds where morality exists in varying shades of grey, which is hinted at in their ethnic identity. Bucky and Lee's German and French surnames are politically and historically significant considering the immediate post-war setting of the novel. It is mirrored in their relationship, which is that of friendship marred by the underlying threat of hostility and violence. Bleichert's attraction to Kay builds because Blanchard appears to be a good friend and the three become a proxy family for each other. His sexual desire is intensified by the guilt he feels surrounding Blanchard's professional and emotional decline.

The discovery of Elizabeth Short's scarred and tortured body, a mere five days after Bleichert's voyeuristic encounter with Kay, once again forges links between sex and death:

> Her legs were spread for sex, and from the way the knees buckled I could tell they were broken; her jet-black hair was free of matted blood, like the killer had given her a shampoo before he dumped her. That awful death leer came on like the final brutality – it was cracked teeth poking out of ulcerated flesh that forced me to look away. (Ellroy 1987: 79)

Kay's pose for Bleichert had been a wordless invitation for sex, which by extension exposed Bleichert to the violence she had suffered at the hands of Bobby DeWitt. Bleichert discovers Elizabeth Short's corpse placed in a deliberately sexual pose after her murder, or at least this is what he assumes. While his relationship up to this point with Kay is expressed through chaste voyeurism, with the Black Dahlia corpse he cannot continue to look at the sexual brutality. Every mark of torture and mutilation on Kay and Short reflect intentional posing which both repulses and fascinates Bleichert. The sexual angle to the investigation is merged with the sexual fantasy of the investigator. The bodies of Kay and Short are both riddled with physical clues as to the psycho-sexual motivation for the violence inflicted upon them. Yet the killer's false tenderness in rinsing Short's hair seems out of place. With Short's 'awful death leer', the killer mocks the suffering the victim has endured, but the phrase also suggests a posthumous rebalancing: her torture-murder had made her an object abused for pleasure, yet her grotesque smile implies a spiritual awareness in the victim herself, a knowing satisfaction that she will be the haunting obsession of the men involved in the Dahlia case.

The critic Joshua Meyer has argued that the discovery of Elizabeth Short's corpse, aside from initiating the main mystery narrative of the novel, is also laced with clues leading to the resolution of the mystery.

The body itself is a symbol of more complex questions of identity and the structure of the novel:

> *The Black Dahlia* is as much a 'who was she' as a 'whodunit' and it is clear that we are not engaged solely with the criminal fable, but also with the fable of identity. Thus, together with Elizabeth Short's mutilated corpse, Bleichert's subjective retelling of the case must also account for Short herself as a cohesive sign system. (Meyer 2008: 10)

The mutilated corpse of Elizabeth Short is literally in pieces, with clues engraved into her skin. Bucky must metaphorically put these pieces together, reassemble her identity, and discover 'who was she' as a means to solving the case. But the 'fable of identity' also concerns Bleichert himself. Bleichert did not experience the horrors of war like many of his police colleagues, and most of his violent encounters as a policeman had begun the week of the Dahlia discovery, with the shootout taking place only five days earlier. Before this, his experience of physical violence was mostly limited to fist fights in the Zoot Suit riots and in the boxing ring. In fact, his discovery of the crime scene was entirely by chance as he was in the area with Blanchard tracking a suspect wanted for a robbery-homicide. Yet his introduction to the case creates a new trinity between himself and the mutilated women Kay Lake and Elizabeth Short, redefining his relationships in the process.

In Ellroy's first major fictional reference to the Dahlia in *Clandestine*, Dudley Smith nurtures an obsession with Elizabeth Short several years after the original investigation. In a revised version of the morgue/warehouse scene first described in *Clandestine*, the police use the corpse as a prop in a killer/detective theatrical game, which plays out their sexual fantasies. In commenting on the treatment of the Dahlia from a feminist perspective, Josh Cohen argues that Elizabeth Short's corpse is employed as a metaphor, not for the murder mystery itself or the structure of the novel as Joshua Meyer has suggested, but for the chauvinism of the male characters:

> It is perhaps the grotesque leer of the mouth, a taunting distortion of the smiling female object, that most graphically conveys this sense of viciously inverted fantasy. Betty Short's corpse, that is, potentially enacts the 'graphic fragmentation' of the feminine wrought by postmodernity's allegorical crisis of seeing. (Cohen 1996: 5)

Bleichert sees Betty Short not just as a 'smiling female object', but as a woman he loves as much as Kay. Betty's death and literal 'fragmentation' means Bleichert will never be able to see or know her completely, which his opening narration concedes: 'I never knew her in life. She exists for me through others' (Ellroy 1987: 3). Bleichert finds himself to be the central figure of unusual triumvirates, namely Kay/Bleichert/Blanchard and later in the narrative, Madeleine Sprague (a wealthy socialite and Dahlia lookalike)/Bleichert/Elizabeth Short. As the critic D.S. Neff has argued, 'Bucky and Lee are safely "neurotic", each held fast within familial and symbolic triangles' (Neff 1997: 323). However, the triangles do not hold fast as Neff claims, even if Bleichert and Blanchard want them to, as they are interchangeable. Bleichert finds himself constantly moving in his role as an interloper, the odd man out in a series of families where his outsider status teases out their hidden roles and secrets.

The importance of family to the narrative is shown, as discussed earlier, in the dedication, but also in the epigraph to the novel taken from Anne Sexton's poem 'All My Pretty Ones': 'Now I fold you down, my drunkard, my navigator / My first lost keeper, to love and look at later' (Ellroy 1987: iii). The narrator is a woman who has just lost her father and is examining a photograph album which traces back generations of her own family, now all deceased. Ellroy also seeks to understand his ancestry by examining records of the past and forging a new narrative. Elizabeth Short's early association with his mother brings her into his family narrative. Thus, the 'family' in the novel becomes a conduit to examine the questions raised by death and mourning.

Bleichert must solve the mystery by following his instincts. He is, like Ellroy, approaching the case emotionally and inchoately. Yet he eventually finds the solution rooted in secrets of a family, the Spragues. Bleichert and Kay attempt to give each other stability and legitimacy in marriage, even though they are haunted by feelings of guilt about the usurping of Blanchard. In contrast, the outwardly natural family, the Spragues, are destructive and perverse. Lee Horsley has argued that *The Black Dahlia* comprises a 'disintegrative narrative' where the mystery storyline is solved and moral conventions are simultaneously destroyed, thus creating deeper emotional questions with less clear resolutions: 'suppressed relationships and unrecognized blood ties are revealed, the family structure is clarified, and we locate the deeper sources of depravity in the patriarchal power structure' (Horsley 2005: 148). The Sprague family itself contains a series of mysteries predating the Dahlia including incest, disfigurement and adultery.

Bleichert blurs the lines between his personal and professional role and becomes involved with the potential suspect Madeleine Sprague, who, ominously, is noted for her extraordinary resemblance to

Elizabeth Short. It is at a family gathering, a meeting with the Spragues, that Bucky detects a sinister undertone to Madeleine's relatives:

> Ramona Sprague was the only one of the three who looked like Madeleine; if not for her I would have thought the brass girl was adopted. She possessed a pushing-fifty version of Madeleine's lustrous dark hair and pale skin, but there was nothing else attractive about her. She was fat, her face was flaccid, her rouge and lipstick were applied slightly off center, so that her face was weirdly askew. Taking her hand, she said, 'Madeleine has said so many nice things about you,' with a trace of a slur. There was no liquor on her breath; I wondered if she was jacked on drugstore stuff. (Ellroy 1987: 142–3)

Although Bleichert is at this stage unaware of the family's complicity in the Dahlia murder, there are already clues that Ramona Sprague is the killer and why. She is 'the only one of the three who looked like Madeleine'. Madeleine does not look like her father, Emmett Sprague, or her sister, Martha McConville Sprague because, as is revealed later, they are not her natural father and sister. She is the result of an affair between Ramona Sprague and Georgie Tilden, a business partner of Emmett's, who ordered Tilden's face to be brutally scarred in revenge for cuckolding him. Madeleine has developed a romantic love for Emmett and murdered Blanchard in revenge for physically beating him. Ellroy gives his noir characters the subliminal desire for sex typical of the genre but the harsh punishments meted out after consummation are almost biblical. All the family, with the exception of Tilden who is a pariah and unacknowledged, are before the detective in a relatively confined space – the family home. Ellroy alludes to the illegitimacy by the unnatural staging of the scene. The family first appear to Bleichert as a 'still-life ensemble' who only respond with 'little nods and smiles' (Ellroy 1987: 142). Politeness is maintained by necessity, but this is also a veil behind which is hidden disease and addiction as Bleichert detects 'a trace of a slur' in Ramona's greeting. Each family member, to varying degrees, is culpable, skewering the reader's ability to guess 'whodunit' and creating a pooling of guilt amongst the unit; the violent and incestuous father abuses his murderous wife and sexually grooms his murderous daughter. Solving the mystery is contingent on seeing through the superficial roles of the family members and identifying their more complicated and incestuously interwoven heritage.

The early reference to Madeleine's looks, and her lack of similarity to Ramona, also alludes to Ramona's motive for killing the Dahlia – her interruption of a hidden family – albeit enough information is withheld from the reader to limit the connection to the benefit of hindsight. By the time Bleichert discovers Ramona is the killer, she is already suffering from terminal cancer and Bleichert sees it as just punishment to leave the 'torturer Mommy' to die slowly from her disease (Ellroy 1987: 347).The name Ramona is of Spanish and German origin and means 'protecting hands', a deliberate irony, perhaps, as Ramona has the hands of a killer and, in her own view, an artist through the slashing of Elizabeth Short's mouth.

In Ellroy's original outline to the novel, Ramona's behaviour is even more psychotic. During her final confrontation with Bucky, she slits her own mouth open from ear to ear, reproducing the crime she committed on Elizabeth Short and transferring the artistic symbolism from victim to murderer (Ellroy 1984e). Ramona's inspiration for the slashing of the mouth from ear to ear comes from two artistic sources, which in turn are based on historical events. Ramona is moved by Victor Hugo's novel *The Man Who Laughs* in which the character of Gwynplaine has had his mouth slashed open by the Comprachios, a group of Spanish bandits in the fifteenth and sixteenth centuries who disfigured children and then sold them to the aristocracy. Bleichert spots a copy of the *The Man Who Laughs* in the shack, which was the murder scene of Elizabeth Short, and it is here that he kills Georgie Tilden, assuming at the time that Tilden is the man solely responsible for the Black Dahlia murder. However, at the Sprague house, he sees a painting which belongs to Ramona of a 'scar mouth clown' (Ellroy 1987: 339). It is a priceless Frederick Yannantuono painting 'The Man Who Laughs', a portrait of Gwynplaine in Hugo's novel, and on his second viewing of the painting Bleichert realizes that Ramona and Tilden together murdered Elizabeth Short.

The dying Ramona confesses her guilt to Bleichert when he confronts her:

> Elizabeth Short tried to run. She knocked her unconscious and made Georgie strip her and gag her and tie her to the mattress. She promised him parts of the girl to keep forever. She took a copy of *The Man Who Laughs* from her purse and read aloud from it, casting occasional glances at the girl spread-eagled. Then she cut her and burned her and batted her and wrote in the notebook she always carried while the girl was passed out from the pain. Georgie watched, and together they shouted the chants of the Comprachios. (Ellroy 1987: 345)

By reliving the murder scene, Ramona's confession reveals how she regards the killing as a communal, almost family act. Ramona is the dominant figure in this pair, with her behaviour toward her partner appearing, significantly, maternal as much as sexual in her reassurances that he will be allowed to keep a memento of Short. To give the murder theatrical aspects, Ramona reads aloud from *The Man Who Laughs*, as though bringing the narrative to life through murder, 'and together they shouted the chants of the Comprachios'. In addition to reading and performing the text, Ramona also writes during the murder, documenting her creation while 'casting occasional glances' at the victim as if to remind herself that the murder is really happening, synching performance with reality. Ramona takes full artistic claim of the body. Georgie merely 'watched' and his actions are limited to what she 'made' him do. The chanting follows the cruelly sadistic laughter of the killers, but it is a laughter which is marked on Elizabeth Short as their signature and which echoes after her death as the victim holds remarkable emotional sway over the men who study her life and death, as Bucky notices upon first seeing on the corpse 'that awful death leer'. Yet the tortured are remembered; the torturer is lost to history.

The distortion of family roles is echoed in the disturbing portrayal of sexual relationships outside the Sprague family. A pornographic 'stag' film is discovered which features Short being sexually abused with a phallic-shaped implement, 'the snake thing' (Ellroy 1987: 169). The images in the film haunt Bleichert, but the consequences for his sexual relationship with Madeleine appear contradictory and ambivalent:

> I was seeing the snake thing. Madeleine tickled me; I twisted round and looked at her to make it go away. 'Smile at me. Look soft and sweet.'
>
> Madeleine gave me a Pollyanna grin. Her smeared red lipstick reminded me of the Dahlia death smile; I shut my eyes and grabbed her hard. She stroked my back softly, murmuring, 'Bucky, what is it?'
> (Ellroy 1987: 169)

There is a curiously circular nature to Bleichert's sexual feelings for Madeleine and Elizabeth Short. He is attracted to Madeleine because she deliberately attempts to mimic the Dahlia's dress style and behaviour. It is this connection which renders their sex energetic but loveless, coming as it does shortly after his viewing of the pornographic film featuring Short. Bleichert tries to compensate for this by forcing Madeleine to imitate an exaggerated feminine, even childlike, innocence: her 'Pollyanna grin'. But Madeleine is not innocent, and even her appearance suggests guilt and complicity. Despite Bleichert's efforts, she continually reminds him of 'the Dahlia death smile'. Unnerved, he wants to make love slowly, but she forces him to be more vigorous, and he distracts himself by not thinking of either woman, 'concentrating on the ripped wallpaper.' However, in spite of Bleichert feeling disturbed by the memory of the Dahlia, Bleichert and Madeleine sexually climax together, leaving Bleichert to 'stanch my tremors', and Madeleine switches to a maternal, comforting role. The role of performance in sexual politics is crucial to the resolution of the mystery, as Madeleine's imitation of Elizabeth Short partially provokes the murder, and the reference to Pollyanna seems cruelly ironic as her semi-incestuous relationship with Emmett motivates her to kill Lee Blanchard. At one point it appears as though the merging of Elizabeth Short and Madeleine in Bleichert's thoughts will drive him to still rougher sex: 'I shut my eyes and grabbed her hard.' But in this instance, Bleichert seeks only Madeleine's emotional reassurance. When Madeleine claims to have had lesbian sex with Short, Bleichert felt 'like I was sinking; like the bed was dropping out from under me' (Ellroy 1987: 170). He is attracted to her because of her resemblance to Short, but he does not want Madeleine to be sexually attracted to the same qualities in Short. Jealousy gnaws away at Bleichert and Blanchard as they try unsuccessfully to freeze women in an unchanging but loving relationship.

Through both sex and consolation, Bleichert moves from one trinity to another. When he finally consummates his relationship with Kay Lake, he uses the language of marriage to symbolize the union, 'So were Kay Lake and I formally joined' (Ellroy 1987: 213). By essentially cheating on his closest friend, Bleichert destroys and replaces the trinity of Bleichert, Blanchard and Kay, which forms at the beginning of the narrative and initially prevents him from sleeping with Kay, and replaces it with Bleichert, Betty and Kay. His first sexual encounter with Kay is on the same night he sabotages the warehouse re-enactment of Elizabeth Short's murder. Prior to this, Madeleine's resemblance to Elizabeth Short creates a superficial trinity of Bleichert, Betty and Madeleine. Bucky uses the phrase 'So Elizabeth Short and I were formally joined' after making love to Madeleine and she reassures him: '"I'll be Betty or anyone else you want me to be"' (Ellroy 1987: 192). But this substitution or false position is similar to Lee's sexless relationship with Kay and will not hold.

The Black Dahlia ends with the mystery storyline resolved, but with the characters reliving the story, both through their memories and their relationships. Bleichert receives two letters from Kay, now living in Cambridge, Massachusetts. The second letter informs Bucky that she is carrying his child. The novel ends with Bleichert lost in thought aboard a plane flying to Boston:

> Nearing Boston, the plane got swallowed up by clouds. I felt heavy with fear, like the reunion and fatherhood had turned me into a stone plummeting. I reached for Betty then; a wish, almost a prayer. The clouds broke up and the plane descended, a big bright city at twilight below. I asked Betty to grant me safe passage in return for my love. (Ellroy 1987: 358)

Although Bleichert is planning a reunion and reconciliation with Kay, he is still obsessed with the Dahlia, tenderly addressing her as Betty as he talks to her in his prayers. It is important to note that this seems to indicate the narration is Bleichert's thoughts and not the written memoir he refers to at the opening of the novel. Ellroy claimed he 'embraced the writing of *The Black Dahlia* with a certain degree of consciousness' indicating that like Bleichert he may have drifted between the need to formally construct the narrative and the desire to emotionally live the story (Silet 1995: 47). This is true even for the killer, as Ramona's confession is her own reliving of the murder.

The viewing of relationships through the sphere of their connection to Short is paralleled by the reader's understanding of the most prominent character outside the main text – James Ellroy. Kay informs Bleichert she is two months pregnant in a letter dated '9/11/49' which would likely put the birth as happening in early 1950, a full two years after Ellroy's birth, but it is an intriguing possibility that Bleichert and Kay's child is metaphorically Ellroy the author. Bleichert will live with Kay not far from Short's hometown of Medford. His strong desire to protect his child, something he could never do for Short, is another form of Dahlia legacy and posthumous justice. But Bleichert's future relationship with Kay is uncertain. Their original separation was partly due to his obsession with Betty, one of the same reasons for Kay and Blanchard's split. Loving Betty is akin to an affair. Yet Bleichert's mental conversation with Short is really Bleichert just talking to himself. The solemnity of prayer has replaced what was once sexual desire, adding another change to the transmogrification. The final scene suggests that Bleichert has narrated the entire story while flying from LA to Boston. It retrospectively gives his prose a floating, dreamlike aura, casting doubt over his ability to adapt to domestic reality, like the bereaved daughter examining photographs of lost loved ones in Sexton's 'All My Pretty

Ones'. By asking the dead for 'safe passage in return for my love', he may be sacrificing his love with the living.

'I wrote the last page and wept': Ellroy's Continuing Black Dahlia Narratives

Before *The Black Dahlia* was even published in 1987, Ellroy had already taken advantage of events which would eventually tie his name inextricably to the Black Dahlia case in popular culture and see the rise of his Demon Dog of American Crime Fiction persona. Ellroy claimed that upon completing the manuscript of *The Black Dahlia*, 'I wrote the last page and wept' (Ellroy 1996: 209). If Ellroy was weeping through the emotional exhaustion of completing the written narrative, he was soon to embark on an equally exhausting oral Dahlia narrative. According to Ellroy's agent Nat Sobel, Ellroy was offered $50,000 for the film rights to *The Black Dahlia* shortly before it was published (Ferrari-Adler 2008). Ellroy contributed the entire proceeds of his share towards financing an ambitious publicity campaign and book tour for the novel:

> I told the Jean Ellroy-Dahlia story ten dozen times. I reduced it to sound bites and vulgarized it in the name of accessibility. I wept at it with precise dispassion. I portrayed myself as a man formed by two murdered women and a man who now lived on a plane above such matters. My media performances were commanding at first glance and glib upon reappraisal. They exploited my mother's desecration and allowed me to cut her memory down to manageable proportions. (Ellroy 1996: 209)

This was Ellroy's first period of significant media exposure and it proved to be a resounding success; *The Black Dahlia* became the first of Ellroy's novels in which the paperback edition reached the *New York Times* bestseller list, albeit only for one week (McDonald 2001: 121). But Ellroy has since described this period as 'glib upon reappraisal', and that his tears were shed with 'precise dispassion'. This latter dismissal of his emotional connection to the narrative refers specifically to the tour and not the completion of the manuscript. Ellroy alludes to two Dahlia narratives; one based upon a genuine emotional transmogrification with Elizabeth Short and his mother 'formed by two murdered women', and the other rooted in dispassionate career advancement 'a plane above such matters'. These two distinct intentions, although successful in career terms, led to a personal dissatisfaction for Ellroy, and as a consequence, spurred him to continue to develop the Dahlia narrative in other forms. Ellroy's first attempts at Dahlia narratives after publication of the novel were quite modest: he resurrected the character of Lee Blanchard for the two short stories 'High Darktown' and 'Dial Axminster 6-400', prequels to *The Black Dahlia* published in the collection *Hollywood Nocturnes* (1994). In retrospect these minor pieces can be seen as the precursor to *Perfidia*, and Ellroy's plans for a prequel Second LA Quartet.

Gradually, Ellroy's continuing Dahlia narrative became more ambitious, as in the complex structure of his unconventional autobiography *My Dark Places*:

> It would be my autobiography, my mother's biography, Bill Stoner's biography, and it would have two basic dramatic thrusts. One, I would go back and re-create the original 1958–59 investigation from official records and surviving witness testimony. Two, if he were willing to help me for a cut of the proceeds, I would enlist Bill Stoner and we would reinvestigate my mother's murder in the present. (Silet 1995: 51)

Ellroy developed five interweaving narratives, three of which he termed biographical and the remaining two 'dramatic thrusts', which implies a fictional aspect to the biography. Overarching these five narrative lines is the transmogrification of Elizabeth Short and Jean Ellroy, and the author's emotional proximity to the two. Although *My Dark Places* resolves some of these narrative lines, the transmogrification is left open for further development, and Ellroy has stated it could not be resolved even if he desired to finish it: 'The only closure is that there is no closure' (Silet 1995: 43). The closing lines of *My Dark Places* allude to how the transmogrification will continue. Each section of the book is preceded by a single stanza of italicized poetic prose, and a final stanza appears as an epilogue, '*I can't hear your voice. I can smell you and taste your breath. I can feel you. You're brushing against me. You're gone and I want more of you*' (Ellroy 1996: 355). Ellroy interweaves his bereavement with the taboo issue of a child's sexual feelings for his mother. He was only a child when she died but as an adult he addresses her as a lover. This is partly a consequence of the similarities between his mother and one of the first women Ellroy sexually desired, Elizabeth Short, and just as the desire is made stronger as it can never be fulfilled the narrative is more powerful through the absence of closure. The importance of the feminine to the transmogrification is heightened by Ellroy dedicating *My Dark Places* to his second wife, Helen Knode, and as Ellroy later remarked, 'My mother and I, as I say in *The Hilliker Curse*, were a love story. We were never a friendship story' (Powell 2009: 197).

However, it would be a 'friendship story' which formed the basis of Ellroy's next attempt at an allusive Dahlia narrative. Ellroy formed a close friendship with the popular American actress Dana Delany. Delany has appeared with Ellroy at book readings and in the documentary *James Ellroy: American Dog* (2006), and she co-authored an article with him for *Interview* magazine the same year. Ellroy named Delany as his first choice for the role of his mother in any future film adaptation of *My Dark Places* (McDonald 2006: 133). There is nothing to suggest that Ellroy and Delany were lovers, but by linking her to his mother, in physical appearance and as a character, he alludes to another transmogrification – again merging platonic and sexual relationships from James Ellroy, Betty Short and Jean Ellroy to James Ellroy, Dana Delany and Jean Ellroy. Ellroy based his character Donna Donohue on Delany. Donohue appeared in the three novellas, 'Hollywood Fuck Pad', 'Hot-Prowl Rape-O' and 'Jungletown Jihad' which form Part II 'Rick Loves Donna' of the collection *Destination Morgue!: L.A. Tales* (2004).

The novellas are a form of neo-noir kitsch following the comic adventures and love affair of LAPD homicide detective 'Rhino' Rick Jenson and the beautiful actress Donohue. The stories feature several allusions to and 'in jokes' from Ellroy's literary career, as seen in the fictitious *Daily Variety* article about Donohue which features in 'Jungletown Jihad':

> She wants to eschew indie cheapies, sexploitation yukfests like *Exit to Ecstasy* and overblown oaters like *San Laredo*. Her plan? To commission a playwright and bomb the boards as pill-popping poetess Anne Sexton.
>
> Sexy Sexton succumbed to suicide in 1974. Deep Donna digs on her as a kool kindred soul. 'I've had two seismic eruptions in my life,' she said. 'One in '83 and one last year. I want to transmogrify them into my role as Sexton.' (Ellroy 2004b: 324)

There may be a risk of reading too much in to what are deliberately comic pieces, but it is possible to see how the Donohue stories fit into Ellroy's Dahlia narrative. Donohue's ambition is to play Anne Sexton on stage. The epigraph of *The Black Dahlia* is taken from Sexton's 'All My Pretty Ones', and Donohue talks of how she plans to make two events of her life, 'transmogrify ... into my role as Sexton'. Transmogrification is important to the narrative, as it is to *The Black Dahlia*, as it alludes to shifting identities. Donohue's reference to 'seismic eruptions' suggests a form of orgasm which is appropriate to the trinities Ellroy creates in which men and women are constantly jostling for position and using each other emotionally, searching for an ecstatic connection.

'Rhino' Jenson is based on Detective Rick Jackson, a close friend of Ellroy's and one of his contacts within the LAPD. However, the romantic relationship between Rick and Donna is more closely based on Ellroy's own feelings for his mother and Elizabeth Short. Jenson's love for Donna is complicated by his Dahlia-like obsession with the real-life unsolved homicide of the teenage actress Stephanie Gorman in 1965: 'he has eschewed marriage and long-term relationships with other women out of a sense of devotion to this woman' (Ellroy: 2004b 325). Rick Jackson investigated the Gorman homicide for the LAPD's cold case unit. At one point Jenson comes across a biography of Donohue titled '*Her Lonely Places: Donna Donohue Deconstructed* by James Ellington', a title which is a clear parody of Ellroy's memoir, and with a sub-title featuring his trademark alliterative style (Ellroy 2004b: 347). The transmogrification is both a meta-fictional comment on Ellroy's career and a meta-narrative to *The Black Dahlia*. Rick has not had successful relationships with women because of his obsessional love for a beautiful murdered actress. Rick falls for an actress based upon Dana Delany, the actress Ellroy most closely associates with his mother, and the fictional Donna dreams of playing Anne Sexton, the poet whose own work and life story Ellroy has tied to *The Black Dahlia* and his mother's murder.

'Now we know who killed her, and why': Ellroy and the Black Dahlia true-crime sub-genre

Apart from texts he has personally authored, it would be the issue of Ellroy's family, and their symbolic connections to the Dahlia case, which would lead to the author's involvement with several true-crime writers who attempted to solidify the link between his mother's murder and Elizabeth Short. During his reinvestigation into his mother's murder, Ellroy was contacted by Black Dahlia researcher Janice Knowlton. With the assistance of crime writer Michael Newton, Knowlton had written the book *Daddy was the Black Dahlia Killer* (1995) in which she claimed her abusive father George Knowlton murdered Elizabeth Short, and that she had repressed this memory only to have it re-emerge years later in therapy. In her letter to Ellroy, Knowlton claimed that besides murdering Elizabeth Short, her father was a plausible suspect in the murder of Jean Ellroy (Powell 2012b: 165), Knowlton's claims were widely derided as implausible, and, sadly, she committed suicide in 2004. She had disappeared from public view in her last years, and her death was not reported until nine months after her suicide when fellow Dahlia researcher Larry Harnisch traced her whereabouts (McLellan 2012). Ellroy dismissed her views out of hand, but her letter to him foreshadowed how events would unravel between the author and other Black Dahlia researchers (Powell 2008a: 165).

There have been multiple true-crime books published about the Black Dahlia case, all written with the intention of doing what the LAPD could not: solve the case. For many years after the publication of *The Black Dahlia* Ellroy did not comment on any of the Dahlia theories, as he seemed content with his fictional portrayal of the case. Ellroy's first public endorsement of the work of a Dahlia researcher marked a distinct change in attitude from the novelist, and came in the documentary *James Ellroy's Feast of Death* directed by Vikram Jayanti. Although it comprises only a brief segment of the documentary, Ellroy endorsed *Los Angeles Times* reporter Larry Harnisch's theory that the LA-based surgeon Dr Walter Bayley murdered Elizabeth Short. Ellroy did not take his endorsement of Harnisch's work much further, and later claimed he regarded it as 'tenuous' (Powell 2008a: 164). Elements of Harnisch's theory faintly echoed the narrative of *The Black Dahlia,* which may have appealed to Ellroy. According to Harnisch, Dr Bayley was in a state of mental decline at the time of the murder and died shortly thereafter: his personal and professional life was falling apart, and Elizabeth Short inadvertently reminded him of a family tragedy which sparked a homicidal reaction, all of which would have been familiar to Ellroy and the connections he weaved between the Sprague family and the Dahlia murder. For the first time since he read Jack Webb's *The Badge* he was beginning to see narrative potential in the work of true-crime writers.

It would not be until the publication of Steve Hodel's *Black Dahlia Avenger* (2003) that the remarkable parallels between fiction and reality in Ellroy's work would emerge. Steve Hodel is a former LAPD Detective turned private investigator. In *Black Dahlia Avenger,* Hodel paints a fascinating and chilling portrait of his father George Hill Hodel – a physician, psychiatrist, businessman, art collector and, according to Steve Hodel, libertine and murderer. Steve Hodel's suspicions about his father began after George Hodel's death in San Francisco at the age of ninety-one. Sorting through his father's belongings, Steve Hodel found two photographs, which he believed to be of Elizabeth Short. This led Hodel to begin an investigation into the possible connection between his father and the Black Dahlia case. Hodel came to the conclusion that his father was the murderer of Elizabeth Short and his mutilation of the body was inspired by the work of the Surrealist artist Man Ray. George Hodel was good friends with Man Ray, and Steve Hodel claims the torture and posing of Miss Short's body was a specific reference to Man Ray's painting *Les Amoureux (the Lovers)* (1933–34) and his photographic work *Minotaur* (1936). Harnisch's work had been loosely similar to Ellroy's fiction, but Hodel's theory that the murder was inspired by a work of art is remarkably similar to the use of the Gwynplaine painting in *The Black Dahlia* and spurred Hodel to describe Ellroy's novel as 'profane and prophetic. It was obvious he had done his homework' (Hodel 2004: 416). Ramona and Georgie kill Elizabeth Short to be like the Comprachios of Hugo's novel, and George Hodel, allegedly, murdered to create Surrealist art. Instead of art referencing death, murder is referencing art.

According to Steve Hodel, it was Ellroy who originally contacted him and suggested he make an endorsement in print, and not the other way round. Ellroy met Hodel at an LAPD author's night function. Hodel was completing the research and writing on the 'Aftermath' chapter for the paperback edition of *Black Dahlia Avenger*, and Ellroy asked to see the new material. Ellroy was apparently so impressed with the new chapter that he offered to help with the publication if he could. Ellroy later commented that he had been 'unconvinced' by Hodel's theory when he first read the hardcover edition (McDonald 2006: 137). Hodel requested that Ellroy provide a blurb for the new edition, but Ellroy responded with an offer to write the foreword. Ellroy was unequivocal in his endorsement: 'We can only glimpse who Betty Short was – but now we know who killed her, and why' (Ellroy 2004a: xix). He also drew attention to the Oedipal dilemma which lay at the centre of both Hodel's narrative and his own: 'This book costs Steve Hodel a father. This book gains him a daughter a generation his senior' (Ellroy 2004a: xxi). Thus by assuming new figures into the Dahlia narrative, Ellroy created the trinity of Betty, Ellroy and Steve Hodel – the author who lost a father and gained a daughter. The transmogrification Ellroy had created in the text of *The Black Dahlia* could be replicated in forms external to the novel with new Dahlia writers.

Hodel was not familiar with any of Ellroy's work at the time he started his investigation and expressed some reservations about accepting an endorsement as the author had contributed to the mythmaking around Elizabeth Short, although 'to his credit, Ellroy never claimed his novel was anything other than "pure fiction"' (Hodel 2004: 416). As a detective, Hodel had a dislike of crime fiction: 'I prided myself in wanting to know things as they are, not as they are imagined' (Hodel 2004: 416). But he eventually read and praised *The Black Dahlia* as Ellroy's vision of LA won him over. Hodel's further investigations revealed more remarkable parallels between the Dahlia case and Ellroy's life and work. After studying *My Dark Places*, Hodel hypothesized that George Hodel's friend and criminal accomplice Fred Sexton was a plausible suspect in the murder of Ellroy's mother. For Ellroy the murder of his mother and Elizabeth Short had always been symbolically linked, but now he had been confronted with the second true-crime writer (Knowlton being the first) to claim the cases were factually connected through the same murderer – a serious blurring of the line between fact and fiction that Hodel claimed had been the source of his initial reservations about Ellroy's work. Ellroy expressed his opinion of this element of Hodel's theory in no uncertain terms: 'Bullshit, bullshit, just bullshit, and I told Steve that. Just bullshit' (Powell 2008a: 165). But Hodel unearthed more connections between his father and Ellroy's work after the publication of *Black Dahlia Avenger*.

In an article published on his website, Hodel noted some of the physical characteristics and biographical similarities between his father and Pierce Patchett, a character in Ellroy's *L.A. Confidential*. Hodel insisted that Ellroy had no prior knowledge of George Hodel before reading *Black Dahlia Avenger* and the connections amount to 'ONLY ABSOLUTE IRONY' (Hodel 2010). Hodel revealed that George Hodel's 1940s LA residence, 'the Franklin House', was used as a set for the filming of several scenes of Curtis Hanson's film adaptation of *L.A. Confidential*, including a montage scene which depicts Pierce Patchett hosting a party where politicians and Hollywood figures are being entertained by high-class hookers. A pivotal scene in which Captain Dudley Smith (played by James Cromwell) suddenly murders Sergeant Jack Vincennes (Kevin Spacey) was filmed in the Franklin House kitchen:

> I recall one of my initial reactions in seeing the film was how very impressed I was with the actor, David Strathairn, who played the character, Pierce Morehouse Patchett. This came primarily from the fact that Strathairn's performance as Patchett was a spot-on impersonation of my own father, Dr. George Hill Hodel. Strathairn/Patchett's sophisticated dapper appearance, his voice, his ability to control any situation, all fit perfectly into my father's real life persona. (Hodel 2011)

Hodel first viewed the film two years before his father's death, and before he began his investigation. There appears to be no possibility that the film-makers, like Ellroy, could have realized George Hodel's connection to the Dahlia case and Steve Hodel described it simply as a 'fascinating coincidence' (Hodel 2014). Hodel claims that the basement of the Franklin House is the crime scene where George Hodel tortured and murdered Elizabeth Short, before moving the cadaver to nearby Thirty-Ninth and Norton. This is the same Franklin House where, seemingly by chance and coincidence, almost exactly fifty years later a film was being shot adapted from a novel by the author who had immortalized and mythologized the Dahlia case in crime fiction.

In *Black Dahlia Avenger*, Hodel identifies Captain Jack Donahue as a 'dark and as sinister a police captain as his fictional counterpart, Captain Dudley Smith' (Hodel 2004: 367). Whether Donahue was a firm or allusive inspiration for Ellroy when he created the character Dudley Smith is an intriguing question, but Hodel does not dwell on it. He paints a portrait of a shadowy figure allegedly involved in much of the corruption that was rife within the LAPD during the 1940s and 1950s. Donahue, the supervisor of the Dahlia investigation, was the Captain of Homicide Division when the murder occurred. Hodel speculated that Donahue may well have been involved in a cover-up of the original Dahlia investigation's findings, but he remained non-committal about the extent of Donahue's involvement. He does add 'Donahue retired fifteen years after the murder of Elizabeth Short and, like the fictional Captain Smith, died a hero to the department and the world' (Hodel 2004: 367). As the inspiration for Ellroy's most famous character it is perhaps fitting that Donahue reappears as a suspect in *The Black Dahlia Files* (2006) by Donald H. Wolfe, another true-crime writer whose dubious findings oddly parallel Ellroy's later work in the Underworld USA series. Completely dismissing Hodel's theory, Wolfe alleges that the Dahlia murder was connected to organized crime, and that Donahue deliberately misled the press in his investigation to protect his friend and associate Jack Dragna, the Boss of the Los Angeles Crime Family from 1931 to 1956. Although Ellroy did not begin thorough research into Dahlia history until 1984, he may have already known of Donahue's allegedly dubious role in the case, as he first fictionally tied Dudley Smith to the Dahlia case with the warehouse re-enactment scene in *Clandestine* published in 1982.

The sheer scale of the reception that Hodel's theory received, both positive and critical, soon made it untenable that Ellroy could in any way control the Dahlia narrative. Ellroy had woven his own brand of Dahlia mythology into formats as diverse as novels, short stories, memoirs, articles, interviews and endorsements, but now true-crime writers like Hodel and Wolfe were taking elements of the Quartet and Ellroy's life for their own narrative. For Ellroy, this would be problematic. The Quartet was his work and his characters were to be used as he saw fit. He had planned to 'leave legal documents so no one can ever co-opt my characters or write an Ellroy knock-off book' (Isaacs 2014). His Demon Dog persona was designed to be dominating: 'I'm too competitive ... I'm out to take over the show' (Powell 2013).

Much of the reaction to Hodel's work was immediately positive. Mark Nelson and Sarah Hudson Bayliss in their book *Exquisite Corpse: Surrealism and the Black Dahlia Murder* (2006) broadly supported Hodel's hypothesis. LA's Head Deputy District Attorney Stephen Kay was convinced by Hodel's findings (Hodel 2004: 439–48). The connections between the Surrealist movement and the Dahlia case had been percolating a few years prior to the release of *Black Dahlia Avenger* and the resultant publicity; the art historian Jonathan Wallis' article for *Rutgers Art Review* 'Case Open and/or Unsolved: Marcel Duchamp and the Black Dahlia Murder' explored the potentially sinister connection between the Dahlia case, Man Ray and Marcel Duchamp's work *Étant donnés* (1946–66), further evidence that Ellroy's narrative, through the Gwynplaine painting, had been closer to the actual facts of the case than he could have possibly anticipated.

Even before Wallis' article was published connections between the art world and the Dahlia were beginning to surface in lesser works such as Mary Pacios' *Childhood Shadows: The Hidden Story of the Black Dahlia Murder* (1999). Although her theory gained little traction, Pacios links the Dahlia murder to artwork and Hollywood. Pacios was a former neighbour of the Short family in Medford and claimed to be a childhood friend of Elizabeth Short. She also claimed the Short family were deeply upset by Ellroy's novel on the case and even considered suing him (Chorney 2000). Pacios, herself an artist who has produced paintings of Elizabeth Short, named Orson Welles as a plausible Dahlia suspect citing his interest in magic and the body-part mannequins which appear in the carnival funhouse climax to his film *The Lady from Shanghai* (1947). Again, a true-crime writer had made literal what Ellroy had rendered metaphorically in fiction. Elizabeth Short's dream of becoming a Hollywood starlet, and her exploitation, as well as that of thousands of young women with similar dreams, makes the film industry accountable for her death in Ellroy's narrative. Short is murdered on one of Emmett Sprague's dilapidated properties in the Hollywood Hills. The setting, as Peter Messent has argued, is not a coincidence: 'For Hollywood, the very symbol of the American culture industry, is portrayed here as in a perversely unhealthy relationship with the young female victims it attracts' (Messent 2013: 197). Even though Pacios is critical of Ellroy, the links between a true-crime genre book exploring the corpse as art and Ellroy's 'Gwynplaine' solution in *The Black Dahlia* reveals the level of influence that Ellroy's fiction has developed. In his novel *Toros and Torsos* (2008) Craig McDonald, who has interviewed Ellroy on his thoughts about Dahlia true-crime theories, develops the theme of Surrealist murders, including the Black Dahlia murder, in a work he claims was inspired by 'haunting concepts put forth by authors Steve Hodel, Mark Nelson and Sarah Hudson Bayliss' (McDonald 2013). By this stage Ellroy had become a major influence in a constant recycling of works linking the Dahlia to Surrealism over which he had little control. The breakthrough in establishing the link between Surrealism and the Dahlia murder entailed that it was not James Ellroy, but Steve Hodel who was now the most prominent Dahlia figure. For years, Ellroy had spun the Dahlia mythology. Hodel had unravelled it, but by doing so he had shown how potentially close to the truth Ellroy's novel had been.

In the article 'My Mother and the Dahlia' written for the *Virginia Quarterly Review of Books* to coincide with the release of De Palma's *The Black Dahlia* adaptation, Ellroy expressed a desire to end his involvement in the spiralling Ellroy/mother/Dahlia narrative:

> I want this piece to redress imbalances in my previous writing about them. I want to close out their myth with an elegy. I want to grant them the peace of denied disclosure and never say another public word about them. (Ellroy 2006c: 215)

In the same essay, he symbolically links director Brian De Palma to author, victim and narrative – 'Now Betty Short's world and my world are his world' – continuing the narrative rather than closing it down (Ellroy 2006c: 220). The link between De Palma and Ellroy is solidified in the film which contains footage of Paul Leni's film adaptation of *The Man Who Laughs* (1929). Blanchard, Bleichert and Kay watch a screening of the film together. De Palma takes the role of a casting director in *The Black Dahlia*, although he does not appear onscreen and only his voice is heard, taunting Elizabeth Short, played by Mia Kirshner, throughout her auditions. This seems to mirror the relationship Ellroy has with Short in their roles as author and character, here evolved into director and actress, although Ellroy would never feel comfortable taunting Short as De Palma does in character as her connection with his mother would not allow it.

By the time *The Black Dahlia* film adaptation was released, Ellroy had clarified his endorsement of Steve Hodel's theory in a more reserved tone, stating that *Black Dahlia Avenger* was only viable because it was corroborated by the original District Attorney Bureau file that was unearthed by *LA Times* journalist Steve Lopez in 2003. The file revealed that George Hodel was the prime suspect of the original investigation. The same file featured a transcript of a covert recording they had taken of George Hodel in which he came close to confessing to the murder. This had been one of the original revelations that had so impressed him in the 'Aftermath' chapter:

> If indeed, as I suspect, that those pictures are not of Elizabeth Short, but he (Steve Hodel) investigates the case at great length, puts together a finally unconvincing case, but it turns out his old man was the number one suspect and admitted it on a tape. That's enough. (McDonald 2006: 137)

Here Ellroy does not reference Hodel's views on the murder of Jean Ellroy or the parallels between his fiction and Hodel's theory. He dismisses the photographs Hodel found, which formed the catalyst for the investigation, as not being Elizabeth Short, and dubs Hodel's case 'unconvincing'. Hodel's work is reduced to being correct by chance, not by the narrative of his investigation. As Ellroy was beginning to distance himself from the work of Harnisch and Hodel, unsurprisingly, both true-crime writers expressed some degree of regret over Ellroy's endorsements, with Harnisch commenting, 'James Ellroy's various endorsements ... have more to do with Ellroy's well-established hunger for publicity rather than genuine support of any particular theory' (Harnisch 2010). Hodel was rather less critical: 'I know for a fact that James truly regrets writing the Foreword to my book. However, I suspect that his real regret is coming not so much *from the heart*, but rather from Ellroy, the businessman. And, believe me James is first and foremost - a businessman. His business is the promoting and marketing of James Ellroy, and he is very good at it' (Hodel 2010). Hodel's distinction between Ellroy's emotional involvement and his business interest in the case overshadows how Ellroy had been genuinely impressed with some of Hodel's research and wanted to add his own narrative contribution to it through endorsement. The regret came when he found himself unprepared for how events developed. Through his involvement with Harnisch and Hodel, Ellroy realized he had lost his prominence in the Dahlia narrative. To move away from the murky world of true-crime theories, Ellroy sketched out a plan through which he would reclaim the Dahlia narrative in fiction.

Perfidia: Ellroy's Black Dahlia legacy

In 2009, *The Bookseller* reported that Ellroy had been paid a six-figure sum to write four novels comprising a second Los Angeles Quartet, the setting of which would precede the first Quartet chronologically and revisit the established characters at earlier points in their lives (Page 2009). This was a major gamble by Ellroy. Now in his sixties, and with the gap between the publication of each novel getting longer and longer due to their epic scope, the Second Quartet was clearly intended as the last major project of his writing career. If the first novel, *Perfidia*, was not a success, then Ellroy had tied himself to writing three more books in the same series. Ellroy was betting everything on the belief that readers and critics would want to return to the fictional universe of the LA Quartet and Underworld USA trilogy so that eventually the 'three series span thirty-one years and will stand as one novelistic history' (Ellroy 2014: 697). As a stylist he risked looking conventional. But after the mixed critical reception of *The Cold Six Thousand* and *Blood's a Rover,* a re-examination of his past successes may have swayed Ellroy to embark on the project. Ellroy himself claimed the foundation of the plotline of *Perfidia* came to him in an epiphany while looking out of his apartment window:

> Novelist James Ellroy prides himself on living in the past, and sometimes his obsessive backward gazing pays off. One lonely Saturday night a few years back, he stood at his window in the Ravenswood — the Art Deco apartment on Rossmore Avenue best known for Mae West's longtime residency — and had a vision.
>
> 'It was handcuffed Japanese Americans,' he purrs. 'In a military vehicle, soldiers up front, going up a snow-capped road to Manzanar in the dead of winter. Bam! The Second L.A. Quartet.' (Timberg 2014)

Ellroy's claim to have decided to write the Second LA Quartet after a vision may be somewhat overstated. A close look at the minor Dahlia narratives Ellroy had authored since the publication of *The Black Dahlia* in 1987 suggests a gradual reintroduction of Dahlia and Quartet narratives in his writing. *Perfidia*, however, would lead to his most expansive revision of the Dahlia narrative yet.

The structure of *Perfidia* evokes narrative connections with all four novels of the Quartet. As the first novel of a new Quartet, *Perfidia* may be the most closely related to *The Black Dahlia* in terms of narrative connections as it features as a principal viewpoint character Kay Lake, as well as Bucky Bleichert and Lee Blanchard in the 'Dramatis Personae' – the same three characters who had formed the three points of the trinity before the discovery of Elizabeth Short's corpse in the novel leads to transmogrification and the constant movement of characters in new trinities (Ellroy 2014: 697). Even the title *Perfidia* is drawn from *The Black Dahlia*, as Blanchard and Kay dance to it on New Year's Eve:

> On New Year's Eve, we drove down to Balboa Island to catch Stan Kenton's band. We danced in 1947, high on champagne, and Kay flipped coins to see who got last dance and first kiss when midnight hit. Lee won the dance, and I watched them swirl across the floor to 'Perfidia,' feeling awe for the way they had changed my life. Then it was midnight, the band fired up, and I didn't know how to play it. Kay took the problem away, kissing me softly on the lips, whispering, 'I love you, Dwight.' A fat woman grabbed me and blew a noisemaker in my face before I could return the words. We drove home on Pacific Coast Highway, part of a long stream of horn-honking revellers. When we got to the house, my car wouldn't start, so I made myself a bed on the couch and promptly passed out from too much booze. Sometime toward dawn, I woke up to strange sounds muffling through the walls. I perked my ears to identify them, picking out sobs followed by Kay's voice, softer and lower than I had ever heard it. The sobbing got worse – trailing into whimpers. I pulled the pillow over my head and forced myself back to sleep. (Ellroy 1987: 64–5)

Perfidia is the Spanish word for treachery. The lyrics of the song written by Alberto Dominguez, and covered by many artists since, refer to a love ripped apart by betrayal: 'To you my heart cries out "Perfidia" / For I find you, the love of my life / In somebody else's arms' (Dominguez 1939). The behaviour of Blanchard, Bleichert and Kay suggests an unusual interaction and reliance on trade-offs. Bucky loses the dance but wins the kiss, and it is the kiss that is the most revealing, as Bucky now knows that his outwardly platonic friendship with Kay is anything but. 'Perfidia' is the perfect background music for Kay and Blanchard's dance, as Bleichert looks on, slowly finding himself falling in love with Kay, and rendering the trinity of Kay, Bleichert and Blanchard riddled with deceit. Communication comes less through words, although Kay says to Bleichert 'I love you', than it does from expressions. Kay's sobs are a signal to Bleichert that he cannot bear to hear.

Further links with *The Black Dahlia* can be found in *Perfidia* through the diary entries of Kay which appear throughout the text. *The Black Dahlia* is structured entirely as the first-person narrative of Bleichert. As a consequence, the reader is not drawn into the thought processes of Kay, but shares Bleichert's external viewpoint of this most pensive of characters. Ellroy cooled on first-person narration after *The Black Dahlia* as his increasingly complicated plotting and epic narratives required multiple viewpoints. *Perfidia* marks a partial return to the first person, as although Ellroy allows other lead characters expression through a subjective third-person style, Kay's perspective is committed to paper through her own words. Her first diary entry is preceded by the line, **'COMPILED AND CHRONOLOGICALLY INSERTED BY THE LOS ANGELES POLICE MUSEUM'** (Ellroy 2014: 24). The detail is intriguing as the novel was billed as 'real-time narration', with the action taking place over three weeks from 6 to 29 December 1941 (Lindquist 2014). To achieve the real-time effect, huge sections of the novel are set over a specific day with one scene beginning at the exact moment in time another scene ends, even if there is a change in viewpoint. Kay's diary and the bureaucratic minutiae which precede the first entry skew the linear timeframe and sense of real time, as Kay is looking back through the written word, and *Perfidia* is potentially linked with the denouement of *Blood's a Rover*, a novel set thirty years later, as Kay's diary could be just another item in Don 'Crutch' Crutchfield's massive archive of files potentially connecting documents which appear throughout Ellroy's historical novels.

Kay writes that she has begun her diary on impulse after seeing from her bedroom terrace 'A line of armored vehicles chugged west on Sunset, to fevered scrutiny and applause' (Ellroy 2014: 24). Knowing that it portends her country going to war, the image triggers a chain reaction of memory in Kay: her upbringing in Sioux Falls; South Dakota, the brutal murder of a black man by the Ku Klux Klan; her ill-fated involvement with Jazz drummer and dope peddler Bobby DeWitt; and how this led her to Lee Blanchard and the heart of the LAPD. The memories stop as the convoy passes out of her view, and the diary entry ends 'Nothing before this moment exists. The war is coming. I'm going to enlist' (Ellroy 2014: 30). Kay's words are prophetic – the following day, the Japanese attack Pearl Harbour – and also reflexive: she reimagines her whole life up to this point as the convoy passes. The story is not dissimilar to Ellroy's claim to have had a vision from his apartment window of a convoy of trucks transporting Japanese-Americans to internment camps. Just as Kay's vision is the catalyst of her reliving a narrative, Ellroy's vision prompted a reliving and revising of narrative. The switching of timeframes is complicated. Action unfolds in both real time and reflection, and an entire life is relived in the passing of a convoy. Kay's sudden decision to stop the reminiscence indicates the changed reality; every character's life will be different now that the country is at war. But it also shows how Ellroy has completely reinvented the Quartet narrative: 'Nothing before this moment exists.' Kay reveals she was in love with Bleichert long before they actually met. She follows his boxing career, 'His circumspection in the ring delights me. I have never spoken to Bucky Bleichert, but I am certain that I understand him', and telephones his house only to hang up when he replies, deferring their moment of first contact until events covered in *The Black Dahlia* and inviting a rereading of their relationship in that novel as a result (Ellroy 2014: 25). Through writing a second Quartet, Ellroy has instigated a reassessment of the first.

A strong link with the narrative of *The Black Dahlia* can be found in the appearance of Elizabeth Short as a living character. In *The Black Dahlia* she haunts the characters and Ellroy himself, leading to the transmogrification with Jean Ellroy which is central to Ellroy's identity as the Demon Dog. In *Perfidia*, she appears in the flesh, and is revealed to be the illegitimate daughter of Dudley Smith. Here Ellroy has delivered a massive upset to the Quartet narrative and taken a significant risk. Smith is not a character in *The Black Dahlia*, so then how will Smith be moved out of the picture when the new Quartet reaches the Dahlia investigation? It would seem completely out of character for Smith not to be involved in an investigation into the murder of his daughter. Smith is referenced as being involved in the Dahlia investigation in *Clandestine* but that is merely a few pages of text in which he describes the failed re-enactment of the Dahlia murder featuring a lookalike corpse. *Clandestine* is not part of the Quartet, and the same re-enactment scene appears in *The Black Dahlia*, only without Smith present. Having made this significant, and potentially problematic, revelation in *Perfidia*, Ellroy does not ingrain it deeply into the plotting. There are many possibilities about the relationship that Ellroy leaves open, possibly for development later in the series.

The most striking scene between Smith and Elizabeth Short comes when he takes her with his lover, film star Bette Davis, to see Orson Welles' *Citizen Kane*. Also in attendance is Short's friend from

Massachusetts, the blind Tommy Gilfoyle. There are multiple viewings within the scene. Short narrates the film for Gilfoyle, who, ironically, as Jim Mancall notes, can see a kindness in her the other characters do not: 'Short's storytelling allows her, momentarily, to mediate the Hollywood spectacle that will ultimately consume her, and in turn, Gilfoyle sees Short's kindness and talent' (Mancall 2014: 88). There is the film star on the screen and the film star in the audience. Davis watches Short as she narrates, observing the similarities she has with her father and absorbing her mannerisms for use in future performance: 'She would know Beth's every tic by suppertime. She would deftly mimic Beth by dessert' (Ellroy 2014: 581). Smith watches the film in a state of agitation. He is the only one not taken in by the 'idiot muckraking and invasive technique', and knows details about Welles' lurid personal life that Beth and Gilfoyle, at least, are oblivious too: 'Young Welles scrounged coon maids off Beverly Hills bus stops. He bamboozled them with maryjane and magic tricks. He plied them with his cricket dick and drove them home to coontown' (Ellroy 2014: 582). Smith's disturbing account of Welles is telling given that Ellroy must have been aware of Mary Pacios' *Childhood Shadows* which alleged that Welles was the Dahlia killer. Although it is doubtful that Ellroy would take Pacios' claims seriously, he is at least prepared to reference them allusively in fiction, and he does have an axe to grind: 'I hate Orson Welles and *Citizen Kane*' (Gogniat 2014). Like Kay with Bleichert, Short has never met Welles but understands his work: 'Beth caught the style and conveyed it frame for frame' (Ellroy 2014: 582).

Smith's parentage of Short is reminiscent of the skewed lines of the Sprague family which led to the Black Dahlia murder. Ellroy experimented with a number of ideas which could link him as author with the bloodlines of his fictional characters before he eventually settled on the Smith/Dahlia storyline. In an interview for *Los Angeles Magazine*, Ellroy tantalized the interviewer by revealing the setting will begin in 1941, shortly before the Japanese attack on Pearl Harbour, and the plot will concern Dudley Smith falling in love with a young nurse by the name of Jean Ellroy: ' "Turns out LAPD officer Dudley Smith, a central player in the earlier books, hasn't gone bad yet", Ellroy says. "He's in love with a striking redhead from the Wisconsin boondocks, a woman by the name of Jean Hilliker." As in his mother, Geneva? "Oh yeah," he says. "Oh yeah! Why not?"' (Wallace 2010). Ellroy abandoned this plan on the advice of his editor Sonny Mehta, but he did not entirely give up on the idea of a character based either wholly or in part on his mother. In *Perfidia*, William H. Parker is obsessed with a redheaded US Navy nurse named Joan Conville. Parker is trying to trace her whereabouts, but his motivation and history with the character is not fully revealed. He employs the investigative skills of LAPD Lieutenant Thad Brown and learns that Conville is 'a home wrecker and more than a bit of a wild one' (Ellroy 2014: 482). In an interview with Chris Wallace, Ellroy claimed:

> my original plan was to base Joan Conville, the navy nurse in *Perfidia*, on my mother, Jean Hilliker—righteous Jean Hilliker. And she and Parker [Los Angeles chief of police from 1950 to 1966, William H. Parker, a central character in *Perfidia*] have an affair the next book. But, do you really want to have Whiskey Bill Parker fucking your mother? Haven't we had enough of this woman? (Wallace 2014)

References to Conville are brief and elliptical. As *Perfidia* ends on 29 December 1941, Ellroy has a number of ways of developing the character further as the Second Quartet moves closer to events in *The Black Dahlia*. The surname Conville links to the grotesque Sprague family as Emmett Sprague's natural daughter with the Dahlia killer Ramona Sprague is named Martha McConville Sprague. The genesis of the Conville surname could be a link to Ellroy: 'this unusual surname is of Irish origin, and is an Anglicized form of the Gaelic "MacConmhaoil", the prefix "mac" denoting son of, plus the personal name "Conmhaoil", composed of the elements "cu" meaning hound' (Anon 2014). Despite changing his plans for *Perfidia* several times Ellroy is still experimenting with tying his own family history to the narrative of the Quartet using his well-established technique of mixed and ambiguous bloodlines. McConville translates as son of a hound, or in this case Demon Dog.

The continuation of the Dahlia narrative through *Perfidia* is an ongoing process that Ellroy began as a child with his dreams, nightmares and fantasies of rescuing Elizabeth Short and solving her murder. The Dahlia narrative became more formal at the beginning of Ellroy's writing career with the brief but important references to Short in his early novels *Brown's Requiem, Clandestine* and *Blood on the Moon*; the publicity tour for *The Black Dahlia* in which he expounded on the symbolic links with his mother's case and further developed his Demon Dog persona; the publication of *My Dark Places*, which detailed his reinvestigation of his mother's murder and included information on the drafting process of *The Black Dahlia*; the short story prequels to *The Black Dahlia* featuring Lee Blanchard published in *Hollywood Nocturnes*; his public friendship with Dana Delany and the novellas this inspired published in *Destination Morgue!*; and his involvement with Dahlia researchers with opposing views on the case – Larry Harnisch and Steve Hodel. In terms of his authorial control, the least successful was the debacle of the Harnisch/Hodel affair, and it was during this period that Ellroy made repeated comments about ending his involvement with the Dahlia legacy. However, this failure has been reversed. Ellroy has reclaimed the Black Dahlia narrative through *Perfidia*, and will continue to develop it in forthcoming novels.

4
Developing Noir: The Los Angeles Quartet

By James Ellroy's own account, the LA Quartet was a remarkable achievement: 'I have finished the LA Quartet. It is considered a monument of some sort—I consider it a great monument, like Mount Rushmore, and so does my dog, my wife, my agent and my current publisher' (Duncan 1996: 74). Ellroy has never been prone to false modesty, and it would not be an exaggeration to state that the Quartet – *The Black Dahlia* (1987), *The Big Nowhere* (1988), *L.A. Confidential* (1990) and *White Jazz* (1992) – made Ellroy a celebrity crime writer and gave birth to a distinct writing style, 'Ellrovian' (Ellroy 2009a). The LA Quartet had three defining features which contributed to its success: a cinematic prose style, a self-referential take on noir and an epic narrative with seemingly endless capacity for continuation. Despite its name, Ellroy has not limited the Quartet series to four novels; rather he has continued to explore Quartet narratives in other formats such as short stories and interviews, culminating in his announcement in 2009 that he would write four prequels to the series.

One of Ellroy's ambitions with the Quartet was to debate the status of noir. Yet despite his clear impact on the genre, his own position as a noir writer is not easy to define. The most pragmatic genre classification of Ellroy's Quartet is that they are neo-noir novels in a classic retro noir setting. However, any label seems too constricting given the level of narrative experimentation in the novels. Ironically, the open-ended, idiosyncratic noir style Ellroy established in the Quartet was nevertheless for him a clear endpoint for the genre, a marker establishing the furthest boundary of noir, leaving no room for future growth.

The extent to which Ellroy's Quartet conforms to genre conventions is debatable. George Tuttle's strict definition of noir fiction would suggest that the Quartet evades easy categorization:

> Noir fiction, in America, can be defined as a sub-genre of the Hardboiled School. In this sub-genre, the protagonist is usually not a detective, but instead either a victim, a suspect, or a perpetrator. He is someone tied directly to the crime, not an outsider called to solve or fix the situation. (Tuttle 2006)

The Quartet's leading men are usually detectives of some sort; however, this does not stop them from being 'tied directly to the crime'. Often, Ellroy's detectives passively allow crime or profit directly from a corrupt system. The Quartet, as I shall argue, is akin to a form of literary film noir wherein the noir era of late 1940s and 1950s LA is reimagined through a radical, cinematic prose style.

The genesis of Ellroy's plans for the Quartet can be found in his contemptuous attitude to traditional series-based crime fiction. By his own account, Ellroy was ignoring the advice of editors who preferred authors to 'write a series character, a sympathetic private eye, British inspector, innocent person who keeps getting caught up in violent intrigue, so that readers can have somebody to come back to and come back to and come back to. I have decided to ignore that rule and forge my own territory' (Duncan 1996: 78). Ellroy had created a Chandler-inspired private detective in his first novel *Brown's Requiem*, but later shifted to a maverick LAPD detective in the Lloyd Hopkins novels.

The structure of the Hopkins series, which follows a fairly rigid chronological and single-character focus, seems orthodox when read alongside the Quartet, which alternates between several leading characters in a narrative timespan of over a decade. By defining himself post-Lloyd Hopkins as against certain restrictive trends in crime fiction, and developing a more idiosyncratic style in the Quartet, Ellroy created a looser, more fluid and more complex series that is, stylistically, distinctly his own.

Intention and reception, however, have also shaped the novels that make up the Quartet. Ellroy only decided to write a series of LA-based historical novels as an afterthought to the success of *The Black Dahlia*, a novel which, as demonstrated in the previous chapter, can be read independently of the Quartet. William Freiburger has argued that Ellroy's second novel *Clandestine* (1982), which includes the key Quartet character Dudley Smith, 'ought to be included with the later novels to make up an LA Quintet' (Freiburger 1996: 95). Freiburger's argument could be taken much further, as in Ellroy's post-Quartet work, he has experimented with minor Quartet narratives, expanding the series beyond the parameters of Quartet or Quintet labels. Ellroy revealed that he had planned to make the leading character of *Clandestine*, Freddy Underhill, the main protagonist of *White Jazz*, a role which eventually became Dave 'the Enforcer' Klein (Swaim 1987: 18). In addition, Ellroy's UK publishers released *The Big Nowhere, L.A. Confidential* and *White Jazz*, the three Quartet novels featuring Dudley Smith, as the *The Dudley Smith Trio* (1999), recasting Ellroy's novels with a defining series character that he had sought to avoid but also, ironically, confirming the fluidity of the series by eschewing the Quartet label. The publication of *Perfidia* (2014), the first novel in Ellroy's Second LA Quartet, is further evidence that the labels of Quartet, Quintet or Octet will never satisfactorily classify Ellroy's series fiction.

The four novels that ostensibly comprise the first Quartet are distinctly noir in style and atmosphere, if not always in narrative structure. Ellroy found more fertile ground for experimentation, and a tradition of moral ambiguity, in noir. To follow the narrative lines of the LA Quartet as a series, it is important to have an understanding of the status of noir as a genre in the era in which the novels are set. The Quartet is set in Los Angeles between 1947 and 1959, which puts both the setting and the timeframe within the classic film noir era. Despite what seems a clear decision on Ellroy's part to set the novels in a distinctly noir period, Lee Horsley has written of the problem of fixing dates to the beginning and ending of film noir in an article which examines the emergence of neo-noir:

> There was for some time a tendency on the part of film critics to argue that the label 'noir' could legitimately be applied only to a specific cycle of post-World War Two Hollywood films, the limits of which were most often fixed as 1941 (the year of John Huston's film of *The Maltese Falcon*) and 1958 (with Welles' *Touch of Evil* marking the end of the cycle). (Horsley 2002)

The timeframe of the Quartet suggests that Ellroy may hold what Horsley deems the conservative view of a noir cycle as lasting from the early 1940s to the end of the 1950s. Ellroy was knowledgeable about the new styles that were emerging in noir films from the 1960s onwards, and his novels, in style and theme, reflect the historical changes in the genre. More than merely replicating historical and film noir genre changes, Ellroy adds complexity to his choice of time period through the application of his own revisionist style, and thus questions the boundaries of noir.

One of the key early critical texts in the study of film noir came in 1955 with the publication of *A Panorama of American Film Noir, 1941–1953* by Raymond Borde and Etienne Chaumeton, in which they argued that film noir's defining characteristic was that it strove for a *'specific alienation'* (italics in original):

> The moral ambivalence, the criminality, the complex contradictions in motives and events, all conspire to make the viewer co-experience the anguish and insecurity which are the true emotions of contemporary *film noir*. All the films of this cycle create a similar emotional effect: *that state of tension instilled in the spectator when the psychological reference points are removed*. The aim of *film noir* was to create *a specific alienation*. (Borde and Chaumeton 1955: 27)

The themes of 'alienation' and 'insecurity' did not start with the Quartet but have existed in Ellroy's work from the beginning: his characters in the Lloyd Hopkins and Avon novels are mostly loners who are rejected by their love interests and are ultimately professional failures. The influence of noir on the Quartet, however, extended the Romantic isolation of characters in the Hopkins trilogy to a more clearly defined historical period and setting, one where missed chances and ill-fated decisions permeate society. Noir gave Ellroy a richer landscape than his previous contemporarily set novels. He was able to transpose the ambivalence, criminality and contradictions that Borde and Chaumeton identified onto a 1980s setting with Lloyd Hopkins, but he was also able apply the same theme in his historical fiction, which although set in the era of Borde and Chaumeton, has an added eighties sensibility in the graphic portrayal of sex and violence. In his depiction of Los Angeles in the 1940s and 1950s, Ellroy combined his interest in popular culture with his parents' history and his childhood fantasies, creating an emotive and very present relationship with the past that does not exist to the same extent in his earlier work.

Ellroy also experiments with noir's cinematic vision in the Quartet. In the Hopkins novels, Ellroy used cinema as a means of physical and psychological torture, for example in *Because the Night*, where a woman is forced to watch a snuff film which replicates her mother's murder. However, in the Quartet, Ellroy incorporated film noir more experimentally, and, most overtly, in *The Big Nowhere* through the device of 'Man

Camera'. Man Camera allows the reader to inhabit the role of investigator and director, spectator and participant, thus going beyond noir's receptive 'co-experience' as described by Borde and Chaumeton. Ellroy goes even further and makes the entire prose style of *L.A. Confidential* cinematic in the way it frames images scene by scene. The streamlined prose style, which removes description to increase the sense of immediate action, reads more like a screenplay than a novel.

Ellroy publicly maintains that he reads very little outside the crime fiction genre, so the extent to which he has studied film noir criticism is something he has kept to himself. Yet his idiosyncratic take on noir, both in fiction and other outlets, suggests a deep knowledge of the genre. Ellroy wrote the introduction to *The Best American Noir of the Century* (2011), ostensibly just a modest anthology of short stories. In his two-page contribution, Ellroy offers a definition of noir, couched in the dialect of the genre, which encapsulates the main themes of the Quartet:

> Noir sparked before the Big War and burned like a four-coil hot plate up to 1960. Cheap novels and cheap films about cheap people ran concurrent with American boosterism and yahooism and made a subversive point just by being. They described a fully existing fringe America and fed viewers and readers the demography of a Secret Pervert Republic. (Ellroy 2011: xiii)

Ellroy's 'Secret Pervert Republic' is a world governed by institutional conspiracies and sexual obsession. It tantalizes because it is secret, base and forbidden, a world which is more attractive to Ellroy than 'boosterism' and 'yahooism'. Culturally, noir may have seemed to be a marginal alternative; however, in narrative terms it is a powerful driving force 'just by being', a theme Ellroy explores further in his Underworld USA trilogy. The true narrative of the Quartet's universe is a noir one, and the real movers are the mobsters, bent cops and immoral politicians. When the secret world does emerge, it leaves readers feeling both tainted and titillated by the glimpse of the forbidden it voyeuristically provides.

Ellroy's reference to the 'Big War' suggests Ellroy recognizes that the themes of noir were percolating through society in the early 1940s before they became more prominent in post-war America. Noir as a genre was the product of a cultural boom arising from the economic boom in cities like LA during this period. The very economy that allowed for 'Cheap novels and cheap films about cheap people' sought to project a more successful and sterile image, and the upshot of this propaganda made noir tales both thrilling and bleak.

Ellroy has expanded the boundaries of noir to include the themes of his own work, but in doing so he is aware of the pitfalls of a fringe genre becoming too satiated in popular culture: 'the concept of noir has been bastardized. It's commonly misused' (Powell 2009: 194). Noir's effectiveness comes from retaining its power to subvert, which Ellroy tries to maintain through continual stylistic experimentation across the Quartet. Ellroy created some stark and pronounced differences between each novel, which ironically stabilized the series. Although radically different when read together, the prose styles in *The Big Nowhere* and *L.A. Confidential* were both recognizably Ellrovian. Yet experimentation can destroy as well as reinvigorate a genre, and Ellroy's final novel of the Quartet, *White Jazz*, in both plotting and prose style, takes noir to the brink of a metaphorical apocalypse.

After *The Black Dahlia*: the evolution of Ellroy's writing process

When planning the outline for *The Black Dahlia*, Ellroy had committed himself to painstaking research into the LAPD investigation of Elizabeth Short's murder and the press coverage of the case. By contrast, Ellroy's plans for *The Big Nowhere* seemed underwhelming. Like *The Black Dahlia*, the narrative focuses on sexually motivated torture-murder, in this case a series of murders. However, Ellroy claimed his inspiration was not a real-life investigation but an almost forgotten film:

> I was influenced by a bad William Friedkin movie from 1980, *Cruising*. It has a great premise. There are a string of homosexual murders in the West Village and Al Pacino is a young, presumably heterosexual cop, who goes undercover and is tempted by the homosexual world. (Rich 2009)

Although he accepts it was a 'bad' film, Ellroy adapted the basic outline of *Cruising* to his narrative structure. Despite this, *The Big Nowhere* is a novel that is not heavily indebted to any one literary or filmic influence. Instead, Ellroy would take the broader history of the period and the noir genre as his inspiration.

In contrast to Ellroy's casual and almost dismissive account of the main influence on *The Big Nowhere*, his drafting of *L.A. Confidential* was much more complex and essential both to the structure of the novel and to his Demon Dog persona. The planning and plotting of the novel was meticulous, and as a consequence, gruelling. Through a 211-page outline, Ellroy structured the novel scene by scene, alternating between the three main protagonists, Ed Exley, Jack Vincennes and Bud White, and including a supporting cast of over 80 minor characters. Despite his extraordinary efforts, Ellroy's first draft, an 800-page manuscript, was deemed too long, and Ellroy was disappointed when '[the editor] wanted me to make cuts for the sake of publishing costs' (Powell 2008a: 159). This editing process would be problematic for Ellroy: after the extraordinary effort he had made in outlining the novel, he had come to regard it as dramatically inviolate and felt the excision of a single scene or character would compromise the entire narrative.

According to Ellroy's agent Nat Sobel, the resolution came serendipitously:

> James came to my house to talk about what we could do about it. I had the manuscript on the desk in front of me, and as a joke I said to James, 'Well, maybe we could cut out a few small words.' I meant it entirely as a joke. But I started going through a manuscript page and cut out about a dozen words on the page. James said, 'Give me that.' I gave him the page. And he just kept cutting. He was cutting and cutting and cutting. When he was done with the page, it looked like a redacted piece from the CIA. I said, 'James, how would they be able to read this?' He said, 'Let me read you the page.' It was terrific. He said, 'I know what I have to do.' He took the whole manuscript back and cut hundreds of pages from the book and developed the style. That editor never knew what we had to do, but she forced him into creating this special Ellroy style, which his reputation as a stylist is really based on. It came from her, sight unseen, saying 'Cut 25 percent of the book.' He wound up cutting enough without cutting a single scene from that book. (Ferrari-Adler 2008)

A closer examination of Ellroy's work as a stylist in his previous eight novels suggests a more gradual evolution towards concision in sentence structure than the near-epiphany Sobel suggests. Ellroy's early novels *Brown's Requiem, Clandestine* and *Killer on the Road*, written from a first-person perspective, contain lengthy digressions by the character/narrator. The three Lloyd Hopkins novels marked the beginning of Ellroy's subjective third-person style which channelled much of Hopkins' mental detection and evidenced a leaner prose style. With the Quartet novels, Ellroy transitioned to shorter sentences, and the density of action and information communicated through a single page increased. The short sentences of the Quartet, however, were the hallmarks of Ellrovian prose, and, notably, Sobel claimed he was only convinced when Ellroy read the text aloud. Performance was key to 'this special Ellroy style', and its language was visual. The opening chapter of *L.A. Confidential* begins 'Bud White in an unmarked, watching the "1951" on the City Hall Christmas tree blink' (Ellroy 1990: 9). Of the several visual images which are conveyed in this sentence the descriptions are minimal. The '1951' is treated as a different object to the Christmas tree, and less an adornment of it. Ellroy's excision of words makes every object stand out in the framing of the sentence. Just as a multiplicity of images can fit into a single sentence, Ellroy was able to make sure that every scene and plot point of his original draft was able to remain in his substantial reduction of the manuscript length.

Ellroy's precise planning of the narratives helped him transition into writing historical fiction. The outline to *The Black Dahlia* was 144 pages and the finished novel came to 358 pages; *L.A. Confidential* had a 211-page outline and was a 480-page novel, and *White Jazz* had an outline of 172 pages and the novel was 359 pages. The ratio between the number of pages in the outline and the pages in the finished novel becomes smaller between the first and last novels of the Quartet, suggesting that Ellroy's outlines increasingly resembled a first draft whereby every character and plot point was so concisely planned that it was subsequently transferred to the manuscript version with minimum expansion. As I will argue, this explains why the screenplay to *L.A. Confidential* so closely resembled the novel in the scenes it directly adapted, even though Ellroy had no role in drafting the screenplay, as the prose style of *L.A. Confidential* convincingly imitated film noir and screenplay writing in its concision.

Despite its strong critical reputation, *L.A. Confidential* is by no means universally accepted as one of Ellroy's great works. Peter Wolfe argues, 'The novel dims much of its luster by being too big, too sprawling, and too full of its own surge' (Wolfe 2005: 183). The surge Wolfe refers to lies in the energy of the lean prose which gives Ellroy's take on noir an exhilarating effect. The downbeat alienation of noir is invigorating in Ellroy's hands, but for critics like Wolfe it leaves the story swamped by the style. Ellroy was leaving himself open to criticism as his developing writing style prohibited or greatly minimized any restructuring of the narrative between the outline and the finished novel. If the outline was flawed, the issues would not be resolved in drafting the novel because few changes could be made. Another factor would be Ellroy's Luddite view of technology: '[Ellroy] writes with a fountain pen on white ruled paper. He edits the draft with red ink before an assistant types it up—he has never learnt to type, let alone use a computer—then goes over it again in red ink' (Sharkey 2009: 207). As the novels were getting longer, the ability to revise plotting during the drafting stage was diminished as there was limited space on the page for revisions before the manuscript was sent to a typist.

The sparse, distinct style Ellroy had achieved with *L.A. Confidential*, which was partly reliant on the removal of what he deemed unnecessary words, such as adverbs, adjectives and conjunctions, would become an issue in the first draft of *White Jazz*. According to Martin Kihn, Ellroy had taken this redacted style so far with *White Jazz* that words needed to be added back into the manuscript:

> The first draft of *Jazz*, for instance, was even more clipped and opaque than the version about to be published. Working first with Sobel, then Knopf editor Sonny Mehta, Ellroy painstakingly added words to the manuscript. 'The first draft was extremely challenging,' says Mehta. 'What James was doing was extremely ambitious. But I think you have to engage people and draw them into the story. And I thought essentially we had to make it a little easier for them.' (Kihn 1992: 34)

Ellroy, however, has offered a different account, claiming he only returned to the clipped style after finding the initial draft of the novel unsatisfactory: 'I started writing *White Jazz*, in a normally discursive, first-person style, but the book felt flabby to me, so I started cutting words' (Powell 2008a: 159). Ellroy's and Mehta's accounts of the drafting process, taken together, indicate that the manuscript underwent a laborious process in which thousands of words were cut and then many were subsequently restored. All of this was done with very few plot changes between drafts, as once Ellroy was satisfied with the outline for a Quartet novel, he largely adhered to it. He did, however, make one major plot change in the drafting of *White Jazz*. Ed Exley commits suicide in the original outline, but in the finished novel he is left alive so as to keep the narrative, and one might suggest the Quartet, open-ended (Ellroy 1992a).

The challenge to both reader and author created by the stylistic experimentation in the Quartet is apparent in *White Jazz*, as Ellroy strove to replicate and reinvent a specific style, which by this time bore his name. Carole Allamand dubbed Bucky Bleichert an example of 'the Ellroyian detective', although Ellroy himself used the term 'Ellrovian' to describe his plotting and prose style in the epilogue to the outline of *Blood's A Rover* (Allamand 2006: 362; Ellroy 2009a). In coining the term, Allamand was referring to the shared obsessions of Ellroy and his leading character, but as a writing technique, Ellrovian could be extended to the channelling of obsession in the style, plotting and prose of the Quartet. In *White Jazz*, Ellroy attempts to engage noir with the surreal elements of Black Bebop Jazz, as shown through the disorientating and fractured first-person voice of Dave 'the Enforcer' Klein. By sharing Klein's viewpoint, the reader is taken on a grotesque journey through a brief but insanely violent period in LA history.

The critical reaction to *White Jazz* confirmed Ellroy's ambition for the novel to be, if not quite the end, then a definitive work in the noir genre, 'I realized that I had taken the police historical novel as far as it could go' (Rich 2008: 185). David Peace described *White Jazz* as the best crime novel ever written: 'His novel *White Jazz* was the Sex Pistols for me. It reinvented crime writing and I realised that, if you want to write the best crime book, then you have to write better than Ellroy' (Wroe 2008). Woody Haut agreed with Ellroy's claim that he had brought noir to some form of perfect conclusion. Yet, as Peace suggested, the end result was reinvention and reassessment rather than the final word on noir that Ellroy claimed it to be. Haut argues *White Jazz* is the dramatic endpoint of a long period of noir, which had become too confined within the limits of its own definition, and was its catalyst for change:

> Neon noir fiction ... reaches its apogee with James Ellroy's *White Jazz*. After Ellroy's fragmented assault, the crime novel would have to reassess its place in the culture. For Ellroy's work suggests that crime fiction is at its most subversive not when it retreats into the confines of the genre, but when it stretches its narrative boundaries and rules regarding subject, style and plot. With its historical resonances, *White Jazz* mirrors the last days of the Reagan-Bush era, and, in doing so, becomes the quintessential noir product. 'The last word in atrocity, cynicism and horror', wrote André Gide in reference to Dashiell Hammett's 1929 *Red Harvest*. He might just as well have been referring to *White Jazz*. But times change. These days, Hammett is the epitome of good taste, while Ellroy has become the most recent example of extremism in pursuit of vice. (Haut 1999: 10)

For Haut, Ellroy's noir style is more subversive than Hammett's as the gradually widening acceptance of the politically subversive crime writer's place in the genre has ironically given him a respectability, albeit posthumously, that Ellroy, as a polemicist, has sought to avoid. Ellroy seems aware that he is reinventing Hammett's own endpoint of noir – what Gide called his 'last word'. Ellroy was inspired by Hammett's perspective of the 'bad men of history, on the leg-breakers, and that in essence is what the Continental Op was all about' (Silet 1995: 43). Ellroy not only reassesses the past, his historical characters are a comment on the present. Murders may be solved and some form of justice achieved, but organized crime and LAPD corruption still remain the dominant social order and individuals work within and largely accept this system. Haut reads this as an indictment of 'the last days of the Reagan-Bush era', but to analyse Ellroy's contribution to the genre through the prism of liberal politics is fraught with risk. Ellroy is an admirer of Reagan, 'one of the greatest American leaders of the past two hundred years' (Powell 2009: 199). Ironically, Ellroy's right-wing sentiment in the Quartet has delivered a subversive effect on the genre similarly to Hammett's communist views in *Red Harvest*.

In *White Jazz*, the social order is restored but not reformed after being on the verge of a complete anarchic breakdown. The brutally violent restoration of order in *Red Harvest* reflects Hammett's pessimistic view of the capitalist system, whereas Ellroy takes a more nuanced, individualistic view with his novel: the cycle of violence winds down, but its protagonist Klein looks forward to his revenge. The continuation of the narrative beyond the last page through Klein keeps the conclusion of Ellroy's noir vision alive with the threat or promise of violence to come. In Klein's closing words, simmering sexual tension is connected to the possibility of violence: '*Love me fierce in danger*' (Ellroy 1992c: 359).

In *White Jazz*, the reader is still a voyeur by the final page, excited by the noir world and its necessity of violence. There is a parallel between the narrative of the novel and the history of the genre as Ellroy sees it. Klein will be going back, hell-bent on revenge, to a very different LA, outside the classic noir age. But the promise of his reappearance embodies Ellroy's retro noir style. Klein, like Ellroy, is an invasive and subversive character in the noir genre.

The Big Nowhere and 'Man Camera'

The Big Nowhere begins a few moments before midnight on New Year's Eve, 1949. The date is significant as LA is transitioning from the grim eras of the Great Depression and the Second World War into a post-war economic boom time. The LAPD is still recovering from the repercussions of the unsolved Black Dahlia murder case. The sadism and torture of the Dahlia slaying serve as a microcosm of the brutality of the wars and revolutions which had plagued the first half of the twentieth century. It also reflects the events still influencing LA at that time, such as the political witch-hunts of suspected communist sympathizers within the motion-picture industry. The hopes and fears of the characters are succinctly described by Norton Layman, LA's Chief Medical Examiner: 'May God bless our new epoch with rather less business than the first half of this rather bloody century' (Ellroy 1988: 6).

Ellroy limns the plotlines of a series of sadistic murders and the 'Second Red Scare' from the point of view of three men: Detective Deputy Danny Upshaw of the Los Angeles Sheriff's Department, Lieutenant Mal Considine of the District Attorney's Criminal Investigation Bureau and Turner 'Buzz' Meeks, an ex-LAPD man turned organized-crime associate. The intersecting of these men's lives parallels the institutional rivalry and paranoia that drives much of the narrative. Whatever the characters' aspirations, 1950 begins with the police responding to a series of incidents ranging from the gruesome to the banal. Upshaw receives the most dramatic call-out of the night when he arrives at the murder site of a man who has been tortured to death. The case bears a striking resemblance to the Black Dahlia murder in the torture details, but when more murders occur, the press gives little coverage as the victims are vagrants and homosexuals who are less newsworthy than the aspiring starlet Elizabeth Short. Layman describes their disinterest as 'reverse Black Dahlia syndrome' (Ellroy 1988: 151). The key word of the title, 'Nowhere', contrasts in its vagueness and negativity with the title of the previous novel, *The Black Dahlia*, which alludes to a single woman, a single murder and a single obsession. The Dahlia is a tangible symbol of the age, whereas *The Big Nowhere* draws on the nihilism of noir: there is no avenger for political and social wrongs, and obsessions prove to be empty and pointless. The philosophy of noir holds the characters in a self-defeating trap, a 'Big Nowhere'. It is the darkness the characters pass through before they enter Chandler's 'Big Sleep'.

The fatalism of noir is that very little changes; people are trapped in recurring impossible problems which makes the society that noir portrays inherently conservative. As Lee Horsley puts it in regard to noir narratives:

> Apparent normality is actually the antithesis of what it seems to be: it is brutal rather than benign, dehumanised not civilised. In the course of the story, it becomes clear that the things that are amiss cannot be dealt with rationally and cannot ultimately be put to rights. (Horsley 2001: 11)

The allusiveness of 'right' is both the basis for obsession and the tragic flaw that leads to an individual's downfall. By contrast, the institutionalized wrong, the collective 'normality' which Ellroy's luckless mavericks face is inescapable. Upshaw finds his case is hampered by jurisdictional rivalry between the County Sheriff's Office and the LAPD and by the prevalent bigotry or indifference his peers show towards the victims. As one policeman tells him, 'let sleeping queers lie' (Ellroy 1988: 162). Offended by the remark (as it is closer to home than he yet realizes), Upshaw refuses to relent in his investigation, living up to his nickname 'Upstart' Upshaw.

Upshaw employs a technique called 'Man Camera', devised by Hans Maslick, which replicates the murder from the killer's viewpoint, thus, reconstructing the crime and developing a profile of the perpetrator:

> In a famous essay, Maslick described a technique he had developed while undergoing analysis with Sigmund Freud. It was called Man Camera, and involved screening details from the perpetrator's viewpoint. Actual camera angles and tricks were employed; the investigator's eyes became a lens capable of zooming in and out, freezing close-ups, selecting background motifs to interpret crime-scene evidence in an aesthetic light. (Ellroy 1988: 94)

Upshaw is a keen student of criminology. However, 'Man Camera', with its visual reconstruction of crime scenes, removes Upshaw from the objectivity of his role as investigator and puts him, cinematically, in the role of voyeur and perpetrator. Ellroy plays with the morally distortive killer/cop scenario he created in his early work, but with no named antagonist, the transmutation of feelings and ideas is more ambiguous. The 'aesthetic light' which Man Camera brings to the crime threatens Upshaw's position as a detective as he experiences the same homosexual desires which make up the image of the 'perpetrator's viewpoint'. The investigation becomes a means of personal voyeurism for Upshaw, and he is homo-eroticized by the criminal case partly as compensation for his failure to convincingly act in a heterosexual role. Asked to go undercover to infiltrate a group of Hollywood-based communist sympathizers by seducing Claire 'the Red Queen' De Haven, Upshaw instead finds himself more attracted to the homosexual pimp Felix Gordean. The irony of Upshaw's character is that the deeper he goes undercover, *double entendre* intended, the more his repressed homosexuality comes to the fore.

Upshaw's authoritative but obsessional use of criminology masks the fact that both Man Camera and Hans Maslick are inventions of Ellroy. Ellroy handles the subject of criminology in the narrative by combining his intuitive knowledge of detective work and his ability to imitate academic language convincingly. He is also subversive with details, as the name Hans Maslick is comically suggestive of an eccentric German scientist. Maslick is said to have developed Man Camera 'while undergoing analysis with Sigmund Freud': ironically his theory was teased out of him by Freud just as Man Camera slowly brings out Upshaw's sexuality. However, despite its outward scientific role, Man Camera is an inherently cinematic device. With Man Camera, Ellroy is parodying both the investigative technique of criminal profiling and his own role as an author or director, creating and 'playing' the roles of detective and killer.

Ellroy is less interested in the science of Man Camera than he is in human weaknesses and emotions revealed in the profiler. The subjectivity of Man Camera becomes a lens through which Upshaw increasingly gives in to his voyeuristic desires, thus the reader co-experiences the slow crumbling of Upshaw's heterosexual façade through his subjective third-person voice, as evidenced in his spying on gay men at an underground homosexual party:

> That close, he got distortion blur, Man Camera malfunctions. He pulled back so that his eyes could capture a larger frame, saw tuxedos entwined in movement, cheek-to-cheek tangos, all male. The faces were up against each other so that they couldn't be distinguished individually; Danny zoomed out, in, out, in, until he was pressed into the window glass with the pins and needles localized between his legs, his eyes honing for mid-shots, close-ups, faces. (Ellroy 1988: 166)

The defects of Upshaw's vision, 'distortion blur, Man Camera malfunctions' occur when his sight is literally impeded, but this oddly parallels Upshaw's inability to see how his repressed sexuality is destroying him. Film noir relies on what is illicit, hidden from view. Upshaw is outside the house watching the party through a large window which is symbolic of a cinema screen, yet Upshaw controls his view, as a film director, manipulating the image to the specifications of his sexual fantasies. The language merges man and machine, and Upshaw's personal feelings are ironically actualized through the dispassionate application of technology: 'Danny zoomed out, in, out, in, … his eyes honing for mid-shots, close-ups, faces.' Upshaw's camera focus is sexually revelatory, even though the window screen is a barrier between participant and spectator. As Upshaw is visually and emotionally drawn closer to events in the picture, the thin line between detective and criminal is blurred.

In noir, sex is more powerful as a subliminal theme. The 'Secret Pervert' Ellroy identifies as the spectator and protagonist of noir experiences sex through voyeurism. Upshaw resists the advances of attractive women, and he cannot consummate his desire for men. When his role as an investigator becomes untenable, he chooses to commit suicide. Upshaw decides that a gunshot through the mouth contains too much phallic symbolism and would invite derogatory remarks. Instead, he chooses the slower, more painful method of slitting his throat. Like Upshaw, several other characters appear relatively celibate and experience sexual feeling only through voyeurism. Felix Gordean experiences sexual excitement by manipulating outwardly straight men into discovering their homosexual feelings, luring them out of the closet. Considine has been twice cuckolded in his two failed marriages and focuses on his career to escape his chaotic personal life. Buzz Meeks appears to be the only sexually fulfilled male character through his affair with Mickey Cohen's mistress. He ends the novel being the only one of the three main characters still alive, but having abandoned the woman he loves for her own protection and in hiding from Cohen, Jack Dragna and Dudley Smith, his chances of survival appear almost non-existent. The fate of Meeks is revealed in the prologue to *L.A. Confidential*.

The visual image is one form of voyeuristic obsession in the novel, but music is of equal importance to *The Big Nowhere*'s narrative, and like Man Camera, is tied to Ellroy's fascination with film noir. Music is both an expression of the character's emotions and key evidence in the investigation. After Upshaw's suicide, Considine and Meeks try to solve the murder case he was working on. They discover that a jazz musician named Coleman Healy is the killer, and they trace him to a nightclub where he is performing. Coleman kills Considine, but then Meeks kills Coleman. After the bloodbath at the nightclub, Meeks locates the dying Dr Saul Lesnick, a psychiatrist and communist informant who had been shielding Coleman for many years. Lesnick reveals the connection between music and the killer's pathology:

> Coleman was fighting his urges inchoately, with music. He was working on a long solo piece filled with eerie silences to signify duplicities. The riffs would spotlight the unique high sounds he got with his sax, loud at first, then getting softer, with longer intervals of silence. The piece would end on a scale of diminishing notes, then unbroken quiet – which Coleman saw as being louder than any noise he could produce. He wanted to call his composition The Big Nowhere. (Ellroy 1988: 461)

'Big' is a well-established noir prefix, appearing in many film noir titles such as *The Big Sleep* (1941), *The Big Heat* (1953) and *The Big Combo*

(1955). Chandler used the word as a reference to death, as Philip Marlowe muses in the closing lines of *The Big Sleep*, 'You were dead, you were sleeping the big sleep, you were not bothered by things like that, oil and water were the same as wind and air to you' (Chandler 1939: 230–1). In noir jargon 'Big' refers to something absolute. Yet Coleman's 'The Big Nowhere' is ephemeral and undefinable. To fight his psychopathic urges, Coleman turns to music to give them a structure which he is able to control. But music only adds to his psychosis, as the 'unique high sounds' are contrasted with 'eerie silences', as his music and his mental state shift between extremes. In a sense Coleman wants his psychosis to be 'Nowhere'. If it is neither vocalized nor actualized, it exists only in his music. But this containment is impossible to sustain. The ending of the novel reads as a punch-line to a noir joke: the characters are looking for a solution to the murders which is ironically revealed in a musical void.

As a meta-reference to noir, the title *The Big Nowhere* oddly implicates Ellroy through association with his killer/musician, as both have chosen the same name for their respective works. The complexity of the plot requires Lesnick's long monologue to clarify events, but this also reads as Ellroy's justification of the narrative. The sly analogies about music give the novel an ambient noir atmosphere and also destabilize the text by placing Ellroy allusively amidst events, the author questioning the status of noir through his text and Coleman's music.

The irony of Ellroy's noir themes is that although author, characters and reader have a shared experience of the voyeurism, they also experience, as Borde and Chaumeton might put it, '*a specific alienation*'. In his introduction to the published *L.A. Confidential* screenplay, Ellroy claimed that his knowledge and experience of cinema rests almost exclusively in the film noir genre: 'My filmic pantheon rarely goes past 1959 and the end of the film noir age' (Ellroy 1997a: xvii). The claim might be somewhat disingenuous as he has also spoken of watching films from other genres during his childhood and after; to give one example, Ellroy had been to a screening of *The Vikings* (1958) shortly before he learned of his mother's death (Ellroy 1996: 12). However, in narrative terms, by presenting an image of his entire cultural experiences being connected to film noir Ellroy channels Upshaw's alienation and his inability to escape his own voyeurism, aligning himself as a speaker for and member of the 'Secret Pervert Republic'. Ellroy recognizes the limitations of noir and the quandary this puts him in as a writer. The boundaries of the genre can be as claustrophobic as the bleak world inhabited by the characters, and Ellroy's duty as a noir writer was to forge new territory through his own noir style.

In *The Big Nowhere*, as in his previous novels *Brown's Requiem* and *Suicide Hill*, Ellroy once again employs the dog motif which usually signals violence in the narrative. When Upshaw begins the investigation, he suspects that the killer is using dogs to desecrate the victim's bodies through his analysis of the bite marks on the corpses. Once he deems that scenario implausible, he speculates that the killer is wearing artificial dog's teeth in his mouth during the murders. His theory rests on the suspicion that the killer is a fellow voyeur, willing himself to have an out-of-body experience so that he can observe the killing committed by a breed of dog. The bite marks are finally revealed to be caused by wolverine teeth which the killer is wearing. Upshaw's suspicion that the killer has a fixation with canines forms one of the most disturbing aspects of the murder investigation, and Ellroy's repeated references to dogs is one of the idiosyncrasies of his writing. But unlike his previous novels, the torture of dogs or their use in torture is merely a stepping stone to a larger, unimaginable evil: the killer's metaphorical transformation into a human/animal hybrid of the rare and sadistic wolverine.

Ellroy's gory depiction of the murders in *The Big Nowhere* is consistent with his portrayal of violence as a constant presence in LA history. In his study of LA, *City of Quartz* (1992), Mike Davis dismissed the Quartet as 'At times an almost unendurable wordstorm of perversity and gore, *Quartet* attempts to map the history of modern Los Angeles as a secret continuum of sex crimes, satanic conspiracies, and political scandals' (Davis 1990: 45). Despite his often unwarranted criticism of Ellroy, Davis does identify the chief paradox of Ellrovian prose: for as much as words are cut from sentences, there is also an excess of words to describe any one issue Ellroy chooses to focus on, hence the 'wordstorm(s)'. When Considine is reading files on the influence of communist sympathizers in Hollywood, Ellroy's description of Considine's angry thoughts employs repetition as he avoids the standard construction of a sentence:

Deluded.
Traitorous.
Perverse.
Cliché shouters, sloganeers, fashion-conscious pseudoidealists.
(Ellroy 1988: 97)

Although verbs and conjunctions are missing from the one-word sentences, Ellroy extends Considine's thoughts through his bad-tempered variation on the same basic theme. Instead of moving the action forward, the description of Considine's thoughts immobilizes action, flooding the page with propaganda. But at the same time, by placing one word in a line, and by extension a paragraph, Ellroy does not allow any room for growth. This has almost comic ends in Considine's work, with his reference to fashion, be it political or in other forms. The prose reflects the political movement Considine has become involved with, which has woefully overstated the communist presence in the movie industry and sees things in words which do not exist in reality. The rhythm of the words is enticing even though the argument is hollow, and it is telling that Considine has chosen to stay late in his office and read these files rather than go home to his wife who will pester him with 'sex offers' (Ellroy 1988: 97). Considine and his wife are not on the same wavelength and he verbally reduces sex to a conjugal transaction, but the rhythm of his thoughts suggests he may be eroticized by his political beliefs.

Mike Davis' claim that the Quartet narratives are comprised of 'satanic conspiracies' is another over-reaction to both the violence and the portrayal of the Red Scare: although the Quartet is extremely violent, Ellroy is able to portray even the animalistic pathology of the serial killings in *The Big Nowhere* with a degree of sympathy. In any event 'satanic' is an odd choice of insult as it is unintentional reminder of Ellroy's Demon Dog persona and his aims as a novelist. Ellroy's writing may be interpreted as a subversive fictional history, wherein widespread conceptions of the past as a more morally conservative age are gleefully destroyed. Ellroy's triumphant distortion, which is also an unveiling, comes from his memory of the past as he lived it as a young boy, merged with documented historical events. This form of historical writing drawn from memory and cultural experience required very little research for three of the four Quartet novels:

> On *The Big Nowhere*, which is about the Red Scare in Hollywood in 1950, I read half a book on the subject, realized I could make the rest of the shit up, and threw the book away. *L.A. Confidential*—I only researched the Bloody Christmas police scandal of 1951 and tossed the rest of the books away. *White Jazz*—no research. (Duncan 1996: 75)

Ellroy rebelliously discards the forms of narrative and the factual details that would constrain him. His comment does not make the distinction between the Second Red Scare he portrays and the First Red Scare of 1919–21. Although he clearly knows the distinction, he plays fast and loose with historical terms in his interviews. The broad scope of *The Big Nowhere* gave Ellroy more liberty within LA history, as it was not merely a popular consensus on the ideas of the time period but his own personal history. It is historical fiction based on a form of fluid, emotional autobiography, and for Ellroy 'autobiography to me is growing up in LA when I did' (Powell 2009: 197).

Historical events such as the Sleepy Lagoon murder, the Zoot Suits riots, the Brenda Allen scandal, and the assassination attempts on Mickey Cohen all form part of either the back story or the main narrative timeframe of the novel. Ellroy does not go into excessive detail regarding these events, but rather uses them as a malleable foundation from which he can construct narrative. By lightly describing historical events as the framework or parameters of his fictional world, Ellroy could create fictional organizations that operate alongside genuine ones, and fictional characters interacting with historical ones. In *The Big Nowhere*, Considine investigates the United Alliance of Extras and Stagehands' role in the Sleepy Lagoon Defense Committee, but only the latter organization actually existed. By pairing fiction with historical people and events, Ellroy runs his content through an authenticating strategy wherein it is difficult to distinguish fiction from historical fact. As Ellroy put it, 'One of the questions I never answer is what's real and what's not' (Taylor 2009: 202).

L.A. Confidential and Ellrovian prose

L.A. Confidential is a key text in the development of Ellroy's prose style, and is also an important work in Ellroy's further experimentation with historical fiction. Whereas in *The Black Dahlia* and *The Big Nowhere*, Ellroy gleaned information from cases in Jack Webb's *The Badge* and from the tabloid scandal magazines he read as a child, in *L.A. Confidential* he reverentially uses these sources as part of the narrative. They are no longer merely sources but fictional contributors.

The title *L.A. Confidential* is a tribute to a source which gave the young Ellroy insight into the secret world. The novel is interspersed with articles from the sensationalist tabloid magazine *Hush-Hush*. *Hush-Hush* was a tabloid magazine, popular in the 1950s, that specialized in the celebrity exposé and sex scandals. The *Hush-Hush* of the novel serves as a composite of the multiple tabloid magazines that his father subscribed to and that Ellroy read as a child: *Confidential, Lowdown, Rave, Whisper* and the original *Hush-Hush* (Ellroy 1997a: xvii). The purpose of the articles is to give updates of events in the novel outside the characters' purview and to offer periodic junctures in the narrative. The articles lend authenticity by appearing to document the narrative.

Given the propensity of the tabloids to rely on rumour and innuendo rather than verified facts, Ellroy appropriately changes details of the historical magazine *Hush-Hush* in his portrayal. The tagline of *Hush-Hush* was 'What You Don't Know About The People You Know', whereas in the novel it is 'Off the Record, On the QT, and very Hush-Hush', a somewhat ironic description as the style of tabloid journalism is neither quiet nor subtle. The lead *Hush-Hush* reporter in the novel is the sleaze-obsessed Sid Hudgens, whose name is a slight deviation on Sid Hughes, a former private detective and one of the most respected LA-based crime reporters of the 1950s who actually worked for mainstream newspapers: 'The *Times*, the *Record*, the *Express*, the *Herald*, the *Examiner* and the *Mirror News*' (Harnisch 2008). By basing Hudgens on Hughes, Ellroy is giving another indication of his admiration for tabloid magazines and their unacknowledged role in investigative journalism.

When asked about the accuracy of his novels, Ellroy remarked, 'I'm not entirely sure how factually valid my books are. My LA Quartet books are certainly a hyperbolized view of police work in the 1950s' (Duncan 1996: 83). Rather than use true crime, Ellroy consciously used *L.A. Confidential* to pay tribute to the sleazy tabloid magazines of the 1950s and mock the highly stylized and idealized depiction of police work in *Dragnet*, as evidenced by Ellroy's overt placement of LAPD Sgt. Jack Vincennes. Vincennes' police work is undermined by his moonlighting as the technical consultant to the fictional television series *Badge of Honour*. Television was the retreat of many noir directors when the Supreme Court ended block booking, a decision that led to drastic cuts in B movies, and Vincennes' presence on the show is one of the many ways he uses police work as a means of personal profit.

Ellroy explores 'the existence of a showbiz/true crime/scandal rag matrix' in *L.A. Confidential* (Ellroy 1997a: xvi–xvii). One of the novel's myriad of sub-plots involves the construction of a massive Dream-a-Dreamland theme park, which Ellroy very pointedly based on the Walt Disney Company, with thinly veiled portrayals of Disney characters such as Moochie Mouse and Danny Duck. The Dream-a-Dreamland storyline is laden with irony as it is connected to a brutal child murder, and in combination with the references to *The Badge* and *Hush-Hush*, it forms a trinity of satirical points which both invites the reader into a secret world and gives the novel, uniquely among the main works of the Quartet, an outwardly comic tone. By comparison, *The Big Nowhere* contains only brief moments of humour, usually in flashes of blackly comic wit by detectives, that alleviate the horrors of homicide investigation.

Humour is derived from a comedy of manners in which the reader observes social norms in a profession where life is cheap and murder is a common occurrence.

In *L.A. Confidential*, Ellroy developed a much more vigorous approach to channelling humour through the greater emphasis on satire. The novel's comic tone also derives from Ellroy's brand of 'Dog' humour. As we have seen in Chapter 1, Dog humour was developed by Ellroy with his friend Randy Rice. It is strongly tied, in name and deed, to Ellroy's literary persona, as he employs Dog humour in his novels and public appearances. In *L.A. Confidential*, Dog humour is present in the *Hush-Hush* articles. Ellroy imbues each article with excessive alliteration, thereby deepening their capacity to offend, which the original *Hush-Hush* did not possess to the same extent. In the short story 'Hush-Hush', published in *GQ* magazine in 1998, Ellroy continued to experiment with Dog humour in the context of tabloid journalism, and featuring plot strands leftover from *L.A. Confidential*. Ellroy transplants the sensationalist prose style of the tabloid articles into the delirious first-person narration of star *Hush-Hush* columnist Danny Getchell. Every sentence Getchell spouts is constructed as an alliterative pattern; although the Jewish Getchell regards this as something of a curse, he laments how 'my meshugenah mom mistreated me. She only let me read one book: a thick thesaurus' (Ellroy 1999: 120). Getchell talks in exactly the same style as he writes. For him, there is no distinction between the written and spoken word. Although this makes him a cartoonish figure, Getchell is also the quintessentially Ellrovian character. He never once deviates from the rhythms of his speech and rules of his writing.

Getchell employs an excess of words in all of his descriptions. He has the hack's gift of being in the right place at the right time in the hunt for good copy. He witnesses at first hand the tempestuous relationship between movie star Lana Turner and Mob hood Johnny Stompanato:

> I beelined to Bedford Drive in Beverly Hills. I Bausch & Lomb'd Lana Turner's backyard. I saw Johnny Stompanato jump on Lana and lash out with limitlessly lewd language. Lana lashed back. She julienned Johnny with jive on his jilt-happy gigolo ways. She spritzed sprite. She shot shit at him shamelessly. She pounced on his pint-sized penis and his wicked welterweight dupe Don Jordan. She called him a guinea gangster and said he poured the pork to her Mexican maid with his poquito pee-pee. She said he pandered and pimped her and got her gussied up in her own Givenchy gown (Ellroy 1999: 116).

The alliteration is limited to one letter phonetically repeated in two or three words and an absence of commas so as not to break the flow of the erratic, excitable speaker. A new alliterative pattern begins with each new sentence. The style is sustained throughout Getchell's narration. Ellroy channels his Demon Dog shtick through Getchell's narrative voice which is indistinguishable from his tabloid style of writing. The result is to create an impression of a spontaneous, improvisational spiel which as a writing style takes tremendous concentration to produce and integrate with the storyline: 'You know how these books are. They're difficult to read. Imagine how they are to write' (Wieners 1995: 37). Although as an outwardly comic form, dog humour has only played a small role in Ellroy's literary reputation, it is still an important, somewhat underestimated, theme in his work. Through dog humour, Ellroy invites readers into a world with different rules, as established social codes of taste and decency are broken down. Inevitably anyone who takes dog humour on the face value of the language is liable to be offended; as Ellroy has said, 'there's people who get it and people who don't' (Powell 2008a: 160). And yet the experience of dog humour is just one conduit into the Secret Pervert Republic, as experiential and thrilling as the rules of noir and secret history which permeate the text. Ellroy is engaging the reader to judge the characters on a different level of morality: 'some people hate my characters because their fascism, racism, homophobia, and anti-Semitism are in no way defining characteristics—they're just casual attributes' (Silet 1995: 49). The racism may be shocking to the modern reader, but it is normative to the world of the characters with whom the reader is supposed to empathize on other levels: 'I show their heroism coexisting with their dubious attributes out of another time' (Silet 1995: 49). Just as dog humour is connected to the bigotry of the characters, it is inherent in the emotional and physical violence which drives the narrative and brings the reader into a world where familiar norms of behaviour do not apply: 'there is a correlation in language and in theme because both violence and dog humour deal with outrageousness' (Powell 2008a: 160). Although the Getchell pieces never deviate from the comic tone or the stylistic alliteration, in Ellroy's novels there is an underlying threat of violence to the prose and the humorous moments which can erupt at any time.

Violence is a common occurrence, and seemingly safe, normal situations can become violent very quickly. The beginning of *L.A. Confidential* shows how a character's attempt to flee the country, which begins without incident, becomes hyperbolically violent within the space of seconds. The prologue to the novel, which reveals the fate of Buzz Meeks and resolves the plot threads remaining from *The Big Nowhere*, is set on 21 February 1950. After having an affair with Mickey Cohen's mistress and stealing a heroin shipment that was being safeguarded by Dudley Smith, Meeks is a marked man. Meeks, who had planned an escape to South America, realizes that his plan has been compromised when he recognizes an ex-cop in the escape team:

> Meeks smiled: friendly guy, no harm meant. A finger on the trigger; a make on the skinny guy: Mal Lunceford, a Hollywood Station harness bull – he used to ogle the carhops at Scrivener's Drive-in, puff out his chest to show off his pistol medals. The fat man, closer, said, 'We got that airplane waiting.'
> Meeks swung the shotgun around, triggered a spread. Fat man caught buckshot and flew, covering Lunceford – knocking him backward. The wetbacks tore helter-skelter; Meeks ran into the room, heard the back window breaking, yanked the mattress. Sitting ducks: two men, three triple-aught rounds close in.
> The two blew up; glass and blood covered three more men inching along the wall. Meeks leaped, hit the ground, fired at three sets of legs pressed together; his free hand flailed, caught a revolver off a dead man's waistband.
> Shrieks from the courtyard; running feet on gravel. Meeks dropped the shotgun, stumbled to the wall. Over to the men, tasting blood – point-blank head shots.
> Thumps in the room; two rifles in grabbing range. Meeks yelled, 'We got him!', heard answering whoops, saw arms and legs coming out the window. He picked up the closest piece and let fly, full automatic: trapped targets, plaster chips exploding, dry wood igniting.
> Over the bodies, into the room. The front door stood open; his pistols were still on the ledge. A strange thump sounded; Meeks saw a man spread prone – aiming from behind the mattress box.
> He threw himself to the floor, kicked, missed. The man got off a shot – close; Meeks grabbed his switchblade, leaped, stabbed: the neck, the face, the man screaming, shooting – wide ricochets. Meeks slit his throat, crawled over and toed the door, grabbed the pistols and just plain breathed. (Ellroy 1990: 5–6)

The prologue consists of four pages: Meeks kills thirteen men and is then killed by the last man standing, Dudley Smith, who seems demonically impervious to the flames enveloping the building: 'Dudley Smith stepped through flames, dressed in a fire department greatcoat' (Ellroy

1990: 6). The scene is written in third-person narration, but the reader views events entirely from Meeks' viewpoint. The chaos and confusion that ensue reflect the thoughts of a man desperately fighting for his life. A more distant form of third person would have slowed events down to clarify, step by step, the action, but Ellroy speeds events up by cutting sub-clauses and giving only thumbnail details to portray men dying by the minute and second. The clipped syntax makes the scene read more like a screenplay than a novel and things end, not in a noir tone, but with a reference to a different genre and period of history: 'Meeks died – thinking the El Serrano Motel looked just like the Alamo' (Ellroy 1990: 6). The speed and level of the violence are more akin to a western than noir, where sex and violence are often subliminal, and yet Ellroy re-establishes the noir tone very quickly in the following chapter to indicate a sharp break from the prologue in both style and narrative. Meeks' perspective, however, is a stylistic carry-over of a key theme of *The Big Nowhere*. As he is in almost constant movement during the shoot-out, the prose reflects what Meeks sees, hears and thinks. The effect is that reading the text is an experience similar to watching events through the lens of a camera. Meeks' viewpoint is cutting quickly from one frame to the next: 'Over the bodies, into the room. The front door stood open; his pistols were still on the ledge.' No detail of the room receives more focus than just a few words. Meeks has become the cornered embodiment of the discredited Man Camera theory practised by Upshaw, but Meeks is a far less cerebral character than Upshaw, who utilized Man Camera as a form of subjective detection. Ellroy's characters do not have to be intellectuals to employ a form of cinematic thinking. Meeks is in a 'kill or be killed' situation and anything that comes within his field of vision is a target.

In the opening chapter, the action jumps forward twenty months to Christmas 1951. The first five chapters trace the build-up to and occurrence of the 'Bloody Christmas' police scandal over a comparatively lengthy twenty pages, and the following chapters deal with the fallout from the scandal at a much slower pace than the prologue. Essentially these chapters bring together the three main protagonists of the novel, Ed Exley, Bud White and Jack Vincennes. After 'Bloody Christmas', Ellroy shifts the focus away from the LAPD's internal politics and towards the mystery storyline: 'the Nite-Owl massacre', a mass murder which relates to the void in organized crime caused by the imprisonment of Mob kingpin Mickey Cohen.

In both plotting and prose, cinema is one of the crossover themes which transitions from novel to novel in the Quartet, and is constantly reflected in violent scenes which are viewed through a filmic perspective of one of the three leading characters, Exley, White and Vincennes. The novel concludes with the premature death of a real-life character essentially cheating Exley of the justice he was hoping for, and the reader of an original ending. Johnny Stompanato is revealed to have a major role in the Nite-Owl massacre. He is placed under constant surveillance by the LAPD and never leaves his lover Lana Turner's house, but before he can be apprehended, Stompanato is stabbed to death by Turner's daughter, Cheryl. Ellroy uses Hollywood lore to play a concluding trick on the narrative. In the short story 'Hush-Hush', Getchell arrives at Turner's house only seconds after Stompanato has been stabbed.

To examine the cinematic themes of the Quartet novels, it is useful to compare the narrative of the novel *L.A. Confidential* to the 1997 film adaptation directed by Curtis Hanson. The screenplay was co-written by Hanson and collaborator Brian Helgeland. Ellroy had very little formal involvement with the production, and he even expressed scepticism that the film could be made: 'I knew my book was movie-adaptation-proof. The motherfucker was uncompressible, uncontainable, and unequivocally bereft of sympathetic characters. It was unsavoury, unapologetically dark, untameable, and altogether untranslateable to the screen' (Ellroy 1997a: xvi). Ellroy, however, did review the seventh draft of Hanson and Helgeland's screenplay and met with them to discuss ideas: 'Some they took, some they didn't' (Blackwelder 1997: 100). Ironically, Ellroy, a writer always willing to play with historical detail, gave advice on where the script was inaccurate in its portrayal of the period: 'I pointed out anachronisms in the script, deviations from 1950s vernacular' (Blackwelder 1997: 100). Yet it would be through dialogue and vernacular that Hanson and Helgeland would triumph in their translation of Ellrovian prose, thereby solidifying the link between Ellroy's narrative and cinema. Although much of the novel's narrative was discarded or truncated, director and screenwriter did attempt to preserve and convey Ellroy's subjective third-person prose: 'We took many liberties with the plot, but we tried to be true to the ones who brought us – Ellroy's characters' (Hanson 1997: x).

Much of the action was transferred from the novel to the screenplay without any significant changes to the wording of the scene. The rescue of Inez Soto and murder of Sylvester Fitch by Bud White reads almost identically between novel and screenplay:

INT. HALLWAY – DAY

Raising the .38, Bud continues along the hall. He looks into an empty kitchen. Up ahead...

INT. LIVING ROOM – DAY

> SYLVESTER FITCH *sits naked on the couch wolfing Rice Krispies and watching cartoons on a flickering TV. He looks up, sees the.38 before he sees Bud beyond it. Fitch sets down his spoon.*
>
> *Bud shoots him in the face. Dead, Fitch just sits there.*
>
> *Bud moves behind him. Pulling a spare piece from his ankle holster, Bud fires back at the door from Fitch's line of fire, then puts the gun in Fitch's hand.*
>
> *We hear a crash against the front door. As Fitch slides off the chair to the floor, Bud dumps the Rice Krispies on him.* (Hanson and Helgeland 1997: 117–18)

The scene is written so that the camera angles reflect Bud's point of view as he slowly walks down the corridor, tense with anticipation. The language is largely dispassionate but there are hints of Bud's nerves being on edge as he does not know which rooms are empty and where he will find Fitch: '*Raising the.38, Bud continues along the hall. He looks into an empty kitchen. Up ahead...*' The italicized prose distinguishes Bud's thoughts from the capitalized directions. Although some of the wording was lifted from the novel, the screenplay's technical details are slower than Ellrovian prose. In the novel, Bud's first glimpse of Fitch is described in just 24 words: 'A fat mulatto at a table – naked, wolfing Kellogg's Rice Krispies. He put down his spoon, raised his hands. "Nossir, don't want no trouble"' (Ellroy 1990: 133). This exact moment is 34 words in the screenplay, and although the scene in the novel employs fewer words to cover the same event, the novel has details which the screenplay omits, such as Fitch pleading for his life, attempting to surrender, and Bud's racist description of him as a 'mulatto'. In a scene-by-scene comparison, it is possible to see how Ellroy has experimented with cinematic techniques in his novels to the extent where he can relay information and portray a confluence of events faster than the filmic equivalent. This is not Davis' 'unendurable wordstorm' but rather an intense collection of events described through short sentences which read quickly: 'Minimalism implies small events, small people, a small story. Man, that's the antithesis of me. Telegraphic means straight sentences—subject, verb, repetitions with slight modifications' (Rich 2008: 188). In Ellrovian prose, shorter sentences lead to a greater density of events, therefore the violence in scenes like Fitch's murder is necessarily brief but more shocking for its immediacy and lack of moral barriers to be overcome.

The influence of cinema in Ellroy's work goes beyond prose style. As Lee Horsley writes in *The Noir Thriller*:

> Ellroy recurrently writes about lives that have been warped by voyeuristic participation in films produced by those in pursuit of wealth and power. The dominance of Hollywood storytelling combined with the addiction to spectacle spurs the disaffected to narrative acts of their own, although it often also means that characters can only conceive of themselves in terms of the conventional roles of the cinema. (Horsley 2001: 214–15)

Bud's behaviour is a response to what he saw as a child but was powerless to stop: his father beating his mother to death. Bud's intervention here reclaims the narrative from the abuser, and the helpless voyeur is now the avenger. Bud is empowered not only through his murderous justice but also from his new control over the narrative. The camera of his subjective third-person narration views and records the murder of Fitch, making Bud as much a film noir character as he is a character in a novel. Despite the LAPD's tacit complicity, the self-destructive urges of the secret noir world which drive Bud to murder Fitch alienate him from the more visible, conventional moral world. Bud's moral code has been shaped by noir. Like Bud, Ellroy's experience of watching film noir from an early age rendered him a child without an innocent period. Yet although Bud is limited as a noir character, Ellroy uses Bud to test the limitations of noir conventions, as even with the latent corruption of the LAPD, Bud's murder of Fitch is risky, both professionally and in the reader's ability to empathize with him.

Due to Ellroy's parallel and overlapping narratives, Hanson and Helgeland faced difficulties limiting the narrative for the screen. Their re-ordering of the narrative led them to reinvent the prologue shoot-out, essentially the ending to *The Big Nowhere*, as the conclusion to *L.A. Confidential* the film. However, these adjustments have created issues for screenwriters trying to adapt a Quartet novel for film. Although two of the four Quartet novels have been adapted to film, the other novels have presented structural problems too difficult to overcome. *White Jazz* was in pre-production for several years and went through many drafts, with Ellroy contributing an early draft. Dudley Smith is killed in the film of *L.A. Confidential*; therefore, it would be difficult for his character to reappear in a *White Jazz* film adaptation without violating the previous narrative. There is also a question of how audiences would respond to Ed Exley, a lead character in *L.A. Confidential*, but only a supporting character in the novel *White Jazz*. Ellroy and Hanson had discussed making 'L.A. Confidential 2', a direct sequel to the first film which would ignore *White Jazz* and partly resolve this problem, but the project never came to fruition (Anon 2013). From these unfinished projects it is possible to see how the endless web of narratives Ellroy has woven has made it difficult for other creative artists to disentangle a Quartet narrative and tell the story in coherent form. Ellroy's byzantine plots are not easily adapted for cinema, but the Ellrovian prose style has achieved a remarkable merging of novel and screenwriting styles.

Matthew Carnahan's screenplay of *White Jazz*, despite never being made into a film, was published on the Internet and is an important work highlighting the potential for other writers to experiment with Ellroy's prose style, as it is written entirely in the first-person narrative voice of Dave Klein:

> Legend: *Recife, Brazil, 1983*
> INT. HILLSIDE VILLA - MORNING
> Stare at my broken face in a gilded mirror. The breaks
> occurred a lifetime ago, healed uneven. I wear a white
> tropical button-down, a Republican-gold Rolex, a pirate-patch
> over what was my left eye.
> ME (V.O.)
> I'm old. And all I have left is the
> will to remember... (Carnahan 2007)

In Carnahan's version of the story Klein is both the lead character and essentially the screenwriter of *White Jazz*. Klein dictates the camera movements which follow his character: 'Stare at my broken face in a gilded mirror', and also cues himself every time he narrates, 'ME (V.O.).' He literally becomes Man Camera. This highly experimental form of screenwriting takes Ellrovian prose to its brilliant, if impractical, stylistic conclusion and was preceded by the parallels Ellroy created in his prose style between novel and screenwriting. Carnahan's Quartet adaptation reinforces Ellroy's position as a stylist of literary film noir.

The Big Nowhere concluded with two of the three lead characters dead and the third facing certain death. *L.A. Confidential* ends with a similar sense of loss: Vincennes has been killed; Bud White is disabled and his police career is over, but he will be cared for by the woman he loves. Exley ends the novel triumphant, having been promoted to Chief of Detectives, but at enormous personal cost: 'Gold stars. Alone with his dead' (Ellroy 1990: 480). Dudley Smith has once again escaped justice and is still protected by his position within the LAPD. The showdown between Exley and Smith forms part of the narrative tropes as the series transitions to the concluding novel *White Jazz*. For this novel, Ellroy dispenses with the rotating three-character structure which he had utilized in *The Big Nowhere* and *L.A. Confidential*. Exley becomes a supporting character, now more ruthlessly ambitious and cold-hearted than ever, who is consequently devoid of any sympathy he may have once possessed. The Exley/Smith rivalry is seen from the first-person perspective of leading character Dave Klein, who moves from observer to participant in a series of events which quickly spiral out of control as the institutionalized rivalries and criminal conspiracies spill out of the secret world and into the public sphere with catastrophic consequences.

White Jazz: apocalypse noir

As a title *White Jazz* references the chaos that engulfs the first-person narrator Dave Klein personally and the increasingly violent events that have almost subsumed the white power structure of LA by the coda. In the Quartet, music often functions as a mirror to characters' obsessions: *The Big Nowhere* takes its name from a jazz piece which parallels the psychosis of its author. *White Jazz*, however, is not a clear reference to a single composition but, to borrow a phrase Ellroy used to describe the Lloyd Hopkins novels, the music the characters are dancing to in their heads. Klein is an overt racist: he uses the word 'nigger' frequently, but his bigotry is complex as ethnic identities are never clear-cut in the novel's Los Angeles setting. The title is echoed in Klein's name, as he feels disconnected from many of his colleagues. His heritage is German, but he laments that his name sounds Jewish: 'I'm a kraut, not a Jew – the old man's handle got clipped at Ellis Island' (Ellroy 1992c: 26). This misrepresentation somehow drains him of the power that a clear ethnic label would give him. Yet Klein's self-consciousness and frustration does not seem to lead to any deep-rooted anti-Semitism. Instead, he chooses a more visibly defined people group, African Americans, as the recipients of his casual racism. But the world he inhabits and tries to control through such prejudice defies him. The music Klein is moving to follows its own rules. It is complex and uncontrollable.

To end the Quartet, Ellroy would integrate music deeply into the narrative rather than just reference it. Bebop becomes symbolic of larger societal breakdown: 'There's a symbiotic frenzy going on among these people at all times. It's very rare that this inward world spills out into the outwardly more placid world. But it does occasionally in *White Jazz*, and the results are hellish' (Silet 1995: 46). To achieve a portrayal of Los Angeles in a state of chaos breaking out of a formerly closed world, Ellroy would have to employ a new style of narrative structure which captures the rhythm of the action from the first page rather than the exposition ending of *The Big Nowhere* which revealed the musical link to the murders.

White Jazz opens with the corruption and conspiracies which connect the LAPD to the criminal underworld, the hidden world, gradually being pushed into the open through a series of horrific crimes. This maelstrom of events leads to LA becoming an anarchic, and in metaphorical terms for the genre, apocalyptic city. There are two prologues before the first chapter of the novel. One is a series of newspaper and tabloid articles which contextualize the plot, and the other is an introductory narration from Klein. Set many years after the events of the novel, Klein's prologue looks back:

> *All I have is the will to remember. Time revoked/fever dreams – I wake up reaching, afraid I'll forget. Pictures keep the woman young.*
> *L.A., fall 1958.*
> *Newsprint: link the dots. Names, events – so brutal they beg to be connected. Years down – the story stays dispersed. The names are dead or too guilty to tell.*
> *I'm old, afraid I'll forget:*
> *I killed innocent men.*
> *I betrayed sacred oaths.*
> *I reaped profit from horror.*
> *Fever – that time burning. I want to go with the music – spin, fall with it.* (Ellroy 1992c: 1)

There are a number of indications that Klein's story will be an unconventional history in which Ellroy employs jazz music as a means of hiding the structure behind a veneer of chaos. Ellroy said of the musical influence 'I'm not a fan of bebop, but I understand it as the means to express confusion and disorientation' (Powell 2008b: 169). Klein is feverish and the prose mirrors his delirium. Also, time has added to his story's incoherence. The detective who is meant to reveal the truth and solve cases now risks being unable to arrange his memories into a salient form: '*Years down – the story stays dispersed. ... I'm old, afraid I'll forget.*' Despite his apprehensions that the material he is about to divulge to the reader is dangerous, Klein is determined that his story should be told. Throughout his narration, Klein makes multiple references to music. The seemingly chaotic, disorientating style of bebop becomes synonymous with Klein's metaphorical descent into hell: *'I want to go with the music – spin, fall with it.'* The prose style mirrors this chaos. Klein is not subsumed by madness, but he is plunged into a frenzy of events totally out of his control.

With *White Jazz*, Ellroy was questioning the widespread perception of an era. He was faced with the practical problem of unleashing an anarchic vision onto his portrayal of 1950s LA which would be, in contrast to his earlier work, completely ahistorical, and yet still not write himself into historical error. Ellroy also had to keep the action of events naturalistic when the style is so surreal it veers close to implausible. It was a difficult balancing act which entailed the book was not as commercially successful as Ellroy had hoped:

> The book is a fever dream—it's a stream of consciousness style—there are no tricks in it—everything is quite literal but, if you blink, you will miss things. You have to get into the rhythm of Dave Klein's head or you won't get the book at all. There are many people who didn't understand the book. The book did not sell as well as the three previous volumes of the L.A. Quartet. (Duncan 1996: 74)

Style had overtaken plot. Yet, to achieve the necessary verisimilitude, Ellroy would have to return to the structure of a plausible crime-fiction narrative to rewrite history.

Peter Schmidt-Nowara has categorized Ellroy's historical revisionism as a method whereby fictional answers are given to historical mysteries: 'By writing about the past, Ellroy can answer the unanswerable; he can solve the unsolved crimes' (Schmidt-Nowara 2001: 118). However, this may be a simplification as many other writers practise this technique, and it implies that Ellroy cannot explore extensively scrutinized events where no mystery, and thus no room for narrative manoeuvre, remains. There are two relatively minor examples of Ellroy revising more than just the 'unsolved crimes' of LA history early in the novel, which act as a precursor to the climactic anarchy of the novel. Through his first-person narration, Klein reveals a substantial back story, including his complicity in a trio of murders which contradict the official versions of police investigations and well-documented events. Klein receives permission from Mob boss Jack Dragna to murder Tony Brancato and Tony Trombino, as 'the Two Tonys' have been harassing Klein's sister for whom he harbours incestuous feelings. After he kills both men, Klein is subsequently blackmailed by Dragna into becoming his enforcer. Jack

Dragna died of a heart attack in 1956, but in *White Jazz* Klein smothers him to death with a pillow on his sickbed. In the fictional murder of Dragna, Ellroy is able to keep the narrative consistent with a documented history but embellishes the event with plausible fictional details.

Ellroy's fictional portrayal of the Brancato and Trombino murders, however, is in direct contradiction of documented events. The 'Two Tonys' were shot dead in their car in 1951; although the case was unsolved for many years, the mobster Jimmy Fratianno confessed to the double murder when he became a government witness in 1977. In his introduction to *Scene of the Crime: Photographs from the LAPD Archive*, Ellroy spoke knowledgeably about the case, although he omitted details which would contradict his fictional rendering: 'Poor Tony and Tony. They trusted their killer. He got in the back seat. He popped off two head shots. Both men look equally dead and relaxed' (Ellroy 2004c: 14). Ellroy's description of the murders corresponds to Klein's narrative take: 'the Two Tonys in a '49 Dodge. I slid in the backseat and blew their brains out' (Ellroy 1992c: 27). By developing the 'Two Tonys' murders along similar lines in both fictional and factually based narrative, Ellroy creates verisimilitude despite events in *White Jazz* being incompatible with the established facts of the case. In Ellroy's follow-up novel *American Tabloid*, there is a conspicuous reference to Dave Klein. The characters Pete Bondurant and Lenny Sands are discussing Hollywood gossip, and when Bondurant asks who murdered the Two Tonys, Sands replies that the killer was 'Either Jimmy Frattiano or a cop named Dave Klein' (Ellroy 1995: 147). Klein is not a character in the novel and there is no further mention of him. It was a sly acknowledgement by Ellroy that he had broken his own conventions of historical fiction with his portrayal of the double murder in *White Jazz*, and he would not return to this form of ahistorical plotting again.

In the outline to *White Jazz*, Ellroy explained to his editors how he would imbue the narrative with a sense of historical validity (Ellroy 1991). A difficult obstacle to overcome was how to portray crime spiralling out of control in LA when this could be contradicted by the crime rates of the period. Ellroy decided to disseminate the horrific violence in the novel through the mediums of film, music and tabloid journalism, and the LAPD's influence over the latter, so that by the denouement, when order is restored, the public has been partially or totally unaware of the gravity of the situation. Cinematic themes are interwoven in the narrative in various forms. Klein is having an affair with Glenda, an actress in a schlock-horror movie titled 'Attack of the Atomic Vampire'. As LA begins to descend into extreme violence, more and more violence is added to the script and shooting of the picture, to the extent that members of the cast and production team feel deeply disturbed by an otherwise inconsequential film. Unbeknown to them, the chief cameraman on the set, Wylie Bullock, is a deranged psychopath, and the increasingly lurid violence of the film mirrors the fantasies he is brutally actualizing outside the studio. Bullock's role as cameraman alludes to Ellroy's Man Camera and the voyeurism it expresses. The murderer's movie thematically echoes the unstructured, mostly incomprehensible 'Big Nowhere' score composed by the psychopathic jazz player Coleman in *The Big Nowhere*.

The violence of the film seems to affect everyone connected to the production. In a heated moment, Glenda knifes to death a man who is harassing her, and Klein covers up the crime. The film is also financed directly by violence, through Mob boss Mickey Cohen, who after being released from prison is unable to reclaim his place as the head of organized crime in the city. It is ironic that Cohen's attempts to do business in the, at least, semi-legitimate world of film production have inadvertently tied him to even more horrific crimes through the cameraman's murders.

Another film within the novel is a snuff film Klein finds himself trapped in when he is drugged against his will on the orders of Dudley Smith. In his intoxicated state, Klein unwittingly murders the police officer he has been investigating, Johnny Duhamel. The scene is described allusively at first, as Klein's dreamlike state makes him think he is back in the war and that Duhamel is a 'Jap' whom he has to kill. Later, when Klein is forced to watch what happened on film, the full horror of events is clarified through cinema:

> I thrashed – futile – sticky tape, no give.
> A white screen.
> Cut to:
> Johnny Duhamel naked.
> Cut to:
> Dave Klein swinging a sword.
> Zooming in – the sword grip: SSGT D.D. Klein USMC Saipan 7/24/43.
> Cut to:
> Johnny begging – 'Please' – mute sound.
> Cut to:
> Dave Klein thrashing – stabbing, missing.
> Cut to:
> A severed arm twitching on wax paper. (Ellroy 1992c: 205)

Klein is horrified at the acts of his filmic self and yet narrates the scene dispassionately, referring to himself in the third person and using technical terms such as 'Cut to' and 'Zooming in'. Klein is aware watching himself that his onscreen actions are being directed by someone else and are not of his own volition. However, he has already experienced the scene as it happened, albeit in a drugged, dreamlike state, and the film clarifies what he had experienced through an intoxicated, blurred vision. He narrates the film as if he was reading a screenplay with a judicious use of words, highlighting incriminating details such as the murder weapon which is a war memento of Klein's. There is only the slightest hint at emotion with the victim mutely begging and Klein thrashing. Bizarrely for a snuff film, as if they were following the Hays code, much of the violence appears to have been cut out, with the film jumping forward to the grisly image of a 'severed arm twitching on wax paper'. The redacted, technical narration of the film within a novel makes the scene more disturbing than if Ellroy had chosen to rely on gratuitous violence. Klein and the reader/viewer are left more shaken by not knowing the full extent of the horrors. Klein states plainly 'I screamed' before drugs push him back into the dream world: 'A needle stab cut me off mute' (Ellroy 1992c: 205). Film has become more powerful than reality, a point reinforced by Dudley Smith's attempt to use the film to neutralize Klein. Both of the novel's internal films imbue metafiction into the narrative as the characters are able to manipulate and clarify events through the medium of film, whereas other characters and the wider public are blind to the connection of violence to film. The ultimate manipulator, of course, is Ellroy, surpassing Schmidt-Nowara's view of historical fiction. Ellroy's portrayal of events remains conversant with history while depicting an anarchic LA that never really existed.

Ellroy also uses *Hush-Hush* as a framing device to authenticate the otherwise ahistorical outbreak of violence and chaos in the novel. Throughout the Quartet, the tabloid prints lurid stories, which although sensationalized, are closer to the secret world than the work of the mainstream press. *White Jazz* concludes with the scandal magazine being censored: a legal injunction filed by the LAPD leaves *Hush-Hush* unable to print a 94-page report written by Klein confessing his own crimes and detailing the corruption in the LAPD and how close the city came to uncontrollable violence. All it can do is run a protest article headlined, 'FREEDOM OF SPEECH GAGGED!!! J'ACCUSE! J'ACCUSE!', which hints at the allegations (Ellroy 1992c: 340). Ironically, the most scurrilous source available to the public has also been one of the most truthful. The secret world is preserved as the tabloid is silenced.

White Jazz ends with an embittered Klein feeling he has only one chance left at revenge and, paradoxically, redemption. Because his report was never published, he still seeks to bring about justice on the men he believes have too long escaped it:

> *I'm going back. I'm going to make Exley confess every monstrous deal he ever cut with the same candor I have. I'm going to kill Carlisle, and make Dudley fill in every moment of his life – to eclipse my guilt with the sheer weight of his evil. I'm going to kill him in the name of our victims.* (Italics in original) (Ellroy 1992c: 359)

Klein's closing thoughts keep the Quartet narrative alive, alluding to repercussions which continue beyond the last page. Yet Klein's thoughts appear to be futile. By this point, Dudley Smith has been incapacitated and is living in a nursing home, but Klein, irrationally, still wants to kill him. Dick Carlisle, a faceless, slow-witted henchman of Smith's throughout much of the Quartet, has become a Mob kingpin by virtue of being one of the few characters left alive at the coda, whom Klein feels obligated to murder even though he bears no real grudge against him. Klein's violent wishes persist even if they are devoid of a legitimate motive. It is the breakdown of logic, 'the jazz' that the characters are moving to.

The sense of continuation beyond the ending, even if it is by implication futile, vindicates Ellroy's choice of a radical prose style for *White Jazz* and shows how he came to the decision of resuming the Quartet narrative in varied forms, significantly more than Freiburger identified when he attempted to classify *Clandestine* in the same series. In previous novels, Ellroy had experimented with a sudden quickening of the pace to denote the onslaught of violence, such as in the prologue to *L.A. Confidential*, but this was usually followed in the next scene by a return to a natural, easily comprehensible pace. In *White Jazz*, the narrative is told at such a breakneck speed that the story ends with energy still to burn, even if the motive for violence has been left behind. The plotting is every bit as complex as *The Big Nowhere*, but as the pace is so fast, *White Jazz* has shorter, less clunky exposition than the second Quartet novel. With *White Jazz*, Ellroy expects the reader to accept its anarchic logic from the beginning and spends little time on retrospective explanation. The further the reader goes into the novel, the more Ellroy bombards them with a greater concentration of events happening in a smaller narrative space. The final chapters are remarkably brief. Chapter 60 is less than half a page and contains two murders.

Chapter 61 consists of five lines. For Ellroy, it was a noir style he had been developing for many years, and it had reached the point where it could not be taken any further: 'That style was suitable for that one book – and I'll never go back to it again' (Silet 1995: 48).

The legacy and return of the LA Quartet

After he had completed the LA Quartet, Ellroy was adamant that he had abandoned noir as a genre and style: 'Noir is a shit-can I'm getting off of' (Wieners 1995: 39). But traces of the Quartet can still be seen in the follow-up Underworld series despite Ellroy's bullish rhetoric that he had completely changed direction. Several characters, such as Pete Bondurant and Howard Hughes, transitioned into the Underworld novels. Ellroy's portrayal of cross-series characters, however, was not wholly consistent between series. *White Jazz* and *American Tabloid* have overlapping timeframes, and the portrayal of characters that appear in both is strikingly different from novel to novel. The main action of *White Jazz* ends in January 1959. The opening scene of *American Tabloid* is set on 22 November 1958. Ellroy begins the narrative of *American Tabloid* exactly five years before the assassination of President Kennedy. *White Jazz* ends with Hughes ordering a reluctant Bondurant to beat up Dave Klein as punishment for his affair with Glenda Bledsoe. Hughes, watching Bondurant pound Klein, is described as dapper, 'in a business suit and wing tips', and is presumably of sound, albeit malevolent, mind and in good health (Ellroy 1992c: 349). However, in the opening scene of *American Tabloid*, set prior to the ending of *White Jazz*, Hughes is injecting drugs into his penis and appears to be a total recluse looked on with pity by Bondurant. He is still Bondurant's employer, but it is clear that of the two, Bondurant has the sharper intelligence and more dominant personality.

The cinematic prose style Ellroy had developed in the Quartet had left its mark on the plotting of Ellroy's historical fiction. Paul Duncan, in an interview with Ellroy in 1996, identified the transition in Ellroy's fiction as mirroring the history of noir films and how they evolved after the end of the classic film noir period:

> You're moving from the crime of the forties and fifties to the politics of the sixties and seventies. This reminds me of the way films stopped being film noirs and started to become counterculture political conspiracy/suspense/paranoia films. (Duncan 1996: 83)

Later in the interview, Ellroy names a major influence: 'the whole trilogy is called the Underworld USA trilogy. (I'm also a bit of a Samuel

Fuller fan—his film *Underworld U.S.A.* came out 1961.)' (Duncan 1996: 83). The plot of *Underworld USA*, in contrast to the complex, interweaving narratives of Ellroy's Underworld novels, is quite simple. A fourteen-year-old boy, Tolly Devlin (Cliff Robertson), witnesses four hoods beat his father to death. When he comes of age Devlin sets out to claim his revenge against the men, who have since risen to the top of a massive crime syndicate. *Underworld USA* falls just outside the classic film noir era according to Ellroy's definition, as it was released one year after the 1960 cut-off point for noir he identified in *The Best American Noir* as 1960, but it is stylistically closer to Fuller's previous films such as *Pickup on South Street* (1953) than the self-conscious neo-noirs that began to appear in the 1960s. Don Siegel's *The Lineup* (1958) falls just in the film noir era and stylistically abides by it, whereas his later film *The Killers* (1964) is much more brash and melodramatic than his earlier film noirs, partly seen in his switch from shooting in black and white to colour. Relatively few crime films were shot in black and white after 1960 as celebrated directors of noir films like Siegel were making stylistic transitions. Ellroy knew his transition from Quartet to Underworld novels occurred at a transitional period in the history of noir as a genre, and the influence of Fuller's *Underworld USA*, which was shot in black and white, is symbolic of how Ellroy maintained a degree of continuity between the series with *White Jazz* and *American Tabloid*. Ellroy still claimed to have started another reinvention of noir as his work was structured to reflect film noir's transition into the 1960s.

Through the LA Quartet, Ellroy created a series of novels in which his writing was undergoing a continuous stylistic experiment. Although he claimed that *White Jazz* was the end of the series and a symbolic end to the noir genre itself, the Quartet narratives he has continued to develop in the Underworld trilogy suggest the new noir style he had created through the series was only in its infancy. The release of *Perfidia* in 2014, the first novel of his planned Second LA Quartet, further highlighted how Ellroy was forging connections between the noir genre and his developing style as a writer. Set in Los Angeles in December 1941, *Perfidia* begins with a transcription of 'The Thunderbolt Broadcast' for K-L-A-N Radio by the real-life historical figure Gerald L. K. Smith. Smith, a clergyman and founder of the far-right America First party, rails against the Jewish conspiracy he believes is dragging the US into the war:

> No sane American desires our participation in a Fight-for-the-Kikes foreign war. No sane American wants to send American boys off to certain peril. No sane American denies that *this* war cannot be kept

off our shores unless we circumvent and interdict it for *foreign* soil. I'm ripsnortingly right about this, my friends – I'm apple-cheeked with apostasy.

We didn't start this war. Adolf Hitler and hotsy-totsy Hirohito didn't start this war, either. The Jew Control apparatchiks cooked up this Red borscht stew and turned friend upon friend, the world over. Are you apoplectically ambivalent, my good friends? (Ellroy 2014: 6)

The right-wing propaganda works on two levels; it sets the tone for the paranoia in the build-up to the Pearl Harbour attacks, which will lead to the internment of Japanese in the US due to fear of fifth-column infiltration, and reads as Ellroy's return to the Quartet world. Smith's creed is not as hyperbolic as Danny Getchell's, but there are traces of Ellroy's fondness for alliteration in the phrases 'ripsnortingly right' and 'apoplectically ambivalent'. Ellroy is now writing in a period setting prior to the post-war tabloid boom which excludes *Hush-Hush* from the narrative. This is not the salacious gossip for mass consumption that *Hush-Hush* specialized in, as the broadcast is labelled 'BOOTLEG TRANSMITTER/TIJUANA, MEXICO' (Ellroy 2014: 5). Ellroy gives the reader a taste of his former style and immediately reinvents it. To begin the novel with Smith's bigoted rant is a typically uncompromising move, and this factor led Ellroy to predict that his portrayal of the complex political machinations of the era would be controversial: 'although the story is very much about the injustice of the internment of the Japanese – most of them innocent – let me say, and this is very un-PC, the f*cking internment was not the Holocaust or the Soviet Gulag' (Isaacs 2014). Smith is skilled in rhetoric after years of hectoring from the pulpit. He uses the phrase 'No sane American' three times regarding the public's desire to go to war, and then, amusingly, seems to argue for just that: 'Yes, the war is coming our way, even though we sure as shooting don't want it. And America *never* runs from a fight.' Smith regards the Jewish race as a bigger enemy for the US than 'Adolf Hitler and hotsy-totsy Hirohito'. Smith's bigotry is only a fringe view compared to the larger forces of prejudice at work. The irony of *Perfidia* is that the paranoia of fifth columns sweeping LA on the brink of war is in large part an illusion, manufactured by factions inside the LAPD to justify property seizures, whereas *White Jazz* had portrayed an affluent, post-war society in which the populace was unaware of how close the city was to anarchy.

One of the characters of *Perfidia* who does not feature prominently in the original Quartet is Hideo Ashida, a Japanese police chemist who is exempt from internment due to his position in the LAPD. One of the tasks for the reader of *Perfidia* is to identify the web of connections Ellroy has spun with the overarching Quartet narrative, which some critics found tiresome. Barry Forshaw wrote that the novel was 'for die-hard enthusiasts only; the casual reader will melt away' (Powell 2014b). Ashida is referenced in *The Black Dahlia*, but he is essentially new to the Quartet world, and is strongly drawn to it. After discussing a case with Sergeant 'Buzz' Meeks, Ashida ponders how '*He chose this male world. He's learning its customs and codes. It's unbearably thrilling*' (italics in original) (Ellroy 2014: 24). Ashida is a closet homosexual, and he finds life in the LAPD thrilling not just due to the violence but also because it is a 'male world'. As a character he never quite fits into any neat classification, being neither fully Japanese nor American, neither a policeman nor a criminal, or even a typically noir or Quartet character. He does possess some Japanese traits, such as a fascination with 'customs and codes'. There is also an emotionless precision to how he assesses the most provocative of situations, such as the constant verbal abuse he receives: 'The driver saw Ashida. Of course – he yelled, "Goddamn Jap!"' (Ellroy 2014: 11). The phrase 'of course' is more damning than the obscenity Ashida receives. Even though he is the recipient of racist abuse, Ashida views it as a natural reaction in males inclined towards aggression. He uses the same phrase 'of course' to describe the abuse a policeman hurls back at the man. Ashida sees immaturity as a logical endpoint of man's character, especially in wartime. He tells his brother Akira: 'There is no proportion. Pearl Harbour took care of that' (Ellroy 2014: 144). Ashida, however, tries to operate within the parameters of the noir world: he feels a strong attraction to Bucky Bleichert, and out of necessity controls his feelings of love and sexual desire as much as he can. Dudley Smith, perhaps Ellroy's most famous character and certainly the most recognizable of the Quartet, does not keep any check on his emotions. His ruthlessness is offset by his similarly strong and open desire for love and sex, which stands in stark contrast to the dour Ashida.

Ellroy brought Smith back to examine the paternalistic, charismatic and expansive side to this otherwise malevolent Quartet character. In addition to his unlikely love affair with Bette Davis, Smith sleeps with the fiery, left-wing radical Claire De Haven:

Dudley lowered his cup. The saucer rattled.
Claire said, 'I smell a woman on you.'
  Dudley said, 'There's a beast in me. I destroy those I cannot control. I must be certain that those close to me share my identical

interests. I'm benevolent within that construction. I'm ghastly outside of it.' (Ellroy 2014: 557)

Ellroy resorts to a comedy of manners, the rattling of the cup and saucer, to elicit sexual tension. Smith, whose hand never shakes when the occasion calls for murder, is endearingly nervous around the alluring De Haven. Describing the split in his personality as both benevolent and ghastly, Smith's claim that he needs people to 'share my identical interests' is ironic considering that his attraction to De Haven is rooted in their opposing political views. Although they are both revolutionaries, Smith fought against the British in the Irish War of Independence. De Haven is a communist whereas Smith describes his views as 'czarist' (Ellroy 2014: 555). It is telling that, once Smith makes the admission 'there's a beast in me', sex follows soon afterwards. For Dudley Smith, sex and love, however sincere and pure as emotions, ultimately become controlling techniques. Through his portrayal of Smith as a man who can slipstream between bonhomie, introspection, seduction and violence, Ellroy reinvents the character within a larger reinvention of the Quartet series. To return to the Quartet may have seemed like a conservative choice for Ellroy as a novelist, but from it the Demon Dog of American crime fiction began an ambitious revisionism of a Quartet which, when the first four novels were originally released, had been itself a radical rebirth of the noir genre.

5
The Narrative of Secret Histories in the Underworld USA Trilogy

The success of the Los Angeles Quartet left James Ellroy with the dilemma of how to make his next project even more ambitious and epic in scope. He could not simply continue to write post-war crime novels set in LA, as noir and its birthplace had become limitations to him. In typically grandiose style, Ellroy declared that any new novels would have to be vastly superior to his preceding works:

> From *The Big Nowhere* on I formed a new covenant with myself—a covenant of consciousness. The covenant goes something like this: every book has to be conceived as bigger, better, stronger, and more stylistically evolved than the book that preceded it. (Silet 1995: 47)

Ellroy believed that he had outgrown noir and LA. His public declaration of his personal 'covenant', however, went further than finalizing his new direction: it also reassessed his hugely popular and highly experimental Quartet novels as lesser works. Yet although Ellroy's statements following *White Jazz* suggest that he would avoid noir entirely – '*Noir* is dead for me ' – his follow-up novels were not the clean break he envisioned but a stylistic reinvention of the genre (Hogan 1995: 54).

In the Underworld USA trilogy, which comprises *American Tabloid* (1995), *The Cold Six Thousand* (2001), and *Blood's a Rover* (2009), Ellroy applies and adapts his revisionist noir style to a fictional overview of American history from 1958 to 1972. The timeframe loosely succeeds the Quartet chronologically, but, significantly, the setting was greatly expanded to include a panorama of American and international locations including Cuba, Haiti and Vietnam. The personal obsessions of LAPD detectives and politics of the city which defined the noir style of the Quartet are reinvented and applied to themes as expansive as the role played by intelligence agencies in US foreign policy. Ellroy heightens this sense of the covert by blending fiction with what appears to be true crime, rewriting the historic record with suppressed or invented details to 'uncover' an alternate history. Official or historical events, often too bleak, too morally compromised or too graphic for public consumption, are the focus of this narrative world. Its main operating force, the 'The Private Nightmare of Public Policy', refers to the nameless conspirators who silently control or manipulate events, and the moral price they pay for the horrific acts they commit to sustain their power (Duncan 1996: 72). Ellroy uses the term 'public policy' in an ironic sense, to encompass covert operations, be they officially sanctioned or illegal or both, yet his use of irony also underpins his main argument. Things are not what they seem, and power lies outside the expected sources.

With the exception of *The Black Dahlia*, Ellroy had done little research before writing the LA Quartet novels. But the historical and geographical scope of the Underworld series required that he hire paid researchers. Los Angeles in the 1950s had been as much a character as a setting in the Quartet, with Ellroy buttressing the text with many incidental details he had accrued as a lifelong Angeleno. But Ellroy had no intention of visiting the foreign locales of the Underworld novels. Research would be almost clinically delivered to him, and he would assess the historic and visual aspect of settings for their dramatic potential, skimming through photographs before deciding on how to portray the setting in his writing: 'If you're a novelist all you need to do is look at a picture and you've got it' (Sharkey 2009: 208). In his portrayal of the Kennedy era and its aftermath, the geographical setting is never as strong and fixed as it was in the Quartet. Instead, the focus is on historical events.

Each novel of the Underworld series features radical stylistic breaks from the preceding work and a more subtle evolution of narrative, as Ellroy fully intended to honour his covenant, but there would still be a large gulf between his original plans and how these plans evolved as the author experimented with a variety of narratives and stylistic techniques which will be examined in this chapter. *American Tabloid* is stylistically indebted to the Quartet, being a revisionist noir but applied to a national setting. By the time he wrote *The Cold Six Thousand*, however, Ellroy had developed a distinct style in the Underworld novels, which he took to extreme lengths through the uncompromising application of his sparse and lean prose style. In *Blood's a Rover*, Ellroy held even greater literary ambitions for honouring his 'covenant of consciousness'. Maintaining the series' chronological aims, Ellroy adapted the historical events to a deeply personal narrative in which one of the leading characters, Don Crutchfield, is based on himself. In contrast to the cold, rigid style of the preceding novel, the Demon Dog's emotional involvement in *Blood's a Rover* echoes the transmogrification in *The Black Dahlia*. The return to an openly personal narrative was the result of a turbulent period in his private life that prompted him once again to stylistically reinvent his work. This can be traced in his second memoir, *The Hilliker Curse* (2010), which deals both with his lifelong obsession with women following his mother's murder, but also an emotional crisis that almost derailed his writing career after the publication of *The Cold Six Thousand*.

American Tabloid

When Ellroy began the Quartet, he was under contract with the publisher Mysterious Press, but the final novel of the Quartet, *White Jazz*, was published by Knopf. The change in publishers indicates the change in Ellroy's critical reputation. Despite the fact that several prominent crime writers had published with Knopf, including Raymond Chandler, James M. Cain, Dashiell Hammett and Ross Macdonald, Knopf had a more prestigious literary reputation than the genre-focused Mysterious Press. By publishing with Knopf, Ellroy could consider himself in the same critical league as the aforementioned giants of American crime fiction, and, so he hoped, realize his ambition to expand beyond the boundaries of genre fiction. In a profile of Ellroy published in 1992, Martin Kihn revealed the full scope of Ellroy's plans: 'He plans a series of as many as ten novels in which he wants to "completely re-create America in the twentieth century through crime fiction. Completely"' (Kihn 1992: 24). In the three Underworld novels, the narrative encompasses the Kennedy years up to the dawn of the Watergate scandal. This falls short of Ellroy's grandiose historical vision as told to Kihn. However, since the completion of the Underworld novels, Ellroy has forged new connections between the Underworld series and the LA Quartet through his latest novel *Perfidia*. Thus, Ellroy seems intent on honouring his pledge by treating the Underworld trilogy as less of an independent series and more of a continuation of his other historical novels which cover a wider timeframe.

Don DeLillo's acclaimed novel on Lee Harvey Oswald, *Libra* (1988), had a considerable effect on Ellroy. Ellroy's reading of the novel 'blew my mind, fucked my soul, and scorched my sexuality', and was the impetus for writing *American Tabloid* (Silet 1995: 49). DeLillo's complex narrative interweaves a fictional biography of Lee Harvey Oswald with the story of CIA agents plotting a hypothetical assassination of President Kennedy. Much of the story is related through a latter-day CIA archivist, Nicholas Branch, who is trying to piece together a more detailed history of the assassination only to find that the abundance of sources contradicts and obscures the historical viewpoint rather than clarifying it. The title alludes to the gap between information about the sources and knowledge of the subject: Libra is Oswald's star sign, but the significance of this detail is negligible. DeLillo occupies this gap as a historical novelist, just as Branch does as a historian. The creative and the historical become intertwined by necessity. Ellroy's reading of *Libra*, much like his reading of *True Confessions* by John Gregory Dunne before writing *The Black Dahlia*, deterred as much as inspired him: 'I felt that, holy shit, now I'm tremendously interested in the Kennedy assassination, but now I can never write about it—because the book is just that seminal' (Silet 1995: 49). Ellroy's solution to the problem would be to write a novel more rooted in the genre than *Libra*, but which would build upon the philosophy of noir to create a narrative in which political conspiracies are deeply ingrained in society, indeed, they are a function of society. Through this, Ellroy would cast doubt, like DeLillo, on the very nature of history.

The influence of *Libra* on *American Tabloid*, however, is a matter of degree. After reading *Libra*, Ellroy came to one objective decision in how to differentiate his historical vision from DeLillo's. Lee Harvey Oswald is central to DeLillo's novel; therefore, Ellroy minimizes his importance as much as possible in *American Tabloid*. By playing down Oswald's role in events, Ellroy buttressed the novel's credentials as a secret history through the absence of the lone gunman and his personification of the simplest, official account of the assassination. Ellroy shows how Oswald, 'the ultimate American loner loser malcontent fucker', is wholly insignificant to his portrayal of the era (Powell 2008b: 172). Ellroy's decision on Oswald mirrors his earlier decision to exclude the Irish-American Dudley Smith from *The Black Dahlia* in order to avoid parallels with John Gregory Dunne's Dahlia novel *True Confessions*, which is deeply suffused with Irish-American culture. Although Ellroy admits to exploiting his mother's death to sell novels, he has displayed a consistently respectful approach to his literary influences.

Ellroy diverged from his drafting style for the LA Quartet in that he was now prepared to make major changes to the outline. The Quartet outlines had read as first drafts featuring exact plotting of the narrative, and Ellroy's sparse prose style did not allow for much extrapolation. In the outline to *American Tabloid*, Ellroy planned for Marilyn Monroe to be an important character, but her presence was eventually reduced to brief references. Kihn indicated how different the first Underworld novel could have been: 'He [Ellroy] hoists an outline he just finished for his next book, *American Tabloid*, about the Kennedys and Marilyn and the Mob. It's 345 pages' (Kihn 1992: 34). This is one of the only references to the importance of Marilyn Monroe as a character in the original outline, who because of her association with the Kennedy family and the rumours surrounding her death, had considerable dramatic potential. But whereas Ellroy does turn the speculation and rumours surrounding the Kennedy assassination into a plausible, fictional account of a conspiracy, in its final version the novel's narrative actually debunks suggestions of a Kennedy/Monroe affair. FBI agent Kemper Boyd begins rumours of an affair by staging a phone call which suggests he is arranging a secret meeting between the two. He knows he is under surveillance by Hoover while doing this, and he has deliberately fed Hoover misleading information: 'He just created Voyeur/Wiretap Heaven. Hoover would cream his jeans and maybe even spawn some crazy myth' (Ellroy 1995: 308). Hoover enjoys the hoax and congratulates Boyd, knowing Boyd has distorted the connection between Kennedy and Monroe for posterity: 'Your Marilyn Monroe aside had me going for quite some time. What a myth you have created!' (Ellroy 1995: 346). The incident serves as an early example in the novel of how the historical narrative has been manipulated and lends authority to Ellroy's version of events as the 'true' historical record.

Although he does not regard rumours of Monroe's affair with John F. Kennedy as completely fictitious, Ellroy has sought to debunk other myths around Monroe in interviews, downplaying her connection to the Kennedy family and dismissing other competing conspiracy theories:

> I think she was just a fucked up, usurious, sad, wasteful drunk and dope fiend. By the way Robert Kennedy did not have an affair with her. The Kennedys did not kill her. She was not murdered for any reason. She OD'd. I always considered it a preposterous story and an over-told story. (Powell 2009: 190–1)

Ellroy's aim is to deglamourize the Kennedy era, but Monroe is too easy a target. Oddly enough, the rumours surrounding Monroe's death might make her story less dramatically viable for Ellroy's purposes as any potential conspiracy theory is 'a preposterous story and an over-told story'. Ellroy does concede that Monroe and John Kennedy had an occasional sexual relationship: 'They met in '54 at the house of a man named Charlie Feldman—a big Hollywood agent that I caddied for on a few occasions. And they probably had seven or eight assignations between '54 and the time of her death in '62' (Powell 2009: 191). It is doubtful, however, that Ellroy ever met the agent Charles K. Feldman, as Feldman died in 1968, and Ellroy did not begin caddying until the late 1970s. Ellroy may just be repeating information passed to him by Fred 'Private Eye to the Stars' Otash who is alleged to have covertly recorded one of Kennedy's and Monroe's trysts (Galloway 2013). Despite Ellroy's downplaying of her cultural impact, Monroe was important to the original outline of *American Tabloid*: in it, she is murdered by the character of Lenny Sands because of her connection with the Kennedys and her death is arranged to look like an overdose (Ellroy 1992a). Ellroy planned to title this section of the novel 'Goddess', a direct reference to the Anthony Summers biography *Goddess* (which examines the possibility Monroe was murdered), and he also appears to have taken material from Donald H. Wolfe's controversial true-crime book, *The Assassination of Marilyn Monroe*. Wolfe's writing on the Black Dahlia case, as discussed in Chapter 3, also had parallels with Ellroy's work. By drawing on two true-crime books on her life, Ellroy sought to legitimize his own account through association. Yet the title 'Goddess' is ironic for Ellroy: Marilyn is deconstructed rather than deified, and his writing repositions the works of history as fiction (and his own work of fiction as the true history). In *American Tabloid*, Ellroy begins the process of tying together a series of historical rumours and allegations until it becomes impossible to disentangle the endless web of conspiracies comprising the narrative from historical fact.

Ellroy's portrayal of J. Edgar Hoover also changed significantly between the outline and the final draft of the novel. Ellroy avoids the more fanciful rumours: 'I had the immediate reaction to all of the Anthony Summers research—"Hoover is an overt fag, transvestite"—preposterous!' (Powell 2009: 190). This is the same Anthony Summers whose work on Marilyn Monroe had been influential in Ellroy's outline. Summers made the allegation that Hoover was being blackmailed by the Mafia because of his alleged transvestism in *Official and Confidential: the Secret Life of J. Edgar Hoover* (1993). Although Ellroy's original outline did not address the transvestism rumour, it did contain a scene in which Robert F. Kennedy chastises Hoover for having gambling debts to the Mafia (Ellroy 1992a). This scene did not make it into the novel, and

Ellroy has since dismissed Summers' work, including the allegation that Hoover was a heavy gambler: 'He was a two-dollar bettor' (Birnbaum 2001). By radically deviating from his original outline for *American Tabloid*, Ellroy made a key stylistic break from the LA Quartet. The prose style he had developed over the Quartet was dependent on there being very few plot changes between the outline and the finished novel. The editing technique he developed for *L.A. Confidential* was dependent on cutting words without cutting scenes. Ellroy was now disregarding this method as the scale of history he was dealing with required frequent plot revisions. This partially accounts for why the prose style of *American Tabloid*, while still lean, is not as reductive as *L.A. Confidential*, as he was no longer excising thousands of words from the manuscript as a way of retaining scenes.

The reasons for the plot changes in the transition between the outline of *American Tabloid* and the finished novel, some of which Ellroy has publicly acknowledged and others of which he has not, is in part a consequence of Ellroy changing the lead characters of the novel and thus reordering the subjective third-person viewpoints. Ellroy had planned to make Freddy Otash one of his main protagonists. Ellroy had discussions with Otash about his experiences as a private investigator in Hollywood, and Ellroy offered Otash money for permission to use him as a character on the condition that Otash would not publicly contradict any detail in the novel: '"Everyone knows you bugged the Kennedys—Wink, wink, wink—Alright, shut your mouth." I didn't trust him not to betray me on this' (Powell 2009: 190). Ultimately, Ellroy shifted Otash into a minor supporting role and created the contract killer Pete Bondurant for the role originally intended for Otash. Bondurant eventually became one of the three characters that support the novel's alternating subjective third-person viewpoint, with the other two being FBI agents Kemper Boyd and Ward Littell. Even after Bondurant transitioned into the Fred Otash role, Ellroy had not intended to make him one of the main three viewpoints.

The original outline for *American Tabloid* shows that Ellroy planned to alternate between four characters' viewpoints: Lenny Sands, Ward Littell, Robert F. Kennedy and a final voice to be revealed in the epilogue, Kemper Boyd (Ellroy 1992a). This structure would have created a completely different narrative than what eventually transpired in the finished novel. Ellroy eventually chose three main 'Underworld' characters, who broadly share a criminal philosophy. RFK was moved to a supporting role, as Ellroy's personal opinion of him grew over time, and the focus switched to characters in or more directly connected with the Underworld. Ellroy described RFK as the 'chief crime fighter of the twentieth century in America and a paragon of moral rectitude' (Duncan 1996: 79). Ellroy thus limited his deglamourizing of the Kennedys to the Mob-connected patriarch Joseph P. Kennedy and the clique surrounding President Kennedy. The Underworld of the novel and its two sequels is never precisely defined, but it broadly refers to elements of organized crime and its collusion with factions of US Intelligence. Both of these institutions, criminal and governmental, operate beneath the surface, the Underworld, of American society. Ellroy brings out the parallels in their hierarchies, moral codes and operations, blurring the divisions between organized crime and the state until their agenda and role in the downfall of a presidency become interlinked.

Despite being publicly committed to write 'bigger' and better novels following *The Big Nowhere*, Ellroy was gradually making the structure of the narrative smaller between outline and the finished novel, which would lead to the key decision of exploring the narrative in further novels. Ellroy's outline for *American Tabloid* includes six sections. The first five sections comprise the bulk of the novel from October 1957 to February 1964, and include the gradual forming of a conspiracy to assassinate Kennedy and its implementation in November 1963. A smaller sixth section would cover the aftermath of the Kennedy murder to the assassinations of Martin Luther King and Robert Kennedy in 1968. Finally, it would conclude with an epilogue dated 19 May 1972, written from Boyd's viewpoint. The date is significant as it is seventeen days after the death of Hoover, and the FBI Director has willed Boyd thousands of classified files which form the substance of the novel (Ellroy 1992a). This crucial detail was amended and only alluded to when the novel became the first of a trilogy, as although the novel is in design a secret history, it does not take the form of other secret history novels such as George Macdonald Fraser's Flashman series or Robert Graves' Claudius novels in which the text is presented as a lost memoir or history which often contradicts historical accounts of the era. Neither *American Tabloid* nor the two follow-up novels precisely fit this classification, although there are similarities as the reader is given glimpses of Hoover's massive archive of classified documents, which are interspersed throughout the narrative, and the fate of which forms the climax of the series.

The biggest single change to the original outline was Ellroy's decision to break the planned 1957 to 1972 timeline of *American Tabloid* into three novels: 'It was a trilogy from about two-thirds of the way through *American Tabloid* when I realized, "Oh shit, it's three books"' (McDonald 2001: 118). Each novel is divided into five-year segments;

thus, *American Tabloid* covers 1958 to 1963, *The Cold Six Thousand* covers 1963 to 1968 and *Blood's a Rover* 1968 to 1972. The first two novels end with political assassinations, and the final novel ends with the death of Hoover, one month prior to the Watergate break-in. Hoover's death and the Watergate scandal cumulatively and symbolically represent the death of the Underworld era. As Ellroy says of the US political system in the years leading up to 1972, 'It was that last gasp of pre-public accountability in America' (Helmore 2001). The narrative ends with the death of the chief architect of collusion between intelligence agencies and organized crime, and the corruption of the era is on the brink of being exposed, although only in part, as the Watergate scandal will lead to a new era of greater accountability.

Given the epic scale of the historical period Ellroy was dealing with, he decided to begin *American Tabloid* with a short, single-page prologue addressing the reader, a practice that he had never used before for a first-edition novel. The text of the prologue is italicized to distinguish it from the text of the novel, and the tone is abrasive in its condemnation of the popular trend to idolize Kennedy and America: '*America was never innocent. We popped our cherry on the boat over and looked back with no regrets*' (Ellroy 1995: 4). The style of Ellroy's direct address is in stark contrast to the prose style of the novel, which is consistently dry, even in its description of extreme violence. Ellroy's prologue places events within a wider time frame: the corruption of the US is an inevitable component of its national character and not a recent moral decline: '*You can't ascribe our fall from grace to any single event or set of circumstances. You can't lose what you lacked at conception*' (Ellroy 1995: 4). But at the same time, the moral shortcomings of one man are paralleled by the failings of a society which worshipped him. From the outset, Ellroy makes it clear that the novel will deconstruct the near sainthood of JFK: '*Jack Kennedy was the mythological front man for a particularly juicy slice of our history*' (Ellroy 1995: 4). The importance of timing, in this case a premature death, supersedes the substance of events and created a martyr in Kennedy, shielded from criticism by the horrific nature of his demise. Timing seems more important than the man, ensuring, through the eulogy of character, that his legacy has been woefully distorted: '*Jack got whacked at the optimum moment to assure his sainthood. Lies continue to swirl around his eternal flame*' (Ellroy 1995: 4). In *American Tabloid,* Kennedy is not only stripped of his reputation as heroic martyr, he is relegated to a supporting character in the events that unfold, unaware of the debt he owes to the Underworld and thus unable to repay it. Martyrs die for a cause, yet Ellroy denies Kennedy this moral significance as the continuation of the Underworld as an economic and political force is the primary motivation of the conspirators, whereas Kennedy only has a minor role in events.

The novel is concerned less with revelations about the assassination than with uncovering other hidden stories of the time. This is just one area in which journalism, or more specifically, the tabloid journalism of the title, is vitally important to the novel. *American Tabloid* reads as a curious blend of history and investigative journalism in which the author gives the reader the inside scoop on the story behind the story. However, one narrative rewrites the other, as the hidden story reveals the true movers and shakers: *'They were rogue cops and shakedown artists. They were wiretappers and soldiers of fortune and faggot lounge entertainers. Had one second of their lives deviated off course, American history would not exist as we know it'* (Ellroy 1995: 4). Political office is shown to be another façade. History is retold from a position of Underworld dominance. Ellroy's vision of the assassination conspiracy is that disparate criminal elements came together in a loose association with the tacit backing of Hoover and rogue intelligence operatives. Ellroy is reordering the historical story. But Ellroy does more than simply uncover a new ruling set who operate alongside historical figures; he also employs optimistic, patriotic language to cynically congratulate them:

> *It's time to demythologize an era and build a new myth from the gutter to the stars. It's time to embrace bad men and the price they paid to secretly define their time.*
> *Here's to them.* (Ellroy 1995: 4)

Ellroy's prologue sets up a new approach, moving beyond the blurred morality present in his earlier works to an open celebration of the Underworld's role in shaping the era. The Underworld may be exalted collectively, but for the people involved in this world *'the price they paid'* is in blood, loss of the women they love and ultimately their soul. The first three chapters introduce these very different *'bad men'*.

Ellroy's subtle deviation in the subjective third-person narration of his three lead characters, Pete Bondurant, Kemper Boyd and Ward Littell, unobtrusively adapts the prose style to suit the personality and viewpoint of each character without changing the consistent tone of the novel. The first page of the first chapter introduces Bondurant with the simplicity and appearance of an official document title 'Pete Bondurant', followed by the sub-title '(Beverly Hills, 11/22/58)'. Bondurant is an enforcer for Howard Hughes, and he is also a voyeur

– an important attribute as he becomes the 'eyes' through which the Underworld is revealed. Through Bondurant, the reader is dropped behind the curtain in full view of one of America's most reclusive men, Howard Hughes. The novel begins with him slyly watching his sickly and disturbed employer feed his drug habit:

> He always shot up by TV light. Some spics waved guns. The head spic plucked bugs from his beard and fomented. Black & white footage, CBS geeks in jungle fatigues. A newsman said, Cuba, bad juju – Fidel Castro's rebels vs. Fulgencio Batista's standing army.
> Howard Hughes found a vein and mainlined codeine. Pete watched on the sly – Hughes left his bedroom door ajar.
> The dope hit home. Big Howard went slack-faced. (Ellroy 1995: 9)

Bondurant's stolen glances heighten the sense of Hughes' shambolic surroundings, as his eyes drift between the TV and Hughes. The juxtaposition is significant as the 'TV light' illuminates but deglamourizes Hughes. From the very first page Ellroy has set up two major themes of the novel: the deglamourizing of celebrity, business and political figures and the impact media outlets have on the public's perception of events. The jumbled news report, which cuts between 'spics' and 'CBS geeks' is both desensitizing and tantalizing: the snippets of information regarding the Castro revolt are communicated to a public who will not be fully informed of its potential consequences. The reader of the novel is aware of the crisis about to unfold. The Cuban revolution, the nationalization of Mob-controlled casinos in Havana, the raids on Varadero Beach by Cuban exiles, the Mob/CIA-backed assassination attempts on Castro, the Bay of Pigs invasion, and the alleged role of Cuban exiles in the Kennedy assassination are all integral to the narrative, but here the portentousness of the news report is underplayed as it illuminates Hughes' dope addiction. Hughes then changes the channel to a programme more to his liking, *Howdy Doody*, a popular children's puppet show. The show is symbolic of Hughes' childlike demeanour and status as a puppet figure, dancing to the tune of his addictions. Drugs and paranoia have rendered Hughes celibate, and probably impotent, and as a consequence, they feed his voyeurism habit. He acquires the magazine *Hush-Hush* and uses Bondurant for 'story verification', a tabloid euphemism for extortion and blackmail (Ellroy 1995: 12). Hollywood celebrity gossip and intelligence work become interlinked as Hughes uses the magazine to curry favour with J. Edgar Hoover who shares Hughes' love of salacious rumour and innuendo.

The third-person style that accompanies the introduction of Kemper Boyd is more reflective of his personality and dialect. Boyd begins the novel working undercover as a car thief for the FBI:

> The car: a jaguar XK-140, British racing green/tan leather. The garage: subterranean and dead quiet. The job: steal the Jag for the FBI and entrap the fool who paid you to do it. ...
> His buyer was standing at the corner. He was a Walter Mitty crime-voyeur type who had to get close.
> The man pulled out. A squad car cut him off. His buyer saw what was happening – and ran.
> Philly cops packing shotguns swooped down. They shouted standard auto-theft commands: 'Get out of the car with your hands up!'/'Out – now!'/'Down on the ground!'
> He obeyed them. The cops threw on full armor: cuffs, manacles and drag chains.
> They frisked him and jerked him to his feet. His head hit a prowl car cherry light –
> The cell looked familiar. He swung his legs off the bunk and got his identity straight.
> I'm Special Agent Kemper C. Boyd, FBI, interstate car theft infiltrator.
> (Ellroy 1995: 22–3)

The reference to the ineffectual fantasist Walter Mitty alludes to a darker fantasy as the buyer, a 'crime-voyeur type', needs to be close to the vicinity of the crime in order to vicariously feel the thrill of stealing. Although Ellroy was publicly claiming to have moved on from noir, Boyd's clipped reductionism shows the prose is still in a hardboiled vein: 'The car: a jaguar XK-140, British racing green/tan leather. The garage: subterranean and dead quiet.' Boyd is mentally processing the details of the scene before him and has only seconds to do it. The scene is a form of visual shorthand or observational notes which reflect Boyd's professional role. This quick-fire style conveys action without leaving space for an emotional response. When Boyd is accosted by the Philly cops, his thoughts and prose black out at the moment of losing consciousness, 'His head hit a prowl car cherry light—', and then reappear, without any emotional interruption, when he comes to in his cell.

Boyd, in contrast to Bondurant, is a sophisticated, adaptable man who for most of the novel is able to slipstream convincingly between a wide variety of roles. As the narrative progresses, he slowly loses the ability to distinguish one from the other, performance from reality. Despite having a higher social status than Bondurant, Boyd still dabbles in crime. He uses his undercover role to illegally skim profits for his own expensive lifestyle, making him wonder whether his arrest was arranged by the FBI in retaliation. His name may also be significant, rhyming with the word void, which aptly sums up his lack of morals. In the prison cell, Boyd mentally clarifies his identity: 'I'm Special Agent Kemper C. Boyd.' Shortly after his release from jail, he meets Hoover who remarks 'there have been times when I wondered how your salary could sustain such a wardrobe', subtly revealing that he knows about Boyd's illegal activities (Ellroy 1995:23). Although Ellroy gives the reader glimpses of classified documents, many more files are alluded to but never shown, including Hoover's file on Boyd. Information is accrued for intelligence purposes, and rests in files unused for years with the mere hint of it enough for Hoover to keep Boyd in line. It is only when Boyd starts to veer from his performance as a Hoover loyalist that his downfall becomes inevitable.

The downtrodden Ward Littell, the last of the three major characters to be introduced, is a very different style of FBI agent to Boyd. Littell is a troubled middle-aged alcoholic who feels he is wasting away investigating Communist sympathizers. Littell's name is symbolic as he is frequently belittled. While searching for fraudulent expense accounts, he is surprised when the suspect's relative returns home. She is not frightened of him, and insults him openly by saying, 'So you people are common thieves now?' (Ellroy 1995: 34). In a later incident he is following a suspect which leads him to a gay bar. When he orders a drink, Littell accidentally drops his FBI badge in full view of all the patrons. Littell tries to humiliate Mob boss Sam Giancana by outing one of his recently deceased underbosses as a homosexual, but the Mob retaliates with the torture-murder of the man's teenage boyfriend. His initial righteousness does not lead to moral vindication; the opposite happens, with good intentions leading to horrific consequences. Over the course of the novel, Boyd and Littell take opposite moral journeys. Littell's deep Catholic guilt (he is an 'ex-Jesuit seminarian') pervades everything he does to the point where he is a nervous wreck (Ellroy 1995: 34). As he becomes cunning and ruthless the fragile, ineffectual side of his character disappears. Boyd's characteristic composure unravels, however, when he develops a strong moral sense. Morality seems to have a negative effect on how Littell and Boyd function. It leads to incompetence and the inability to fulfil multiple roles, an essential requirement for their clandestine activity.

After the viewpoints of Boyd, Bondurant and Littell, Hoover's archive of confidential files is the most frequent viewpoint Ellroy employs. From the brief glimpse of Lloyd Hopkins' psychological evaluation in *Suicide*

Hill to the newspaper headlines and diary entries in *Killer on the Road*, and latterly the appearance of *Hush-Hush* in the Quartet (see Chapters 1, 2 and 4), Ellroy had been continually expanding the roles of reports, transcripts, files and dossiers to illuminate and legitimize events in his novels. Hoover appears in a few scenes at the beginning of the novel. Otherwise, his presence is limited to transcripts of telephone conversations he conducted with Boyd and other agents. Transcripts of covert wiretaps 'Recorded at the Director's Request' appear at the beginning and end of certain chapters alongside other 'DOCUMENT INSERTS' such as newspaper articles. Ellroy intentionally blurs the line between the archive presented within the novel and the novel itself. The sense of bureaucracy is buttressed by the structure of the novel, which is so precise that in some ways it resembles a historical document: the narrative timeframe covers five years to the day, and each chapter's sub-heading introduces the location and date. One hundred chapters are divided into five sections with relatively bland, objective titles: Part I, SHAKEDOWNS, November–December 1958; Part II, COLLUSION, January 1959–January 1961; Part III, PIGS, February–November 1961; Part IV, HEROIN, December 1961–September 1963; Part V, CONTRACT, September–November 1963. Authenticity is projected through a quasi-official collation of information, and yet Ellroy is ultimately attempting to challenge the reader's preconceptions of a history they have come to regard as authentic. The archive also reflects Hoover's taste for salacious rumours and scandals: *Hush-Hush* articles suggest Hoover's addiction to acquiring information is far from being a dry, bureaucratic ambition. Instead, it combines his lust for power and the forbidden, titillating glimpse of the secret world that noir provides. Inspired by DeLillo's blurring of the line between the vital and inconsequential details in sources in *Libra*, Ellroy is also questioning the nature of history itself. A wide variety of sources appear containing endless reams of information and speculation, so that it is almost impossible to separate truth from distortion.

Hoover employs *Hush-Hush* to spread anti-Castro propaganda, a campaign which backfires disastrously when the magazine prematurely announces the Bay of Pigs invasion to have been a great success:

COWARDLY CASTRATO CASTRO OUSTED!

RETREATING REDS WREAK RAT-POISON REVENGE!

His rancorous Red reign ran for a rotten two years. Shout it loud, proud and un-kowtowed: Fidel Castro, the bushy-bearded beatnik bard of bilious bamboozlement, was determinedly and dramatically deposed last week by a heroically homeland-hungering huddle of hopped-up hermanos righteously rankled by the Red recidivist's rape of the nation! (Ellroy 1995: 410)

The *Hush-Hush* articles deviate from the clipped prose of the main text in their lurid writing style, which is dependent on endless alliteration and more concerned with following the rules of its own rhythm than informing its readers. Ellroy affectionately lampoons tabloid journalism by displaying how the verbose style is more important than fully coherent reportage. Hoover is outraged by the article and suspects its author Lenny Sands of treachery. He reprimands Hughes drily: 'I would advise you to tell Mr. Sands to get his facts reasonably straight. *Hush-Hush* should not publish science fiction, unless it's directly in our best interests' (Ellroy 1995: 411). Disinformation is a technique Hoover wants to tightly control. The debacle questions Hoover's omnipresent authority. *Hush-Hush*, always a disreputable publication, is downgraded even further when it becomes a '*private* skank sheet. The sheet would feature skank too skanky for public skank consumption. The sheet would be read by two skank fiends only: Dracula and J. Edgar Hoover' (Ellroy 1995: 417–8). Dracula is a reference to Howard Hughes and his desire for pure Mormon blood. His dubious quest for purity is contrasted with the unpublishable *Hush-Hush* articles latterly printed privately for Hughes and Hoover: it is significant that these ultra-secret editions do not appear in the novel, as the allusion to more confidential documents outside the reader's purview containing secrets, scandals and conspiracies, no matter how lurid, buttresses the novel's credentials as a secret history.

The Bay of Pigs *Hush-Hush* article is presented as an FBI document which has been accumulated, studied and filed at the request of Hoover. Ellroy changes the narrative function of *Hush-Hush* between the Quartet and the Underworld series, as in the latter *Hush-Hush* is distinctly labelled as a historical document. The magazine acts as bridge between organized crime (both Hughes and Lenny Sands are 'connected'), and the intelligence agencies. Through the transition of *Hush-Hush* from a sleazy tabloid magazine to a valuable historical source, Ellroy questions the concept that historical validity is determined based on the number and quality of the primary sources, since all information is distilled, filtered and distorted through the mediums from which it is relayed.

As with so many of the themes of *American Tabloid*, Ellroy's reading of *Libra* was a key influence in his portrayal of the limitations of history as a discipline. In *Libra*, the rogue CIA agent Win Everett engages in much mental theorizing as to how an assassin of the President could be created and presented to the public:

> He would put someone together, build an identity, a skein of persuasion and habit, ever so subtle. He wanted a man with believable quirks. He would create a shadowed room, the gunman's room, which investigators would eventually find, exposing each fact to relentless scrutiny, following each friend, relative, casual acquaintance into his own roomful of shadows. We lead more interesting lives than we think. We are characters in plots, without the compression and numinous sheen. Our lives, examined carefully in all their affinities and links, abound with suggestive meaning, with themes and involute turnings we have not allowed ourselves to see completely. He would show the secret symmetries in a nondescript life. (DeLillo 1988: 78)

By searching for and creating the character of Lee Harvey Oswald, Everett assumes the role of author/historian. He is essentially writing the history of events before they take place by prophesying how the American people will react to the character of Oswald when he is presented. He knows that a manipulation of the established facts surrounding a man's life can lead to all sorts of circumstantial evidence indicative of guilt: 'We lead more interesting lives than we think. We are characters in plots.' The public will help construct the right identity for Oswald. Looking back on events the CIA archivist Nicholas Branch examines the connections and is frustrated in his efforts to achieve a coherent narrative of the assassination. The abundance of sources could possibly suggest any number of scenarios. The name Branch symbolizes the many connections endlessly sprouting off one another.

For Ellroy, writing historical fiction encompasses more than just the need to fictionalize historical events, it becomes a conduit for his vision of history as an evolving concept. As John Scaggs has argued in relation to Ellroy's work:

> Reading historical crime fiction from a realist perspective, there is a tendency to distinguish between literature, which is subjective and somehow 'untrue', and history, which is objective and 'true.' This results in a fundamental conflict at the heart of historical crime fiction. On the one hand, a premium is placed on verisimilitude and 'realism', while on the other hand fictive demands are evident in such realist devices as a reliable narrator, a well-structured plot,

converging story-lines, and a tidy narrative transition from beginning to end that echoes, in its narrative order, the restoration of the social order initially disrupted by crime. (Scaggs 2005: 120–1)

Scaggs identifies the same concept as Ellroy, verisimilitude, as an essential component of historical fiction. In his prologue to *American Tabloid* Ellroy used the phrase '*reckless verisimilitude*'. The distinction is important as Ellroy strives for a probable truth in a deliberately provocative tabloid fashion. He achieves 'realism' through a clipped noir prose style which is journalistic in its exactitude, whereas the *Hush-Hush* articles are experimental and expansive with language. However, Ellroy radically diverges from the Scaggs model which stipulates the ending must include 'the restoration of the social order initially disrupted by crime'. By contrast, the denouement of *American Tabloid* portrays a social order restored by crime through the Kennedy assassination. Indeed, as an Underworld novel, the social order *is* crime. Kennedy is killed because he is oblivious to how much he is indebted to Underworld figures and unwittingly fails to honour his debts. Ellroy put it succinctly: 'Kennedy fucked with some people and they fucked him back' (Wieners 1995: 37). The list of crimes Ellroy stacks up against the Kennedy clan in *American Tabloid* are culled from a long list of historical rumours to achieve verisimilitude: most significantly, Joseph P. Kennedy's links to organized crime dating back to the Prohibition era, Sam Giancana's secret donations to Kennedy's 1960 election campaign and organized crime securing union backing in key states. Ellroy also uses outright fictitious scenes to smear Kennedy: an unguarded comment Kennedy makes to his mistress after sex inadvertently leads to the murder of a Mob informant. Kennedy's biggest crime in Ellroy's portrayal is to be passive to events. The Underworld is more historically influential than the presidency.

The precise details of the assassination conspiracy are never fully revealed as this would leave the narrative vulnerable to historical falsification. None of the three main characters actively has a role in the assassination, although they all know when and where it will take place. Boyd, Bondurant and Littell's plan for Kennedy to be killed in Philadelphia is cancelled at the eleventh hour:

> One of the chief ironies of the book is that Boyd, Ward, and Pete get fucked out of the assassination; they don't get to kill him. These guys all start out enamoured of Jack to one degree or another, and all end up hating him. Their motives for killing him are really very personal,

but they are in the grip of events bigger than themselves and don't even get to kill him. (Hogan 1995: 54)

The reader is privy to suggestions that a plot is brewing through Hoover's audio surveillance of Mob figures whose anger is building towards Kennedy. Hoover disobeys instructions from Bobby Kennedy to hand over all his audio surveillance, instead only passing on sanitized tapes so that Kennedy is unaware of an impending assassination. Through this process of suggestion, which avoids clarification, Ellroy achieves the 'verisimilitude' and 'realism' of Scaggs' definition of historical crime fiction.

The impending assassination of Kennedy is paralleled with the deaths of several leading and supporting characters. Kemper Boyd spends his last day alive trying to contact several of the departments which have ostracized him:

> He called the White House and the Justice Department. Second-string aides rebuffed him.
> His name was on some kind of list. They cut him off midway through his salutations.
> He called the Dallas SAC. The man refused to talk to him.
> He called the Secret Service. The duty officer hung up.
> He quit toying with it. He sat on the patio and replayed the ride start to finish.
> Shadows turned the hills dark green. His replay kept expanding in slow motion.
> He heard footsteps. Ward Littell walked up. He was carrying a brand new Burberry raincoat.
> Kemper said, 'I thought you'd be in Dallas.'
> Littell shook his head. 'I don't need to see it. And there's something in L.A. I do need to see.'
> 'I like your suit, son. It's good to see you dressing so nicely.'
> Littell dropped the raincoat. Kemper saw the gun and cracked a big shit-eating grin.
> Littell shot him. The impact knocked him off his chair.
> The second shot felt like HUSH NOW. Kemper died thinking of Jack. (Ellroy 1995: 581)

This scene is set two days before the assassination, which makes Boyd's telephone calls all the more ambiguous. Boyd may not be fully sure what he is trying to achieve: 'He quit toying with it.' It is fitting that he is cut off in every phone call he makes, the final aborted call occurring only moments before his life is abruptly cut short. The darkness enveloping the rural Mississippi landscape is symbolic of Boyd's impending murder. Boyd's admiration for the landscape reflects a final desire to embrace his Southern roots, which he has spent a lifetime repressing for career purposes. As if returning to the South were a form of conversion, his new-found righteousness has manifested itself in civil rights activism, but it also inflames the darker side of his character as he is prone to extreme acts of violence against Klan members. In his final moments, he reflects on his life, 'the ride', as though watching a film, which Boyd can 'replay' and expand in 'slow motion'. The scene faintly echoes the Zapruder film, which captured the literal and symbolic end to 'the ride'. Suggesting images of a fairground attraction, the 'ride' is evocative of the epic spectacle of the novel. Boyd's death scene, written from his own subjective third-person viewpoint, forms a cul-de-sac of consciousness. Boyd is about to be murdered, yet his thoughts are of Kennedy's impending assassination. Likewise, he sees his murderer, Littell, as the man he once was. Boyd had once admired Littell for his righteousness, but chastised him for his incompetence. Now Littell is amoral and highly competent, and Boyd is washed up. The mental image of Kennedy helps ease the suffering in Boyd's dying consciousness: 'The second shot felt like HUSH NOW.' 'HUSH' naturally evokes the tabloid magazine integral to the narrative and it gives the word a profundity it had heretofore not possessed as Boyd dies 'thinking of Jack'. The final irony of Ellroy's portrayal of Kennedy is that despite his rather vacuous personality – even as an adulterer he is an underwhelming 'two-minute man'– he inadvertently sparks wildly different passions in people: Boyd had wanted an active role in the assassination conspiracy, but his final thought of Kennedy is rather nostalgic (Ellroy 1995: 86).

Peter Wolfe argues that Ellroy portrays the assassination as a 'sporting event at which the spectators discover, to their horror, that they've come to the wrong game' (Wolfe 2005: 216). This is oddly paralleled by characters who have a foreknowledge of events and are all strangely drawn to consider their own mortality on the day. Although Hughes would live for another thirteen years, Ward Littell views him on his symbolic deathbed in Beverley Hills: 'Bugs were floating in a bucket filled with piss. ... His bed sagged under the weight of a dozen disassembled slot machines' (Ellroy 1995: 583). Littell views Hughes' mental and physical decline as a consequence of his addiction to power and rampant paranoia. Littell's motivation for seeing Hughes on the day Kennedy is shot is ambiguous. He has nothing practical to gain from being there, and when an orderly he bribes in order to see his reclusive employer asks in stupefaction, "You just want to *see* him?", the response appears in capitalized text: 'I WANT TO SEE THE PRICE' (Ellroy 1995: 582). Littell must see the moral price of his new identity. In Hughes, that price is an old decaying body with no semblance of virtue to act as consolation. Littell has only a brief moment to gaze on his decrepit employer, as the orderly must smuggle him in and out before Hughes' Mormon minders return. Knowing this, Littell mentally speeds up time and then freezes it, 'His head raced two hours ahead and locked in to Texas time', so that his viewing of Hughes will be synchronous with Dallas, which is two hours ahead of California. Another mental leap of time will put him at the scene of Kennedy's assassination, which happened two hours and twenty minutes after his viewing of Hughes. Kennedy's exploding head, Hughes' rotting body, and Littell's realization of his own damnation all transcend time zones to merge into a voyeuristic image as Littell 'pressed up to the wall and looked through the doorway' (Ellroy 1995: 583).

Ellroy moves from the moral death of Littell to the physical death of another Underworld figure. Bondurant visits the dying gangster Heshie Ryskind on the day of the assassination. Ryskind is an immoral, perverted and for most of the story, insignificant character who through his simple venality elicits more sympathy in Ellroy's narrative than the exalted, martyred president. Like Ellroy's vision of America, Ryskind has never possessed any innocence to lose and appears beyond redemption, and yet in his desperately weak, cancer-stricken condition he acts as a moral coda to the novel. Bondurant comforts Ryskind with the news that he can watch the build-up to the assassination from his hospital window, and this provides him solace in his last hours:

> The dope hit home. Heshie unclenched and eked out a smile.
> Pete wiped off the needle. 'It's happening about six blocks from here.Wheel yourself to the window about 12:15. You'll be able to see the cars go by.'
> Heshie coughed into a Kleenex. Blood dripped down his chin. Pete dropped the TV gizmo in his lap.
> 'Turn it on then. They'll interrupt whatever they're showing for a news bulletin.'
> Heshie tried to talk. Pete fed him some water.
> 'Don't nod out, Hesh. You don't get a show like this every day.'
> (Ellroy 1995: 584)

Although the reader is only familiar with Ryskind's perverse character, in this brief glimpse Ellroy changes the tone from the journalistic portrayals of violence to a touching scene where morality is turned upside down. Empathy and complicity to murder become inextricably linked: Ryskind's dying wish is seemingly granted in Kennedy's death, and Ryskind's death, humanized through Bondurant's kindness, becomes more resonant and sympathetic than Kennedy's.

There is a strange double viewing of the assassination as Ryskind watches it through two screens. The hospital window acts as a symbolic cinema screen, through which Ryskind will first see the presidential motorcade. The second screen is the television, which both criminals know will be interrupted with an announcement that will confirm the event to a national audience. This double viewing alludes to the two different perspectives, Underworld and public, which Ellroy sets out in the novel. The characters consistently view events from their morally dubious Underworld perspectives, yet they hold a more accurate knowledge of events than the public view. Ryskind is so ill he could die at any moment. This will be the last thing he sees, if he lives long enough. Bondurant's parting words put the reader in a position whereby they desire Ryskind's final wish to be fulfilled: 'Don't nod out, Hesh. You don't get a show like this every day.' The 'show', a series of tumultuous political events over the course of five years, culminates in a spectacle arranged for a mass audience. It is a double viewing for Ellroy himself as his father had his first stroke in late 1963 and was discharged from the hospital on the day of the assassination (Ellroy 1996: 119). The decline of his father's health and Kennedy's death would have been strongly connected in Ellroy's memory of the event which suggests there is an allusive autobiographical thread to Ryskind's deathbed scene.

After displaying a rare act of kindness in helping Ryskind view the assassination, Bondurant heads to a rundown nightclub close to Dealey Plaza to watch his girlfriend Barb Jahelka perform in a very different 'show':

> The combo mauled an uptempo number. Barb blew him a kiss. Pete sat down and smiled his 'Sing me a soft one' smile.
>
> A roar ripped through the place – HE'S COMING HE'S COMING HE'S COMING!
>
> The combo ripped an off-key crescendo. Joey and the boys looked half-blitzed.
>
> Barb went straight into 'Unchained Melody.' Every patron and barmaid and kitchen geek ran for the door.
>
> The roar grew. Engine noise built off of it – limousines and full-dress Harley-Davidsons.

They left the door open. He had Barb to himself and couldn't hear a word she was singing.

He watched her. He made up his own words. She held him with her eyes and her mouth.

The roar did a long slow fade. He braced himself for this big fucking scream. (Ellroy 1995: 584–5)

The glamour and power of the Kennedy administration lies in stark contrast to the dirty, cheap nightclub Bondurant chooses to visit at the moment of the assassination. Bondurant fell for Barb when he was setting her up as one of Kennedy's mistresses in an attempted sting. Again, there are two viewings taking place in this scene: Bondurant is watching the woman he loves, and the people on the streets are watching the presidential visit. The patriotism and excitement of the crowd contrasts with their blindness as to what has really happened over the past five years, and their ignorance of what will happen next. The noise from the crowd outside is so loud that Bondurant and Barb cannot hear each other in the club, but they still communicate silently: 'Barb blew him a kiss. Pete sat down and smiled his "Sing me a soft one" smile.' The novel ends at almost the exact moment the assassination takes place as the excited cheers of the crowd fade, and Bondurant anticipates the reaction which will echo across the nation. The change in music from an 'uptempo number' to the slow ballad 'Unchained Melody' parallels the change in the tone of events. Barb sings an elegy of a lost love as the Underworld characters are able to sync performance and reality, but the public are violently shaken from performance into reality. The roaring crowd becomes 'a long slow fade' moments before the unmelodic 'big fucking scream'.

The Cold Six Thousand

By the time of the publication of the second novel in the Underworld USA trilogy in 2001, Ellroy was at the height of his literary celebrity. In his study of the genre *Nice and Noir: Contemporary American Crime Fiction* (2002), Richard B. Schwartz wrote of the Demon Dog:

Ellroy's reputation is at its zenith. His very presence in Los Angeles (characteristically at the Pacific Dining Car as a base of operations) initiates a spate of rumors and second guesses. (Schwartz 2002: 44)

Schwartz's high regard for Ellroy unknowingly lets slip the problem Ellroy was facing. Expectations for the second novel were high, but from the beginning of *The Cold Six Thousand* publicity tour, Ellroy seemed plagued with bad luck. Manuscripts were sold on the Internet before the official release, and the reviews were not the unqualified praise Ellroy had become accustomed to. In *The Observer*, Tom Cox mocked the prose style, a reversion to the extremely pared-down writing of *L.A. Confidential* and *White Jazz*, with the sub-heading, 'James stops. James thinks. James writes a sequel' (Cox 2001). This captured the general tone of criticism; the complex structure was seen as meticulously planned, but the reductive prose style produced a narrative that was too mechanical. Reviewers were beginning to associate Ellroy's public persona with his changing literary style, and not always positively. Chris Petit questioned the ongoing value of Ellroy's Demon Dog persona: '*The Cold Six Thousand* is pretty much the Ellroy show, and a further example of how he has turned himself into the star of his recent work' (Petit 2001).

Literary stardom was beginning to wear Ellroy down. The book tour began in France before moving to Italy, Spain, the United Kingdom and then to North America, and Ellroy was scheduled to return to Europe. In addition to this gruelling work schedule, Ellroy was dealing with several personal problems. His marriage to Helen Knode was under strain, and his behaviour was becoming unpredictable and erratic: he started to believe he was suffering from melanoma and developed an addiction to painkillers which led to a spell in rehab. It was affecting his performance in interviews as his usual brand of 'Dog humour' seemed more tetchy and argumentative. An interview with M.G. Smout for *The Barcelona Review* captured Ellroy's volatile behaviour during this period and the health issues which fed his paranoia:

> He also has a frightening array of vitamin pills and supplements lined up on the table. These he washes down with copious amounts of green tea which he has brought along for the tour, producing bags from his pockets to plop in hot water after testing the temperature with his finger. The fear of illness, the upheaval of traveling (alone) and being on a tight tour schedule, calls for strict cautionary measures to help combat a persistent apprehension over health matters which leads to nervous check-ups in hotel mirrors. Every blemish, mark on his skin, wheeze, or whatever urges him to seek transatlantic phone help from his wife, writer Helen Knode. (Smout 2001:105)

Although he did not know it at the time, the issues Ellroy was facing would lead him to make a complete stylistic and narrative overhaul of the Underworld series when he came to outline and write the concluding volume of the trilogy, which in turn would lead to the author virtually disowning *The Cold Six Thousand* from his body of work.

In May 2001, Ellroy was interviewed by fellow crime writer Craig McDonald and confessed, 'I'm tired of myself, if you want to know the truth' (McDonald 2001: 120). Two days after the McDonald interview, Ellroy released a statement cancelling the rest of the tour:

> It is with great regret that I have had to cancel appearances on my U.S. book tour. I have been on the road since March 12 and the effect of this global tour finally caught up with me in Chicago. (McDonald 2001: 115)

For Ellroy, even after the tour was cancelled, the emotional turmoil would continue, eventually leading to a nervous breakdown (Peace 2010: 214). This harrowing period of his life had a profound effect on Ellroy personally and led to the longest period of time yet between the publication of two of his novels. *Blood's a Rover* was published eight years after *The Cold Six Thousand*, which attests to a period of relative inactivity for Ellroy as he wrestled with his personal problems. But the delay was also due to the scale of the challenge of redesigning the series.

Right from the very first page, and first line, *The Cold Six Thousand* is confrontational work: the novel begins with the introduction of a new character, Wayne Tedrow, a Las Vegas Sheriff and Mormon, on a plane bound for Dallas. The opening line reads, 'They sent him to Dallas to kill a nigger pimp named Wendell Durfee. He wasn't sure he could do it' (Ellroy 2001: 3). Ellroy justified the line to Craig McDonald: 'This book scares people ... paragraph one, the word "nigger" is a warning' (McDonald 2001: 117). Ellroy knew the word was more loaded than the plot device of the contract killing, which is introduced in the same sentence, and it gives a foretaste of the dark morality of the novel. When McDonald expressed admiration for the novel, Ellroy replied, 'you're among the 30 per cent and the brave' (McDonald 2006: 146). As with *White Jazz*, *The Cold Six Thousand* reaches a stylistic apex that was also a limitation. Ellroy had taken his brand of reductionism to its logical conclusion: 'there's not a word out of place in this entire book' (McDonald 2001: 117). This careful, merciless precision also affects the novel's structure: 'There is not a plot thread that isn't buttressed. There isn't a thread of incident or circumstance or character that isn't layered-in seamlessly' (McDonald 2001: 117). These structural and stylistic changes influence the narrative thrust of the novel, as characters and events are propelled inexorably to the violent endpoint of 'public policy'. Thus, both prose and plotting convey Ellroy's view of the five years of American history that the novel covers as a national dead-end.

The racism of the times is firmly embedded in the prose style. Aside from the use of the word 'nigger' in the first sentence and frequent repetition thereafter, there are deliberate mis-spellings with racist connotations such as 'Lincoon Coontinental' and 'Martin Luther Coon'. Ellroy also replaces the letter 'C' with 'K' in certain words. This was common in the naming of the Ku Klux Klan Klaverns, here depicted at the peak of their struggle with the civil rights movement, and Ellroy uses it to convey the mind-numbing, inflexible racism of their philosophy: 'The White Knights. The Royal Knights. Klextors/Kleagles/Kladds/Kludds/ Klokards. Klonklaves and Klonvocations' (Ellroy 2001: 215). From the outset of the novel, racial terms are embedded at an accelerating rate, yet the mis-spellings are distinct from racist invective in the dialogue, suggesting a layering of bigotry. However, the novel does contain more emotionally palatable plot threads. Pete Bondurant begins to withdraw from the Underworld due to failing health, and Ward Littell makes an ultimately fatal attempt at redemption.

Between *American Tabloid* and *The Cold Six Thousand* there is a distinct shift in tone: *American Tabloid* ended almost at the exact moment of Kennedy's assassination; *The Cold Six Thousand* begins the same day. When Tedrow arrives at Dallas airport he discovers Kennedy has been shot, which suggests the assassination took place while Tedrow was on the plane. Indeed, it may have taken place at the exact moment the novel begins, giving direct succession between the two Underworld novels. Tedrow's opening journey between time zones is a metaphor for the transition the country will go through upon the death of a president. The Underworld is less hidden after this pivotal moment, and the battle between Hoover and the civil rights movement, and the escalation of US involvement in Vietnam become increasingly apparent in a now openly divided country. Thus, Ellroy is not trying to deglamourize the era as with *American Tabloid* but to maintain a downbeat tone from the first page.

Ellroy described the Kennedy assassination as 'but one murder in a long series of murders', and so the novel begins with murderous continuation as Tedrow has accepted a contract to kill a pimp, in stark contrast to the murder of a president which closed the previous novel (Duncan 1996: 78). However, just as the Kennedy assassination haunts the narrative, Tedrow's intended victim Wendell Durfee has a massive effect on Tedrow's life over the subsequent five-year narrative. It is

Tedrow's first contract killing, and the title references his fee. Durfee has unknowingly drawn Tedrow to Dallas, which instigates Tedrow's involvement with events following the assassination. Tedrow's inability to kill Durfee backfires disastrously when Durfee murders Tedrow's wife and then disappears. Tedrow's ambiguous, but nonetheless sincere love for his wife is established in the opening scene on the plane when he is contemplating the Durfee contract. Tedrow flirts with an air stewardess, bragging about being a Sheriff and telling her of his duty to find Durfee, but leaving out the fact that he plans to murder him. When the stewardess suggests they take things further, Tedrow angrily snaps back, 'I don't cheat on my wife' (Ellroy 2001: 4). Murder sparks gloomy indecision in Tedrow, but while he is happy to flirt, the thought of adultery makes him indignant.

When Tedrow later discovers Lynette's defiled corpse, he attempts to commit suicide, realizing his inability to kill Durfee has led to her murder:

> He kicked the door in. He looked down the hall. He saw the bedroom light. He walked up and looked in.
> She was naked.
> The sheets were red. She drained red. She soaked through the white.
> He spread her. He cinched her. He used Wayne's neckties. He gutted her and shaved her. He trimmed off her patch.
> Wayne pulled his gun. Wayne cocked it. Wayne put it in his mouth and pulled the trigger.
> The hammer clicked empty. He shot his full six at the dump.
> (Ellroy 2001: 164)

In this moment of initial discovery, the name Lynette never comes to Tedrow in his thoughts, nor does Durfee's, as the prose style and narrative are so cold that even grief seems emotionless. The clipped sentences suggest Tedrow is tightly controlling information, only revealing as much of the horror as he can handle. The avoidance of feelings makes the action distinctly cinematic with the emphasis on a single colour akin to a storyboarding of visual images: 'The sheets were red. She drained red. She soaked through the white.' Blood is an unwelcome colour intrusion into an otherwise dour world. Tedrow's instinctual response to commit suicide would absolve him of the consequences of failing to kill Durfee. Putting the gun in his mouth is a potent phallic symbol. In *The Big Nowhere*, Danny Upshaw decides against this method of suicide, worrying that people might associate it with his homosexuality. It may be a sexual image mirroring the violation of Lynette, or it may just stop Tedrow from screaming in the moment, as Ellroy offers no elaboration on his emotional reaction. However, he is cheated out of suicide as he shot his 'full six', the phrase oddly reminiscent of the title, earlier in the night.

The click of the hammer indicates both a scene change and a cinematic cut to a different visual image. It also indicates a change in Tedrow. He will not shirk his duty through suicide but immediately leaves the scene to murder three of Durfee's associates. In his grisly fashion, Durfee had taken Tedrow's role as the possessive male through the murder of Lynette, cutting her pubic hair as a memento and even using Wayne's neckties to cinch the body. Wayne will posthumously reclaim Lynette through Durfee's murder. Tedrow's frustration at being unable to properly earn the advance of $6,000 imbues the narrative with a sense of incomplete business. Even though Tedrow soon finds himself caught up in conspiracies which determine the future of his country, on a personal level, Tedrow needs to avenge his wife and earn the payment, and so he periodically returns to hunt Durfee. Durfee's sheer existence torments Tedrow, as he is completely irrelevant in every way other than being the target of his revenge. Even his name 'Durfee' is almost completely devoid of stature or dignity as a character. Durfee is phonetically similar to 'doofus' and the first syllable of his forename, W(h)en-dell, illustrates Tedrow's inability to find him. Durfee becomes a symbol to Tedrow, who channels his energy in perpetuating racist acts to undermine the civil rights movement. Although he detests the racism of his father Wayne Senior, he tries to imagine every black man, including Martin Luther King, as Wendell Durfee. This allows him to 'hate smart', a concept whereby racism is quantified according to its personal and political benefit. Tedrow tries to legitimize his actions by distinguishing himself from more extreme forms of bigotry exercised by Klan members who 'hate dumb'. Tedrow's hunting and hatred of Durfee is at root a commercial enterprise, despite the personal nature of the crime.

Tedrow finally locates Durfee in LA in March 1968. Once again, the confrontation is notable less for being the climax of Tedrow's quest to avenge his wife than for the banality of their exchange:

Wayne stood there.
Wendell said, 'You look familiar.'
Wayne stood there.
Wendell said, 'Give me a hint.'
Wayne said, 'Dallas.' Wayne almost threw up. (Ellroy 2001: 620)

Ellroy's sparse dialogue and use of their similar first names, 'Wendell' and 'Wayne', make the two men almost undistinguishable. Yet beneath the plain dialogue, a storm is brewing in Tedrow. Tedrow suppresses the urge to vomit, disgusted by the squalor of the surroundings and disturbed by past actions, but Durfee regards the past casually, even nostalgically. The only thing of note Durfee can think to say could be interpreted as affable in a different context: '"That was some weekend. Remember? The President got shot."' Once again Ellroy draws a parallel between the murder of the president and the contract killing of a pimp as the Underworld operates on every level of society (Ellroy 2001: 620).

There is a correlation between a lack of emotion in the characters and their propensity for extreme violence. Even in the revenge killing of Durfee, Tedrow remains emotionless as he tortures the man and then watches him bleed to death. Andrew Pepper has connected the themes of violence in Ellroy's work to the 'dominant social order':

> The idea or hope that 'crime' can be controlled is wilfully abandoned in Ellroy's fiction, not least because every aspect of the dominant social order and those who occupy positions of power and privilege is satiated with an oppositional logic; that individuals do not really know themselves, do not understand the tangled mess of repressed neuroses (usually of a sexual nature) which compel them to perform acts which might otherwise be seen as 'disgusting', 'perverse' or 'sick'. (Pepper 2000: 29)

Here Pepper is writing specifically about the LA Quartet, but his argument applies equally to the violence in the Underworld novels. The idea that 'individuals do not really know themselves' is taken to absurd levels in the novel as Tedrow and Durfee do not really know themselves or each other. Durfee does not really know who Tedrow is, whereas Tedrow is disappointed to discover that after such a long search there is nothing interesting to know about Durfee. Durfee at this stage is so drug-addled he has all but forgotten about the murder of Lynette, but adds 'I've fucking widowered more than a few' (Ellroy 2001: 620). Tedrow's grief is not unique, Durfee's murder of Lynette was not personal. Durfee murders out of psychopathic compulsion. Tedrow's murder of Durfee is ultimately the fulfilment of a business contract, the six thousand of the title, as much as a revenge killing. Tedrow does not 'understand the tangled mess of repressed neuroses' which affect him after the death of Lynette, nor does Durfee help enlighten him as to the reason for her murder. Tedrow's initial orders from the Casino Operators

Council to kill Durfee are vague: 'Nobody *said* it: / Kill that coon. Do it good. Take our hit fee' (Ellroy 2001: 3). The word *said* is italicized as it indicates the veiled communication of conspiracy. Money changes hands and information is relayed to murder an individual without reference to specific details. The only relevant fact Tedrow knows is that the Council want Durfee dead after he 'shivved a twenty-one dealer' in Las Vegas (Ellroy 2001: 3). An Underworld conspiracy takes shape with individuals shielded from one another through buffers and operating on deliberately limited information. Although conspiracies drive the narrative, they are not masterminded to account for every possible scenario. Instead, Ellroy's intricate plotting allows events to unravel in a way which is more complex as the connectivity is loose and unpredictable. By the time of Durfee's murder, Tedrow and his country have inexorably changed since the Kennedy assassination. Durfee's death is significant only to Tedrow.

Ellroy consistently parallels the duel between Tedrow and Durfee with the larger, national struggles in the narrative. He also applies a dual approach by undermining some aspects of conspiracy theories, while still questioning the validity of the official record. In the novel, Hoover creates a fabricated report on his surveillance of the civil rights movement which will eventually become available to the public, but the real operation is detailed only in the archive contained within the novel. As the critic Jonathan Walker put it:

> The historically documented 'Operation Zorro' (as it is designated in the novel) is presented as something that exists only on paper, a fabrication created specifically to distract attention from a far more insidious initiative controlled directly by J. Edgar Hoover himself. (Walker 2002: 204).

Hoover's plans to undermine and infiltrate Martin Luther King's entourage and his organization the Southern Christian Leadership Conference are dubbed 'Operation Black Rabbit'. Even in the title of the operation, Hoover is expressing his racism as he chooses the name in reference to the 'sex drive, prowess and heedlessly puerile demeanour of our long-eared friends' (Ellroy 2001: 350). The operation is as complex as the codenames are farcical: Ward Littell is 'CRUSADER RABBIT', Dwight Holly is 'BLUE RABBIT', Dwight's brother Lyle is 'WHITE RABBIT', Pete Bondurant is 'BIG RABBIT', Wayne Tedrow Senior is 'FATHER RABBIT'. King is 'RED RABBIT' and his aide Bayard Rustin is 'PINK RABBIT'. Every codename reflects the characteristics of the subject, thus red for King's socialist views and pink for Rustin's homosexuality. There is also a sense of blackly comic farce to the operation. All of the characters are running around like rabbits. Hoover seems to give himself up to the childlike absurdity of the situation, listening but not learning from the targets rabbiting on endlessly while his hatred grows for the 'very bad bunny' Martin Luther King (Ellroy 2001: 592).

Operation Black Rabbit is a failure, and Dwight Holly, who appears in the following transcript by the initials of his codename BR, notices the effect it has on Hoover. Whereas he once seemed strong and shielded by appearing only in transcripts of recorded telephone conversations, he latterly comes across as paranoid, and tacitly concedes that the only way he can beat King is to have him assassinated:

DIR: I am at my wits' end, Dwight. I do not know what more I can do.
BR: There's a counter-consensus brewing, Sir. I know you've been reading the bug transcripts.
DIR: I would define that consensus as too localized, too little, and too late.
BR: Some men are offering a bounty.
DIR: I would not be overly perturbed to see it happen.
BR: The concept is very much out there.
DIR: I would not like to be stuck with the task of investigating such an incident. I would be inclined to work for brevity and do what was best to put it behind us.
BR: Yes, Sir.
DIR: Unreasonable actions and unjustified rage serve to spark reasoned and measured responses. (Ellroy 2001: 592–3)

Thousands of hours of surveillance of King have proved worthless. Hoover knows Holly wants to plan King's assassination by piecing together a small group from the anti-King factions, 'The concept is very much out there', but Hoover understands that although a conspiracy can form through disparate elements coming together for a single purpose, it can just as easily come to nothing. The consensus is 'too localized, too little, and too late.' Hoover refrains from giving a direct order to plan the assassination; instead, he resorts to bureaucratic jargon full of irony. He regards the reformer King as fuelling 'Unreasonable actions and unjustified rage', whereas violent racists will give 'reasoned and measured responses.' To Hoover, progressive change is extremely negative, but reactionaries are benevolent and moderate. As with the Kennedy assassination, Hoover cannot be tied to the crime outside of the archival documents, rather he uses the power of his office, through Holly, as an invisible hand to briefly unite the loose factions long enough for the assassination to be planned and implemented.

The failure of Operation Black Rabbit challenges Hoover's authority in more than just the main narrative of events. Documents begin to appear which cast doubt over Hoover's omnipresent view of events and bring up the wider issue of whether the reader is viewing documents outside Hoover's domain, which suggests a paranoid narrative of conspiracies pitted against other conspiracies. Almost all of the transcripts which appear in the novel are marked as being recorded on Hoover's orders; however, a series of conversations between Dwight Holly and Wayne Tedrow Senior, 'FATHER RABBIT', are recorded by Holly himself and begin with the minutiae '"FBI-Scrambled"/ 'Stage-1 Covert'/ "Destroy Without Reading in the Event of My Death". Speaking: BLUE RABBIT, FATHER RABBIT'. Holly disparagingly refers to Hoover as a 'dopehead' and an 'old poof', and when Tedrow expresses fear that Hoover could be monitoring the call, Holly replies, '"He's not God"' (Ellroy 2001: 548–9). The balance of power begins to shift away from the increasingly senile and drug-dependent Hoover in the Underworld narratives. Hoover's decline, however, is clouded in ambiguity. Like the endless possibilities which stem from the sources Nicholas Branch reads through in *Libra*, the transcripts only reveal certain information while leaving open multiple interpretations. How is the reader able to view both Hoover's files and apparently rogue files? Ellroy provides an allusive answer in the concluding Underworld volume *Blood's a Rover*, and it ties to the one character of the series who most closely resembles the Demon Dog himself, Don 'Crutch' Crutchfield.

The Cold Six Thousand ends five days after the assassination of Bobby Kennedy. The political narrative parallels the previous novel in concluding with various Underworld figures securing their position through conspiracy-led assassination. However, *American Tabloid* ends at the moment of the Kennedy shooting, whereas Ellroy prolongs the narrative after the assassinations of King and RFK to resolve an emotional sub-plot. Tedrow embodies the oedipal drama of *The Cold Six Thousand*, which played out on a grander political scale with the Kennedys in *American Tabloid*: '"Bobby Kennedy's Oedipal drama that resulted in Jack's murder. Bobby had a strong moral sense, and he understood that the gangsters he was chasing were his father once removed"' (Silet 1995: 50). The Tedrow family resemble a dynasty due to their immense wealth and traditional Mormonism, but Tedrow Junior detests the idea that he has become like Tedrow Senior after having embraced some of his racial views and having an affair with his father's wife, his stepmother, Janice. Tedrow Snr viciously beats Janice for her many infidelities despite taking voyeuristic pleasure in having her encounters secretly filmed. Her physical pain from the beating masks her cancer symptoms until it is too late. The final scene of the novel replicates the political drama on a personal level, with Wayne Jnr and Janice taking their revenge on the father and husband they so hated:

> The car pulled up. The car stopped. Janice got out. Janice weaved and anchored her feet.
> She twirled a golf club. Some kind of iron. Big head and fat grip.
> She walked past Wayne. She looked at him. He smelled her cancer breath. She walked inside. She let the door swing.
> Wayne stood tiptoed. Wayne made a picture frame. Wayne got a full window view. The club head arced. His father screamed. Blood sprayed the panes. (Ellroy 2001: 672)

The murder which ends *The Cold Six Thousand* is more grisly in tone than what Peter Wolfe describes as the 'sporting event' of Kennedy's assassination in *American Tabloid*, where Ellroy cuts away from the murder before the excitement of the crowd turns to horror (Wolfe 2005: 216). Tedrow Snr's death is a macabre spectacle by comparison, although it does reference one sport. Janice uses all of her remaining strength to beat Tedrow to death with a golf club after Wayne handcuffs him to a bar-rail in his house. Janice is a passionate golfer which makes her choice of weapon both brutal and personal. Death is an aphrodisiac for Wayne, just as Janice's adultery gives Tedrow Senior voyeuristic and sadistic pleasure. Wayne smells Janice's 'cancer breath' as she strolls past him to commit murder, and it acts as a sexual turn-on before the main act for the son who has set up his father.

Wayne watches the murder through a window which gives him a 'picture frame' view not dissimilar to the window view Ryskind has from his hospital room of the Kennedy motorcade. The detail that Wayne 'stood tiptoed' is reminiscent of a child trying to grasp or look at something that is forbidden. This serves as a metaphor for a television or cinema screen allowing Wayne to see his father's death in terms of narrative, in this case a microcosm of the Oedipal narrative of the Kennedy family. The screen is also a reminder of the influence of film noir on the novel as the scene is still oddly emotionless despite the brutality of the act. Wayne is excited, Janice musters all her physical strength and Wayne Senior is screaming in agony and terror but the absence of dialogue once Janice appears makes the confrontation deliberately flat. Revenge, the most hot-blooded of emotions, is the motive but the execution of it is merely another transaction between characters in Ellroy's vision of noir. The novel begins and ends with murder, but Tedrow, who was on a flight to Dallas when Kennedy was shot, did not learn of the event until he landed. He witnesses his father's death in real time, however, but he only has a partial viewing as 'Blood sprayed the panes'. Murder has become part of the spectacle by the conclusion of *The Cold Six Thousand*, and the Underworld has been slowly forced into the open. In *Blood's a Rover*, the climax of the series concerns the fate of Hoover's archive of files, a plotline which reveals the nature of Ellroy's secret history.

Blood's a Rover

The final volume of the Underworld USA trilogy is another work of epic historical fiction by Ellroy, but it is also a personal history which is deeply informed by the author's turbulent emotional state during the drafting stage. Ellroy adapted his personal difficulties both into the text and also as a separate narrative performed and extrapolated through interviews and through his memoir *The Hilliker Curse*. Ellroy has not revealed much of how he originally conceived *Blood's a Rover*, other than that it was to cover 1968 to 1972 and it would end the series. Ellroy originally considered 'Police Gazette' as a title which suggests his continued interest in forms of journalism as a theme (McDonald 2006: 146).

The eventual title, *Blood's a Rover*, is intentionally awkward: it begins with a contraction and continues with a noun which does not clarify the subject. The uncertainty adds to its suitability. The title is taken from the A.E. Houseman poem 'Reveille' a quotation from which forms the epigraph of the novel:

> Clay lies still, but blood's a rover;
> Breath's a ware that will not keep
> Up, lad: when the journey's over
> There'll be time enough to sleep. (Ellroy 2009: iii)

Houseman's verse encapsulates Ellroy's vision of his Underworld characters. They travel (rove) and shed blood. Blood is also a symbol of life, with the blood which courses through the veins of a human body also serving as a metaphor for the body politic. Characters in *Blood's a Rover* are reborn politically as radicals, moving to a different Underworld, and yearn not for more destruction but for the restoration of order on a personal level through fatherhood with the women they love. It also reads as Ellroy reprimanding himself, 'Up, lad' for the journey is not over, the writer returning to his work after an eight-year hiatus.

Changes in Ellroy's personal life are reflected in the openly emotional tone of the novel, a stark contrast to *The Cold Six Thousand*. As Ellroy's marriage to Helen Knode disintegrated, they agreed to try an open relationship. Ellroy adapted two of his extra-marital relationships into fictional form: 'the last two women who broke my heart and kicked my ass' (Powell 2008a: 164). The relationship which finally caused Ellroy's marriage to end was with a woman he has only publicly identified as Joan. On occasion he has referred to her as 'Comrade Joan' or 'Red Goddess Joan', which is also the sobriquet of the character in the novel drawn from the affair, Joan Rosen Klein. Ellroy has not revealed Joan's real surname in order to protect her identity. The dedication of the novel reads, '*To J.M. Comrade: For Everything You Gave Me*' (Ellroy 2009b: i). Ellroy's relationship with Joan was intense, and at one point they even discussed marriage. It was an intensity heightened by their personalities being so opposite to one another: 'She was Jewish, I'm Gentile. She was Marxist, I'm a Tory. She was atheist, I'm religious. She was bisexual, I'm straight. It was a very passionate, wild, all-encompassing thing' (Sharkey 2009: 208). Just as the real-life Comrade Joan caused Ellroy to radically overhaul his writing plans, the fictional Comrade Joan politically radicalizes the characters in *Blood's a Rover*. Through their love for strong women, three leading men, Tedrow, Dwight Holly and Don 'Crutch' Crutchfield, become sickened by their Underworld roles.

Aside from Comrade Joan, Ellroy based another leading female character on a woman from his chequered love life. Karen Sifakis is a character inspired by a married woman Ellroy had a brief relationship with after Joan, and like Joan, he has identified her in interviews simply by her first name, Kathy. Ellroy's relationship with Kathy had strong literary significance as it led him to return to LA after living away from the city for 26 years. According to Ellroy, Kathy was pregnant when they first met (Peace 2010: 214). The issue of illegitimate parentage occurs in the novel: Holly is convinced he is the father of the married Karen Sifakis' child. Parallel to the themes in the novel, Ellroy laments he never had children in *The Hilliker Curse*. Ellroy had returned to California in 2002, as part of a failed attempt to save his marriage to Helen Knode (Ellroy 2006b). He briefly lived with Joan in San Francisco and returned to LA with the faint hope that Kathy would agree to a more permanent relationship in spite of her marriage. Kathy declined.

Ellroy's last break-up led to the realization that the overarching narrative of his travels throughout the US in the last 30 years was his pursuit of women: '*Cherchez la femme*. I chased women to suburban New York, suburban Connecticut, Kansas City, Carmel, and San Francisco. But I ran out of places, and I ran out of women, so I ended up back here' (Rich 2008: 176). *Blood's a Rover* is the culmination of this sexual obsession transplanted into a historical and political narrative. To make the personal aspects of the narrative more coherent to the reader, Ellroy released his second volume of memoirs, *The Hilliker Curse*, which broadly explores his lifelong obsession with women, particularly his relationships with Comrade Joan and Kathy. Ellroy was repeating a stylistic technique he developed with *My Dark Places*, the memoir which detailed his reinvestigation into his mother's murder and narrative engagement with the Black Dahlia case. Just as his first memoir is a parallel narrative to the novel *The Black Dahlia*, *The Hilliker Curse* is not a straight autobiography but a narrative closely associated with *Blood's a Rover*.

As the novel was to be constructed as an intensely personal work, Ellroy felt obligated to repudiate the impersonal narrative of *The Cold Six Thousand* which he had come to regard as a career nadir. Contrary to his earlier defence of the novel, Ellroy embraced the negative reviews: 'I think that the book is too complex and somewhat too long and that the style is too rigorous and too challenging in its presentation of a very complex text' (Powell 2008a: 159). Ellroy's constant dismissal of the novel's literary value led the *Guardian* to print an article asking, 'Is James Ellroy the best judge of his own novels?' which cast doubt on the sincerity of Ellroy's volte-face on its literary merit (Evers 2009). By switching from an abrasively defensive tone to a relentlessly negative public dismissal of *The Cold Six Thousand*, Ellroy was performing a narrative external to the novels, a renewed 'covenant of consciousness', which structured the transition between the two works, preparing the reader for the new style he had embraced. It was a strategy fraught with risk, and judging by the critical response only partially successful, as readers and critics started to wonder: if the author does not take his past work seriously why should they his regard his future work more kindly?

'Comrade' Joan and Karen act as a radicalizing influence on the men who fall for them. On this point, however, Ellroy, has been specific in differentiating fiction from reality: 'I wanted to honor in this book the lessons learnt from a woman whose beliefs were inimical to mine and to talk in the abstract about the necessity of conversion and of revolution. But I have not moved left. I have just described the journeys of people who have done so' (Peace 2010: 216). Tedrow's and Holly's conversion occurs when they discover in themselves the capacity to love strong women, which triggers in each man a moral rebirth as they try to push America out of the grip of the Underworld. It is difficult to gauge Ellroy's political beliefs as he has expressed many outrageously right-wing views as part of his Demon Dog schtick. At times he appears to publicly endorse right-wing 'Establishment' attitudes, which are deconstructed in the text, essentially causing a schism between Ellroy and the characters of *Blood's a Rover* who are ultimately repulsed by their Underworld existence. Ellroy is certainly more conservative than many of his colleagues in publishing and Hollywood, but as he believes the term 'right-wing' is loaded he has developed a malleable, contrarian political identity which he alluded to in his article for the *L.A. Times* 'The Great Right Place':

> L.A. had overdosed me. Extreme stimulation had fried my brain pan. I had raped a beautiful place. I had usurped its essence to tell myself sick stories. My mind was infused with an L.A. virus. Wrong L.A. thoughts and undue L.A. stimuli could unravel me.
>
> I believed it then. I don't disbelieve it now. I was a tory mystic then, and I remain one. (Ellroy 2006b)

With the term 'Tory Mystic' Ellroy is both rejecting social liberalism and placing himself outside the sphere of conservatism. Although still heavily used as a colloquial term for a conservative in the United Kingdom, Tory is wholly redundant in American political terminology. Ellroy's Toryism is literary rather than exclusively political: it is specific to the 'stimuli' and the 'sick stories' of the 'L.A. virus'. In the article, Ellroy talks of the tumultuous years of his life that led to his moving back to LA. He employs words which are direct references to past and present, 'then', 'now', 'was', and ends on a note of 'Tory' consistency surviving through the turmoil: 'I remain one'. This developing literary and political identity, rooted in the mysticism of LA and the classic noir age, entails an ongoing connection between Ellroy and his noir characters which transcends any movement from right- to left-wing. In narrative terms, whether Dwight Holly is the reactionary of *The Cold Six Thousand* or the left-wing convert of *Blood's a Rover*, Ellroy can empathize with both aspects of his extreme views by imbuing them with differing strains of romanticism.

Aside from the theme of conversion, Ellroy brought another autobiographical element to the novel through his portrayal of a real-life character. Ellroy decided to make Hollywood private detective Don Crutchfield one of the three leading characters of the novel. Crutchfield was in many ways a successor to Fred Otash among private detectives in LA. Ellroy resurrected the plan he had originally intended for Otash in *American Tabloid*, offering to pay Crutchfield money for permission to use him as a character on condition that Crutchfield did not publicly contradict any of the events in the narrative: 'he and I will never say what's real and what's not. Did he really go to the D[ominican].R[epublic]. and kill all those people, kill a lot of Castroite Cubans? Well, maybe, maybe not' (Taylor 2009: 202). Ellroy's deliberate manipulation of history stems from his desire to lay bare his personal life through the proxy figure of Crutchfield.

In order to make the narrative of the novel more closely parallel his personal history, Ellroy began to embellish the connections between his own life and Crutchfield's. Crutchfield first met Ellroy at the Starlight Bookstore in Hollywood in 1996. From the beginning of their acquaintance, it was clear to both men that key events in their lives had been interconnected: 'I liked the way he conducted his research. I experienced and lived some of those stories he wrote about' (Crutchfield 2012). Crutchfield signed his autobiography *Confessions of a Hollywood P.I.* for Ellroy, writing, 'I not only loved your book, I lived it' (Crutchfield 2012). In their first conversation, Crutchfield discussed his work as a 'Wheel Man', tailing cheating spouses, on divorce cases in the late 1960s, and it is in this modest role that Crutchfield is introduced in the novel. Crutchfield is seven years Ellroy's senior, but Ellroy adjusted the fictional Crutchfield's age down by four years to bring it closer to his own for the 1968–72 setting. Also, Ellroy adds a psychological motivation for Crutchfield's investigative work rooted in sexual voyeurism and perversion. Gradually, Crutchfield's voyeurism transcends his sexual desires and encompasses a unique view of America's secret history of the period.

Crutchfield's evolution mirrors Ellroy's own obsessions with history, stemming from his unconscious sensing of history during the 1960s to his revisionism of history through fiction as a novelist. The time period of the novel covers some of the worst years of Ellroy's addictions, yet this was also the time when history and writing became important to him: 'I read and nurtured notions of being a great writer. And I sensed history bombing around beside me. I knew I was living through tumultuous history. And I had a sense, even then, of the human infrastructure of big public events' (Peace 2010: 215). Ellroy was able to present his darkest days as an act of narrative, to be revived through autobiography and fiction. He was looking forward, even then, to the adaptation of his life and events into historical fiction narratives.

Crutchfield is referred to in casual conversation by his nickname Crutch, a mobility or emotional aid. Crutch does not hold the same stature in the Underworld/Intelligence community as Tedrow or Holly. He is an outwardly flawed and pathetic character, yet he is a crutch for others, providing stability through his pure, childlike love of the ideologue Comrade Joan. Crutch is also similar phonetically to crux, which is appropriate as the character who ties the narrative to Ellroy's own life through his voyeurism and love affair with Joan. Crutch also symbolizes the resolution of the historical mystery of the Underworld series, as his fate as a voyeur becomes inextricably linked to Hoover's archive of secret files:

> *AMERICA:*
> *I window-peeped four years of our History. It was one long mobile stakeout and kick the door-in shakedown. I had a licence to steal and a ticket to ride.*
>
> *I followed people. I bugged and tapped and caught big events in ellipses. I remained unknown. My surveillance links the Then to the Now in a never before revealed manner. I was there. My reportage is buttressed by credible hearsay and insider tattle. Massive paper trails provide verification. This book derives from stolen public files and usurped private journals. It is the sum of personal adventure and forty years of scholarship. I am a literary executor and an agent provocateur. I did what I did and saw what I saw and learned my way through the rest of the story.*
>
> *Scripture-pure veracity and scandal-rag content. That conjunction gives it its sizzle. You carry the seed of belief within you already. You recall the time this narrative captures and sense conspiracy. I am here to tell you that it is all true and not at all what you think.*
>
> *You will read with some reluctance and capitulate in the end. The following pages will force you to succumb.*
>
> *I am going to tell you everything.* (Ellroy 2009b: 9)

Crutch combines the role of historian, private eye and sexual voyeur, '*I window-peeped four years of our History.*' The form of this prologue deliberately echoes Ellroy's direct address to the reader in *American Tabloid* in its italicized text, its theme of verisimilitude and its demythologizing of the past. Although as the timeframe has moved from the Kennedy to the Nixon era, Ellroy is less concerned with stripping away idealism than rebuilding it through a positive portrayal of political conversion, as the hidden conspiracies of the Underworld are gradually exposed to an angry nation. Ellroy merges historical and literary sources with a tabloid sensibility. It is the work of both *'literary executor'* and *'agent provocateur'*. It is both *'Scripture'* and *'scandal-rag'* in its content, thus the salacious becomes authoritative. Crutch regards this secret history as a form of seduction: *'reluctance'* will be followed by the need to *'succumb'*. It is a bold statement from Ellroy, warning the reader that in its focus on conspiracies in the shadows of history, the story might seem highly improbable, but by the end of the novel he will have won them over, making them 'window-peepers' as well. The window is the screen through which the secret history will be revealed.

The first-person narration is only temporary. But although Ellroy quickly switches the perspective to third-person, Crutch's control over the narrative remains considerable as the documents the reader will view and the events described are to an indeterminate extent arranged by him. Hoover had ordered transcripts to be compiled from the covert recordings which appeared in the previous novels and was, to an extent, their author. Crutchfield cannot create documents; instead they *'[derive] from stolen public files and usurped private journals'*. The legacy of *Libra* to the Underworld trilogy is that documented sources do not necessarily offer a clearer picture of events. The paper trail that has led Crutch to this point could have obscured his view of events rather than clarified it. That being said, the revelation that Crutch has an endless supply of forms of documents is another indication of how as a character he is closely modelled on Ellroy in the text, able to trace the development of the Underworld narrative from its inception.

The novel begins prior to Crutch's monologue with a hyper-violent armoured car heist which takes place in Los Angeles on 24 February 1964:

> SUDDENLY:
> The milk truck cut a sharp right turn and grazed the curb. The driver lost the wheel. He panic-popped the brakes. He induced a rear-end skid. A Wells Fargo armoured car clipped the milk truck side/head-on.
> Mark it now:
> 7:16 a.m. South L.A., 84th and Budlong. Residential darktown. Shit stacks with dirt front yards. (Ellroy 2009b: 3)

The opening scene breaks with the established timeframe of the trilogy and jumps back four years, depicting an event which is independent of the events in *The Cold Six Thousand* but runs parallel to them as a series narrative. This is indicated in the very first word in the text: *'SUDDENLY'*. Not only is it italicized, whereas the bulk of the text is not, it is also the only word to appear on the first line, indicating a sharp, unexpected break in the narrative which has detoured from the established chronology of the trilogy by going back in time. This abrupt break followed by a colon leads into the violent events which unfold in the next paragraph. Ellroy forces the reader to consider the effects of the past on the present, as the complex structure of *Blood's a Rover* goes beyond its 1972 cut-off date in the epilogue to, presumably, the present day with Crutch's direct address to the reader.

As part of its shifting, malleable timeframe, *Blood's a Rover* contains a subtle homage to John Gregory Dunne. Dunne's *True Confessions* begins with the section heading 'NOW', which is followed by the long first-person monologue of Tom Spellacy. An aged Spellacy is ruminating on the events of the 'Virgin Tramp' murder of 1947. The next section is titled 'THEN': a third-person narrative of the murder investigation in the 1940s setting forms the bulk of the text. The novel concludes with NOW and returns to Spellacy's monologue, concluding the story in the present day. *Blood's a Rover* takes Dunne's interweaving narrative of past and present and adds greater complexity. The first section is titled THEN, and the first scene is the 1964 armed robbery. In this instance, THEN refers to a past event separate from the 1968–72 timeframe of the main action. As with *SUDDENLY*, THEN implies a break from one action to another. However, as it appears at the beginning of the novel, the only preceding action the reader is aware of would come from the other novels, but Ellroy has already deviated from the timeframe of the trilogy. The robbery scene is followed by another section titled NOW. By contrast to Dunne's novel, Ellroy's novel contains a very short monologue of less than a page. The monologue is followed by THEN as it returns to the 1968 setting where Ellroy left *The Cold Six Thousand* and by extension the natural chronological order of the trilogy. The novel concludes by returning to the present-day monologue NOW. In his opening monologue, Crutch promises to link the *'Then to the Now in a never before revealed manner.'* There are essentially three time periods of the novel. Here again is the restructuring of the historical narrative from within, creating new connections and associations between past and present. One of these connections is a specific day, 24 February 1964, and the violent events of this day reverberate throughout the narrative. Consequently, there is a very different tone between the settings of the novel. The heist sequence is described in less than four pages. Seven people are killed, four guards and three robbers, and only one man survives. The confluence of violence is crammed into a small space and a small window of time: 7.16 to 7.27 a.m. on 84th and Budlong. When the narrative transitions into the novel's main 1968–72 setting, the pace slows and the violent scenes are dispersed. Crutch's NOW monologues are also distinguished by being the only present-day direct address to the reader.

Aside from the monologues, Crutch's impact on the narrative can be seen in more allusive ways. Both *American Tabloid* and *The Cold Six Thousand* are divided into sections with dry, single-word titles such as, 'SHAKEDOWNS', 'COLLUSION', 'HEROIN' and 'CONTRACT.' However, *Blood's a Rover* contains much more colourful two-word titles which are idiosyncratic of Crutch's personality: 'CLUSTER FUCK', 'SHIT MAGNET', 'ZOMBIE ZONE', 'COON CARTEL', 'THROWDOWN GUN' and 'COMRADE JOAN'. The titles reference Crutch's role in the narrative through his eventual possession of the *'massive paper trail'*, which, in his hands, are less formally bureaucratic and more reminiscent of pulp crime fiction. The genre feel Crutch brings to the novel refers back to Ellroy's identity as a crime fiction novelist, and the role of crime fiction in his historical vision. Ellroy considered using other section titles: 'SHINE GAMES', 'TACO RUNS', 'HATE SCHTICK', 'PUPPET PAWNS', 'GREEN ICE' and 'CATHY'S CLOWN' (Ellroy 2009a). The final unused section title is a reference to his earlier novel *Blood on the Moon*, showing that despite Ellroy's constant desire for reinvention and experimentation, there is still a repetition of ideas at play.

In *Blood on the Moon*, Theodore Verplanck becomes a serial killer partly because of his unreturned love for Kathleen McCarthy. Although connections between *Blood's a Rover* and Ellroy's earlier Lloyd Hopkins novel are slight, a parallel can be drawn between narratives as they both deal with the consuming, irrational nature of love leading characters to violent acts. For Ellroy, the chaotic personal life he describes in *The Hilliker Curse* links to the themes of turbulent love affairs and political conversion in the novel. The epigram of *The Hilliker Curse* is the Beethoven quote: 'I will take fate by the throat' (Ellroy 2010: i). Ellroy's admiration for the Romantic composer seeps in to both narratives:

> What I love is the worse it got, the greater he got. ... It's just almost unfathomable courage. And the older he got, and he was dead at fifty-six, the more unfathomable and great and uncategorizable his music. ... What Beethoven asks of you, will you ascend to my example? (Powell 2009: 196)

Ellroy attempts to evoke parallels between himself and Beethoven through the idea of a personal or emotional disintegration fuelling a transcendent narrative. By refusing to reveal Comrade Joan's real identity, he is shadowing Beethoven's famous letter to the unidentified 'Immortal Beloved'. Ellroy, however, characteristically creates a darkly comic version alongside this elevated one in his relationship with the married Kathy. Ellroy's memoir *The Hilliker Curse* refers to Kathy's husband as 'WHAT'S HIS NAME'. This clear insult carries over from *Blood's a Rover* where Karen Sifakis' husband is also referred to in this way. In the novel, Karen plays Beethoven's music, which Dwight Holly listens to silently on her porch, unable to enter the house as her husband is home, a scene drawn from his memoir with Ellroy standing outside Kathy's house. Presuming the scene did happen as Ellroy describes in his memoir, the choice of Beethoven's music and philosophy, as opposed to Bruckner's in *Brown's Requiem*, is still important dramatically for the scene in the novel: 'What Beethoven asks of you, will you ascend to my example?' Ironically, for Ellroy the ascension comes from a submission to worldly desires, followed by its assumption into the narrative of the novel. The personal narrative, however, may be compromised as it is ongoing, unlike the historical narrative which Ellroy neatly cuts off in 1972. *The Hilliker Curse* is less a memoir of Ellroy's life than of his love life, as indicated in the sub-title 'My Pursuit of Women'. It was dedicated to Ellroy's then lover Erika Schickel. Unfortunately for Ellroy, as he conceded to this author at a book reading in Manchester on 5 November 2014, his relationship with Ms Schickel ended before the book was completed (Powell 2014a). His determination to plough on with the memoir indicates its greater importance as a companion piece to *Blood's a Rover*.

If love can inspire artistry and irrational acts, then so too can the politics of the era. The directly political aspect of the historical narrative is focused on Hoover's COINTELPRO campaign to discredit the Black Panther movement, which is paralleled by the Mafia's attempts to re-establish casinos in the Caribbean through its courting of the right-wing dictatorships of the Dominican Republic and Haiti. The irrational hatred and increasing senility that fuel Hoover's campaign against the civil rights movement are mirrored by the Voodoo paranoia which props up François 'Papa Doc' Duvalier's personality cult regime in Haiti.

Hoover's physical and mental demise is symbolic of the Underworld's decline. The Watergate scandal will usher in a new era of increasing accountability, and Ellroy drops a few subversive clues about the impending crisis. In a recorded transcript, President Nixon requests

Hoover's assistance for an illegal bugging operation against the Democrats:

> RMN: The Democrats will field a good team. I'd like to get some derogatory poop on them in a timely fashion.
> JEH: Uh... what type of-
> RMN: 'Black-bag job,' Edgar. Don't go coy on me. Don't pretend you didn't pull that shit with Lyndon Johnson. (Ellroy 2009b: 444)

Hoover later reveals to Dwight Holly that he procrastinated with Nixon in order to try to wring more concessions out of him, implying that Nixon's entourage will have had to look elsewhere to hire covert operatives. The long-term consequences of such a move would be well known to the reader. Ellroy does not take the Watergate references any further as he does not particularly need to. He expressed scepticism regarding its dramatic potential: 'Watergate bores me. The scandal has been done to death' (Libby 2001). However, the deeper the reader goes into the novel and its early 1970s timeframe, the stronger the consciousness of the scandal becomes. Ellroy allows the reader to draw their own connections between the webs of conspiracies in the novel and the defining political event of the era. By doing so, he keeps the narrative in continuum with the expectation of more political revelations after the novel ends.

The novel moves towards a climax similar to the assassination codas of the previous two novels as Dwight Holly draws up plans to assassinate Hoover. Holly becomes radicalized from a far-right racist to a left-winger convinced that Hoover needs to be killed for the crimes he has committed during his near 50-year tenure as Bureau Director. Holly creates a false paper trail which will set up the black, LAPD officer Marshall Bowen as the fall guy for Hoover's assassination. Like Operation Black Rabbit, all of the documents that have been conceived, drafted and planted are partially redundant as the mission is abandoned. This reverses Jonathan Walker's argument that the documents reveal events closer to reality than the public's viewpoint, rather they show a reality that never comes into being, but Holly believes that this fictional paper trail will ultimately expose Hoover's lifelong racist campaign. Holly's plans for revenge on Hoover carry a delicious irony. Hoover had shielded the conspirators behind the assassinations of JFK, RFK and Martin Luther King partly by not sharing information that was privy to him about the assassination conspiracies. If Holly's plan had been successful, the documents he planted would both create a narrative leading to Hoover's assassination and expose him as the chief architect of the Underworld. Holly has a change of heart when he sees a senile Hoover being cared for and fed by two FBI agents in a Washington restaurant, and all of the narrative energy leading towards an assassination to close the trilogy dissipates when Holly is in turn murdered by the corrupt LAPD detective Scotty Bennett. Hoover's death finally comes at the hands of Don Crutchfield:

> Crutch reached in his pocket and pulled out the emerald. Mr. Hoover trembled and homed in on it.
> The sparkle was incessant. It eyeball-magnetized. The green glow grew and grew. Mr. Hoover weaved and drooled. Mr. Hoover clutched his chest and staggered upstairs. (Ellroy 2009b: 632)

Crutch has broken into Hoover's house with explosives and a 'heart attack potion' (Ellroy 2009b: 633). However, although he is able to use the explosives to destroy Hoover's vaults and his archive of files, the syringe he was carrying to administer the lethal dose has been crushed and the poison has spilled in his duffel bag. The ailing Hoover dies of a heart attack precipitated by the shock of seeing Crutch and the sight of the emerald. As the emerald's beauty seems to grow, so does its violent power: 'The green glow grew and grew.' By destroying Hoover's files Crutchfield attempts to erase and conclude the Underworld history, and yet he is about to be the recipient and custodian of an equally massive archive of files.

Conclusion: 'I have paid a dear and savage price to live history'

Crutch's closing monologue strengthens his position as the character that most strongly links to Ellroy as the author of the Underworld series. Although Ellroy has begun a second LA Quartet that will buttress the links between the Quartet and Underworld series, he has already given, through Crutch, the end of his secret history. Crutch is the recipient of files, a voyeur-custodian of archives, who shares the experience with the reader:

> *Documents have arrived at irregular intervals. They are always anonymously sent. I have compiled diary excerpts, oral-history transcripts and police-file overflow. Elderly leftists and black militants have told me their*

> stories and provided verification. Freedom of Information Act subpoenas have served me well. ... 'Your options are do everything or do nothing.' Joan told me that. I have paid a dear and savage price to live History. I will never stop looking. I pray that these pages find her and that she does not misread my devotion. (Ellroy 2009b: 639–40)

As Hoover's grip on power, and life, slowly slips away, the fate of his secret files becomes the most important consequence of his impending death. The key is in the transition of power from a Hoover-regulated history, to one that is compiled by the leftist radicals of a different Underworld. As Jim Mancall states in his review of the novel, 'The epilogue reveals that Crutchfield is the master narrator; his is the hand that assembles the documents that make up *Blood's a Rover*' (Mancall 2014: 50–51). Crutch both destroys files and acquires new ones. The merging and blurring of files allude to the difficulty of reading history and determining authorship. Are the files that appear in the previous Underworld novels 'Recorded at the Director's Request' all destroyed by Crutch or did some of them come into his possession after Hoover's death? The triumphant destruction of Hoover's files vindicates Ellroy's anti-history approach in that he shows how recorded history is as transient and vulnerable as the characters who live through it. Boyd, Littell and Tedrow all had a role in shaping history but are killed and replaced by other Underworld figures. Hoover's identity, and his representative status, has always hinged on the power he wields. He has no personal life as such, other than a few insinuations of homosexuality. Whereas Holly, Tedrow and Crutch all find their redemption through women and by extension fatherhood, even if it is by proxy, Hoover has only political power through the control of information. The theft of classified files from the FBI office in Media, Pennsylvania, and their distribution throughout the country, confirms the FBI's anti-dissident COINTELPRO program. This event foreshadows Crutch's acquisition of files upon the death of Hoover, an ending reminiscent of Hoover willing the files to Kemper Boyd in the original *American Tabloid* outline.

The files sent anonymously to Crutch give him a unique insight into American history. But the burden of history has been compounded by the tragedy of lost love. Crutch's search for Joan has radicalized him almost to the extent of madness, touring warzones hoping to find the revolutionary: '*I have been to Nicaragua, Grenada, Bosnia, Rwanda, Russia, Iran and Iraq*' (Ellroy 2009b: 640). Perhaps Ellroy goes too far in giving Crutch this claim, imbuing the character with an impressionistic, even fantastical tendency towards reminiscence which potentially undermines his reliability as a narrator. However, Crutch reveals details about the real Don Crutchfield which re-establish his plausibility: '*I run a successful detective agency in Los Angeles. My firm bodyguards celebrities and verifies stories for tell-all rags.*' By slipstreaming between the absurd and the plausible in his portrayal of Crutch, Ellroy brings the character closer to his identity as the Demon Dog, part-fantasy, part-reality. Ultimately Crutch is unable to fulfil the promise of the opening monologue, '*I am going to tell you everything*', as history is, by its nature, always incomplete (Ellroy 2009b: 9). The more files he receives, and the greater his knowledge grows, the bigger the sense of emotional loss and dwindling hope he will see Joan and their child: '*She's eighty-three now. Our child is thirty-six. Instinct tells me it's a girl*' (Ellroy 2009b: 640). Ellroy ends the Underworld trilogy by merging the secret files with the novel's narrative: '*I pray that these pages find her and that she does not misread my devotion*' (Ellroy 2009b: 640). His reference to '*these pages*' suggest the history he has conveyed is an authored document or rather a collection of documents and narratives and that the Underworld novels are a huge fictional archive anchored on an obsession with women. In Ellroy's earlier work the tabloid sensibility of the *Hush-Hush* articles had imbued the text with a sordid focus on the sex lives of public figures, but by the end of the Underworld series the characters' desire for love has become their redemption.

Ellroy has described *Blood's a Rover* as a tribute to 'Comrade' Joan and, like Crutch, he hopes the narrative will lead to a reunion: 'All I really want is to get her one [the novel] up in San Francisco. I still have her address. I just want to put it in her hands with all my love and an expression of my thanks. And then maybe see her at a book gig and just wave to her across the room' (Taylor 2009: 204). Over the course of the three Underworld novels and the fifteen years of history that they cover, the narrative evolves from what Ellroy terms 'the private nightmare of public policy', the obsessions which drove Kemper Boyd, Ward Littell and Pete Bondurant to violent, ultimately self-destructive acts, to an alternative history which reads as a public narrative of Ellroy's private life. The nervous breakdown on the publicity tour of *The Cold Six Thousand*, followed by his extra-marital affairs, led him to reinvent characters Dwight Holly and Wayne Tedrow, and adapt Don Crutchfield, as characters looking for their redemption through love and radical politics. In his early novels for Avon, Ellroy had adapted his harrowing life as Lee Earle Ellroy, the periodically homeless, alcoholic drug addict, voyeur and petty criminal, into narrative. Characters such as Freddy 'Fat Dog' Baker and Martin Plunkett were relatively autobiographical inventions with fictional embellishments. As Ellroy developed his Demon Dog persona he was able to imbue his novels with a greater level of narrative complexity, culminating in the coda of *Blood's a Rover* and the disposition of the files which reads as a subversive revealing of Ellroy's role as author.

Complexity evolves from simplicity. For Ellroy, it was a long journey from creating 'Dog' humour with Randy Rice to the completion of the epic Underworld USA series where the Demon Dog persona is triumphantly present at the coda. But no matter how far Ellroy had developed and utilized his literary persona; for him, the Demon Dog identity was quite a simple creation: 'I'm just James Ellroy, the self-promoting Demon Dog. It comes naturally to me. You call it swagger, I call it joie de vivre' (Rich 2008: 187).

Bibliography

Abbott, M. (2002) *The Street Was Mine: White Masculinity in Hardboiled Fiction and Film Noir* (Basingstoke: Palgrave Macmillan).

Allamand, C. (2006) 'A Tooth for a Private Eye: James Ellroy's Detective Fiction', *Journal of Popular Culture*, 39:3, 349–64.

Anon '40 Sequels That Never Happened', *Shortlist.com*, http://www.shortlist.com/entertainment/films/40-sequels-that-never-happened, date accessed 28 Mar 2013.

Anon (1992) 'Author's biography', in *Murder and Mayhem: an A to Z of the World's Most Notorious Serial Killers* (London: Arrow).

Anon 'Dr. John Biography', *Rolling Stone Magazine*, http://www.rollingstone.com/music/artists/dr-john/biography, date accessed 15 Jun 2011.

Anon 'Last Name: Conville', *The Internet Surname Database* http://www.surnamedb.com/Surname/Conville, date accessed 1 Dec 2014.

Berten, H. and D'haen, T. (2001) *Contemporary American Crime Fiction* (Basingstoke: Palgrave Macmillan), p. 96.

Birnbaum, R. (2001) 'James Ellroy' *Identity Theory*, http://www.identitytheory.com/james-ellroy/, date accessed 8 Oct 2010.

Blackwelder, R. (1997) '"Confidential" Commentary' in S. Powell (ed.) (2012) *Conversations with James Ellroy* (Jackson: University Press of Mississippi), pp. 99–103.

Borde, R. and Chaumeton, E. (1955) *A Panorama of American Film Noir, 1941–1953* (San Francisco: City Lights Books).

Caleb (2013) 'Guns of the Los Angeles Police Department', in *Gun Nuts Media*, http://www.gunnuts.net/2013/10/08/guns-of-the-los-angeles-police-department/, date accessed 06 June 2014.

Carnahan, M. (2007) 'Carnahan's Scripts' *Joblo.com*, http://www.joblo.com/movie-news/carnahans-scripts, date accessed 9 Dec 2010.

Chandler, R. (1939) *The Big Sleep* (London: Hamish Hamilton).

Chandler, R. (1944) *The Simple Art of Murder* (London: Hamish Hamilton).

Chorney, J. (2000) 'Citizen Killer?' *Salon*, (16 October), http://www.salon.com/2000/08/16/dahlia/, date accessed 14 Jan 2013.

Christopher, N. (2006) *Somewhere in the Night: Film Noir and the American City* (Emeryville: Shoemaker and Hoard).

Cobley, P. (2000) *The American Thriller: Generic Innovation and Social Change in the 1970s* (Basingstoke: Macmillan).

Cohen, J. (1996) 'James Ellroy, Los Angeles and the Spectacular Crisis of Masculinity', *Women*, 1:7, 1–15.

Cox, T. (2001) 'Powders, Treason and Plots', *Observer*, (22 April), http://www.guardian.co.uk/books/2001/apr/22/crime.jamesellroy, date accessed 22 Sept 2011.

Crutchfield, D. (2012) 'James Ellroy', *Crutchfield and Associates*, http://www.pi4stars.com/jameselroy.htm, date accessed 20 Jun 2012.

Davis, M. (1990) *City of Quartz: Excavating the Future in Los Angeles* (New York: Verso).

DeLillo, D. (1988) *Libra* (New York: Penguin).
Dominguez, A. (1939) 'Perfidia Lyrics', *Linda Ronstadt*, http://www.ronstadt-linda.com/perfidia.htm, date accessed 12 March 2012.
Duncan, P. (1996) 'James Ellroy: Barking', in S. Powell (ed.) (2012) *Conversations with James Ellroy* (Jackson: University Press of Mississippi), pp. 61–91.
Dunne, J. (1977) *True Confessions* (New York: Pocket Books).
Eliot, T.S. (1942) 'Little Gidding', in *Four Quartets* (London: Faber & Faber).
Ellroy, J. (1980) Colombia, University of South Carolina, MS Correspondence, Business (16 October 1980) 4, 1–4.
Ellroy, J. (1981) *Brown's Requiem* (New York: Avon).
Ellroy, J. (1982) *Clandestine* (New York: Avon, 1982; repr. New York: Perennial, 2002).
Ellroy, J. (1983a) Colombia, University of South Carolina, MS *The Confessions of Bugsy Siegel*, unpublished typescript: 1–398 outline (four folders: 100, 3–6).
Ellroy, J. (1983b) Colombia, University of South Carolina, MS [*Suicide Hill*] *L.A. Death Trip*, corrected manuscript, photocopy, 7, 2–5.
Ellroy, J. (1984a) *Because the Night*, in *L.A. Noir* (London: Arrow, 1997).
Ellroy, J. (1984b) *Blood on the Moon*, in *L.A. Noir* (London: Arrow, 1997).
Ellroy, J. (1984c) Colombia, University of South Carolina, MS Correspondence, Business (18 Nov 1984) 4, 1–4.
Ellroy, J. (1984d) Colombia, University of South Carolina, MS *The Cold Six Thousand*, outline typescript, 'Volume IV of the Quintet Hopkins in Jeopardy', title page, 33–84, 66,1.
Ellroy, J. (1984e) Colombia, University of South Carolina, MS *The Black Dahlia*, story outline, 9, 5.
Ellroy, J. (1986a) *Killer on the Road* (New York: Avon, 1986; repr. London: Arrow, 1990).
Ellroy, J. (1986b) *Suicide Hill*, in *L.A. Noir* (London: Arrow, 1997).
Ellroy, J. (1987) *The Black Dahlia* (New York: Mysterious Press, 1987; repr. New York: Warner Books, 2006).
Ellroy, J. (1988) *The Big Nowhere* (New York: Mysterious Press).
Ellroy, J. (1990) *L.A. Confidential* (New York: Mysterious Press).
Ellroy, J. (1991) Colombia, University of South Carolina, MS *White Jazz* story outline, author corrected typescript, 30, 3.
Ellroy, J. (1992a) Colombia, University of South Carolina, MS *American Tabloid*, notes, outline corrected manuscript 39, 2.
Ellroy, J. (1992b) 'Introduction', in *Murder and Mayhem: an A to Z of the World's Most Notorious Serial Killers* (London: Arrow), pp.1–10.
Ellroy, J. (1992c) *White Jazz* (New York: Knopf, 1992; repr. London: Arrow, 1993).
Ellroy, J. (1995) *American Tabloid* (New York: Knopf).
Ellroy, J (1996) *My Dark Places* (New York: Knopf).
Ellroy, J. (1997a) 'Introduction', in B. Helgeland and C. Hanson *L.A. Confidential: the screenplay* (New York: Warner), pp. xv–xx.
Ellroy, J. (1997b) 'Introduction', in *L.A. Noir* (London: Arrow), p. i.
Ellroy, J. (1999) 'Hush-Hush' in *Crime Wave: Reportage and Fiction from the Underside of L.A.* (New York: Vintage Books) pp. 97–122.
Ellroy, J. (2001) *The Cold Six Thousand* (London: Century).
Ellroy, J. (2004a) 'Foreword', in S. Hodel, *Black Dahlia Avenger: A Genius for Murder* (New York: Perennial) pp. xix–xxi.

Ellroy, J. (2004b) 'Jungletown Jihad', in *Destination Morgue!: L.A. Tales* (New York: Vintage Books), pp. 321–89.
Ellroy, J. (2004c) *Scene of the Crime: Photographs from the L.A.P.D. Archive* (Los Angeles: Harry N. Abrams).
Ellroy, J. (2006a) 'Hillikers: an Afterword to The Black Dahlia', in *The Black Dahlia* (New York: Warner Books).
Ellroy, J. (2006b) 'The Great Right Place', *Los Angeles Times* (30 Jul 2006), http://articles.latimes.com/2006/jul/30/magazine/tm-ellroy31/6, date accessed 22 Sep 2011.
Ellroy, J. (2006c) 'My Mother and the Dahlia', *Virginia Quarterly Review*, 82:3, 213–22.
Ellroy, J. (2007) 'L.A.: Come on Vacation, Go Home on Probation', *Zocalo Public Square Lecture* [podcast] 11 September 2007, http://zocalopublicsquare.org/fullVideo.php?event_year=2007&event_id=13, date accessed 5 July 2010.
Ellroy, J. (2009a) Colombia, University of South Carolina, MS *Blood's a Rover* [*Cold Six Thousand*], outline, preliminary, 53, 3.
Ellroy, J. (2009b) *Blood's a Rover* (New York: Knopf).
Ellroy, J. (2010) *The Hilliker Curse: My Pursuit of Women* (London: Heinemann).
Ellroy, J. (2011) 'Introduction', in J. Ellroy and O. Penzler (eds) *The Best American Noir of the Century* (London: Windmill, 2011), pp. xiii–xiv.
Ellroy, J. (2014) *Perfidia* (London: Heinemann).
Everly, D. and Everly, P. (1960) 'Cathy's Clown', http://www.azlyrics.com/lyrics/everlybrothers/cathysclown.html, date accessed 5 Dec 2011.
Evers, S. (2009) 'Is James Ellroy the Best Judge of his own Novels?' *Guardian* (24 Nov), http://www.guardian.co.uk/books/booksblog/2009/nov/24/james-ellroy-best-judge-own-novels, date accessed 20 Jun 2012.
Ferrari-Adler, J. (2008) 'Agents & Editors: A Q&A with Agent Nat Sobel', *Poets & Writers* vol. 40, http://www.pw.org/content/agent_amp.editors_campa_agent_nat_sobel, date accessed 8 Mar 2011.
Flügge, A. (2010) *James Ellroy and the Novel of Obsession* (Verl: Trier Wiss).
Freiburger, W. (1996) 'James Ellroy, Walter Mosley and the Politics of the Los Angeles Crime Novel', *Clues: A Journal of Detection*, 17: 2, 87–104.
Galloway, S. (2013) 'Rock Hudson's Wife Secretly Recorded His Gay Confession', *Hollywood Reporter* (6 June), http://www.hollywoodreporter.com/news/rock-hudsons-wife-secretly-recorded-562508?page=2, date accessed 3 Oct 2013.
Gogniat, V. (2014) 'James Ellroy: "I always want more women and more money"', *Les Temps* (Apr 5), http://www.letemps.ch/Page/Uuid/4acc30d8-bc0c-11e3-992b-e6aa952f4c35/James_Ellroy_Je_veux_toujours_plus_de_femmes_et_toujours_plus_dargent, date accessed 6 Jun 2014.
Hanson, C. (1997) 'Foreword', in B. Helgeland and C. Hanson, *L.A. Confidential: the screenplay* (New York: Warner), pp. ix–xi.
Hanson, C. and Helgeland, B. (1997) *L.A. Confidential: the Screenplay* (New York: Warner).
Harnisch, L. (2008) 'Sid Hughes dies at 50; The Daily Mirror mourns', *The Daily Mirror* (11 Nov), http://latimesblogs.latimes.com/thedailymirror/2008/11/sid-hughes-dies.html, date accessed 10 Jan 2011.
Harnisch, L. (2010) 'The Pitfalls of the True Crime Genre', *Venetian Vase* (22 Mar), http://venetianvase.co.uk/2010/03/22/the-pitfalls-of-the-true-crime-genre, date accessed 10 Nov 2011.

Haut, W. (1999) *Neon Noir: Contemporary American Crime Fiction* (London: Serpent's Tail), p. 10.
Helmore, E. (2001) 'Out of the Dark', *Guardian* (20 Apr), http://www.guardian.co.uk/books/2001/apr/20/crime.jamesellroy, date accessed 8 Oct 2010.
Hodel, S. (2004) *Black Dahlia Avenger: A Genius for Murder* (New York: Perennial).
Hodel, S. (2010) 'An Open Letter to French Journalist Stephane Boulan re. James Ellroy and Black Dahlia Avenger', *Steve Hodel's Squad Room Blog*, [blog] (25 January), http://207.56.179.67/steve_hodel/2010/01/cut-author-james-ellroy-some-s.html, date accessed 1 Feb 2010.
Hodel, S. (2011) 'Hansen's *L.A. Confidential*; Scorsese's *The Aviator*; George Hill Hodel's Franklin House; ART IMITATES LIFE', http://stevehodel.com/2011/02/hansens_la_confidential_scorse/, date accessed 2 Mar 2014.
Hodel, S. (2014) 'FAQ 6', http://stevehodel.com/wp-content/themes/hodel-s/faq/FAQ06.pdf, date accessed 6 Jun 2014.
Hogan, R. (1995) 'The Beatrice Interview: 1995', in S. Powell (ed.) (2012) *Conversations with James Ellroy* (Jackson: University Press of Mississippi), pp. 53–60.
Horsley, L. (2001) *The Noir Thriller* (Basingstoke: Palgrave Macmillan).
Horsley, L. (2002) 'An Introduction to Neo-Noir', *Crime Culture*, http://www.crimeculture.com/Contents/NeoNoir.html, date accessed 24 Jan 2010.
Horsley, L. (2005) *Twentieth Century Crime Fiction* (New York: Oxford University Press).
Isaacs, B. (2014) 'James Ellroy', *Shortlist*, http://www.shortlist.com/entertainment/books/james-ellroy, date accessed 15 Nov 2014.
Jayanti, V. (dir.) (2001) *Feast of Death* [film].
Johnston, I. (2014) 'L.A. Unbound: James Ellroy Interviewed', The Quietus, http://thequietus.com/articles/16855-james-ellroy-interview-perfidia-crime-la-quartet, date accessed 16 Dec 2014.
Jud, R. (dir.) (1998) *James Ellroy: Demon Dog of American Crime Fiction* [film].
Kihn, M. (1992) 'Doctor Noir,' in S. Powell (ed.) (2012) *Conversations with James Ellroy* (Jackson: University Press of Mississippi), pp. 25–35.
Libby, B. (2001) 'Interview: James Ellroy', *Willamette Week* (23 May), http://www.brianlibby.com/interviews/james_ellroy.html, date accessed 20 Jun 2012.
Lindquist, M. (2014) 'James Ellroy's *Perfidia*: dark doings on the eve of WWII', *Seattle Times*, http://seattletimes.com/html/books/2024460599_perfidiajamesellroyxml.html, date accessed 6 Sep 2014.
Lowe, J. (1956) 'Green Door', http://www.kovideo.net/lyrics/j/Jim-Lowe/Green-Door.html, date accessed 12 Sep 2010.
Mailer, N. (1980) 'Before the Literary Bar', *New York Magazine* (10 Nov), http://nymag.com/arts/books/features/50435/, date accessed 22 Aug 2010.
Mancall, J. (2014) *James Ellroy: A Companion to the Mystery Fiction* (Jefferson: McFarland & Company).
McDonald, C. (2001) 'James Ellroy: The Tremor of Intent', in S. Powell (ed.) (2012) *Conversations with James Ellroy* (Jackson: University Press of Mississippi), pp. 114–24.
McDonald, C. (2006) 'James Ellroy: To Live and Die in LA', in S. Powell (ed.) (2012) *Conversations with James Ellroy* (Jackson: University Press of Mississippi), pp. 132–48.

McDonald, C. (2013) 'The Black Dahlia: A Dark Anniversary', *Craig McDonald* (13 Jan), http://craigmcdonaldbooks.blogspot.co.uk/2013/01/the-black-dahlia-dark-anniversary.html, date accessed 14 Jan 2013.

McLellan, D. (2012) 'Janice Knowlton, 67, who asserted her father was the Black Dahlia killer', *Los Angeles Times* (20 Dec), http://www.boston.com/news/globe/obituaries/articles/2004/12/20/janice_knowlton_67_figure_in_famous_black_dahlia_murder_case_in_los_angeles/?page=full, date accessed 30 Jun 2013.

Meeks, F. (1990) 'James Ellroy', in S. Powell (ed.) (2012) *Conversations with James Ellroy* (Jackson: University Press of Mississippi), pp. 20–24.

Messent, P. (2013) *The Crime Fiction Handbook* (Hoboken: John Wiley & Sons).

Meyer, J. (2008) 'Haunted Subjects: Fragments of the "Sexual Mosaic" in James Ellroy's Los Angeles', *Philament*, 13, (Dec), 57–79.

Miller, L. (1996) 'Oedipus Wreck', *Salon* (9 Dec), http://www.salon.com/1996/12/09/interview961209/, date accessed 19 Nov 2010.

Milward, J. (1997) 'L.A.Beyond Your Wildest Nightmare', *Los Angeles Times* (7 Sept 1997), http://articles.latimes.com/1997/sep/07/entertainment/ca-29564/3, date accessed 3 Aug 2010.

Mulholland, G. (2005) '"Rapture Riders" by Blondie v the Doors' *The Observer* (20 Nov),http://www.theguardian.com/music/2005/nov/20/3, date accessed 5 Jun 2012.

Neff, D. (1997) 'Anoedipal Fiction: Schizoanalysis and The Black Dahlia', *Poetics Today*, 18.3, 301–42.

Page, B. (2009) 'Second LA Quartet to William Heinemann', *The Bookseller*, http://www.thebookseller.com/news/second-la-quartet-william-heinemann.html, date accessed 10 Nov 2011.

Peace, D. (2010) 'James Ellroy and David Peace in Conversation', in S. Powell (ed.) (2012) *Conversations with James Ellroy* (Jackson: University Press of Mississippi), pp. 212–18.

Pepper, A. (2000) *The Contemporary American Crime Novel: Race, Ethnicity, Gender, Class* (Edinburgh: Edinburgh University Press).

Petit, C. (2001) 'National Enquirer', *Guardian* (28 Apr), http://www.guardian.co.uk/books/2001/apr/28/crime.fiction, date accessed 22 Sep 2011.

Powell, S. (2008a) 'Engaging the Horror', in S. Powell (ed.) (2012) *Conversations with James Ellroy* (Jackson: University Press of Mississippi), pp. 158–68.

Powell, S. (2008b) 'Coda for Crime Fiction', in S. Powell (ed.) (2012) *Conversations with James Ellroy* (Jackson: University Press of Mississippi) pp. 169–75.

Powell, S. (2009) 'The Romantic's Code', in S. Powell (ed.) (2012) *Conversations with James Ellroy* (Jackson: University Press of Mississippi), pp. 189–200.

Powell, S. (2012a) 'Introduction', in S. Powell (ed.) (2012) *Conversations with James Ellroy* (Jackson: University Press of Mississippi), pp. ix–xii.

Powell, S. (2012b) '"Betty Short and I Go Back": James Ellroy and the Metanarrative of the Black Dahlia Case', in V. Miller and H. Oakley (2012) *Cross-Cultural Connections in Crime Fiction* (Basingstoke, Palgrave Macmillan), pp. 160–76.

Powell, S. (2013) 'Unpublished James Ellroy Interview', *Venetian Vase* (9 Feb), http://venetianvase.co.uk/2013/02/09/unpublished-james-ellroy-interview/, date accessed 9 Feb 2013.

Powell, S. (2014a) 'James Ellroy in Manchester: In my Craft or Sullen Art', *Venetian Vase* (6 November 2014), http://venetianvase.co.uk/2014/11/06/

james-ellroy-in-manchester-in-my-craft-or-sullen-art/, date accessed 6 Nov 2014.

Powell, S. (2014b) 'Perfidia Reviews: The Good, the Bad, and the Ugly', *Venetian Vase* (October 13), http://venetianvase.co.uk/2014/10/13/perfidia-reviews-the-good-the-bad-and-the-ugly/, date accessed 1 Nov 2014.

Rich, N. (2008) 'James Ellroy: The Art of Fiction', in S. Powell (ed.) (2012) *Conversations with James Ellroy* (Jackson: University Press of Mississippi), pp. 176–88.

Rich, N. (2009) 'James Ellroy, The Art of Fiction no.201', *Paris Review* 190 (Fall 2009), http://www.theparisreview.org/interviews/5948/the-art-of-fiction-no-201-james-ellroy, date accessed 28 Sep 2010.

Rowston, K. (2012) 'On the Low-Down and Very Hush-Hush: A James Ellroy Primer', *Lit Reactor* (20 Nov 2012),http://litreactor.com/columns/on-the-down-low-and-very-hush-hush-a-james-ellroy-primer, date accessed 30 Nov 2012.

Scaggs, J. (2005) *Crime Fiction* (London: Routledge).

Schmidt-Nowara, P. (2001) 'Finding God in a World of "Leg Breakers" and "Racist-Shitbirds": James Ellroy and the Contemporary L.A. Crime Novel', *Western American Literature* (Summer), 117–33.

Schwartz, R. (2002) *Nice and Noir: Contemporary American Crime Fiction* (Columbia: University of Missouri Press).

Sharkey, A. (2009) 'Star of the Noir: An Audience with *L.A. Confidential* Author James Ellroy', in S. Powell (ed.) (2012) *Conversations with James Ellroy* (Jackson: University Press of Mississippi), pp. 205–11.

Silet, C. (1995) 'Mad Dog and Glory: A Conversation with James Ellroy', in S. Powell (ed.) (2012) *Conversations with James Ellroy* (Jackson: University Press of Mississippi), pp. 40–52.

Simon, A. (2001) 'James Ellroy: The Hollywood Interview', *The Hollywood Interview*, http://thehollywoodinterview.blogspot.com/2008/02/james-ellroy-hollywood-interview.html, date accessed 14 Feb 2010.

Smout, M. (2001) 'Lunch and Tea with James Ellroy', in S. Powell (ed.) (2012) *Conversations with James Ellroy* (Jackson: University Press of Mississippi), pp. 104–13.

Spinks, L (2008) 'Except for Law: Raymond Chandler, James Ellroy, and the Politics of Exception', *South Atlantic Quarterly* 107:1, 121–43.

Sublett, J. (1997) 'Dead Women Owned His Soul', in S. Powell (ed.) (2012) *Conversations with James Ellroy* (Jackson: University Press of Mississippi), pp. 92–8.

Swaim, D. (1987) 'Don Swaim's Interview with James Ellroy', in S. Powell (ed.) (2012) *Conversations with James Ellroy* (Jackson: University Press of Mississippi), pp. 11–19.

Taylor, A. (2009) 'James Elroy Previews *Blood's a Rover*', in S. Powell (ed.) (2012) *Conversations with James Ellroy* (Jackson: University Press of Mississippi), pp. 201–04.

Timberg, S. (2014) 'James Ellroy talks up his new L.A. Quartet', *L.A. Times*, http://www.latimes.com/books/jacketcopy/la-ca-jc-james-ellroy-20140907-story.html#page=1, date accessed 5 Sep 2014.

Todorov, T. (1966) 'The Typology of Detective Fiction', in *The Poetics of Prose* (New York: Cornell University Press), pp. 42–52.

Tucker, D. (1984) 'An Interview with James Ellroy', in S. Powell (ed.) (2012) *Conversations with James Ellroy* (Jackson: University Press of Mississippi), pp. 3–10.

Tuttle, G. (2006) 'What is Noir?' *Noir Fiction*, http://noirfiction.info/what.html, date accessed 10 Jan 2013.

Von Mueller, E. (2010) 'The Police Procedural in Literature and on Television', in C. Nickerson (2010) *The Cambridge Companion to American Crime Fiction* (Cambridge: Cambridge University Press) pp. 96–109.

Walker, J. (2002) 'James Ellroy as Historical Novelist', *History Workshop Journal*, 53:1 (Spring), 181–204.

Wallace, A. (2010) 'The Ladies Man', *Los Angeles Magazine* (Sept 1), http://www.lamag.com/longform/the-ladies-man/, date accessed 28 Nov 2010.

Wallace, C. (2014) 'James Ellroy', *Interview*, http://www.interviewmagazine.com/culture/james-ellroy#, date accessed 23 Dec 2014.

Webb, J. (1958) *The Badge* (New York: Thunder's Mouth Press), p. 35

Wieners, B. (1995) 'Interview with a Hepcat', in S. Powell (ed.) (2012) *Conversations with James Ellroy* (Jackson: University Press of Mississippi), pp. 36–9.

Wolfe, P. (2005) *Like Hot Knives to the Brain: James Ellroy's Search for Himself* (Lanham: Lexington Books), pp. 15–16.

Wroe, N. (2008) 'The History Man', *Guardian* (10 May), http://www.guardian.co.uk/books/2008/may/10/fiction, date accessed 25 Mar 2013.

Index

Abbott, Megan, 3–4, 216
Allamand, Carole, 102, 137, 216
Avon (publisher), 5, 8–9, 14, 24, 33–4, 38, 46–51, 132, 214

Beethoven, Ludvig van, 9, 15, 22, 209–10
Bellow, Saul: *The Adventures of Augie March*, 33
Berten, Hans, 3, 216
Black Dahlia, The (film), 92, 120–1
Bruckner, Anton, 22–3, 32–3, 46, 210
Bush, George H. W., 138–9

Cain, James M., 171
Carnahan, Matthew, 156, 216
Castro, Fidel, 179, 182, 205
Chandler, Raymond, 5, 14–15, 18, 20, 24, 55–6, 79, 130, 140, 144, 171; *The Big Sleep*, 143–4
classical music, 5, 12, 14–15, 20, 22, 38
Cohen, Josh, 104, 216
Cohen, Mickey, 143, 147, 151–2, 161
Cromwell, James, 117
Crutchfield, Don, 124, 171, 199, 202, 205–7, 209, 212–14, 216

Davis, Bette, 125–6, 167
Davis, Mike, 145–6, 154
Delany, Dana, 2, 93, 113–4, 127
DeLillo, Don, 171–2, 182–4; *Libra*, 171–2, 182–4, 199, 207
De Palma, Brian, 92, 120–1
D'haen, Theo, 3, 216
Didion, Joan, 99–100
Dragna, Jack, 118, 143, 159–60
Donohue, Jack, 118
Double Indemnity (Film), 82
Dunne, John Gregory, 96–7, 99–100, 172, 208; *True Confessions*, 96–7, 99, 172, 208

Eliot, T.S., 34, 68, 217
Ellroy, Armand Lee (Ellroy's father), 1–2, 9, 27, 30, 36, 43, 91, 93, 147, 189
Ellroy, Geneva Hilliker (Ellroy's mother), 1–2, 5–6, 9, 25, 27–8, 30, 36, 39, 43, 47, 91–6, 98, 100–2, 105, 111–15, 117, 120–1, 125–7, 144, 171–2, 203, 218
Ellroy, James
  criminal acts, 2, 9–10, 13, 36, 40
  family, *see* Ellroy, Armand Lee; Ellroy, Geneva Hilliker; Knode, Helen
  health, 2, 9, 11, 13, 17–8, 191–2, 205, 214
  influences, 1–2, 4–5, 11, 14, 20, 30–1, 47, 53, 55–6, 71, 90, 93, 96, 99, 132, 134, 155, 158, 160, 164–5, 172, 183, 200;
  literary persona, 2–3, 7, 9–10, 12, 18, 24, 31, 35, 47–8, 51–4, 56, 69, 73–4, 87–8, 90, 93, 111, 119, 125, 127, 134, 146, 149–50, 168, 171, 190–1, 199, 204, 214–15
  military service, 9
  political views, 138–9, 202–4
  religious views, 11, 18–9, 21–2, 85, 202
  research, 93, 98–9, 118, 134, 146, 170, 174, 205
  works: *American Tabloid*, 6, 35, 160, 164–5, 169–178, 183–5, 193, 199–200, 205–6, 209, 213, 217; *Because the Night*, 49, 69–79, 81, 83, 90, 132, 217; *The Big Nowhere*, 129, 131–4, 139–148, 151–2, 155–8, 161, 163, 169, 176, 194, 217; *The Black Dahlia*, 2, 4–6, 53, 90–118, 120, 122–5, 127, 129–30, 134, 136, 140, 147, 167, 170–2, 203, 217; *Blood on the Moon*, 49, 51–69, 73–4, 80–1, 83–4, 90, 98,

Ellroy, James – *continued*
127, 209, 217; *Blood's a Rover*, 34, 122, 124, 137, 169–71, 177, 192, 199, 201–15, 218; *Brown's Requiem*, 2, 5–6, 8, 11–26, 29, 31–3, 46–7, 55–6, 74–5, 78, 97, 127, 130, 135, 145, 210, 217; *Clandestine*, 5, 8, 23–33, 46–7, 50, 75, 97–8, 104, 118, 125, 127, 130–1, 135, 163, 217; *The Cold Six Thousand*, 33, 55, 71, 88–90, 122, 169–71, 177, 190–204, 207–9, 214, 217; 'The Confessions of Bugsy Siegel', 33–4, 54, 217; *Destination Morgue!: L.A. Tales*, 93, 113, 128, 218; *The Hilliker Curse: My Pursuit of Women*, 37, 43, 49, 113, 171, 201–3, 209–10, 218; *Hollywood Nocturnes*, 112, 127; 'Hush-Hush', 149–53, 217 *Killer on the Road*, 5, 8, 33–48, 52, 135, 182, 217; *L.A. Confidential*, 6, 89–90, 117, 129, 131, 133–4, 136–7, 143–4, 146–57, 163, 175, 191, 217; 'L.A. Death Trip' (*see also Blood on the Moon*), 49–50, 52, 54, 59, 66–8, 78, 88, 90, 217; *My Dark Places: An L.A. Crime Memoir*, 43, 112–13, 117, 127, 203, 217; *Perfidia*, 92–3, 99, 112, 121–8, 131, 165–7, 171, 218; *Silent Terror* (*see also Killer on the Road*), 34; *Suicide Hill*, 49, 63, 74, 78–90, 145, 217; *White Jazz*, 6, 90, 129, 131, 134, 136–9, 146, 155–66, 169, 171, 191–2, 217

film noir, 1, 3, 78, 81, 94, 130–3, 136, 142–4, 155–6, 164–5, 200
Flügge, Anna, 61–2, 218
Freiburger, William, 130–1, 163, 218
Freud, Sigmund, 27, 141–2

Giancana, Sam, 181, 185
GQ (magazine), 149

Hammett, Dashiell, 138–9, 171; *Red Harvest*, 138–9
Hanson, Curtis, 117, 153–6
Harnisch, Larry, 2, 93, 1151–6, 121–2, 128, 148
Harris, Thomas, 55, 69
Haut, Woody, 138–9, 219
Helgeland, Brian, 153–5
Hodel, George Hill, 115–18, 121
Hodel, Steve, 93–4, 115–22, 128, 217
Hoover, J. Edgar, 173–9, 181–3, 186, 193, 197–9, 201, 206–7, 210–13
Horsley, Lee, 3, 105, 131, 140, 155, 219
Houseman, A.E., 33–4, 201
Hughes, Howard, 164, 178–9, 183, 187–8
Hush-Hush (magazine), 147–9, 153, 162, 166, 179, 182–3, 185, 214

Jayanti, Vikram, 18, 115, 219
Jenson, Rick, 113–4
Johnson, Lyndon B., 211

Kennedy, John F., 164, 170–9, 185–90, 193, 197–201, 206, 211
Kennedy, Joseph P., 176, 185
Kennedy, Robert F., 173–6, 199, 211
Kihn, Martin, 1–2, 10–11, 17, 24, 39, 51, 54, 66, 137, 171, 173, 219
King, Martin Luther, 176, 193, 195, 197–8, 211
Kinsey, Alfred, 72
Kirshner, Mia, 120
Knode, Helen (Ellroy's second wife), 113, 191, 202–3
Ku Klux Klan, 124, 187, 193, 195

L.A. Confidential (film), 117–18, 136, 144, 153–6
Lopez, Steve, 121
Los Angeles, 1, 7, 36, 91, 94, 99, 115, 118, 122, 124, 126–7, 129, 131–170, 190, 207, 214, 216, 218–20, 222
Los Angeles County Sheriff's Department (LASD), 140–1
Los Angeles Police Department (LAPD), 1–2, 12, 17, 22, 24–6, 28, 32, 47, 54, 61, 63–4, 68–9, 75, 79–80, 84, 86, 88, 97, 100, 1131–6, 118, 124, 126–7, 130,

134, 139–141, 148, 152–3, 155, 157–8, 160, 162, 166–7, 169, 211–12, 216
Los Angeles Times, 94, 115

Macdonald, Ross, 7, 35, 43, 58, 67, 170
MacMurray, Fred, 82
Mailer, Norman, 53, 220
McBain, Ed, 24
McDonald, Craig, 30, 35, 111, 113, 116, 120–1, 176, 192, 201, 219; *Toros and Torsos*, 120
Mehta, Sonny, 126, 137
Messent, Peter, 5, 119–20, 220
Meyer, Joshua, 103–4, 220
Mitchum, Robert, 82
Monroe, Marilyn, 53, 173–4
Mysterious Bookshop, 50–1

New York Times, 111
Nietzsche, Friedrich, 32–3, 37–8, 71, 75
Nixon, Richard M., 206, 210–11

Oswald, Lee Harvey, 171–2, 184
Otash, Fred, 174–5, 205
Out of the Past (Film), 82

Parker, William H., 126–7
Peace, David, 138, 192, 202, 204–5, 220

Penzler, Otto, 3, 49, 50–2, 54, 67, 88
Pepper, Andrew, 3, 196, 220

Reagan, Ronald, 62, 138–9
Rice, Randy, 3, 17–8, 31, 47, 149, 215
romanticism, 6, 19, 21, 49–50, 53–4, 56, 59–63, 65, 68, 72–3, 132, 204, 209

Scaggs, John, 184–6, 221
Schwartz, Richard B., 190, 221
Sexton, Anne, 105, 110, 113–14
Sexton, Fred, 117
Short, Elizabeth, 2, 6, 90–8, 100–21, 123, 125–7, 134, 140, 220
Siegel, Don, 63, 165
Sobel, Nat, 49, 51–2, 54, 67, 88, 111, 135–7
Spacey, Kevin, 117
Stoner, Bill, 112
Summers, Anthony, 174–5

Todorov, Tzvetan, 18–20, 221
Tucker, Duane, 24, 36, 52–4, 56, 58–9, 62, 75, 221

Wagner, Bruce, 2
Watergate scandal, 171, 177, 210–11
Webb, Jack, 2, 93–5, 115, 147; *The Badge*, 2, 93–5, 115, 147–8
Wolfe, Donald H., 1181–9, 136, 174
Wolfe, Peter, 4, 13, 25, 66, 136, 187, 200, 222

Printed and bound by CPI Group (UK) Ltd, Croydon, CR0 4YY